I0577586

quarterback scramble

By M L Chambers

Quarterback Scramble

The Marriage Offensive

Two-Date Warning

Flag on the Date

Red Hot Zone

Ineligible Receiver

The Heart Hand-Off

Champagne Problems

On the Rocks

Fools Dive In

Kendry the Vicious

quarterback scramble

Book 1
Mountaineer Footballers

M L Chambers

For those sitting on the edge of their seat for a different reason.

Chapter One

Victoria Steer, best, brightest, and *only* recruiter for the Vermont Mountaineers, hovered at the threshold of business and pleasure. With a deep breath, she shoved deeper inside the Allgood Lounge, palms sweating, heart racing, her eyes flared at tonight's fine selection of footballers. Even in her most sinful candy apple red dress, not one paid her a passing glance. Their focus stuck to the half-dressed women writhing and twisting on the dancefloor.

Pushing through the mix, striding in time with the thumping, grating drop of the bass, Victoria spied the object of her most ardent affection.

Target acquired.

If it weren't for the puckering mosquito bites lining her legs, she'd think she was in Miami. Humidity tangled her hair, sucked the curl from her bangs. Sweat licked down her chest, her arms, as bodies ground against hers, hands fondling where they liked. Gone were the pearls and coiffured hair. These women were no southern ladies. They came for euphoria and pleasure. They came for release. On hands and knees.

Victoria hadn't labored in line for over two hours to be a show-girl.

This is what Houston called a hard place to get into. The Allgood Lounge entertained only the exceptional: unscrupulous senators, vengeful divorcees, and those who thought Texas was a sovereign nation. And what was it that drew attention? Peanut shells littered the floor. A splintered bar sat low enough to serve flashes of the bartender's daisy dukes and belly button rings.

Victoria hiked her own dress higher. Competition.

She wasn't the prettiest girl in the room. The fine—*okay, thin*—hair and average—*slightly above*—height were made up for by the double heaping of hips and tits. Best of all, at the ripe age of twenty-five, Victoria no longer had qualms about the way she dressed. Especially not on nights like this.

What did professional athletes like? Tits and ass. In excess. Especially the one caught in her crosshairs.

She'd been on his trail for four weeks.

Calling, stalking, dropping names, handwriting letters to his friends, kissing the envelopes. The man was untouchable. Until Victoria heard a whispered giggle between two yogis in the Starbucks bathroom, regaling how they stole the attention of the king himself at this very establishment.

God, she loved good intel.

There he was. Behind a thick, black crushed velvet rope and three raised steps. Long legs stretched out in front of him, golden hair glimmering, an even tan, and dangerous near black eyes.

She couldn't actually see through the crowd, the flickering lights, the shadows blocking his face, but she'd memorized his player profile. The puppy dog grin to camera. Midas, they called him.

Because of his almost unnatural, damn near unattainable, golden sheen. Because he was a gift on the field, the quarterback that made gold of mere men. The darling of the league venerated and worshiped. A chill broke up her back, causing a shiver. When she got him, *she'd* turn to fucking gold.

She knew it.

Problem: everyone wanted him.

Watching him, she felt her predatory instincts surge. The promise of the hunt's end made her mouth water. The gold king sat in the fold of other starters, a line of overconfident spread knees, thick thighs, and expensive over-white sneakers. Women paraded in front of their velvet rope, yearning to be hailed, like willing virgins for sacrifice.

Victoria wasn't a sacrifice. Not only because she wasn't a virgin—sorry mom—but because she was a hunter.

A killer.

She'd been methodically, meticulously stalking her prey, and now she would take him down by his haunches. Force him to submit.

Easy.

Already, the glowing pleasure of a victory glossed up her arms, over her legs, tickling at her, teasing. She'd hand off the papers, tell him he was the most wanted bastard in all of football, and she'd come to make him a legend, a goddamn hero. People would weep when they heard the name Midas.

She'd practiced the pitch in her head over the past few weeks, mouthing the words every time he slipped from her clutches. Every time she stormed back into her gilded hotel room, crammed a chair under the door and screamed into her pillow.

Victoria never failed. Still hadn't. Not Yet.

Texas.

How she hated Texas. Especially this far south. Painfully hot in the summer.

"Are you going to get a drink or are you just going to stand there? Because I only get paid if you drink."

She glanced over her shoulder. Evidently, there were male bartenders too, but as this was Texas, her eye candy was buttoned up. Tragic. At least his burgundy flannel was tight, though she'd love to tip the cowboy hat off and rub her heel in it. A checkered rag dangled from the pocket of his jeans, white stained with bright UV blue. Tall, dark eyes, a youthful mouth, and overlarge nose. A full head of cropped dark hair. Cute, except for his dopey drawl.

"Who are those guys up there?" she asked, sliding a twenty across the counter.

"Those are the Texans."

Forcing a smile, she fished another twenty from her purse and stacked it on the other. "I was talking about the guy controlling the rope. How close are you two?"

"You want to bed a Texan?"

Victoria set her chin in her hands and batted her lashes. "I flew all the way from the East Coast to find one."

"They're my best customers," he said, taking the forty. "And you seem like trouble, so let's say I *don't* know the rope guy."

She pursed her lips. Maybe she could talk to one of the dancers, tell them the truth. That she was here for work. The forty was a business expense. She'd sooner fuck a confederate cowboy than she would the players. But... it'd take time, she'd have to answer questions, risk a press leak.

Girding herself, she waved a fifty. Big guns. "I'd *really* like to get behind the rope. Trust me, the boys will be happy to see me. Downright grateful."

"You're from New York, ain't you?" he asked as he plucked the cash from her. "In New York, people are out for themselves, but in Texas, we're Texas strong. We protect our own. Those boys, they come in every week. Your skinny ass isn't getting up there."

Victoria almost shredded the money just to piss him off. "Have you ever been to New York? Because if you had, you'd know I'm not from there. The East Coast isn't one big apple, just like how Texas isn't the center of the universe. Drop the preacher act. You've got your own problems that I don't even want to begin to discuss." She felt her skin tighten, her fists clench, and closed her eyes. No. Focus on the mission.

Fighting through a grimace, she added, "Also, thank you for calling me skinny. I'd like a margarita."

The hunt had not stopped, she reminded herself, glancing over her shoulder to make sure Midas hadn't seen her outburst. A splash of lime splattered her back. Baby boy bartender wasn't happy. Twenty to one, her drink would be ice, lime, water, and a La Croix splash of tequila.

So be it. Wasn't like she'd tip him any more. Unhelpful ass. When her glass hit the bar, she snagged it and sauntered to her nemesis, the velvet rope. Before it, women gyrated in tandem, movements lewd and graceless, greedy and desperate. Through their turns and spins, the whip of perfumed hair, their gazes stayed locked on the elevated VIP table. A show. That's all they were.

All she had to be.

If Victoria hiked her skirt up further, she'd be arrested. Time to work the other way. Moving the lowball glass between her palms, she yanked down the top of her dress until the scalloped edge of her bra showed. Spinning, she dared a sip and—*holy fuck*—her eyes burned. She coughed, choking on salt and lime, stumbled forward.

Dazed and dizzy, crunching ice to stop her throat from peeling, she found refuge across the room.

Fuck. Why was it that each time she neared Midas, chaos ensued? No more. She'd burned through her deadline. It was now or never. Firming her lips, she clenched her jaw.

Get Midas. Sign Midas. Bathe in the spoils.

Gomez wanted someone splashy. She'd bring him a whale. The big name. The star.

She refused to go home without him.

Straightening her spine, Victoria threw back the so-called margarita and hissed through the burn. Focused, intent, she shook out her hands, pulled her skirt up to indecent, and charged back into the feeding pit.

Gun cocked.

***

"CLOSE IT," WARREN told the barkeep. One round and he meant it. That's what his budget allowed for. One fucking round in this fucking ridiculous place.

Why did he keep coming? Week after pathetic week. Overpriced, overcrowded, the constant stench of desperation and sweat. It wasn't even the bartenders in their uniform swimsuits. It was everyone else.

Men and women abound, all frantic to touch Midas. To share a room with the golden god, to breathe the king's air.

His name was *Doyle*. Doyle Heark.

Not that the kid would ever admit it.

Warren turned, two ten dollar IPAs in tow, and smashed into a whirling dervish of licorice red and decadent curves. Her gasp broke through the thumping music as four bucks of beer sprayed her neck, her chest, and—

Christ—were those real?

"Come on," a sultry voice groaned. "Beer?"

The accent yanked Warren's focus from the endless voluptuous... assets. One not often heard around these parts. The sharpness, the quick edges, and separated words. She spoke with hurried detachment. As if each word took too much time.

In Texas, words tangled together. Gelled and became lyrics. Didn't matter how dumb or foul the sentence, it became a poem when you had a drawl. Red's words didn't float on a whispered harmony. They didn't sing at all. She was a drum, big enough to stand on its own, harsh enough to make his ears bleed and yet...

Blue eyes ensnared his. Warren smiled. She smelled faintly of sunscreen and sand, as if she'd been tanning on the beach and naming the clouds.

"I guess drinks are on me," she said, half mocking, and then she was looking down, plucking at the silky red material of her dress, folding it to hide the wet spots, completely unabashed.

Warren stared, chin dipped like hers, no more than a foot between them.

He couldn't stop looking at her. He had the feeling if he blinked, she'd disappear, return to his fantasies. Her hair an oil slick black, flashing deepest blue when the strobe hit right. The ends swept back and forth over bare shoulders, covering her face as she fixed her dress, letting Warren's gaze wander where it liked. The trim of a navy lace bra, the tan knee-high boots, the milky white thighs. His heart smashed against his ribs, blood thundering. Please God, tell him the flash of navy between her legs wasn't what he thought it was.

"It looks like I spit up on myself." She huffed. "Just great." Her face lifted to his, eyes a shocking blue made even brighter by sweeps of black across her eyelids. Beautiful, a heart shaped face with a delicately pointed chin. Her symmetrical red lips were downturned, her hip jutted to the side.

He recognized the stance: mad.

Shit. Warren caught both bottles in one hand and patted her down with the corner of his cotton shirt. Damage control.

The dress, as short as it was, looked expensive and *holy shit*, Warren could *not* afford dry cleaning, he could barely cover the drinks.

"I'm sorry." He tried to sound earnest through the husky pitch, stepping closer to wipe away the drops, erasing his mistake before it became a bigger one. He had a habit of that.

But his hands felt bulky and rough against her small frame. As he dried, her gaze drifted over him, followed the trail of his hands as if they left scorch marks behind.

"Are you giving me a mammogram?" she asked with warm amusement. "Because if you tell me you're a doctor, I'm going to demand a medical license."

Warren dropped his shirt, raised his hands. "I'm not."

"I know." Her head tipped to the side, like a dog intent on understanding its master. "No doctor has a six-pack like that. Congrats." She adjusted her dress again, right there in front of him, shamelessly shifting the cups of her bra. Two lucky thumbs lifted her breasts until they were perky and high, a display of carnal delight.

"I think it'll be fine," she told him. "Isn't this what guys want? A beer covered woman?"

He didn't know if anybody wanted a woman to smell like hops, but tasting like one...

"Hop flavored nipples," she said, reading his mind. "That's got to be a thing. GQ probably sells it as a body spray."

He shrugged, waiting for her anger to return, for him to stumble into a trap. She couldn't be making a joke, could she? "Seems like it's your thing now."

"Guess you're right." With a sardonic arch of her dark brows, she patted his elbow. "Thanks for the drink, stud."

She froze, hand digging into his arm, nails biting skin.

Warren flinched, opened his mouth—

And clenched his teeth.

Red stared as a line of Texans swaggered to the exit, snatching women and dragging them with. A mane of golden hair led the pack.

Not one bothered Warren with a look, a goodbye, a fucking glance.

Who cared about Warren when they were in the company of a myth? Doyle laughed and the flashing lights dimmed, as if he stole the electricity himself.

Lungs tight, Warren fisted the bottles in his hand and averted his gaze. Red's lips were parted as she balanced on the toes of her heeled boots, eyes wide at the sight of the golden boy.

A hand came to her chest, the pulse in her neck jumped.

Of course.

Of *fucking* course.

Raw desire flanked those sweet blue eyes.

"You're here for him," Warren said, swigging from his bottle.

Of course she was. The hottest fucking woman in the bar. The only one that sparked his interest, and she'd come for Doyle, prettied herself up for the king.

Next, his mother would superimpose Doyle's face on his for the Christmas card.

"We have business," Red said, voice thinner. She bit her lip, still clutching Warren's arm as panic splayed over her delicate features. "No," she muttered as Doyle left. "Not yet."

There was no sympathy in Warren's stony heart. Only rage as she dragged hungry eyes back to his.

"Let me guess." He took another slug. "You're his wife." She had the body, the face, the fucking smile to score the king of the south.

She held up her hands, wiggling unadorned fingers. "Never even been to a church."

"You're pregnant."

"You better shut your mouth or I'll think you're suggesting something about my body." Her hip cocked again, hand settling at the small curve of her waist.

Warren swallowed his tongue.

"Come on," she goaded. "I'll buy you a drink and you can keep guessing." Mood flipping, she pulled on the front of Warren's shirt, guiding him forward. She walked them backward, leading him to the bar, watching him with none of the desire she'd shown Doyle. "If you're lucky, I'll let you pour it all over me." A wink.

But her eyes had dulled, cleared.

Warren's jaw locked. "I'm here with someone."

Immediately, Red let go. "I wasn't proposing, and you were staring at my tits a lot to be here with someone."

"I'm single, I'm—"

She cut him off. "Save it. I don't have time for a circuitous, phony explanation on why you're flattered, but you don't want me. How I'm too X for your Y. Blah Blah bullshit. I was looking for a hot lay with no strings attached. Someone to lick all this beer off me and while you could've filled that hole, *pun most certainly intended*, I'll find someone with less hesitancy."

***

"I'M SURPRISED YOU came back," Cole said, nodding his thanks as he accepted a half empty beer.

Warren tossed a look over his shoulder, immediately finding Red slinking into the crowd, body swaying to the music. Making good on her threat to find somebody.

"She's not from here," Warren said. As if it was a reason not to fuck her. Truthfully, he was tired of sleeping with women because their better options had fled. He was second in everything.

Fuck, Doyle's betrayal had left him bitter. After taking the golden prick under his wing, the bastard had usurped him without a muttered *thank you* or *sorry*.

But that's what people did.

Warren knew that. He'd had his ass handed to him enough times to know everyone was the same. They only cared about themselves, and it didn't matter who they had to stab to get their way.

He'd caught the same ruthlessness in Red's sweet blues. After he'd torn away from those amazing tits.

"I thought she was going to slap you, not offer to sleep with you."

"That's the thing," Warren said as they watched Red wedge into a party of men, smiling, twirling her fingers. "She didn't really seem mad that I spilled on her." Which hadn't seemed odd until now. Most women would've freaked out, demanded him to pay for their dress. Left in a huff, hiding themselves.

He watched her ass arch over the bar, waving a twenty, big stain on her chest. She didn't care at all.

"Name?" Cole asked. The offensive tackle was soft-spoken. He didn't need words to get his point, and when they were required, he preferred to keep it minimal. He'd been a Texan for three years, drafted from nowhere Utah for his size and uniquely calm demeanor.

While he was large and stocky, like most of the O-line, Cole Seeder didn't fit the mold of a professional athlete. He kept his chestnut brown hair long pulled back in a ponytail. His face was always clean shaven, dark eyes gentle. The odd tattoo slinking down his arm was the only hint that he wasn't an oversized high school guidance counselor.

It didn't surprise Warren that through the pulsing music, the chink of glass, the pounding of feet, and thumping bass, Cole had caught every word of their conversation.

Warren would've accused his best friend of eavesdropping had it not already happened a dozen times.

Cole's act for listening, learning, was what made him a phenomenal athlete. He could read between the defense with closed eyes, pick up on things happening behind him, to his sides, in the stands thirty-five yards away.

He always knew where Warren was and planned for it.

Now he protected Doyle.

"I didn't get it and she didn't ask for mine."

"No name sex." One eyebrow on the massive athlete's face lifted.

"She'll give *them* her name," Warren said, twisting to look away from her, running his fingers over the wood tabletop and nodding at the VIP area. That's who she really wanted, who she'd imagine while he touched her, while he fucked her.

The first time a woman had cried out *Midas* as she came on his cock, he'd been embarrassed. Four of those later, it felt like a lashing on his back, invisible whips tearing at skin below the surface.

"She said she has business with the king."

Cole nodded acknowledgment, having heard it already. He dropped his beer to the table and his other eyebrow went up, expectant. "Empty."

It was on the tip of his tongue for Warren to tell Cole to go lick it off Red. But he found even the idea of such a tease made him irritable, had his hands fist. Even if he wouldn't be her substitute, he wouldn't share. He'd liked the interest she'd given him.

The first interest he'd entertained in what felt like ages.

"We need to stop coming here," Warren said abruptly, pressing the neck of his beer to his temple, closing his eyes to calm down.

Allgood Lounge stiffed for no other reason than the Texans frequented its dank halls. Charging through the nose didn't shorten the line out the door. Everyone wanted a piece of the Texans.

At least those who played.

As a professional athlete, Warren was in better shape than most, but when in the shadow of Midas and his loyal flock, no one paid him any mind. He was no one. Nothing. Less than nothing. He might as well fold their laundry. He faded away.

Fans long forgot the number under Warren's name. He was a faceless man on the sidelines, a body taking up air, staining the jersey. Funny how he'd grown up in the shadows and never gotten used to it.

Each day it chafed.

In small Abilene, Kansas, Warren's older brother had been the first and last male model. A charmer baby face that jetted off to San Francisco, trading farm fields and scarecrows for palm trees and supermodels. The town knew Warren as handsome Bricks' little brother.

At eighteen, Warren couldn't wait to escape it. When he ran off to a college states away, he found football. And his life changed, newfound skill propelling him onto a national stage. Young, gifted quarterback, headlines read. The spotlight narrowed during the draft, brightened during his first game as a Texan. The rookie starter.

Five good fucking years.

Ancient history.

It hardly felt real. His past had become someone else's dream, his nightmare, as if he'd woken up in the middle of it, never been worthy of it. Now, he was thirty-one living in the shadow of a twenty-four-year-old who roared like an actual lion at every pass completion.

"Fuck, maybe I should go. I'm not feeling it tonight."

The frown on Cole's face was a familiar sight. "We don't need to come here," he offered. Had repeatedly offered. "I only come to be your sparkling companionship. Plenty of bars serve watered down beer."

Forcing a grin, Warren finished his bottle. Cole would leave now if Warren requested it. But the offensive tackle had one of the most recognizable faces on the team. Brimming with talent, stoic and mysterious, there were entire forums dedicated to breeding his babies.

Hailed the Norse God by everyone but himself, Cole dismissed his Scandinavian army as a blip, soon to end. At least when they drank at Allgood, Cole was, by comparison, average in the sea of footballers. Anywhere else, Warren's best friend would vanish in a sea of pussy.

That is to say, Warren would disappear in a bigger, burlier shadow while Cole suffered through the affections of the fairer, more vicious sex.

"No. It's me. I have to head out, but let's do burgers tomorrow."

"Steaks," Cole said. "I bought them already." He spun his thumb around the lip of his beer. "You go on. I'm staying. I have some pent up energy." He swallowed, averting his gaze.

Cole didn't date. And he didn't fuck around like the other players. He didn't keep a few prime cut women on rotation. He found a woman, brought her home, and then never spoke to her again.

Usually he could go two, maybe three weeks, and then he'd have a night like this. Where he'd sit back and wait to make eye contact long enough for some girl to recognize him, to offer her body as the next sacrifice, and Cole would disappear.

The next day, there'd be dark bags under his eyes, tension wrinkling his forehead.

To Warren, it seemed like a chore. As if sex was a part of Cole that Cole hated. Detested. His desire for contact, to fuck, abhorrent. It was like he did it because man had done it for thousands of years. He had an evolutionary need to feed his innermost beast without ever satiating it. Scratch an endless itch.

"Good luck to you." Tomorrow, Cole would be a cold husk, quiet, trapped in his head, overthinking, suffering.

Abruptly, the offensive tackle pushed back from the table, his chest swelled the same time his shoulders knocked back. "Trouble," he warned, looking past Warren's shoulder.

Dread pulsed into Warren's bloodstream at the sound of Red's voice. The confident staccato slipping between drops in the music.

"Get off me, you big ape," she said sharply. "I'm not here for you."

Warren twisted to stare as a rough hand caught hers, and a cowboy, one missing manners, pinned Red to the bar.

Cole moved.

Warren stopped him. "Mine."

CHAPTER TWO

"WHAT PART OF 'FUCK no' is incomprehensible to you, you tiny dick?" Victoria wiggled her wrist, but the guy was part mammoth. A Mac truck. Disgusting and enormous.

This was why she preferred short men. They never made her feel weak, never rubbed a hard dick into her stomach and got confused when she didn't instantly come. Wrenching back, Victoria bared her teeth at her assailant. Texas formal in a cowboy hat, he reeked of chewing tobacco and had a brain half the size of his penis. That is to say: microscopic.

"Come along baby, I seen you dance for me all night."

"Oh, gross, as if I'd dance for a fucking hick. Move. You're blocking my view." She tried to look over the cowboy's shoulder, squinting to drown out the music. Was that Christoph O'Connor the running back? He was on her list.

Midas had left, but she could still salvage this evening.

First, she had to get rid of micropenis.

"Baby, listen, I'll give you free weed if you take a ride." His blackened tongue flicked out over his bottom lip, a chunk of packed chew flashing. Revolting.

"I wouldn't take a brick of gold," she said, closing her hand into a fist and sliding it from under his paw. She saw salvation before the cowboy could react.

Rescue came from none other than her beer guzzling denier. The one with the half drawl that didn't seem to grate.

She didn't usually like men that played hard to get, but he was hot enough for her to give chase.

The height should've turned her off. He put the towering in tall, had to be six-three at least, but he was pleasantly lean. The slightly thinner upper lip granted him a mischievous crooked smile with perfect teeth, adorned by sexy little fangs and a deep, highly lickable, dimple in his left cheek. Strong and even features, dark brown hair thick and messy on top, trimmed at the sides.

He was throw your hair up and get on your knees gorgeous. Especially the eyes against his suntanned skin. Caramel brown and deep set, tucked behind dark, sinister lashes.

"I'm with somebody," she told the cowboy, throwing an elbow to his groin as she rushed to meet Dimples halfway.

He wasn't smiling. Wasn't walking. Wasn't looking at her. He was storming, unstopping, on a collision course with the cowboy. Didn't even slow when Victoria caught him, her hands on his cheeks, feet tangling with his. She pulled his face down and surged to her toes. Tall guys were so much work.

Only when their lips touched did he freeze.

That's what it took to stop the rampage. A kiss.

He went rigid under her hands, lips hard against hers. He tasted like she smelled. A hint of beer with something clean and fresh underneath. Arching up, Victoria luxuriated in the softness of his thick, brown hair. Did she unlock a new type? Tall guy with a savior complex?

Pushing closer, she became aware of the hands limp at his sides, the gap of air he maintained between their bodies. A new wave of irritation lashed. Yanking him down, closer, she pinched the back of his neck and bit into his lower lip.

"You're being kissed," she panted against his mouth. "Kiss back."

He'd said single, right? When they were talking. She'd listened, not fantasized. Maybe both.

"Come on," she whispered against his lips. "Show me you want me." Raking her nails over his scalp, she meant to trigger a little passion. Wanted a spark next to her wild flame. Anything to show the cowboy she hadn't been lying. A dose of possessiveness would make the cowboy back off.

A man challenging a woman, he didn't think twice, but man-to-man, especially with a man as big as Dimples, the cowboy would rub those two brain cells together and reconsider.

Again, frustration swelling, Victoria pressed closer to Dimples, nuzzling into his hard chest, biting at his lower lip.

He moved then, his hand marking the back of her waist, sweeping down her spine to grip the curve of her ass. Firm, hot. A sharp dash of lust lit her veins. she moaned encouragement as he yanked her closer, covered her body with his and locked her there. His mouth opened, tongue tasting hers, and then her back hit something hard.

The wall? Victoria didn't dare open her eyes, didn't foil her show. Couldn't stop the feeling pooling in her stomach. Not as his leg nudged between her thighs and lifted her until she was sitting on him, splayed over him, her lace covered core resting on thick, warm jeans.

Every inch of her skin heated. A strong hand came to the nape of her neck, tilting her until he found the angle with a direct line to her lady parts. And bit it.

The kiss stopped being her escape route and transformed into her tropical paradise. Hot, steamy, wet.

First kisses were bad.

This one was a showstopper. Maybe she'd known it. Why else had she quit the hunt early? It wasn't like her to give up. However, throwing in the towel to drag Dimples to the hotel and lick over every taut muscle as he drove wildly into her was textbook Victoria. Girl had to eat.

And she was starving for him.

No one ever matched her need, but she was following *his* lead, chasing *his* mouth, gasping when *he* bit, groaning when *he* stopped. Victoria pulled him closer, trying to reach all of him at once.

I want him now, came a lust drowned thought. She'd beg for it. He could make her, watch her crash to her knees on the peanut shell floor and plead.

Clutching at his biceps, she kissed him harder, pressed tighter and began, slowly—achingly slowly—to ride his thigh.

Paradise.

He jerked back.

A brush of cold air struck her.

Her heels met the floor with a near silent thud. His hands went to her skirt and yanked it down. Dazed, disoriented, Victoria blinked.

She *was* against the wall.

Dimples turned as if he'd just remembered why he'd approached her in the first place. Jaw tight, he found the cowboy and glared.

The redneck watched wide-eyed, hand on the belt, like he was about to jerk-off to them.

"You should kick his ass," she goaded, subtly tracing the ridge in his jeans.

Dimples' head dipped, as if he agreed, as if he considered it. As if he took her word and was now going to make it happen. Enshrine it on a tablet in the fifteenth century and command people to follow it for hundreds of years.

Fingers playing, she tipped her head against the wall and heard herself say, "Or you could kiss me again."

***

WHO WAS THIS woman? Warren fought to hold his glare. He wouldn't look back. Couldn't. Because he'd take her up on the damned tempting offer. Not the first, though it was equally enticing. Anyone who dared to touch a woman, especially one as lovely as her, ought to know what the bottom of his boot tasted like.

It was the second fiery offer, the one whispered with husk and sin, he avoided.

He'd take it too far.

Crush her to his mouth and take her right here, against the wall.

He'd fuck her right in front of the cowboy, in front of everyone. Stake a barbarian claim on her. Already, she'd unraveled his composure. Hard as granite in his local bar, snarling at a regular, ready to throw down.

Her featherlight touch grazed his dick as if it were a long-lost friend.

"Red," he warned, catching her wrist, holding it far away from him. Her pulse leaped under his grip, stirring liquid heat through his body. Christ, she'd like it. Like if he was brutal, if he crowded her into the plaster and shredded those lace panties.

Swearing, he beat down the fantasy, released her wrist.

He didn't even know her name.

What kind of asshole didn't ask a lady for her name, he berated, hoping it might tamp down the excruciating erection scraping his zipper.

No such luck. A thousand names populated his mind, from sugar sweet Mary Lynn to strip club sexy Kandy. Without thinking, his gaze dropped to her. Warren ran his tongue over his teeth. He'd coax the name out of her, a strip search for every detail of her life. Drape her across the bar until he had a portfolio named Red.

No. A tremor rocked his body as he wrenched back a step, bared his teeth at the cowboy, and pretended blood wasn't rushing in his ears.

No more looking.

He'd get arrested. Jail. Fines. Repercussions he couldn't afford. The truth of his situation kept him glaring at the cowboy.

If he couldn't fuck, he might as well fight.

Feet spread, shoulders pushed back, Warren blocked Red with his body, splaying a hand over her nape. Possessive. Proprietary. Things he'd never before been.

His thumb caught the thump of her pulse, and his body throbbed. She hadn't cooled, calmed. He wondered if her mind ran like his, fitting them together in different alcoves, across different tables.

Soft, she was so soft, so light and pliable. And the racing heart couldn't be faked. Which meant her desire for him was real. Warren dropped his head, muscles straining. He wasn't a fighter. Not really. He was big enough that he'd never had to be. People didn't challenge hulking athletes. And he wasn't one to prey on the weak.

But with one question, a whispered rush, he saw blood.

Saw the wannabe cowboy following him out to the parking lot, wading through the humid night. The two of them and the hum of locusts under a flat, midnight sky. He'd lead left, a warning shot before the power landing with the arm that got him a third round pick. Only when the cowboy was quiet, collapsed on the gravel, blood pooling, would Warren issue his warning.

He fucking dared to touch Red? Dared to ignore her? To seize her? Take something she hadn't offered?

She wasn't shy about what she wanted. That was for fucking sure. Nor was she shy about what she didn't want.

"I should break his hand," Warren muttered under his breath. That'd be a good quid pro quo. The cowboy had touched her with it. Therefore, he didn't deserve to use it.

Red's hand drifted up Warren's chest, fisted the fabric of his shirt and pulled until he saw blue.

Blue.

Was that her name? Bestowed when she first parted those dark lashes.

"That's hot as fuck," she purred. "But I think you should just kiss me again."

He planted a hand on the wall to stop her from dragging him closer, and forced his elbow straight. "No. Not going to happen."

She groaned once and let go. "I fucking hate Texas. I hope I never come back. Every man thinks he's Walker Texas Ranger and we're all damsels waiting to get split on his dick."

"Christ." Warren let out half a laugh. She had a mouth like she was on the team, maybe worse. "Everybody talk like that where you're from?"

"Course not." She smiled sardonically. "*I* don't even talk like that where I'm from, but this is a seedy bar in the worst city in America, so I'm doing as the Romans do, letting it fly."

This girl was honest and funny and Warren fucking liked that. He liked a lot about her. "Where are you from?"

"Bartender said New York." Her brow arched in silent challenge.

It was a good guess. One he himself would've voiced when they first met, but he'd tasted her now, swallowed her moans, felt her body quiver under his hands. Setting his teeth, he assessed her. Too funny to be a New Yorker, too forgiving. A New Yorker would be colder, closed off. She was an explosion of fun and foul words. "Not New York. He was wrong,"

"He was." She smiled, trailing fingers down her narrow dress straps. "I'm from the best damn city in the country. Newport, Rhode Island."

It caught him so off guard, he laughed.

"You think I'm wrong?" she asked, arms folding in defense.

So much damn fire. Warren shook his head. "I've never actually met anyone from Rhode Island."

"Once you meet one, it's like you've met the whole family." Her smile returned, threatening his decency. "We don't get out much. Who would want to leave?"

"Rhode Island." He was incredulous. What were the chances?

"Newport," she corrected. "And we're a hell of a lot more evolved than this crowd. Excluding present company."

"Why are you here? America's worst city bingo? Blew your spring break in Detroit?"

She snorted at the question, grading him ridiculous. Like he'd asked if it would snow on this balmy Texas July night.

"Are you really not going to kiss me again?"

"No."

Sighing, she waved at the high top tables. "Then let's get a drink. Your friend left by the way."

Warren turned. She was right. Cole was gone, likely not alone.

Red ordered Warren a beer. The same overpriced brand he'd been drinking. Sharp. Then, waving a twenty, she ordered a margarita, light on the marg.

Explained the lime and salt taste he'd sucked off her tongue.

Ignoring his offer, she paid, plus a hefty tip. Licking at the rim of her glass, she turned to face him. Frowned. Her thumb rubbed his cheek, his bottom lip. She cringed. "Dragon Girl red sticks," she said. "You could be a drag queen. The color suits." Totally at ease, she bent her knee across the pleated barstool, deliberately taking up room. "Is that why you don't want to have sex? You can come out to me. I don't know any of your friends. I don't even know your name."

He dragged dark eyes over her, pinning the rise of her ass. "I'm not gay."

She smiled, as if pleased by the answer, and went back to her drink, licking the salt off the rim and not chasing it.

"I bet you're a good kisser," she said.

"You bet? We kissed."

"Technically. But it was for evasion, not passion. You were nothing but a mouth for my own nefarious purposes." At his dumbstruck stare, she smirked. "It was cute. Very noble, a home-grown Texas savior. But hardly proof of skill. I bet if you really wanted to kiss somebody, just kiss them because you wanted to, you'd do well."

"Are you saying I was bad?" Why was this, of all things, getting him hard?

Suddenly demure, her shoulder lifted. The tease.

His hand was in her hair, pulling her across the stool before he realized he was forcing her lips apart, tasting her tongue, stealing that salt.

Hands flattened against his belt, and she rose, kneeling on the leather, arching toward him. He encouraged it, fanning corrosive flames, pulling her closer. Until it wasn't close enough. Groaning into her Dragon Girl lips, he yanked her waist until she was flat against him, feet hovering above the floor.

"The bar," she gasped, hands frantic in his hair, tugging. "Put me on the bar."

The image burned. Red seated on the bar, skirt bunched at her waist, pussy wet, soaked and on display for him. He'd been picturing it since the moment he met her and realized he was out of fucking control. He forced himself to pull back, to run a hand over her ass and yank her dress down.

Christ, he would kill for this woman.

She didn't seem to notice that he covered her, gently touching her lips as she stumbled to sit, legs askew. The first time he'd seen her truly graceless.

"Yeah, you're good at that." She closed her eyes and exhaled slowly before she looked at him again. "Practice?"

"Are you asking if I've kissed somebody before? No."

She smiled against her fingers. "How degrading. A man who fucks without kissing."

He'd said he was leaving. Now he was on his second beer, staring at her, his entire body electrified. Red licked more salt and he clenched his fist to not taste it off her tongue. Suddenly he had a deficiency.

"Who said I wasn't a virgin?"

"You're not a virgin. No one as good looking as you could get away with that. Even if you signed a purity pledge, you wouldn't make it."

"Do you say everything that pops into your head?"

She grinned, running her tongue along her teeth, flicking at her lip. "How do you know Cole?"

Everything locked down and went rigid in Warren's body. The sudden openness, the flirting, the way her attention fixed to him, but lingered occasionally to the VIP section.

He understood it now. He'd been a fly on her wall when they met. Then, like an idiot, he'd mentioned his friend, told her they were together. Of course, she'd recognized *the* Cole Seeder.

She was using him.

She wasn't even trying to hide it.

He didn't know if that pissed him off or turned him on.

Both.

What had he become? A stepping stone to better men? A man who had potential, but never quite met expectations.

Warren feigned nonchalance, taking a swig, finding it lacking. "How do *you* know Cole?"

"We use the same shampoo, though my hair never captures the same effortless shine he manages. I blame the NFL for today's skyrocketing beauty standards. What about you? High school friends? College?" She tipped her head, waiting.

Christ, she was good at that, being charming while she furthered her agenda.

She wasn't going to let it drop, so he said, "We work together."

Red didn't ask another question, just pursed her lips, attention drifting to his mouth.

After another drink, she stiffened, swallowed, faced the bar. "Does he like Texas?"

"Not as much as you."

She arched an eyebrow.

Fuck. This had become an interview for his best friend. And she'd kissed the fucking sense out of him because he wasn't ending it. "Honestly, I don't know. He can be hard to read, but he's a hick, likes to live rurally. Went to college in Provo. There's a chance he misses the cold."

Another drink. "Good to know."

"You're not even going to ask me if I like it?" He sounded bitter even to his own ears.

"I don't know if you'd like being anywhere. You seem content to make yourself miserable. Why else would you say no to me?" She slid her drink to him. "All yours." Then she was walking away.

Leaving.

No goodbye. No number. No name.

Chapter Three

"Mr. Gomez, it's so good to see you." Veronica's voice had transformed into her fake phone call voice. The one used when you're in the supermarket talking with your mother and she's begging you to take home that nice Jewish boy who's always alone on Christmas and you want to tell her straight that you watched him mainline pencil lead in middle school but a rosy-cheeked grandmother is already frowning at the sheer quantity of *her-pleasure* condoms in your cart and you don't want to seem like the *worst* fucking person to shop at a Hannaford's, so you say, 'Oh yeah, Mom. He'd love to sit and watch us open presents. I'll get his number from the phone book.'

It was the voice you held until you got to the parking lot and alphabetized the reasons Joshua Morris would, under no circumstances, enter your family home.

The esteemed Fulgencio Gomez, however, could not be as easily escaped with a swipe of her credit card and a tight smile.

The East Coast had yet to get out of bed and Gomez had already ruined Victoria's day.

Channeling bond villain, the Mountaineers' owner, wore an expensive, double-breasted, camel coat indoor during summer in Texas. Rich people didn't sweat from what Victoria gathered during her childhood, watching trust fund kids stomp down the boardwalk in leather pants and Anthropolgie sweaters during the Fourth of July.

If he did sweat, one of the hotel staff would claim the ceiling spontaneously sprung a leak and whisk him away, already on the phone with dry cleaning.

They hadn't breathed since Gomez stepped into the pretentious lobby.

Gomez hotels were renowned for their opulence. For extravagance and excess. They were not a home away from home. They were *better* than home. They were palaces, mansions that demanded gentle, almost reverent voices, and delivered on high expectations. Marble Venetian floors, arched self-darkening windows, and massage chairs came standard in every suite.

Custom art was commissioned for each hotel, watercolor landscapes, charcoal portraits, ceramic figurines. The Gomez Houston's sweeping three-foot hand-blown glass lilies were on Yelp's top ten sights to see.

Victoria's hands were sweating. She felt a headache root. She wanted to run, to hide. He'd caught her by surprise, flying down here.

Gomez's surprises were known to induce ulcers and alcoholism.

He's not a god, Victoria reminded herself. Without the luxury clothes, without the hand of solid gold rings, the exorbitant wealth, Fulgencio Gomez was markedly average. A few years short of retirement, his body was shutting down early, speckled gray hair, a shock white mustache overhanging his mouth, wrinkled brown skin.

"I only wish I could say the same." Gomez, despite deep, solid roots in Madrid, had no semblance of his native accent. Trained away. Along with human emotion, Victoria expected. "When I called Midas' agent this morning to congratulate him, he said he did not know what I was speaking of."

"Midas and I have yet to connect, but I am—"

"Then what, pray tell, has occupied your time for the past four weeks, my dear? I have allowed you a unique opportunity to be in charge of my recruiting. Do this well and you have your pick of career options. But you seem intent on tying my hands. How badly must you want to fail to avoid Midas in his very own city?"

"I'm working on different leads until Midas gets back to me." A nervous shiver went through her. Why, today of all days, had she worn her miserable black dress? "Specifically, I'm speaking with Cole Seeder. Once I've connected with one member of the team, it'll be easier to finagle a meeting with Midas."

"Cole Seeder?"

"An offensive tackle, sir. Toby likes him, so does Foss."

He bristled. "Must I remind you that the GM and Coach do not pay your fee? I do, and I want a star. I want the stands to be filled for my first American football game. I want jerseys on back order, and do you know, dear Miss Steer, what sells tickets and jerseys?"

She refused to look down. "Midas."

He ignored her. "Midas. Named for a king because he is one and he's going to be a king on my mountain. Midas in green."

"Yes," she said, her fake voice rising. Another pitch and she'd break glass.

Beside them, the concierge hovered in the doorway in case Gomez were to lunge for it.

Never mind that she'd hauled her own suitcase across the gleaming lobby just four nights ago, chasing the Midas tip. "Mr. Gomez, I assure you I am handling the situation and taking all of your needs into consideration."

"I have but one, and it is Midas." Gomez's hands slid into his pockets. "I will sell jerseys that say Midas. My family will wear them for the holiday."

"A family affair," Victoria schmoozed, hating herself, wondering if it sounded as shrill to other people as it did to her own ears. She couldn't fuck this up. He was right.

She was in this, all or nothing, for better or worse, cards face up. Knock this job out of the park and have her whole life fall into place, every opportunity hers to seize. Doors would never close on her. Calls would never go unanswered.

Or she could fail, destroy her reputation, lose her paycheck, become a pariah. Black listed, ghosted, ridiculed, unfit to work. She'd be lucky to recruit for the Canadian football league, spend her years putting ketchup on mac and cheese. The ultimate nightmare. No shattered glass ceiling, no vengeance, no recognition for the grief she'd endured.

The name Victoria Steer would be another in a wretched pile of women who tried and failed to join the boys.

Well fuck that.

"I'm signing Seeder today," Victoria told Gomez, chin raised. "You caught me on my way to print off the contract."

Overconfident? Yes.

But she'd bawl at Seeder's feet, bolt herself to his door to make it true. By any means. That's what Morgan had taught her. That's what it took to survive.

"Very Good," came Gomez's crisp reply. "Confirm the offer with Zither. Aim low. We'll need more room in the cap to afford Midas. Gold, I don't have to tell you, is not cheap."

"I have quite the stack set aside." Never mind that Toby Zither, the team's GM, had given her full access to the cash, told her to use it, when necessary, not once mentioning rationing for the king.

"Training camp is a week away, dear. And I haven't seen a single story regarding our acquisitions."

She struggled to stop herself from saying, *have you been living in a hole? Does ESPN not play on private jets?* "Don't worry. I'm saving the best for last."

"I enjoy a bit of drama, Miss Steer." His tone indicated nothing of the sort. "But at the end of the night, I prefer to know I have what I want under lock and key." Without a farewell bid, without a handshake, he turned on his oxfords, stalking through the open door.

Alone, Victoria let out a full body shudder.

It'd be less stressful to swap recipes with the grim reaper.

On a mission, she went directly to the hotel bar.

Tiered mimosa towers and over-garnished Bloody Marys lined the glistening white bar top, waiters in mauve soda shop shirts claimed the best for their waiting tables.

Winding through a hungover bachelorette party dedicated to their schedule, Victoria snagged a stout pedestal table for herself, slinking into the plush chair and scanning the neat row of televisions overhanging the quartzite bar. Instantly, she found ESPN, third from the left.

She made her office there in the syrup scented air, setting out her laptop, her folders, a stack of yellow sticky notes, and her headphones. Placing a silky amaranth napkin over her bare legs, she tucked into the bowl of candy coated almonds next to the stunted bouquet of white roses.

Scrolling through her spreadsheets, she fidgeted.

Gomez was an extravagant man. He'd bought peacocks for his third wife, and when the prettiest one tried to flee via a willow tree, he'd shipped the whole parade to the New York Zoo.

Thousands of dollars spent and lost in three days. Because he could.

He'd bought the Mountaineers to prove he wasn't the same Spain bound hotel magnate Fulgencio Senior was.

No, Junior was fresh and full of ideas. He spread his hotels across the United States and with his earnings, bought the most American thing in the world.

An NFL team. Centered around none other than America's blonde sweetheart.

Not the typical American Dream, but one, nonetheless.

Reflecting on her progress, his dream seemed closer to fantasy.

Gomez was not the only person Victoria needed to please.

As GM, Toby wanted an even talent spread across the team and prioritized polishing rough materials over time. Similarly, Coach

Foss feared missing pieces. In their last call, he threatened murder at the prospect of a safety doubling as an outside lineman.

Both refused to authorize the amount of cash necessary to secure Midas. Too limiting, too much.

Yet all these men, with different priorities, agreed Midas would be a welcome addition.

Therefore, Victoria would get him.

There was no hope of finding him until tonight when the Allgood Lounge opened. Until then, she needed results. Physical results.

She needed Cole.

His stats were a thrill to read. High-impact player, limited injury record, excellent man-to-man coverage. It took less than twenty minutes to compile a respectable offer. If Dimples was right and Cole didn't like Texas, he wouldn't need much incentive to accept.

For Gomez's sake, she emailed a copy of the offer to Toby for review.

A coaster grazed her pinky, jolting Victoria from her work.

"Can I get something to drink?" The gruff, southern drawl raised the fine hairs on the back of her neck.

"An apple juice with a straw," she said, tearing away from her screen to smile at the handsome, dark-skinned server. "Quick question." She nodded at the television. A highlight reel from last season. "Are you a fan of Midas?"

"Everyone is." His tone was too hard to believe he was included in everyone.

Victoria draped a hand over the back of her chair. "He's a good player for sure, but do you like him? Do you have his jersey? Watch his post-game interviews?"

"Kid's a little cocky," said the server, Marcus, according to the copper embroidery on his Gomez Bar and Lounge shirt. He leaned close to spill his guts like a sinner at confession. "A real Texan wins without dancing up and down the field."

"What about his back-up?" She flipped to his report, stomach clenching. "Rose?"

Rose. A horrible name for such a powerful man.

A man she still tasted. A man she hadn't even recognized.

Marcus scratched his chin thoughtfully. "Rose was good back when. Haven't seen him since Midas walked out. Seemed solid, steady hand, short in the pocket."

Victoria fought back a grin. She may not like Texas, but she appreciated a Texan. Every one had near religious opinions about football.

"Yeah," she agreed, picking through Rose's numbers. He hadn't started a game in almost three years, but before that... wow.

Popping a lavender colored almond into her mouth, she sank back in her seat. She'd bag two today.

***

HAND RAISED, VICTORIA squinted against the sun's glare. Forty minutes outside Houston and it felt like a different world.

It wasn't the ocean from home, but she greeted it like an old friend, a scratch of yearning twisting her stomach. The familiar tingle of salt hit her nose as she listened to the calls and cries of pelicans and seagulls performing acrobatics feet above the clear, blue water.

She almost closed her eyes to absorb it, to sink back ten years when the sea was as familiar as her reflection. Almost.

There were problems with the Gulf sea. For one, it was a fuck lot hotter than Newport ever got. The water near bubbling, the air thick and heavy. And it was missing the tumultuous ocean waves forged over miles of open sea. In the Gulf, the breakwater didn't sting your cheeks like errant shards of ice. Swells didn't swallow bobbing boats.

Mindful not to catch a heel in the cracks of the dock, Victoria checked the notes on her phone and stopped in front of the *Circe*.

A thousand guesses and she wouldn't have said cheap midsize fishing boat with a sagging hammock strung across the stern.

"You live on a boat?" she called. The familiar whimper of fiberglass compressing bumpers was her only response. They said he'd be here. Warren Rose. Dimples. Quarterback. Boat captain.

There was no front door to knock on, no bell to ring on a fucking boat, and it felt much too piratey to swing herself onto the narrow deck. Never mind that she had her tongue wrapped in his the night before.

Memories she'd reveled in last night, alone in her hotel room, watching the welcome channel loop through blurred vision, her hand between their thighs.

He'd said no to her. Gone cold. Closed himself off. Damn her need to impress, the denial only excited her more.

No.

No touching, fondling, or admiring, she reminded herself, glancing up and down the dock in case a crowd had formed to read her filthy mind. Throw tomatoes at her. Over chilled apple juice and sugared nuts, she'd shut that fiery yearning inside a lead box, locked it, and tossed it to sea.

A slam punctured the air. Hinges creaked, and the very man she'd sworn off climbed to the deck of the *Circe*, long limbs attacking the creaking ladder.

He was big in a bar. Tall. Imposing.

On a boat, he was enormous. Tanned body rising like Poseidon from a parted sea, her knees begged to hit the floor, to worship. Warren Rose made the *Circe* look like a raft fashioned of twine and turtle shells.

No shirt. Bare feet. Low rise, light wash jeans.

"Can you even fit a bed in there?" She peered around him to catch a glimpse of the cabin below, attributing the flutter in her stomach to rapidly fermenting apple juice. "One that fits you, I mean?"

Light brown eyes glided to her and snagged, snapping down her fitted black dress.

His skin loved the sun, shone with it, seizing wayward rays and greedily consuming them. Victoria fixated on his jeans, the baseball cap sitting backward on his head, dark strands escaping through the eyelet.

Were those the same jeans from last night?

Her heart surged. Was there a wet spot on the left thigh, evidence of how—

No. She lifted her chin, smiled. "Remember me?"

He turned, giving her his back, ignoring her, telling the water, "You make it sound like a bad thing. Living on a boat."

In two strides, he was on the opposite side of the bow, spreading distance between them as he adjusted the lines of three massive fishing poles.

"It is," Victoria told the shifting muscles in his shoulders, trying to not to stomp her foot and yell *look at me!* "It smells like fish and oil." And it didn't matter to her at all because she'd discovered twin dimples right above his ass.

A thirst to trace them, to splay her hands across the indents and pull as he thrust into her rose.

She stiffened her jaw, unsure what spell he had her under. He wasn't even her type. Never mind that he was a football player, making him resolutely off limits.

He was wrong for her.

Too tall, too nice. A hero complex. His smile wasn't one that dazzled, but lazily crept up on you. Stealthily imprinting on your memory. She could return home and not remember a single face, but his smile would stick to her skin.

Most players—they were too headstrong, too loud, too arrogant to be tempting. Quarterbacks were an even more conceited breed. Completely intolerable.

"Why call it the *Circe*?" she asked despite herself.

As he turned, he asked with a rumble, "Did we make plans or something?" In seven sweeping steps, he was across the bow. With the water lapping at the wood planked dock and the *Circe*'s swollen hull, they met head on.

Victoria lifted to her toes until they were nose to nose.

"How did you find me?" Warren asked, voice icy, muscle jumping in his cheek.

"You gave yourself away, Warren. Or is it War? You could go by Rose, by any other name would be—"

"So what..." His stare was detached, lifeless. "You figured out who I am, and you regret blowing me off, is that it?"

"You almost did it," she said, boldly planting a hand on his shoulder to help herself onto the *Circe*'s deck. "I'll admit you snuck right under my radar, but Cole gave you away. Friends with him, we work together. I googled *tall, dark, and handsome* plus *Houston*, and you popped right up, top of the list." She brought her hands together, beaming with pride. "One call to the team, claiming I'm looking for the father of my unborn child and bam, they gave me your address." She paused, glanced back at the dock. "Or slip number."

Though a slow clap would have been appreciated, it wasn't expected.

Neither was Warren's foul stare, the force with which he ripped off his hat and hurled it on the floor, hand scrubbing down his face. "Christ, you're fucking crazy. I didn't think women like you actually existed."

"Oh, we do." Victoria retrieved the hat, straightened the bill and held it to him, smiling when he snatched it back. "You should be glad we do. We're the ones who get things done."

"By lying."

Brows raised, Victoria strolled the perimeter of the deck. Who would've guessed Dimples had such a bite? And on such a beautiful day. Fascinating.

Aware of his trailing gaze, she kept her steps smooth, her posture relaxed, and switched tactics. "Relax." She traced along an almost invisible fishing line, plucking it with her nail. "You're no fun. I told the team the truth."

A rough, caustic laugh broke from his throat. The same timbre he'd groaned into her skin. "Which is that you're psychotic?"

"Rude."

"Go on," he insisted, regarding her with disdain. "What possible reason could you have for coming? Don't tell me you're my long-lost sister?"

Victoria perched on the squat bulkhead, spreading out to cross her business casual highlighter yellow heels, wicked smile curving her lips. "If we were related it would explain why we're both so good at kissing."

Warren faced her like an enemy. Tanned, strong shoulders hard with tension, folded arms high on his chest, a firm, unflinching wide stance.

Chin lowered, voice hard, he warned, "Red."

Hiding her smile, Victoria peered over the boat's edge. The water was brighter, sharper than it was at home. A cerulean canopy for a bed of seaweed.

"I called you Dimples," she told her reflection before pushing to her feet, stepping into his space.

Fresh soap and sea salt.

Her skin prickled. "Unfortunately, we're past nicknames now. I'm Victoria Steer and I'm going to make your dreams come true."

"Victoria." He tasted it on his lips, honey eyes skimming her, matching the name to the face. Carefully, his hand spanned her shoulder, warm skin coaxing a shiver up her spine.

Bending—he was so tall he had to bend—he asked softly, "Did you do all this to fuck me?" He didn't sound mad. Intrigued, maybe. Definitely interested.

"No." She sighed, sidestepping out of his hold. Flattering and once mutual, but she had rules. "That opportunity has passed. I'm going to make you a star quarterback again."

***

RED BEAMED AT him, smirk twisting her soft, sinful lips. She had a million-dollar smile and smirked instead. Warren should've guessed. Victoria. A name suited for her. Beautiful, dashing, rare.

Diabolical.

At last, he understood the glint in her eyes. She was one of an army whose purpose was to use him for their own gain. Another in a long line of self-serving backstabbers. The more success he yielded, the more vipers slipped from the woodwork.

The fact that he hadn't recognized her instantly, hadn't taken one look at the dress of sin, the sultry smile, and pinned her as dangerous, showed how far he'd fallen. Shaking his head slightly in silent reprimand, Warren blew out a suffering exhale, seeing Victoria in a new light.

Not a seductive hellion, but the devil. She'd even worn black. Prim molded black to match her hair and soul.

She waited for him, suddenly patient and amiable, palms extended, as if she were offering him hope, a dream.

Their gazes clashed, brown versus blue. Land and sea. "No," he said curtly, voice so guttural it scraped his throat. "I don't deal with devils."

He was finished with this, with her and her perverse game. He went to leave, to escape, to breathe in exhaust fumes until he forgot the way she smelled like sunscreen and sin.

He stopped. "Dammit, this is my boat. You get out."

Victoria jolted with surprise, approaching him like a wild animal, eyes gentle, movements cautious. A wave rolled the *Circe*, the hull hit wood, Warren braced.

Red didn't. She jerked sideways on her ridiculous—sexy—shoes.

Instinct forced him to lunge, to catch her, spinning to absorb her momentum until they were pressed against the pedestal steering wheel.

He never expected to live on a fishing boat. Have one, yes. He'd vowed on it when he first signed with the Texans. One twice the size of the *Circe* laden the highest end reels, graphite fiberglass composite rods, and a full-time driver who knew where to buy the best cigars. His fantasy boat had a pretentious name, something like *Tax Refund* or *Money Pit*, and he'd waste every off-season weekend trolling for sailfish.

Three years ago, Warren had bought the *Circe* in a bid of desperation over a series of shady cash deals. There were no property taxes on a boat. There was no mortgage to pay off. No costly electrical bills. He even got a free parking spot with his slip.

Her problems were aplenty. The engine leaked oil. The hull was encrusted with barnacles. When it rained, water pooled on the deck and funneled straight down the stairs to flood his living quarters. His bed frame sat on cinder blocks and the whole cabin smelled suspiciously of mold.

It had taken him an entire week to carve out the doorways to stop smacking his forehead on the frame, and not just his feet, but also his ankles and calves hung off the end of his mattress. The old gal wasn't perfect, but at least he never had to worry about finding the cash to mow a lawn, heat the house, and once he fixed the starter and clogged the oil leak, he could fish his life away.

Alone, just him and the sea.

"Isn't Newport on the water? Is this your first time on a boat?" Feeling her smooth, soft skin made his tone sharp and sullen. He wanted to recoil, but he couldn't make himself let go.

Crystalline blue pierced him. "Did you look it up," she teased, "or figure it out on your own that places with port in the title reside on the water?" It didn't sound acerbic. As if she really wanted to know if he'd thought about her after she took off last night.

Christ, had he. He clenched his jaw to keep from admitting it.

"I've been on boats," she continued. "Custom yachts, grand, imposing sailboats, enormous catamarans. No dinghies like this. Not on the real ocean. The *TB Circe* would get crushed."

There she was. The firecracker, his hellion had returned, gathered her poise.

With immense effort, Warren peeled his arms from her, maintaining a firm grip on her bicep to keep her steady. "Allow me to show you to the exit." He spoke through locked teeth, waving his finger in a circle around them. "Goodbye."

"You don't even know what I'm offering."

His nostrils flared, muscles jerking in an enraged frenzy. "I saw the way you were eyeing Doyle. Ergo, I'm not interested in whatever you have to say. I've had this talk before. Let me show you how it goes. I don't have his number. I don't know where he lives. We play together, we're not buddies."

Narrowed gaze never leaving her, he pulled her close, letting her feel how powerfully he meant what he said. In a falsely quiet voice, he told her, "I wish, how I fucking wish, I could give you his information because I'd much rather he dealt with you, but I don't have it. Feel free to take the dock or the water back to shore. Watch for the hooks."

Using Warren to get to Doyle was a waste of both of their time.

Rather than snap or defend, rather than jerk from his punishing hold, Victoria said in a pleasantly amused tone, "As if you'd be so lucky to see me wet."

He coughed a dry laugh. "I have."

A flick of her brow was a gentle concession.

Fire lit through him.

"I don't buy it," she said, not moving an inch, the brush of her arm between them somehow erotic. "The woe is me quarterback attitude. The NFL is mean, women use me to get Doyle sad story. It's garbage and not at all relevant. I don't want him, I want you."

Warren snorted. "I'm not strapped for ass. I don't take leftovers."

"I said the offer's off the table. I'm here on business."

"That's why you kissed me?"

"I didn't recognize you." She pushed from him, shaking out her fingers. "You don't have the classic meatiness of a football player." She was careful not to look at him. "I don't care about Midas."

Warren shook his head. He'd heard that before. Heard coaches tell him not to worry about Midas, heard girlfriends say they didn't even know him before hopping into his bed. "Leave."

Indignant, she sat between his fishing poles, nails trilling against the bulkhead. "Did I go to Allgood for him last night? Yes."

Warren threw his hands out. "An admission. Finally."

"But I found you instead and now—"

"Now you're willing to settle. You found out he doesn't take any pretty girl that throws herself at him."

Lush lips twitched into a frown. "You're cruel. I'm gorgeous, not pretty. And sex is off the table, remember? I want you to play him, not fuck me."

His hands curled into fists. "Play him? Play Doyle? What the hell are you spewing?"

In an elegant whirl, she rose, absentmindedly dusting off her neat, black skirt. "I'm here on behalf of the Vermont Mountaineers. You may have heard of us nestled up north in picturesque Burlington, with our shiny never-before-played-in stadium. The first expansion to the NFL in twenty years. I'm their recruiter."

He stared at her, waiting for the lie to come. Waiting for her to laugh and say *kidding*.

She didn't.

She reached into the wallet sized purse on her hip and retrieved a sleek white card.

He didn't even look at it. The way she held it out. So obvious. Blatant. Arrogant. He wouldn't be surprised if it said, *believe me, you fucking idiot.*

Flipping it between her fingers, she said, "I haven't found a quarterback yet. Well... until right now." She wiggled the paper again.

He let it dangle, staring, completely disoriented. He'd heard of the team, the focus of the upcoming season. He knew they were amassing players. But learning it was *her* hiring them. He froze. "You came here for Midas and now you want me? Why?"

"Why not?" She threw back without hesitation. "Is there something I should know? I watched your reel tapes. You're solid. Everybody likes you. I can offer you an attractive contract. Three times what you're making now."

"But..." He fumbled for words, blinking rapidly. Hands numb and loose at his sides. "Why?"

"Because I want you. Because it's my choice, my team that I'm putting together, and you'll be the perfect addition." Powder blue eyes flashed to him, a devious smile edged her mouth. "I want you like that too, but not anymore. You're business now and I don't fuck where I eat. So say yes, Warren, and I'll be your fairy godmother."

His mind raced. His mouth opened. "No."

Chapter Four

"Listen." Victoria angled her laptop screen so she could simultaneously watch the news, ESPN, the Real Housewives of Salt Lake City, and two of her three bosses while keeping her beer out of the shot. "We can get Laughlin, Asher Laughlin, the wide receiver, if we skip on Midas." She held Toby's stare as she spoke. He understood money.

And, evidently, good lighting.

Their conference calls didn't keep to a schedule. Especially with Victoria on the road. Today, she'd set the meeting during her lunch, which a couple time zones away meant Toby was still in his morning tracksuit, a steaming *I love my Grandpa* mug of coffee blocking half his face.

Coach Rodney Foss leaned back in his chair, hands bracing his head. The wall behind him appeared to be in a dungeon of sorts, layered cinder blocks and no windows. A singular white light shone on his narrow, tanned face. "What does Gomez think?"

Victoria's lips pursed. "He doesn't understand the logistics or cash-flow like we do. He wants flash when we need a team."

Flippant, Foss said, "Nice story. Doesn't stop him from firing us if we don't deliver."

Toby nodded his agreement, white squares reflecting on his glasses. "Fulgencio wants Midas."

"We can give Rose a cool new nickname. We'll call him—" Dimples came to mind, then Sweetcakes, then Flowers, and holy fucking hottest guy in the world. "Zeus. He's better than Midas. We'll tape a lightning bolt to his jersey. Teach him Greek."

Foss's laugh crackled through her headphones.

"He's just as good as Midas," Victoria went on. "I've seen the play tape."

"If he's just as good, why isn't he playing?" This from Foss, pragmatic bastard.

Of her three bosses, she felt closest with Toby, so she implored him, leaning in to fill the screen. "Because of stupid player politics. Midas outmaneuvered Rose off-field somehow. Since he started, Rose hasn't played. Rose hasn't moved teams once in his entire career. I bet he's desperate for a change. He'll come if we compile a fair offer."

Didn't matter that he'd said no just two hours ago.

Warren's answer had surprised her enough to make her leave, come back to the hotel, back to her table, and skip the apple juice for something stronger. No, he's said. He hadn't meant it. It was a lapse in judgment, a mistake. One she'd rectify.

Covering her camera, Victoria took a swig of her IPA, hating the bitterness, loving the memory. Swallowing, she bolstered herself. She'd change Warren's mind as soon as she finished changing everyone else's.

"Well which is it?" Foss needled. "Are we going to save money on him or are we going to give him a good offer?"

Maintaining an even tone, Victoria offered a fake smile. "Both," she said. "We could easily double, even triple, his salary and it wouldn't even scratch the amount we'd spend on Midas. We'll have enough left over to negotiate during the season and entice some bigger names to the team. Better receivers, a solid tight end."

Before she finished, Foss was shaking his head.

Victoria went into attack mode, teeth clenching. "I guarantee Laughlin will come to Vermont."

"You want to double Rose's salary?" Toby clarified, forehead a mess of wrinkles. "What is he making down there?" The GM kept his tone placating, having witnessed many a fight between Foss and Victoria. Tired today, his eyes instructed her to sit back and calm down. This wasn't the fight to pick.

"It's horrendous." Victoria softened her tone and checked her notes, pulling the salaries she'd gathered that morning. For a quarterback... she was starting to understand the boat. "They've been short changing him for years."

Toby sipped his coffee. "Why?"

"The rumor mill mentioned a difficult agent. Not open to negotiations, hard to find, bad communicator. Altogether lackluster."

Rocking in his chair, Foss remained unimpressed. "Agents reflect players. If we even wanted him, how'd you do it?"

Victoria ignored the familiar sinking in her stomach, shooting acidly, "Most recruiters don't have double Ds, Rodney."

"Jesus." His hands shot up like she had a gun to his temple. "Can you not say that? That's exactly what coaches get fired for."

Her smile was positively poisonous.

"Calm," Toby interjected. "Here's how we'll do it. Make Midas the same offer as Rose. We'll send them out together. Whoever accepts gets on the plane."

Victoria stiffened. "Absolutely not. If I lowball Midas, he'll get pissed and never talk to me again."

Foss sat forward, dragging a hand through his shorn, dark hair. "Toby's right. Do it. That way, we can tell Gomez that Midas blew us off and go forward with Rose."

She bit the inside of her cheek, toes curling. *No.* They were thinking like coaches, like GMs. Like two men secure in their positions. Victoria was twenty-five. This was her first real job. She couldn't afford to antagonize a star quarterback.

"It's settled," Toby nodded. "I'm out of here." His screen went black and then Foss's frown took over.

"Watch him play the Seahawks," Victoria asked of the coach, extending a wilted olive branch. "He's good."

"You had me at Laughlin. I've wanted him since his college years." His screen went black.

Victoria ripped off her headphones, letting the quiet chatter of the bar suck away at her energy.

It was shit working for three bosses. Three men. With vast egos and no concept of compromise. It was half the reason she'd gotten the job. No one else would touch it.

The idea of pulling a team together, finding fifty-three men to play the most competitive sport in the world from scratch was enticing, alluring, lovely.

Building it with a chain around your ankle, a blindfold, and handcuffs left Victoria sweating. She'd hand over more than sweat, she'd give rivers of blood, spit her teeth out. She'd finish the job. Stamp her name on a legacy, become synonymous with football.

Like Atlas, she'd carry the mountain on her shoulders.

And come September eighth, her resumé would be four words: I made the Mountaineers. As soon as the season began and contracts were signed, she'd split, ink still wet.

On to the next.

She could work anywhere, do anything. No one would double check her references, ask her to get coffees, assume she was the secretary. Never again would she be dismissed, mistreated, disrespected.

Coaches, agents, even players would scramble to shake her hand.

Whispers in restaurants would follow her. *She built the Mountaineers. She's a legend.*

Sipping the last third of her beer, Victoria pictured it, warmth bubbling up her chest. The glory, the retribution. The look on Morgan's stupid face. She'd write a book, start a cool catch phrase, trademark a badass nickname, like *The Shark* or *The Sniper*, become a regular on SportsCenter, host a special show on draft day.

She could taste it. Now all she had to do was finish it.

***

WARREN PAUSED HALFWAY out of his car door. A violent rush scoring his skin. His body tensed, thoughts contracting, heart pounding. He felt his teeth grind, a saw rattling his sanity.

Only one sound could coax such a flurry of feelings.

Caught between the urge to laugh and punch something, Warren slammed his door shut.

Whatever Victoria had dosed him with in her kiss had left him brash, impulsive, and emotional. He burned. Burned for the most confounding, intoxicating woman he'd ever met.

A woman who wanted him and didn't.

Who abandoned him and stalked him.

A woman determined to use him.

Still, he burned, blazed at the prospect of seeing her again, watching her pupils dilate, like storms shrouding the ocean.

Usually Warren's desire was binary. If she had an ulterior motive, he wasn't interested. Why then, when Victoria opened her mouth and doomed herself, when she admitted her bid to use him, did he get hard at the mere sound of her voice, did he crave salt and lose focus?

Collecting the plastic bags from the backseat, Warren took a deep, steadying breath and snaked around the side of Cole's house. If it could indeed be called that.

The ranch sat on sixty acres, and the house was sized to match. An emasculating six-thousand square feet.

Enormous. Outrageous. The *Circe* could fit in the laundry room. Vaulted ceilings, custom woodwork, corbels at every threshold. Surprise, the best offensive tackle in the league made mad money.

It was a home for a family, Warren had realized when Cole showed him the blueprints. Master suite on the first floor, on the second, a cluster of smaller bedrooms, jack and jill bathrooms, a bonus game space with a loft.

Cole wanted a family. To be a father, a husband. And something stopped him. In their three years together, Cole had never mentioned a date, a woman. No strings for Cole, no attachment, only tormented one night stands.

Naturally, Cole was silent about how much went into the house. When Warren asked what he needed the space for, his friend had shrugged, before saying thoughtfully, "I need more room than most."

Words from other men would've been smug, implying his size, his wealth merited more space. Required it.

No one could accuse Cole of arrogance.

Three hundred pounds, six-foot-five. He hardly fit through regular doors. Of course he needed a bigger house, bigger rooms, extra space. And, of course, he hosted their weekly dinner. Saved Warren from cleaning out the *Circe*'s bilge pump.

From the moment Warren added a chilled, overpriced six pack to his bag at the Stop & Shop, he'd been bracing for Cole's foul mood. For the deep, unrelenting line between his eyebrows. Mentally, he'd prepared himself to listen to crickets and watch his friend recover from the night before.

But laughter trickled across the freshly cut lawn, bounced off the glistening pool and shattered like glass, spraying the hand laid terracotta tiled porch with warmth.

Sunlight spilled across the back porch, long slants of a dimming yellow cast wild shadows onto the metal patio set.

Victoria's feet dangled in the water, kicking gently as Cole handed her a frosted glass. How she convinced the brute to make her a margarita, Warren would never know. Salt lined the rim, a freshly cut lime floated on the ice.

As Warren climbed the stone path, he caught Cole's low voice. "Rhode Island is made of many islands, right? I always thought that was confusing. Call it Rhode Islands." Absurdly, Cole sounded chatty.

Victoria's shoulders shook as she giggled like a schoolgirl passing notes, as if the offensive tackle was a secret admirer intent to charm. She was in a new dress, not red or black. She'd gone for the kill in a dark steel blue. Knotted at her waist, the satiny material flared around her, forcing Warren to picture her bare skin, those lace navy panties resting on the hot tile.

"Not many people know that, but I should've never underestimated you. From what I understand, the less a man speaks, the more intelligent he is."

"Is it the same for women?" Warren asked.

Ignoring the liquid fire in his veins, he strode directly past her to drop the groceries on the eight foot wrought iron dining table.

Setting a hand over her brow, Victoria grinned. "You'd love it if I were dumb, wouldn't you? I would have slept with you."

Desperate to quell the rising fire in his chest, Warren spun the cap off a beer. Reminding himself who she was, what she wanted, he drank until his indignation resurfaced, his resentment piqued. "I recall being the one who turned you down."

"And I took you at your word. Anyone less intelligent would've begged. I mean, look at him." She faced Cole, stirring her ice with the crook of her pinky. "He looks like the tuxedo man on the cake topper. We should smother him in frosting."

Cole smiled.

The bastard smiled.

Not once had Warren coaxed a smile from him on his dark days. No joke, no story, not even a bit of self-inflicted pain was able to wake Cole from his misery.

Victoria did it with ease, didn't seem to be trying, didn't realize she'd performed a miracle.

Some of Warren's anger fled. He would tolerate her company for Cole, for his friend. To have him smile.

Helping himself to a chair, metal scraping tile, Warren asked, "What are you doing here?"

"Isn't it obvious?" She withdrew her legs from the water, flashing pink toenails as she stood. Warren's brow quirked at the soft color. "I'm scouting. I told you this morning when you were embracing me on your boat. Though you do talk a lot, one may wonder how much you actually listen."

Uncapping his own bottle, Cole brushed his long hair over his shoulder and raised dark brows at him. Silent judgment speaking volumes.

"Vic visited me at the docks this morning," Warren explained.

"It's Victoria," she cut in.

Cole's lip rose, just barely, and Warren read it as a tease. "You're a busybody," he accused her while glaring at Cole. "You can't give me a single minute of peace."

"Oh, this body is very busy," she replied, smoothing down her dress, shaking off her feet. "Don't look so glum. I'll be gone tomorrow. Besides, it's not like you two have plans. You're twiddling your thumbs until training camp, and I cook a mean steak."

Warren tensed. "She's staying for dinner?"

Still smiling, Cole shrugged, hand stretched flat over the imposing grill to check the temperature. "I bought three steaks."

Two for Cole, one for Warren. Always.

"Perfect," Victoria said, clearing the salt from her glass with a lick before dropping it on the table beside Warren's beer. "You two relax, I'll cook and then we'll break bread together like a good southern family."

"Grill's touchy," Cole warned, courteous as he handed over metal tongs.

Victoria waved dismissively. "I've used this model a thousand times. I've got it. Based on the daggers Warren's shooting at my back, he wants to talk to you alone."

They made it ten, eleven steps into the yard, grass whipping at their ankles before Cole lifted his hands, all innocence.

After a charged silence, he told Warren, "I only invited her because she told me she was eating alone. I like her."

"You *like* her?" Warren couldn't keep the scorn from creeping into his tone. "When was the last time you liked a woman?"

Tension bracketed Cole's face. Last night's shadows lingered under his eyes, his jaw clicked.

Shit. Warren let out a ragged breath, tugging at his collar, guilt and jealousy battling. "I'm surprised," he managed to say without vitriol. "She's a talker."

And mine.

"Fills the silence."

Warren gave him a questioning glance. "You love silence."

"No." Cole looked out over his land, at the lines of dark and light green hiding the dips, the holes, the imperfections in the lawn. "I just can't find a way to fill it."

Guilt held Warren's throat. For three years, four, the two had been silent together. Bonded in their misery, broken parts collecting dust. In one day, one evening, Victoria understood Cole better than him.

An unaccountably long pause ensued. "How'd you meet her?"

Last night? Warren almost asked. *Did you find each other in the moon draped parking lot, humidity sticking to your skin?*

Had he watched Red push through Allgood's doors only to step into Cole's arms?

Cole read his mind. "Not like that." Sensing Warren's short, tight leash, he quickly added, "She called my agent, made an offer. I accepted. She swung by to drop off the papers."

Warren nearly dropped his beer. "Accepted?"

A distant feeling stung him, one he'd thought he'd outgrown. He tried to shake it off, but it pierced deep, cleaving with expert precision against the tender spot. Suddenly, it was five years ago, Warren was in the PT office, stretching his shoulder, helmet within reach. Opening game of the season at home, versus the Cowboys. Bigger stakes didn't exist, but he was focused, unruffled by the hollering, the cheering, the pre-game scrambling on the other side of the door. The win felt close, almost within reach.

He'd stood as Coach Nale pulled open the door. To this day, Warren couldn't say if Nale had seen him or looked right through as he seized Warren's helmet, and called to the hall, "I found one." Warren remembered tearing after him, livid, when Keith Louden, the GM, stopped him. He remembered the bleak, succinct speech. *Benched, going a different direction, valued player.*

The team had fined him for missing the kickoff.

Abandoned. They'd abandoned him and now so was Cole.

"When were you going to tell me?" Warren asked, clenching his bottle to keep from smashing it. "What the hell, man? You're leaving me?"

Cole's expression went remote, mouth tense. "Four years in the mountains, a nice bonus. I'm tired of the heat. Tired of this."

Only a rich man could be sick of a ranch built less than two years ago.

Shaking his head, Warren slugged back another drink. Giving up this place, a solid spot on a good team, he couldn't imagine.

"I'm tired," Cole repeated, iron in the word, as if admitting it exhausted him further. "It's the same color year round. I tried, but it's not working. I miss the cold, the mountains, the smell of pine, I miss—" he broke off. "Victoria said she made you a fair offer."

Glaring at his empty bottle, Warren sucked in a sharp breath. "If she told you who killed Tupac, would you believe her?"

"People are full of secrets."

***

HE'D BE PICKING char out of his teeth for the next month.

Victoria was not the cook she claimed to be.

Scorched corn. Blackened steaks with icy centers.

Lousy food, they'd run out of beer, and the mosquitoes had crept out, brave as night swept in. Neither Cole nor Warren had time to complain. Not with Victoria's questions bouncing off them.

How did you two meet? What's it like living in Texas? Have you ever wrangled a bull? What about a pig?

She had Cole's years one through ten memorized by the time the steaks hardened past the point of no return.

A churning sky, red bleeding to orange and gold, blanketed the yard and stained the pool. Remote as the property was, set back from the road, the night was quiet, almost somber in its serenity, save for the whine of mosquitoes, the occasional hand slapping skin.

For a man who detested the quiet, Cole had built himself an effective torture chamber. How many nights had he and Cole sat watching dust drift through the air as the shadows lengthened and built, only the roll of distant thunder speaking.

Miserable. He must be. That's why he'd said yes.

A peal of Victoria's laughter warmed the air, drawing a near blush to Cole's cheeks as she tucked his long, unruly hair behind his ear.

"Feathered hoops," she was saying through wheezing breaths. "They'll call you visionary."

"Or a masochist." Cole's face was shiny, dark eyes slit with a twinkle of mischief.

Her laugh went soundless, her shoulders shaking, "Imagine." She gasped for air. "The fans in their matching sets."

They were off, cackling like drunken best friends. There'd been no talk of football. Expertly, Victoria steered the topic away whenever it was brought up. Collapsing back in her chair, rubbing her arms for warmth, she beamed with the same effervescent light she had at Allgood, like a bonfire floating on the sea. Her every bewitching word injected life in the evening.

Warren had to ask, "How did Doyle say no to you?"

He couldn't picture a man that could say no. The way she curled her bare feet into the seat beneath her, clutched at her empty glass as if it were a hard-won trophy, rolling the bare rim against her salt swollen lips.

The sunset soaked her in orange. A melted creamsicle sugar coating on her skin.

What would she look like if she stayed in Texas? Would her pale skin darken, freckle? Would she trade the dresses for cutoffs? Let her hair grow out to frizz in the heat? Warren struggled to see it, couldn't imagine her changing for anything, not even nature.

"I haven't spoken to Midas yet," she said once her voice returned. "Doyle, no wonder he wanted a nickname." Her nose wrinkled. "It's like he's got his own Secret Service and I don't have a high enough security clearance. I thought I'd catch him in his natural habitat."

Cole nodded. "Drinking."

She tipped her glass to him. "And getting ass. You wouldn't believe how many football players live in bars and clubs."

"He's trash," Warren said, bunching up his napkin.

Victoria lifted an eyebrow. "Don't get all high and mighty. I found you there, too."

Cole's gaze shot to his feet, either embarrassed or guilty.

Shit, Warren was a terrible friend. Quickly, he said, "I don't care how many women he sleeps with. His personal life doesn't matter. It's his fucking behavior."

Pink lips set in a line. "Because he took your spot?"

"Because I taught him everything. I took him under my wing. I showed him how the entire sport worked, how the games are faster, the players stronger, harder." A dark, roiling emotion smothered the night. Warren flexed his fingers, pulse building. "And at the very first opportunity he had, Doyle stepped on my back to replace me. No fucking *thank you*. No *I'm sorry*."

"Would you be happy then?" Victoria interrupted his rant, leaning back in her chair. "If he said thank you, would you be happy to be a second string quarterback?"

A simple question, dragged down by lead weights. He heard the forced brightness in her tone, caught the sharpening of her eyes.

A rock landed in his stomach.

They weren't friends sharing dinner. She was interrogating them, in bare feet and chlorine soaked calves, a margarita in her stomach. This was how she got answers. By lowering their guard. Playing the Trojan horse.

Warren tore his eyes off her to glare at the horizon, sealed his lips.

"Come to camp," she said softly, her hand folding on top of his. Soft, warm. "Don't sign anything. Just give it a chance. Don't you want to play again?"

Asking a man in space if he wanted oxygen would be a less obvious question. Warren lived to play, to walk out onto the field and stare down eighty yards, to march, step by grueling step, if he had to.

Five years since he'd felt that rush. Five years he'd waited on the sidelines. Nobody asked for him, nobody subbed him, sent him out. Nobody wanted him.

Why did she? Why would Vermont?

Because they couldn't get Midas. That was why.

He ripped his hand from hers.

From the end of the table, Cole said, "He can't."

"Why?" Victoria went straight in her seat, hands closing over her ribs as she glanced between them.

"It's your agent," she deduced carefully. "You think he'll say no. He won't. Cole's practically wept when I called. I'm expecting an invitation to Rosh Hashanah."

Cole stood. "I'm going to wash the dishes."

"What's the problem here? What am I missing?" Astute, Victoria twisted back and forth in her seat, searching for the answer.

Embarrassment forced Warren to stare down the sun, a shred of brandished brass hiding at the base of the sherbet sky. "If I'm not playing, I won't get hurt, lower odds of retirement. I'm a sure thing, a steady paycheck." Pressing his palms against the steel table, he said darkly, "I didn't become a bitter fucking bastard because of Midas. It's because of people like my agent, like you."

Blue heat sliced to him. "People like me?"

A born competitor, he welcomed the gentle challenge in her tone. "Who pays your bills, Vic? Me. After you convince me to leave, to uproot my life, change everything, you walk off and count your money. Doesn't matter what happens to me."

She didn't look at him as she replied flatly, "Victoria. That's my name. Victoria. Not Vic. Not Tory. Not Red."

She rose a different breed. Not the seductress of last night, not this morning's thorn. Even the charmer had fled. Shoulders back, chin high, she laid her hands on the table to match Warren's aggressive pose. A fighter. "Of course I get paid to sign you. I got a check for Cole. A big one. In exchange, he never has to suffer through a hot muggy Texas summer with you. I'm not a leech, Flowers. What I'm offering is mutually beneficial."

"I've heard the sales pitch."

Her fingers slipped between the gaps of the metal grate tabletop, gripping tightly. "Not from me."

"And how are you different?"

She opened her mouth, a flurry of fire storming forward.

Heartbeat raging, he spoke first. "Because you dance like sin? Because you taste like paradise? You're still the same. Worse. You're a fucking Venus fly trap. Beautiful and deadly, drawing men in to eat them alive."

Victoria became very still, the hands on the table turning white, a harshness scraping her delicate features. "I didn't know who you were when I kissed you. Had I, I never would've touched you. Rest easy knowing I've come to regret it."

With every word, Warren's jaw locked tighter.

Had she convinced herself of the lie? Forgotten her true nature?

Bending until his face was mere inches from hers, he said, "Liar." Before she knew better she'd told him directly she dressed like that, in skintight red, for Midas' attention. Asked him if it was what men wanted, if *she* was. Her purpose made abundantly clear. Seduction. A card she played well.

Not against him.

He could sniff out betrayal before it came. It had only taken a dozen knives in his back.

For the first time since he'd met her, Victoria seemed to be at a loss. Unsure how to combat the truth.

Justice stroked over Warren. He pushed back from the table, ready to find Cole, to change his friend's mind.

"If I broker a deal with your agent for a starting spot on the Mountaineers, will you say yes?" The boldness had seeped out of her voice, but it didn't waiver, didn't soften.

Warren's thoughts became as scattered as the bugs. The candy color sky darkened and dulled. She was offering him freedom. She wanted him to say something. To respond.

"If you get Randell to stop fucking strangling me, I'll follow you wherever you want for the starting spot."

She looked like she wanted to add something, make a declaration, mount a defense, call him words he'd heard before. She turned instead, jaw set. "Then, pack your bags." Cold.

She'd gone cold for him.

Pushing off the table, she bound into Cole's house.

The sun vanished.

He'd missed the sunset. Gawked at it and seen nothing, imagined how the colors would reflect on perfect creamy skin. Behind him, slipping through the screen door, rattled Cole's deep chuckle.

Warren wished he didn't know better. He wished he had to search for her deceit, uncover it, spend hours sifting through sand for one crystal darker than the rest. If only to have Cole happy for a while longer.

With all of his might, Warren couldn't ignore what she had laid bare. How she shined like his nightmares, dazzling and intense. Knives glinting in the darkness.

Lovely. Until they drew blood.

Chapter Five

Victoria stayed away from Warren for twenty hours.

A record since she'd met him. One that made her skin itch.

Thin trails of rising smoke cloaked the bar in a bitter haze, yellowing the drop tile ceiling.

Nose twitching, Victoria knew she'd found the right place. Clunky gambling machines blocked the front windows, stopping the afternoon sun from cutting through the gloom. Wooden stools lined a long counter, steel-toed boots chinked on the heavy brass foot rail.

Victoria regretted wearing her little black dress. Five minutes in Duncan's Place and it'd be soaked in the stench of stale cigarettes. Drawing the lapels of her blazer together as a willing sacrifice, she searched the time warped bar for her contact.

There.

Why she bothered to look professional, to pin her bangs, tame the wing in her cat-eye was beyond her. Her beer drenched mini would've suited, as would her chlorine dipped sundress. Alas, after wasting weeks on the trail to El Dorado, the only clean clothes left in her suitcase were a miniskirt Foss once called phlegm green and a handful of panties.

In her brief investigation of Randell Cresset, she'd learned that Warren's elusive, stubborn agent was not an agent at all.

No other clients, no work number, no business card. He liked to leave scathing google reviews for Chinese buffets that tossed him out, laden with racist ramblings and posted around three a.m. The community, as a whole, rated them widely unhelpful.

Divorced. Father of two. He rented a condo in the suburbs and posted on Facebook thrice daily, gracing his handful of friends with long, hate filled rants about softening society and snowflakes.

In short, Randell was repugnant. And sitting at the bar.

Like a jungle cat with night vision, Victoria observed him through the smog, watching him scratch at lotto tickets with uncut yellow nails. He was as frail as the cigarette dangling between his lips. His neck barely held up his wide brimmed white cowboy hat.

Her initial assessment of Randell was, sadly, confirmed as he roared at the sad eyed bartender for the excess foam on his beer. Imperious and coarse, he sneered more than he smiled. Graying scraggly beard, jeans with shredded, stained hems.

He was so vile, so odious, Victoria couldn't imagine him being in the same room as Warren. Much less having the balls to coerce Warren into a merciless contract.

After studying their original contract, she'd tossed and turned in her bed, understanding Warren's outburst. Randell had stolen his negotiating rights, claimed a veto in decision making, and tacked on outlandish, regularly rising fees.

Warren would have more autonomy in a prison.

"Randell Cresset," Victoria greeted, brandishing a good-natured smile. The empty bar stool beside him became a dumping ground for her snakeskin Coach purse. Her hands braced the tattered wood.

"Who's asking?" Randell grunted, not looking up. "You a cop?"

Yeah, she thought sarcastically, *Watch out. There's Kevlar and cuffs hidden beneath the Ann Taylor blazer.*

"You represent Warren Rose. Is that correct?"

"Ah." Sniffing out a payday, Randell's shoulders uncoiled as he tugged on the front of his rhinestone Harley shirt. "What do you want with my boy?"

"I read your deal with him." Another smile, less kind. "Good work there. You've been together almost ten years." Which meant Randell had signed Warren when he was twenty-one, preying on a naïve kid.

Showing off overcrowded, shiny white Chicklet veneers, Randell smirked, all ego.

"Too bad he's getting old," Victoria said indifferently. "You could've lived off him for another couple of years."

"Shows what you know. He barely plays and quarterbacking is a long game."

"Strange," Victoria mused. "I visited him yesterday and he could barely move. He was so tired. That's how the game works, though. Coaches run the back-ups in scrimmages to keep the starter fresh. Midas relaxes while Rose gets pummeled. Nothing we can do about it." To the bartender, she signaled for a beer. "Not sure he'll make it much longer."

Randell's dull eyes shifted, his back hunching. "He can't do nothing else. You know what he told me ten years back? Football was his true love. He'll retire when they have to remove him from the green. Ain't going to be for years."

"You're so right." The kegs pipes groaned as the bartender pulled a golden lager into a dusty pint glass. "He'll go to the practice squad before then, make a fraction of what he makes now. There will be a natural decline over the next five years." As if in thought, she looked up at the ceiling. "Thinking about your contract details. By then you'll be making, what, ten grand a year off him?" Commiserating, she grimaced at his losing tickets. "He's your only client, right?"

He covered the scratchers. "I got others in the works."

"Of course." Victoria accepted her beer, leaving a generous tip despite the thick head. "An industrious man would. Only an idiot would depend on an aging player. I'd like to help Warren navigate these last stages of his career."

"Who are you?"

"My name is Victoria, and I don't have an official job title. I freelance with a few teams."

Randell regarded her with suspicion. Something in that slithering, probing look made her want to scrub her skin with bleach.

"What do you want with Rose? He's like a son to me. I'm protective of him."

"As you should be, he's getting near fragile." She leaned over the bar, thumbs dragging through the condensation on her glass. "I'd like to take him off your hands. He could fill a spot somewhere new. The Bills, maybe. Ease off his practice requirements. Lengthen his career. Quarterbacks aren't made every day."

Randell chuckled. "You think you're the first rat to crawl into my alley? I'm not letting him go. He's got another year on his current contract, and the only way he and I split is if he buys me out, which I know he can't."

Victoria shrugged, sipping calmly, nose twitching at the foam on her tongue. "I can."

"You don't have enough." Taking a rip on his cigarette, he blew out a stream of smoke. "I've got life handled as it is."

"That's good enough for you? Covering bills? What about going on vacation? Taking time off? If you got rid of Rose, no rats would bother you again."

He was shaking his head.

Victoria pounced before he could run. "I'll give you fifty grand right here, right now. Invest half and it'll make more than ten grand next year."

The math was off, probably. She needed a calculator and twenty minutes. But he didn't correct her, didn't look offput.

"He makes fifty if he starts."

"Midas is twenty-four," she replied smoothly. "The only thing that's going to stop him from playing is an act of god."

"We call that blasphemy round here."

Victoria held his gaze, refusing to apologize. To demonstrate weakness during negotiation was to lose.

Randell took another puff, gaze sweeping up and down her. "Offer me something better. Fifty grand ain't nothing to you."

"The best I can do is eighty. It's all I'm at liberty to give. He's not worth much."

"A hundred."

"I can't do it," she lied, pushing her near full beer back across the bar.

Randell stood, itching the back of his neck, panic setting in. "Ninety."

Victoria remained motionless, expressionless, ruthless, as she delivered the last blow. "The older Rose gets, the more attention he's going to need. Others might come, but they'll offer you much, much less. A stallion only has a few good years before it's shot dead."

***

THE LAST TIME Warren felt this guilty, he'd been starving.

It'd been Thanksgiving. His rookie year, driving in his brand new, two-streetlights-off-the-lot King Ranch F-150. Houston's take on the Bugatti. Country music thumped from the speakers, the smell of new leather and polished wood made his head light. Fingers tapping on the steering wheel, knee jumping.

Then his mom called.

A proud third grade teacher married to a retired firefighter trying to make ends meet in a dying town. She'd begged him to pick up a turkey on his way home. The prices had skyrocketed, and she couldn't afford it this year.

Over and over she'd said, *I'm sorry. It won't happen again.* As if a forty-dollar bird would strain him.

Pulling over in the El Pollo Loco parking lot, clipping his left rearview mirror clean off on the dumpster, Warren had sat, stewing in self-hatred, in bone deep loathing. Ten minutes, he ruminated, slumped against the calfskin seat, avoiding the mirrors, his phone, the frayed wires dangling off his door.

He never got the turkey.

Warren went to the bank, set up recurring payments.

Ten years later, his truck had rusted wheel wells, gaping tears on the shifter where he tugged too hard. He still liked it. It reminded him why he went in every day. How even the darkest shadows could produce life.

This guilt, today's clawing guilt, was different.

Ten years ago, he'd been ignorant.

Yesterday he'd been cruel. Sending Victoria to Randell. He couldn't imagine the chaos they'd create. Randell's lethargic sexist ass. Victoria's brutal confidence.

Part of him wanted to warn Randell there was a damn Kraken on his tail. *Get lost or get bit.* But curiosity entangled with his ominous thoughts. How would she take it when she lost?

Aphrodite shoved off her pedestal. Would she be humbled? Violent? Indignant?

Tough shit.

She needed to learn not everyone could be bought or bewitched. It didn't matter how short her dress was or how big her smile, some people were immune. She couldn't survive on plump lips and a wicked tongue. Eventually, the truth would prevail, and everyone would know she's a user, a manipulator, an imposter.

Pushing up his sunglasses, Warren massaged his nose and tried to think of anything but her. Why should he feel guilty for unleashing the real world?

Fishing, he reminded himself, *you're fishing*. He turned, shaking his head.

Green smacked him in the face.

"I'm not a tailor." Victoria's voice purred like the roar of a well-oiled engine. "But I think that's pretty damn good."

Warren caught the fabric in his hands. A jersey the color of dehydrated grass. ROSE was taped on the back in blue painter's tape, peeling at the edges.

"Congratulations," she called, overconfident, cocky. "You're mine now. Say thank you and invite me aboard for a toast."

Blinking, fisting the shirt, Warren faced her and unlocked a new kink. Between her narrow aristocratic nose and rounded cheeks, Victoria was stunning. Add anything below the neck and she could enslave half the population, maybe more. Today, she'd certainly score above fifty percent.

He'd never seen her so covered up. Thighs hidden, chest concealed. It was the tease of what lay underneath that crucified him. A sweetly wrapped gift waiting for his filthy hands to tear it apart.

As if she realized her modesty, forgot herself, the seductress returned, stripping.

First the boxy blazer, the top three buttons of the same black dress from yesterday morning. She teased the headband from her hair and bent to unzip her heeled red boots.

The jersey slipped from Warren's hands. The sun stopped setting. The waves stopped rolling as he watched, helpless against her, his throat tightening, hands itching to serve.

To stop her.

To speed her up.

He yearned to fall to his knees right there on the sun bleached boardwalk and set her foot on his shoulder, draw his knuckles down her calf and unzip her himself.

"I said you could thank me now, Flowers."

Reality struck him in the chest, air rushing into his lungs. "What…" He glanced at the puddle of nylon on his deck and couldn't compute. "What is this?"

"It's a Peewee hockey jersey I found at the gas station," she said, tiptoeing onto the ledge of the *Circe*'s bulkhead, teetering on bare feet, pink toes flashing. "I didn't know you guys had ice down here."

He reached to balance her, scold her.

She leaped out of his range, feet smacking the *Circe*'s deck. "It was the closest they had to Mountaineer green, which is much darker, much manlier. Don't worry. But I enjoy being dramatic. Don't put it on, you'll rip right through it with those shoulders."

Helping herself to his only deck chair, she shut her eyes and tipped her head back to bask under the lowering sun, black hair draping over the chair back.

"Two sunsets in a row. Am I on vacation in Hawaii?"

He pictured it. A white bikini, her racing into the waves, yelling something lewd, throwing said bikini into the surf, curling a finger toward him. *Come join me.*

"What the fuck?" Warren moved to stand in front of her, a black cloud swallowing her sun. "What are you doing here?"

One blue eye snapped open to glare. "My buddy Randy signed the release forms. You're a free agent or he is, rather."

Lying, she was lying.

"No," Warren said emphatically.

She was grinning. "No?"

"No. You didn't get Randell. Bullshit. He'd never even talk to you."

"What like it's hard?" She popped up, sidestepping his form to steep her skin in pinks and oranges.

The scent of sunscreen made the inside of his cheeks water.

Unaffected by his denial, she flipped her hair back, taking stock of the *Circe*. "Start packing for training camp. Honestly—" she dared a look in his Home Depot orange chum bucket. "Probably just throw all this out. I'll buy you a new vomit bucket when we land in Burlington. Preferably one with a lid."

She patted the bulkhead fondly. "Oh, you'll be remembered sweet *Circe* for your perseverance and stench." A glance back. "What do we think of Viking funerals?"

"You want to torch her?"

A huge smile broke over her, widening her cheeks, crinkling her eyes.

Warren looked away, no distracting him. "I'm not packing. I'm not going to Vermont."

"Yes, you are. I bought us tickets."

He shook his head so fast his sunglasses almost shot off.

"Yes, I did. You said you'd come if I got Randell to let you go. He did. Let's go."

"To Vermont?"

She nodded.

"Just like that?"

"No, not *just like that*. This took a tremendous amount of work. I have a blister on my ankle and I'm probably developing the early stages of lung cancer right now." She pinched the bridge of her nose. "It doesn't matter. We fly out tomorrow. Be there or I'll make you wear the Peewee shirt in your first game."

Warren's thoughts scattered.

Ten years under total tyranny. Of regret, shame, humiliation. Holy shit, she'd done it.

His arms fell limp at his sides, his chest drummed.

She'd freed him.

He pushed his sunglasses off, tugged at his shirt, wanting to rip it off and swim to the islands, wrestle a shark, make use of this exploding energy.

"How'd you get him to say yes?"

"Don't ask." She sighed, fingers walking up and down her nose. "I don't see you packing."

Warren's muscles locked. He snatched her hand, keeping his grip gentle as his voice became steel. "Victoria, what did you do?"

Under the sunscreen, she smelled like beer and cigarettes, and bad decisions. He pictured Randell's hands on her and wanted to break his slimy neck.

Her black brows furrowed, half her face shadowed, half sparkling in the sunset. "I spoke with him."

"Like you *spoke* to me?"

She shoved on his chest, propelling herself backward, legs smacking the bulkhead. "I didn't touch him, if that's what you're insinuating. As if I'd ever let him touch me. Thanks for assuming, but I'm actually good at my job. You judgmental—"

He stopped hearing her, stopped hearing everything. The water folding against shore, flags snapping in the wind. Gone.

All he heard was freedom.

A beautiful trill singing into his very soul. He was free. Victoria had freed him.

Then he was touching her again. Gripping her shoulder, reeling her into his chest, pulling her up, bare feet stretching as his arms circled her waist, as he pressed their lips together.

His tongue dove into her mouth before he could stop it, regret it, and once he tasted Victoria—salt and sin—there was no stopping.

His body surrendered to desire without giving his brain a chance to object. Plans unfolded as he kissed her, a little too roughly.

He'd have her slow and then fast, have her gently in the paling sunset and then hard, rocking the boat, listening to the tie downs scrape once night fell.

On the bow, in his bed, with enough balance and creativity, he'd take her on the stern.

He'd known her two days and he drafted plans for fifty.

Lost to the burning helplessness curling inside him, he whispered her name, sucked at her lips. Her body bowed to meet his. He grabbed, he gripped, caressed, and touched. And touched and touched, exploring the curves and hollows of her body, the soft swells of Victoria.

Not enough. He wanted her closer, wanted her up, wanted her tied around him with nothing on.

His hands trailed up her spine, no wandering or teasing, no exploring, his movements were determined as he folded over her, gripped her nape and tilted her to taste her more thoroughly.

"No." A breathless cry against his mouth.

It broke through the fog of lust, he stopped himself from finding salvation in her lips. His hands trembled over her skin.

"No," she said again, ripping her body back, stumbling, pushing away. "No, absolutely not." She twisted from him, hands covering her face.

Three breaths shook her back and then she faced him, chin stubbornly high. Eyes cold. Unaffected. The sharp lines of her eyeliner extended like black spikes into her hair, as if she'd been rubbing her eyes.

That quickly.

Her taste had unraveled him, and she'd felt none of it.

Warren's throat tightened. He thought he might be sick.

"Conflict of interest," she said. Not to him, but to the water, the air around them, a reminder, an explanation.

"You don't want me? Because you sure as hell—"

"As soon as you said yes, you became my client." To his astonishment, one corner of her mouth curled with contemptuous mockery. "And contrary to what you may think of me, I don't fuck my clients."

"You're the one who propositioned me."

"That was before I knew who you were, before you were even on my radar."

He stumbled back. Of course he wasn't on her radar. The woman who worked with football players hadn't even recognized him. A nobody, a random person. Nameless, faceless, at least when there were real golden trophies filling the bar.

"Isn't it your job to know footballers?"

"It's my job to find the ones recommended by my employers and sign them through whatever means possible." She crossed her arms, hands stroking her biceps, trying to warm off the goosebumps roused by his touch.

Good fucking luck, Red.

"There are hundreds of players in the NFL, even more potential recruits. I can't memorize them all."

The truth hurt Warren better than another knife in the back.

One in a sea of many.

Unimportant, not worth remembering. Not her target. If he hadn't spoken of Cole, she wouldn't even be here.

If she'd gotten to Midas, he and Cole would be preparing for a hot, miserable Texas training camp.

"Pack your bags," she said in a soft tone. "Sell the *Circe*. I'm never going to let you come back to her."

Coldly, he mocked, "Pack. Sell my boat, leave my life."

"You agreed already." A bite in her voice. "Cole flew out this morning, and he didn't complain half as much. Pack. It's not like you have other commitments."

"When do I leave?"

She flashed a nefariously sweet smile. "*We* leave tomorrow."

Chapter Six

It was an easy morning for Houston Hobby. The terminal was saturated with the quiet rustle of clothes, the whine of scanners, the zip of suitcases, and one annoying voice.

"Warren Rose. Picked seventh in the third round, a bona fide Texan. What are you doing with Vic?" Dark blonde eyebrows lifted to inspect Warren.

With a stiff nod, Victoria greeted the man, "Morgan." Clutching her slick boarding pass, she leaned into the interloper's arms, patting his back.

Warren couldn't help but notice they fit well together, her chin on his shoulder, no arch in her back. The man, Morgan, was short, stocky, broad with a thick neck. Like he snorted protein powder before his morning gym selfie.

It chafed how they seemed like a matching set.

His harsh Boston accent, fashionable tapered suit the same midnight shade as her hair. Despite the early hour, they both vibrated with energy and alertness. Cell phones fastened to their hands, devilish glints in their eyes. They were three steps ahead and Warren was still browsing the rules.

After a mild violation from security, Warren had found Victoria waiting with a failing paper sack of breakfast sandwiches dangling from her fingers.

He'd watched porn like that.

A blue eyed Venus in a short, tight black dress being strip searched by TSA agents.

Warren had shut down the thought, strangled it with unreasonable violence.

"Gate four," she'd said in lieu of hello, spinning on her needle thin yellow heels and expecting him to follow.

What other choice did he have? He'd issued her a challenge, counting on her to fail, expecting to live on in constant melancholy, and to everyone's surprise, she'd picked up the gauntlet and drawn first blood. Beat him on home soil.

The promise of starting, of leading a team again... Warren had slept for twenty, thirty minutes total. The rest of the night he'd pounded out push-ups in between serpentined pacing. He wanted to start, coveted the idea, and now that it was close, a hunger had woken in him, a chasm of roiling energy.

Only two things could fix the deepening hope in his chest.

Un—fucking—believably, he suspected one was cradled in the arms of a Boston bro.

Shifting on his feet, Warren wished he could look away from her, ignore the elegant curve of her back, the fine, pullable hair streaming down her shoulders.

No genies in Houston Hobby.

He stared, wanted.

Hated.

Himself, yeah, for being weak enough to lust for a backstabber hellion. But he hated Morgan too, for touching what he wanted. She'd reduced Warren to a selfish four-year-old, wanting to make Morgan eat sand for taking his toy.

Morgan wasn't an athlete. Dark blonde, edging on brown, hair cut close to the skull, a flat nose, shrewd eyes, a green so pale they were hard to watch. Heavy diamond studs in his ears. He held his chin so high, the tendons in his neck strained.

Maybe he had the arrogance to compete, but not the rest. Not the drive, passion, the discipline, the iron will to press on even when you were outmanned and outplayed.

Morgan didn't possess the severe edge of competition, the obsession of a true athlete.

Saying something in his ear, Victoria slowly retreated. She jerked as Morgan swept in for a kiss.

Warren surged forward, objection raising his fists.

Victoria was faster, smarter, shoving at the blonde, swearing. "Fuck, Morgan. I hate that. Don't put your mouth anywhere near me. No one should kiss before seven a.m. It's un-American."

"I really wouldn't know." Morgan was grinning, not embarrassed or ashamed. "You always avoided me in the mornings after." He met Warren's seething gaze and winked.

A quiet fury rolled down Warren's back as he stepped forward to break Morgan's hand. *And really*, his savage muse whispered, *why stop there?*

"Don't," Victoria told him, reading his mind, adding curtly, "Morgan thinks it's rude to stay after everyone's finished. Afraid cuddling might make him a genuine southern gentleman."

Fisting his hands, Warren demanded, "Change topics."

Morgan laughed, back bending. Comfortable. As if he were hosting friends in his parlor, not blocking the terminal screens before sunrise. Checking a diamond encrusted watch, he said, "Vic thinks anything south of Portsmouth is *the* South."

"Victoria," she cut in.

He ignored her, saying to Warren, "Morgan Turaco. I hear through the most beautiful grapevine that you're looking for an agent." A wink to Victoria.

"Rose," Warren supplied, ignoring the outstretched hand.

"Soon to be a Mountaineer." A smirk. "Where did our delicious Vic discover you?"

"One more time, and Flowers is witnessing a murder."

A faint smile curved Warren's lips as he looked down at her, his fingers sliding into the back of her jacket collar. Although his tone couldn't be considered civil, it lost its vitriol. "We met in a bar."

Morgan lifted his brows, looking smug. "That's our Victoria. By any means." A business card crowded Warren's face before he could blink. "I'm currently welcoming new clients. I've brokered downright nasty deals for the biggest names in sports and I'm always eager to renegotiate. If you're playing well."

Snatching the card, Warren flipped it. *Morgan Turaco* was foiled in gold, shining under the airport's fluorescent lights. Three phone numbers were listed, each a digit apart. "Plus, Vic and I work incredibly well together, isn't that right?" He winked at her again. "That's an added bonus for you."

"Say goodbye to Morgan now," Victoria cooed. "Fortunately, he'll be ingesting poison soon." Landing a sizzling glare at the agent, she took Warren's elbow. "We have to go. Our flight's boarding."

There was an hour before takeoff. Not that Warren corrected her. He wanted away.

"I'll get your bag," he offered, grabbing her Gucci suitcase, and leaving Morgan—gold leaf—Turaco in the dust.

"Wait up." Victoria jogged to his side, clinging to his steps.

"No kiss goodbye?" he gritted out, jealous. Jealous fucking monster. For what? Victoria threatening homicide with an ego-tistical asshole? Of course, that was her type. A sleazy schmoozer with no tact, just black suits and business cards and three phone numbers.

She breezed over his fit, saying, "You don't want Morgan as your agent. He's cold-blooded."

Purposefully antagonistic, Warren said, "Maybe I do want him."

"No," she dismissed easily. "You don't. He's too busy to pay attention to you because unfortunately for society he wasn't lying, he's got a two page list of high-profile clients. In turn, he gives each a tight sixteen minutes of his precious time every two weeks. And we *don't* work well together."

"You just sleep together," Warren pointed out gruffly, plastic luggage handle digging into his palm.

As they stepped around a snaking queue waiting for McDon-alds to open, Victoria lifted her head, regarding him with a faint arch of her dark eyebrows.

"We dated," she said, glancing away. "For a while. Until I knew better. Longer than I should've."

Rather than question her sanity or mock her choices, he softened toward her. The burn of his own exes stripping down his anger. Withdrawing Morgan's card from his pocket, he ripped it in half and threw it into a green recycling bin. "Consider him dismissed."

"Thank you."

Victoria smiling because of him was Warren's new favorite sight.

Nearly empty, Gate Four sat between the smoking lounge and a hall of vending machines. The mass bracketed seats hung low over the patterned carpet, smelling of coffee and sweat. There were no outlets, no televisions, only a steady stream of feet shuffling past, heels clicking along the worn tile.

Each click beat at him, became a pounding in his head. His gaze darted, trying to locate the source, banish it.

Unperturbed, Victoria picked a seat and kicked her feet up onto the top of her suitcase, lounging as she peeled the flimsy yellow parchment off her sandwich. Bacon and eggs, and a thick cut of cheddar cheese smashed between a pressed sesame bagel. Black lashes dusted her cheeks as she breathed in the grease and melted butter.

"Sit and I'll share," she said with her eyes still closed, as if she sensed his hovering.

They ate with single-minded determination, no decorum or bashfulness, catching falling scrambled eggs midair to stuff them back in their mouths. Licking salt and melted cheese from their fingers as raw, yellow sunlight slashed through the white artificial airport hue.

Sitting there next to Victoria, watching as the terminal filled and bustled, metal armrest biting, legs cramped, Warren couldn't recall a better breakfast.

"Why not Vic?" he asked, crumpling his paper into a neat ball, holding his hand out for hers.

Stuffing a final bite into her mouth, she covered her mouth and told him, "Rhymes with ick."

He sat back, folding her trash over his. "Worried about a scathing comic strip in the *Post*?"

Her hands knotted together, but she shrugged, casual, her voice near flippant. "No reason to give them fodder."

Sensing a buried landmine, Warren dropped it, walking to toss their trash at Gate Five. When he returned, she was on her phone, thumbs scrolling, eyes glazed. Probably telling the commissioner she was after his job.

Restless, he leaned against her suitcase, fingers folding over the handle. Checking the time, he chewed on his cheek, heart rate ramping up. In jeans and a sweatshirt, he became hot and then cold, then tired and then wired in anticipation.

His foot drilled against the carpet. He tugged at his hood, tied the strings, untied them.

Fed up, Victoria asked, "What's your problem?"

Not realizing he'd been stewing over it, he spoke without hesitation. "What did you mean? When you said you found names on the list, what list?"

And why wasn't he on it?

"The Mountaineers are starting from scratch. No players, no trades, no draft picks. My boss"—she rolled her eyes—"my three bosses made player wish lists for each position. They hired me to sift through those lists and build a team while managing the budget."

"And I wasn't on that list."

"The quarterback list ran very shallow." Wetting her lips, she wrung her hands together. "The owner Gomez, you might recognize the name, he's been vocal and stubborn about who he wants. One name. Didn't leave me much wiggle room."

"Midas." It came out like a curse.

Her nod punched a hole in his stomach.

"And what will you tell him when we get there, and I'm still me?" She was setting him up for failure, feeding him to the wolves. No agent, no team. No football.

Her voice was steel. "Calm down." Her feet slid to the floor. "I'll tell him the truth. That you made Midas, and the original is always better than a copy." She fell silent, tension wiping from her features, softening her eyes to a robin's egg blue. "Warren, I—"

"Are you Warren Rose?" A bright Rockets jersey stood in front of them. "You played for the Travelers? That's my school."

A pen appeared, along with a hat. "Can you sign this? I'm a big fan."

A sense of unreality drifted over Warren as he beheld the man. After taking a quick look at Victoria, her face cast down, wiped blank, attention on her phone, he said hesitantly, "Yes."

Warren signed his name, his number. Took a picture and then before he could even check on Victoria, ask what she'd been about to say, an old woman was smiling at him, asking for his photo.

Then another.

Warren got lost in the handshakes, hugs, the blinding flashes until Victoria said, "It's time."

Taking the bag from her hand, mind whirling, he asked, "Did you do that? Did you tell them who I was? Did you pay them to ask for my signature?"

Her sarcasm came as a barbed whip. "Yeah, they were all under-cover actors. I had to pay extra for the little kid to lisp. Come on, this isn't our gate."

***

"PAY THEM," VICTORIA muttered darkly.

How would Warren react if she told him the truth? Would he accuse her of sleeping with them, too?

Obviously, he didn't think bribery was above her.

Maybe it wasn't.

But not for something so inconsequentially dumb. By any means.

Not by all incoherent, cash burning ideas that flocked to her head.

She was ruthless. But only when necessary. She had to be. It was a dog eat dog world and women were mice.

Less than mice.

They were freshly iced peanut butter pumpkin dog treats.

Out of college, she'd chosen to become a sports agent. It's what she'd studied in school. Business courses, negotiation seminars, internships every summer.

Qualified, competent, eager, she was laughed out of rooms, blocked, shoved into corners, ignored.

Morgan, even when they were together, hadn't stopped it, hadn't gotten mad when she did.

"This is how it is," he'd told her. "Toughen up or find a different job."

It was worse when doors weren't slammed in her face. When hands crept over her knees, trailed up her leg. Vengeance and anger woke her up every morning, like two Godiva extra dark chocolates on her pillow.

She toughened up. Threw out the rules, stopping trying to join the exclusive club. She started her own. Made herself President, CEO, and Prime Minister Steer.

Her credo: by any means.

No longer would she hide her tits, braid back her hair, dip her chin, or suffer late nights with no recognition.

Every tool in her arsenal was kept primed and sharpened, and she had quite the depth for convincing.

There was a singular advantage to being alone in a man's world. Attention. Commonly overlooked, or misjudged, attention was power. She could wield it like a soldier and her gun. Loading the barrel with the proper dresses, cocking the pin with a flirty smile.

She could make it to point blank range, convince a player to give her five inconsequential minutes and—bam—spin it into an hour, a signature, a bullet in the brain.

Bond had nothing on her.

She knew how good she was, how far she could go, and as soon as she finished this job, as soon as Gomez gave her the nod, the *good job*, the *you've done it*, everyone else would know it.

Even now, it was deliciously sweet to watch Morgan attempt to poach Warren. An accidental slip of his hand that revealed he respected her.

The respect of a snake. Useless.

She'd never forget what he'd done. Never forgive.

She'd hoped Warren would be protected in the armpit gate of the airport, but any time she flew with these massive guys, the fans discovered them. It was expected for one as panty drenching as Warren Rose fresh out of bed, eyes sleepy, thick hair devilishly mussed to be recognized.

The adoration? A pleasant welcome.

Another star on her resume.

The swarming? A surprise.

As her bag mule excused his way through wannabe paparazzi, snapping photos, waving, pronouncing their love. Victoria gave herself a raise, sent herself an oversized bouquet of wildflowers, and became employee of the month.

People liked him, remembered him.

Did Warren remember?

Had life secluded on his boat, on the bench soured a good seed? She could see white all around those caramel irises. Surprise, disbelief, shock slowing him down. If he forgot this, what about the rest? Had he forgotten how to lead, to call plays?

The weight of immense scrutiny could crush if one wasn't prepared.

Sidestepping a chittering family, Warren looked distracted enough to have a breeze level him.

Gomez was a tornado.

What if she'd made a mistake? What if Gomez was right and there was only one quarterback for this team?

No. Victoria forged ahead, checking the departure time on her ticket and quickening her pace. Doubt could kill. Worry tortured.

So what if she hadn't recognized Warren? She'd been laser focused on Midas and his ungodly golden mane. She'd been stalking him. Eating, sleeping, breathing gold, desperate to touch, to feel.

Gollum wanted gold.

She'd fucking craved it.

The moment he'd escaped her, there'd been a change, something like relief. The pressure off. She couldn't follow him home. She was off duty.

And Warren had been hot.

Third-degree burn hot and right in front of her in the heat of the dance floor, beer in his hand, lazy crooked smile. No Grey Goose bottle service, no model dangling off him. The slight drawl.

And she'd wanted him.

It'd been easy to overlook why he was so built, so broad, muscled, and handsome when her stomach tightened under his warm brown sugar gaze.

Again, her eyes found his with a glance. Connecting, lingering. He looked good in gray, dark and mysterious, the lack of color made his tan stand out, his eyes warm into melted caramel. Heat curled in her stomach.

"Come on, we need to hurry." She yanked his shirt until their steps aligned.

"It'd be easier if you told me where we were going. I thought we were at our gate."

"We're not going straight to Burlington." She hid their tickets, guiding him forward. "We're making a quick stop. It's nice to see you're missed, though. Isn't it?"

His jaw clenched. "They don't know who I am. They saw one guy take a picture with me and mistook me for someone famous, someone else."

"Please." She didn't have time for his fake humility. "They knew exactly who you are. You've been tagged about a million times on Instagram already. I've been shutting down rumors that you're leaving the Texans until they make their official statement."

Tucking her hair back, gut wrenching, she took her suitcase from him with a yank. "I should warn you. New Englanders are not like this. In Vermont, high schools don't have tiered football stadiums. It's not Friday Night Lights, and there sure as fuck will not be a hundred thousand people banging down the stadium doors. Football isn't standard. The Patriots are an exception because they fucking win. I didn't grow up checking scores, studying rosters, making sure my guys were playing. You're going to start over up there. You're going to have to make your own name. Are you prepared to do that?"

She stopped for his answer.

For a second, he didn't say anything, peering over her head, gaze distant.

Fuck.

Before he could retreat, she said, "Never mind. It doesn't matter what you think, I know you can do it." Her conviction grew teeth. She caught his chin, balancing on her toes as she forced him to face her and listen. "I know you can. That's why I picked you."

Her nerves tingled with awareness as she stared into his eyes, the gentle striations of brown so pure that they appeared to be painted.

She let go of him, walking again, chest tight, suitcase nipping her ankle. "We're leaving from Gate Twenty-Nine."

He caught up with her easily, long legs devouring the distance. He'd checked his bags, leaving his hands free to scrape through his hair, rub his eyelids.

His usual even voice turned to gravel. "What did you do on Sundays?"

Having expected denial, she blinked. *That*'s what he'd heard in her speech? Not the warning, or her guidance. She'd been ready to groom his ego, stroke his pride, become his number one fan, and he'd asked to hear about her childhood.

She almost tripped. "Sundays were for sailing."

"Sailing." He peered down at her, surprise lighting his eyes. "Like big pirate ships with massive black sails, skulls, and peg legs?"

"I definitely wouldn't call myself a pirate, but I wouldn't deny it either. I had an uncomfortably long phase with an eye patch. Only child syndrome."

He laughed, and it was so beautiful, like snow flaking over a tin roof. She continued, "My dad raced a sixty-five foot sailboat around the world. It's a sport unto itself, especially in Newport. They host regattas every weekend. His ship was the *Victoria*."

"Named after you?"

"I should be so lucky. The boat came first back then." Gently, she elbowed his side. "You never told me why you called it the *Circe*."

"Seemed fitting." He was closer now, breathing her air. He'd shortened his strides to match hers. "She called to me once, and I knew I'd never leave." He shook his head. "Doesn't seem as prolific now."

She felt a smile fill her cheeks.

"How'd you get into football?"

She grinned at her feet, watching her heels fly across the white airport tile. "I went to Georgia for college. I thought sorority life, how fun. I was wrong, sororities were terrible. I bleached my hair when I was a freshman, and it all fell out."

Her hallmates called her a ghost for the entire year.

"I made zero friends. No one liked that I said *fuck* instead of *bless your heart* and I'd get a rash anytime someone mentioned chapel. But I didn't need friends to enjoy a football game."

She'd felt like she was surrounded by friends every Sunday. The games livened her, intrigued her. "I liked that my Sundays were full again. I liked that the team paraded around on campus, and everyone knew their names. I liked knowing their stats, the odds of a win. I'd cheer until I went hoarse. I wanted to be a part of it. I stuck out the worst city in America for football."

Warren shook his head at her.

"What?" she said, caustically. "A girl can't like football?"

"No. I was trying to imagine you saying, 'bless your heart'." He stared at her. "You couldn't have had no friends."

"Don't make me defend my own pitiful past."

He was grinning, dimple on brilliant display.

She gripped her suitcase with two hands.

"I can't imagine it." he told her, voice lowering, as if he was talking to himself out loud, "You alone. It's like the sun without the moon. People flock to you, to warmth."

Victoria wanted to keep those words. Protect them. She wanted to write them down in the margins of her player notes, cross out names on her list and replace them with his words.

Warren's sweet, drawled words.

"Tickets," a terse voice interrupted.

She jolted, spun, and handed the gate agent their tickets like she was turning over contraband.

"Where are we going?" Warren could have looked at the screens, grabbed his ticket and read it. Instead, he stared at her, at her lips, waiting.

"A stop." She turned away, squinting, biting at her lip. "Washington."

He shut his eyes. "Please say DC." A pause. "Victoria."

Her name on his lips.

She white knuckled her bag. "Sorry, I've got a tight end that's dragging his feet and you're the perfect way to sell him. I'll give you three guesses as to who."

Apparently, he was as smart as he was handsome because he said, "Kilbride."

***

THE CRINKLE OF chocolates told Warren that Victoria wasn't a casual flier.

The way she'd ripped through the plastic wrapped blanket and settled the cheap nylon over her legs. The way she'd loosened her seat belt until she lounged cross-legged, thumbing through the in-flight magazine as if it were a Pulitzer.

Her knee rested on his thigh.

He tried to focus on it, the feeling of her touching him.

He said nothing when she raised the armrest, leaned over, and opened his window to watch the ocean fade away. Her hair smelling like exotic flowers, her chest warm against his bicep.

Her bulky blue purse became the center of his universe. The wardrobe to Narnia, Santa's goody bag. Headphones, hand wipes, ChapStick, snacks, an inflatable neck pillow, and a thin polished wedge of pink rock she smoothed up and down her jaw.

This was her domain.

As much as his was out on the field, ball in his hands.

Victoria's domain was the skies, was first class. Champagne in plastic flutes and requesting seconds of the Biscoff cookies.

He watched her layer thick slabs of milk chocolate between the shortbread and vibrate with uncontainable excitement.

"An FAA approved s'more", she called it before taking a bite, catching the crumbs with her hands, licking her lips, eyes fluttering closed.

He clenched at his thighs, digging into meat and muscle, fingers inches from her knee, from taking her thigh and clutching it, stroking it.

She relaxed as if she was on a private yacht cruising the Mediterranean.

But she wasn't.

She was on the *Titanic*.

One frayed cable, one loose bolt, a missing gallon of fuel, and their last words would be: "Why do people think it's acceptable to drink tomato juice on planes?"

He forced his head forward. Away. She was a distraction.

Not a good one.

"You actually like this," he accused, avoiding the window, avoiding the seatbelt sign flashing above their heads. The smell of plastic and imminent death.

Against his will, his attention drifted back as Victoria began her routine anew. Jiggling in her seat, layering cookie, chocolate, cookie.

"Flying. Hurtling through the air with no parachute or back-up plan. It doesn't bother you?"

"I *love* flying," she said. "It's the only time no one can contact me. Flight attendants behave like doting mothers, filling my glass, watching my purse, gently waking me up when we land. My phone's on airplane mode, giving me blissful silence. And all the television I've watched in the past year has been on airplanes."

Her lips parted when he made some sort of sound in his throat. "You don't like it," she deduced, shaking her head. "How? Don't you travel with the team?"

"I'm a back-up quarterback, not a water boy."

Pulling out of her happy bubble, she scoured his white knuckles, the vein in his forehead, the way he shoved back into his seat, preparing for impact.

She gathered the excess fabric of her blanket and shifted to face him. "Does this happen every time?"

He knew what she was asking.

Is this why you got cut? Because you can't stomach simple fucking air travel?

"No," he said quickly. "When we're on the team plane, I'm concentrated on the game, memorizing plays, and the windows stay down."

He looked at it angrily. No land in sight.

Just clouds. Vaporized water. Nothing to slow the plunge.

He tore his gaze away, arms shaking.

Somewhere, miles below, a pedestrian could look up and see them on fire and confuse it for a shooting star. They'd wish while he burned alive. "Now, I'm very aware that geese like to fly at this altitude."

"We're way too high for geese or any birds," she pointed out. "The air is too thin."

"*Christ*," he swore, sucking his chin to his chest. He shut his eyes, body trembling, sweat beginning to coat his hands. Just what he needed to think about: no air.

"Oh God," Victoria twisted, the blanket gliding off her lap to reveal heaven.

Bare legs, skirt indecently high.

His breath skipped. He choked.

Her voice became low and soothing in his ear. "It's okay." She stroked his shoulders, his cheek, laid a hand over his forehead. "We're okay."

Her nerves exacerbated his. He failed to get another breath.

Uncrossing her legs, she let her bare feet hit the carpet. "I think we should get up. Yes. That's right. Come on, let's get up."

Her steady hands knocked away his to unbuckle his seatbelt.

He couldn't breathe at all now.

"Quick," she whispered, her hands caressing his stomach, his ribs, searching for a wound that didn't exist. "I need... I need a water," she said loudly, announcing it as she hauled him from his seat.

"Let's go get some water," she blared again, thrusting him into the aisle, shoving him back and back. Blurs of narrowing blue pleather seat passed. Passengers watched with rapt attention, staring at the pale faced man and the barefoot hellion holding him at gunpoint.

He was going to faint.

He couldn't breathe.

He couldn't get any air. His knees buckled with every step.

Victoria pushed him harder, faster. A door opened, and then he was crammed into the lavatory. A tinier space. Less oxygen. His back bumped into the folded changing table as Victoria snuck in after him, locking the door.

The lights sprung on. A fan whirled.

He'd die like this.

"Breathe." Her hands were moving over him again, not as gently, she gripped him, cupping, squeezing his hands, massaging a path up his arms. "It's okay, just breathe."

Fingers kneaded his shoulders, her bare foot landed on the toes in his tennis shoes. "Do you want to splash water on your face?"

Warren needed to breathe, to get out of the coffin sized bathroom.

He looked up at the ceiling and found it an inch from his face. The walls were getting closer.

He made for the door.

Soft hands pushed at him, clasping, shoving.

He needed to knock them away but didn't. He froze under fathomless blue.

"You can't leave like this. A quarterback can't panic." Victoria's voice was soft but firm, her hands comforting as they moved over him again, caressing, brushing.

"*Fuck.*" He'd lose his job. Become homeless, useless, worse than before. He wrenched on his hair, gasping, lungs brittle, empty, knees weak. "That's not helping me. I'm going to pass out."

He tried drawing air in. Forgot how.

Victoria spun to search for answers, knocking him back against the wall with her hips and came up with nothing. Her eyes went wide. She was panicking too.

The air was thin. So thin and they were sharing it. The only air in the tiny bathroom.

His eyes shuttered closed.

Lips brushed his. Hands curled in the hood of his sweatshirt, stroked against his neck. Victoria.

She pressed into him, body soft and insistent against his squeezing chest.

He couldn't breathe, his eyes wouldn't open.

Victoria didn't quit. She took his mouth again, moving her lips over his. Kissing life into him. Blindly, he lowered his head for her, wanting more. If he died of asphyxiation, he wanted it to be because of Red.

She kept at it. Pulling back, kissing again, hands roaming over him, tasting of chocolate and spiced cookies, like the bubble of champagne, and the sting of coarse salt. As if she carried a flake on her tongue just to tease him, to haunt him.

She tasted like release, like heaven. His fingers laced into the straight, satiny locks of her hair, molded against her scalp.

She tasted like something he hadn't known he craved. One lick, a single sample and it transformed his composition.

A tremor broke across Warren's back. Bending his frame over hers, he took command, hands clutching her hips, yanking her closer, his breath rushed out against her soft skin.

He deepened their kiss, wanting to devour her, every part all at once.

She made a sort of gasp when he came to life for her, surrendering, her head knocking back in offering while she clung to him, knee lifting, dragging up his hip as if she wanted to climb him.

Yes.

Undiluted lust whipped his chest. Palming her thigh, caressing and kneading, Warren lifted her, set her on the sink, and took handfuls of her bare legs, kissing down her throat as her head fell back against the mirror.

This.

This was how he'd wanted to take her at Allgood.

Teeth grazing the tender skin beneath her jaw, he pushed up her skirt, uncovering holy ground.

He'd wanted her from that first moment. Hadn't stopped since. His dark addiction.

She moaned against his skin, breath hot. He dragged her ass to the edge of the sink, delighting when her hips ground against his, her skirt sliding up to band round her hips.

When was the last time he'd been desperate? Wholly desperate. Die if he couldn't have her.

"Warren," she panted against him, rolling her hips, eyes closed tight. Had another name ever sounded so good? Had a mouth tasted as sweet?

A sharp noise split through the fantasy, a palm smacking the door.

A second passed. The lock jiggled.

Chapter Seven

For three hours, Victoria avoided Warren.

Not easily accomplished when trapped on a plane together, splitting an armrest. Not that such limitations deterred Victoria Steer. She could stay dry in a hurricane, stop a tornado in its tracks. Cajole Brady out of retirement. Again.

No longer did Warren fear the thin air, the loosening of bolts and screws. He was wholly and entirely distracted by Victoria. And hard as fucking iron.

Didn't matter that she tried to be the least distracting woman on the planet. Legs no longer crossed, but folded neatly beneath her, tense and compact. Elbows fastened to her hips. She treated the armrest stamped down between them like it was lava.

As if touching him would cause a plague, a swarm of locusts, the end of mankind.

Warren couldn't bring himself to speak, to break the wall she'd built. Dammit, *she'd* kissed *him*. This was no alternate universe. Two people had been in that bathroom, had participated. They each knew what happened.

Fidgeting, struggling to stay tucked, to evade him, Victoria tilted her laptop screen to the aisle, hiding her notes. Failing.

Jaw locked, Warren watched her torch through names on a spreadsheet. Some familiar, some foreign. Five seconds a name, jotting down questions, comments, and then she was moving to the next. Half didn't make it past two seconds before she was deleting the entire row, erasing them.

A viper. Killing not to eat, but for sport, for prestige.

She hacked a black line through a young running back writing: temper; big penalty yards; bad fit.

Warren's fingers curled around his ice water, the plastic flexing inward.

If he'd been on the list, what would she write? *Decent spiral, can't fly, forgettable kisser.*

For the remainder of the flight, work took priority, Victoria's focus consumed until the wheels touched down. Then it'd been a frenzy. Deplaning, bags, car service. With batting lashes and a caress of her stomach, Victoria charmed her way into the front seat of their ride. "Car sick," she'd lied.

Last one, Warren decided bitterly.

Now she couldn't ignore him. Not as he hauled her bag from the trunk and strode past a marble fountain of a life size bucking Clydesdale spraying water from its hooves. The hotel's glass doors were set with golden inlays in the shape of curled *G*s.

A Gomez holding. Figured. Inside, guests congregated around a wall of shimmering water, pouring from the ceiling, splashing against a cropping of jagged obsidian protruding from the dark wood floors.

An indoor waterfall.

What was next? A manufactured sunrise? An artificial dune?

The lobby was crowded with excess. Coffered ceilings, cherub sconces, a twenty foot glimmering onyx reception desk, too narrow to hold a sheet of paper. Soft piano music wafted from a lounge area of deep gray leather couches and thick black rugs.

The splatter of water on the rock seemed to cease when Warren's scuffed tennis shoes hit the floor.

No.

When Victoria did.

Conversations ended, the reception's printer broke, even the pianist's hand cramped when Victoria Steer arrived. He wasn't the outcast in his rumpled plane clothes. *She* was. Black dress sculpted to supple curves, neon heels, blazer hanging off her arm, bangs ruffled, a hypnotizing gleam in her eyes. Warren froze mid-step for her to slip against his side.

He dared someone to utter a single salacious word.

The pianist was the first to recover.

"I hate Seattle," Victoria muttered to Warren, her sunscreen and salt scent obliterating the delicate floral notes of the hotel. She didn't seem a bit flustered by the gawking as she strode past the waterfall, gesturing for him to follow.

Warren was losing his damn mind keeping up with her. No. She'd said no. No while her hands clutched at him, while her heart raced, her eyes fought to stay open, while her hot breaths tickled his hair.

For three hours he'd suffered her ice out, and now they were buddies again? He was getting whiplash. Trailing her though the lobby, Warren vowed to get her alone, to make her look at him. Stop the Tilt-A-Whirl

He'd done his own research in the car, chasing down every lead to stamp out the taste of Victoria. Fulgencio Gomez was a real estate billionaire who outbid four of his fellow magnates to become sole owner of the Mountaineers. Reporters fondly called the eccentric Spaniard hands-on, ambitious, and eccentric. None cited innate football knowledge or background, none mentioned friendliness or competency. No mention of leniency.

Uncertainty gnawed at Warren's stomach lining, acid leaching into his bloodstream. He wanted to shake Victoria, to kiss her, to ask her if she knew what the fuck she was doing bringing him to fill Doyle's tiny gold shoes.

Was she so cocky she thought she could change the wind direction in the middle of a dust storm?

"Two rooms, reservation under Steer." Victoria tapped her fingernails on the onyx specked granite, reciting her credit card number to the check-in attendant as she read and reread the backlit silver *Gomez Seattle* nameplate flush with the wall.

Warren dropped his elbows onto the counter. "What floor is the gym on?" He plucked a local eats pamphlet from the display and paged through it.

"We don't have time for the gym," Victoria said, grabbing the brochure and putting it back. It seemed her kiss had stolen the stress of flying from him. Now, his anxiety shackled her, made her motions robotic, her face tense. "Training camp is days away. We need to be in and out. I want you in Burlington on the soonest flight possible."

"If you want me to be a starter, I need gym time. All I've done today is sit on a plane."

Lightning blue eyes darted to him, slipped to his lips. *That's not all you did today*, she seemed to say.

"You're telling me there was a gym on the *Circe*?" Her lips quirked. "I thought not, Flowers."

"Swimming's great exercise. As were the weights at the Anytime down the block." *Look at me*, he wanted to order. He wanted to grab her, line her body up against his. *Look at me. You kissed me. Why?* Because he'd lost it? Because she'd wanted to?

Had his panic been an excuse to fulfill her desire?

Victoria regarded him impatiently. "Fine. I can catch up on some emails for an hour, but then we're out. I don't like it here." Her mouth curved into a faint frown. "I feel like I'm in a mausoleum."

The noise all around them, the rushing water, the clack of heels and loafers against polished wood, the swipe of hotel cards all receded as they both turned to behold the morose grandeur. Ebony floors, faded olive walls. Floor to ceiling umber curtains blocked the afternoon sun.

The fine hairs on the back of Warren's neck rose as he turned to her, as they became the only two people in the room. "We're going to die here," he whispered.

A slow smile spread on her lips.

The attendant stomped forward, brandishing room keys and an information sheet, passing them along with a terse, "Enjoy your stay."

Holding his key hostage, Victoria warned, "Nothing risky. No bench press, no kettlebells. Run. Don't sprint. Warm up and cool down. If something hurts—"

Warren cut her short. "Are you going to tie my laces, too?"

"If you get hurt, I'm leaving you here. I don't care if I can see bone, if the fountains run red. You won't get so much as a band-aid from me. I'll incinerate your tugboat and steal your identity. Understand me, Flowers?"

Warren responded with a snort of amusement, wrapping his fingers over the plastic key card, crowding her. "Oh, I understand completely. You're not worried about me. You're worried you won't be able to deliver."

"I *always* deliver." Her smile held savage truth. "You might think you have cards to play in this game, that my life somehow depends on you, but you're mistaken. I've got a stack of fifty-two plus jokers, got it? I *own* you."

Warren's gaze drifted to her mouth. He stepped closer.

She jerked backward, letting go of the key. "Two hours and then you, me, and Kilbride are wearing matching sweaters, posing for his contract signing."

Fitting the key card into his palm, Warren fought to hold the distance between them. She wanted him to be her show pony, his entire future hinging on her.

He'd been in similar situations, felt the prongs of a cattle prod on his naked skin as he was herded to the pen for slaughter.

This wasn't one.

Whether she could admit it or not, their fates were entwined. If one failed, so would the other.

"Four hours," he told her, pushing back from the desk, tucking the key in his pocket. "And then you and me? We're having a fucking talk."

***

WHILE WARREN LIFTED heavy metal blocks and set them back down for lifting again, Victoria made herself useful. Preparation was the secret to winning. Another life lesson Morgan had bestowed the hard way.

At thirty-five, Burton Kilbride was the third oldest tight end in the league. It wasn't luck, destiny, or a daily acai bowl that kept him on the field, it was down and dirty stubbornness. Once he made up his mind, Burton was immovable. Which meant she had only one chance to steal him away.

Ideas bloomed and withered as she showered the plane off her, ate all the crinkle cut chips from the minibar, and sorted through her pitiful array of clothes. She needed to go home and restock. When was the last time she'd been in Newport? In her apartment?

Long enough that her rosemary plant had likely graduated from dead to desiccated.

Long enough that she'd paid three electricity bills for less than twenty bucks. She'd be better off paying for a storage unit.

In Gomez branded slippers and a complimentary white silk robe, Victoria perched on the edge of her rich mauve bedspread. She'd requested a basic room. To Fulgencio Gomez, basic included a king-size bed canopied with gossamer cream drapes, a fifteenth century writing desk, and a 4k television designed to look like a Monet that matched the soft natural colors of the wood floors and ecru wallpaper.

Flopping onto the tufted comforter, hair still dripping wet, Victoria schemed.

Notoriously blunt, Kilbride would respect honesty, being straightforward, but shaking his hand and asking him to move his entire life across the country would surely immolate any beneficial outcome. On the other hand, hesitating, procrastinating might make him distrusting, uneasy.

Blue, Victoria decided, the silk cobalt dress with the cutouts.

A thud hit her door.

On instinct, Victoria reacted, rolling off the bed, scrambling for her purse, ripping down the zipper.

Weapon reverberated in her mind. *Weapon, weapon, weapon.* Sharp, dangerous, jagged, and grotesque. She overturned her bag. God damn TSA and their god damn rules. She clutched at her nail clipper, extending the file toward the door, grasping at it like a switchblade.

The air in her lungs expanded, her heart hammered as she waited, bracing for the wood to crash in, collapse, for shards and splinters to shower her.

A pound hit the wall opposite her bed.

With a terrified gasp, Victoria's shin smacked the bed frame as she jolted, weapon at the ready, gulping. They'd infiltrated the room next door to tunnel inside. Guerrilla warfare. The beginning of the end. The muscles in her legs tightened, preparing to run.

No. She fisted clammy hands. No running.

The flat, white door across from her bed shuddered.

Victoria braced.

Warren pushed through the threshold, gaze traveling over her splayed suitcase, the rumpled bed. "We have adjoining rooms."

Heart beating painfully in her chest, Victoria flung her nail clippers at him, furious to see the sliver of steel bounce off the taut muscle of his abs. Furious and relieved.

Sidestepping to him to keep her eyes locked on the main door, she swiped the remote from the sideboard and held a finger to her lips. "Someone's outside," she whispered, adjusting her grip on the remote for ideal smacking and stabbing.

Immediately, Warren tensed, met her halfway. His mouth hit her ear, voice low. "How do you know?"

"They pounded on it, trying to break it down." She snuck closer to Warren. A meat shield.

He didn't whisper again. "That was me. I forgot which room was mine."

"What."

"I forgot which room was mine. Are you okay? Your skin is—" Honey brown eyes scoured her from head to toe, darkened and then disappeared, went distant, locked onto the chair blockading the door.

"Victoria?" He became a wall between her and the door. "Who's there?" he called out.

It was stupid to be embarrassed. She refused to be, even as her cheeks flushed. "No one's there." She shoved at his back, feeling hot all over. Her neck, her face, ears. Potato chips turning to chalk in her stomach. Yanking on the ends of her belt, she hurried to her suitcase, grabbing at things randomly.

"Who pounds on the door like that?" she asked defensively. "You interrupted a brilliant brainstorming session. All for the world's most obvious break in." Heat spread from her cheeks down. She clutched a white knee high sock.

Softly, Warren said, "I'm sorry." His wary gaze met hers.

She forgave him. Maybe the second he smiled at her. Definitely once she noticed his lack of clothing. The t-shirt stripped of its sleeves, sliced to the waist to reveal powerful, sculpted muscles. Sweat tripped down his arms, following the sinew to slide between strong, callused fingers.

Watching her intently, Warren strode to her side, tossing his key onto her bed. "I didn't mean to scare you." His hands cupped her biceps, warm even through the silk sleeves of her robe, so warm and strong.

She felt the abrasion of his calluses down to her toes. "I'm not scared. I don't like uninvited guests barging inside."

"I knocked."

She sliced him with a glare.

"Never again," he conceded. "I won't barge in. I won't even knock. I'll sing all my entrance attempts."

Absurd. She was behaving absurdly. He had knocked. Knocking was fine. She'd freaked out, been ridic—

"Do you need me to kiss you?"

Victoria blinked, suddenly aware of her trembling, the cold encasing her fingers and toes. "What?"

"Do you want me to kiss you?" He coaxed damp bangs to the sides of her face. "It calmed me down."

Victoria pushed Warren back but didn't get far before he caught her wrists. "I'm not having a panic attack." Not anymore, at least. The mere mention of having her breath stolen with Warren's tongue had killed it, calmed her. Her vision was no longer infrared, her heart slowed.

Warren tugged her closer, dragging her from the depths of her fear. "I don't have to kiss your lips." His thumb caressed the pulse in her wrist, proof he knew her reaction to him, felt her heart skip, her skin turn molten.

She jerked away. "Go shower. We're leaving in fifteen minutes."

It seemed like he wanted to ask her something, but instead, he gave her a curt nod and motioned to his door. "Door open or closed?" Warren waited at the threshold, asking ten questions buried in one.

Could she keep her distance without a wall? Was her will strong enough? Victoria regarded his back, corded with muscle, hardened and beautiful. "Open," she said, as if his presence, sharing a room, didn't affect her. His presence was inconsequential. She didn't need a physical boundary, her mental one was stalwart.

She wouldn't cross the line again.

Her one time emergency exception had nearly undone her. Never again. Each time they were close, each time she felt the comfort of his hands, his voice, felt his eyes sear her, a different, ever evolving, incredibly potent lust struck her deeper, dragged her under the spell.

Closed. That's what she should say, demand, as Warren plucked his shirt at the back of his neck and dragged it over his head.

She clenched her teeth, prickles roving over her skin as Warren disappeared into his bedroom.

"Stop it," she muttered. She couldn't risk messing up this job. Not now. Not when she was so close.

Warren Rose was decidedly off-limits.

Once, shame on her. Twice, she'd be watering the same dead plant for the rest of her life.

***

AS HE BORE holes into the bathroom door, Warren paced the lush lilac runner in front of Victoria's bed.

Fifteen minutes. He'd been ready in eight, and then rapped his knuckles against her open door before daring to enter.

New thoughts clouded his mind, dark ruinous thoughts with claws and teeth. So ferocious they made airplanes a safe haven, a fiery plane crash a lucky departure from earth.

She'd shook, trembled, her skin gone pallid, her sizzling blue eyes had faded.

What could scare an impossibly tough Victoria so much that she'd barricade her door? What could suck the color from such fair skin?

She'd been so afraid, she'd lied about it.

The idea that a woman as vibrant, capable, damn ferocious as Victoria could be scared infuriated Warren. A creature had woken in him, risen from the recesses of his mind, desperate to vanquish any who dared strike fear into Victoria's stubborn, piercing eyes.

Questions clogged his mind, dominated his thoughts, and he had only one answer as to why he cared: he liked her.

More than he previously thought.

More than a basal connection. More than savoring the way she tasted, how right she felt pressed and arched and tucked against him. He liked the parts he couldn't see, couldn't quantify.

Her lascivious wit, shrewd business sense, the passion she garnered for football, for community while hating the masses.

Victoria was alluring in the way the darkest part of the night was. Striking at first, then chilling, the glossy black hair and spiked heels behaving like opaque shadows hiding dark terrors. Slowly though, your eyes adjusted to the darkness, stars winking into existence, revealing a dazzling beauty that could only shine in true darkness.

She'd helped him when he was at his worst, brought him back. Didn't make fun of him or bring it up.

He'd thought her callous, but she'd been respectful.

Something sweet and hot, like spiced oranges and jalapeños slid under the bathroom door, wound around him, and sharpened his mind. Warren had a feeling nobody saw Victoria when she was in a bad way. He'd caught a glimpse, seen a harrowing chink in her faultless armor and she'd run.

There was a muffled ring of glass colliding, followed by a sigh. Pulling at his damp hair, Warren started back to his room, missing the fake flower smell, tired of imaging Victoria shrouded in steam, naked and—

"Ready," she called, door swinging open, bouncing off the stop. She caught it with a familiar yellow heel.

Warren latched onto the neon like a loose jersey thread, unraveling his way up the curve of her ankle, the dip of her knee, the long span of exposed thigh. His nostrils flared. His throat thickened. He jerked his gaze away, looked at the ceiling, the floor, pierced a hole through the duvet to avoid staring, memorizing.

Glaring at the cream piping on the pillowcase, he shook his head. "Go change."

Nothing crushed him like the sound of her smile falling. "Minus one, Flowers. The right greeting was 'are you *the* angel from Charlie's angels?'"

"You're no angel." Warren scrubbed at his face, pressed his shoes firmly into the carpet. "Angels have modesty."

Exasperated, her arms shot out. "This is modest. You can't even see my tattoo." A waft of sweet citrus made his mouth water as Victoria spun, the sapphire miniskirt crawling higher on her thighs. It was a departure from the layered silky red number. Rather than cling, the blue draped, skimming her curves, fluttering against creamy skin. Narrow, magical straps wrapped over her shoulders and crisscrossed down her back.

"Go. Change," Warren repeated, fingernails biting into his jeans. Where was her tattoo? *What* was it? A fire-breathing dragon? The devil's trident? The name of her ex? If Morgan was etched onto her skin...

"You're not wearing that." His teeth clamped together as he scoured her body. A small tattoo. Had to be to hide under the scrap of sapphire tied around her.

Victoria gave a short, mocking snort as she plucked a glittery white purse from the bed, flashing fuchsia pink panties.

Warren turned to face the wall.

Ended up completing a full three-sixty.

"This is what I wear when I'm recruiting," she explained, searching the pockets and zips of her bag. "If anyone's changing, it's you. Jeans, Flowers? For a business meeting? We're not in Texas." She cut off with a pleased exhale, withdrawing a square of metallic blue foil marked *Dove*.

The arteries going to his heart kept were collapsing, one after the other. He'd die like this, seeing her in glistening blue, red lips splitting open to savor a chocolate square, eyes fluttering closed, body languid.

He craved to see her post orgasm.

"No," he said. No one would see her like that, like sin and sex and fantasy. Dreams spun to life. Lust incarnate. "No. I'm recruiting with you now. No need for the costume. Go change."

"This isn't fairy-princess-dress-up-pretend-time, Flowers. I'm signing a tight end today. This is how I do it. Men are simple creatures with short attention spans. If I don't wear this, he's looking somewhere else, and that means he's not listening. I want him to listen." She twisted the chain of her purse around her wrist and hooked her palm at her hip in a no-nonsense display. "Let's go."

"No one's looking at you in that." Warren planted his feet. "Change."

"Can't." She shrugged, not at all apologetic. "You ruined my red dress and the black one has soap stuck to the ass. This is it. This is the look. Shield your eyes if it offends you, Flowers. Though"—her gaze dipped to his jeans—"I doubt it does."

Sucking on his teeth, Warren adjusted the rigid length to stop hacking at his zipper. At Victoria's indulgent smirk, he asked, "Are you a cheater?"

"What? No." Her voice was edged in steel.

"Are you a thief, a liar? Are you swindling him out of a good deal?"

"Of course not."

"Then. Go. Change. Burton's a brute, but he's got scruples, and he's married. He's a good man."

"You're all"—she made air quotes—"'Good men'. But everyone, whether or not they can admit it, marvels at a little eye candy."

"You're not eye candy."

"Tell that to your erection."

Swiftly, Warren caught her elbow and pulled, yanking her across the hardwood. "Forgive me, if I misspoke," he said softly. "You are devastating in that dress, not that you aren't aware. But I've been hard since I saw you in that blazer this morning. You don't need to wear this to get attention."

Her chin lifted, shiny hair slipping from her cheeks to kiss her back. "You and Burton ever talk about women? About conquests and epic stories?"

Warren thought his teeth might break from the tension in his jaw. "Doesn't matter."

"It does. It's bonding, swapping stories. I can't do that." Her arms crossed, tongue swiping at her teeth. "We can't bond over that, but we *can* bond over what he likes to see. And I've got two big ones."

Warren swallowed a groan, keeping his gaze on hers, refusing to take the bait. Fuck, he was miserable.

Grabbing both of their room keys, Victoria threw back the door lock and unwedged the chair from the handle. Another flash of pink.

A hex on his soul.

"Change. Please." He'd get down on his knees.

"Why? Why do you care?" A sardonic smile crossed her face. "Because it worked on you, and you regret it?"

"Do you really want me to say it?" For once, she didn't have a comeback as Warren stalked forward to crowd her into the door. Her eyes flared, her hand slipped to the doorknob. "Do you need me to admit that the idea of other men looking at you pisses me off? The thoughts running through my head right now, Victoria... I don't want anyone else having them. I don't want to share this."

Wide eyes found his. Her breath sped and shallowed. "I'm not yours."

"You're right." He stepped closer, against her, knuckles scraping up her arm. "You own me." He kept his tone purposely gentle as their skin brushed, as his hand traced the arch of her shoulder, inched down her exposed back. "And I'm a fucking handful." He ripped then, snapping the thread-thin straps.

She gasped, slapping a hand over her chest, trapping the silky fabric in place, passion warping into fury. Surprise dominated by indignation. "Are you kidding me?" she erupted, free hand shoving and fighting, backhanding his chest, pinching his stomach, not moving him back an inch from her prison against the door. "This is my last dress."

"Good." He wouldn't have to burn the rest of her clothes.

"Good?" she mocked. "This is all I have to wear. What's the plan, Warren? I meet Burton Kilbride, the Boar of the North-woods, naked? That's what you wanted?"

His jaw ached, his body hummed with want. Not for that. He backed off. One step, two. Admiring the disheveled hair, the exposed line of her cleavage, her bare shoulders, he said, "Wait here."

Chapter Eight

BURTON KILBRIDE SAT ON the bottom step of his grand staircase, a pinched look on his face.

Scores of men, movers, might as well be called thieves, lumbered in and out of his house.

His home.

One he'd built from the ground up, pored over every detail to delight his fanciful wife. A woman who had seen his rough edges and not tried to smooth or soften them. She'd never asked to change him, claimed to love him for his flaws and the beast trapped within.

Bridgit repeated it in her vows. In their Christmas letter. She told him on Valentine's Day and screamed it through the confetti when he won the Super Bowl.

Never change.

She loved him for him, not the money, not the cars, the extravagant trips. Because of that, he'd given her everything. He knew he could be a hard man to love. The Irish often were. Crass in the tongue, blunt, spectacularly short-tempered.

It didn't help that he'd birthed from the O'Doherty clan. Known for their size, heights close to towering. Shoulders like hulking stones. In grade school, they'd called him the Boar, roared it when he swung fists in the lunchroom.

Teachers called him indelicate, told him boys without manners had no place in the classroom. He'd get relegated to sit alone in the hall, and when he couldn't keep still there, they banished him outside like a feral wolf. That's what they expected him to be, with his rigid brow and hard jaw.

He gave them what they wanted.

Years later, when he traded fighting for fucking, the whispers changed, but the sentiment remained. A brute. An animal. Unfit for society, but fun for a turn. He was less sophisticated, dumber, simpler regardless of his education.

It was his face, Bridgit told him on their honeymoon, caressing the freshly caught black pearl necklace hanging off the nightstand. She'd slid across the satin sheets and stroked his cheek. Knuckles kissing the hard, rigid lines that left him boxy, a strong brow, hard cheekbones, a jaw cut from steel. Features passed straight from his father that he now kept hidden under a coarse, auburn beard.

A prominent *fuck you* to Bridgit.

Her one stipulation after his proposal. Shave. His thick hair scratched at her delicate skin. She wanted to see the beast beneath.

Never change.

Bridgit became the exception to all the whispers. She loved his stony face, his lack of manners, his impropriety. She loved him for all he was. For six years, he shaved in the morning and again in the evening to please her.

Now he knew the truth. Had found himself face to face with a parade of Bridgit's lovers. She didn't dislike beards. She liked control. The game of manipulation, making the savage beast bend and bow for her. A play in power, proving he was nothing but dirt under her thumbnail.

Now, he enjoyed the slightly ruddy beard he saw in the mirror. It reminded him of the bitch he'd married, the trust obliterated, the liar, the cheat, an emblem of all women. He stroked at the beard as he counted the tiles in the foyer, an endless barrage of dark thoughts swirling.

Which one had Bridgit fucked during his knee surgery? The silver fox Cuban? Perhaps the nerd, with glasses and a watch face wider than his wrist. Probably both.

The Irish put clan before everything. There was no greater honor than protecting your own. Burton had married Bridgit with a band of the O'Doherty plaid, offered the checkered blue and green like it was his blood and soul. A sacred, pagan honor.

Now, a scrap of the original offering burned in his back pocket. The cleaners had found it forgotten in the depths of her closet, next to the wedding dress she just *had* to keep. The cost of a home for some. He hadn't blinked at the price. He'd have paid whatever she wanted to welcome her into his clan.

Stupid. How stupid he'd been. He deserved to be alone.

The urge to break, to destroy, to tear down the walls festered inside of him. He had a certain darkness caught in his soul. One that made it impossible for him to lie and impossible to stomach one as well.

He wasn't virtuous by any means, but he kept his damned vows.

There was a need to dig into his pocket, smooth the plaid with his fingers, and study the face of betrayal. He fisted his hands, glaring at the band of light skin where his ring used to sit. The skin, the finger itself, seemed narrower there after six blissful years of marriage.

Years that permanently changed him. Not for the better.

"Must ye take everything?" Burton asked, pushing to his feet to chase after the movers hauling the desk from his office. One he'd taken Bridget over after their trip to St. Barts. The way she'd cried out his name, he heard each time when he opened the drawers. He'd murmured *Mrs. Kilbride* to her skin, gushed about how he loved her, loved making her family.

At the end, there was certainly no love, but he'd always enjoyed coming home to a house with a voice in it, something warm on the stove. The NFL could be hard on families, the abrupt moves, weekends away, the sheer physical toll.

He'd been near brought to tears when Bridgit followed him from Cincinnati to Seattle. Elated when they bought the land together, designed the house. He'd decided this was it. He'd retire in the mountains and rain, never make Bridgit move again.

"She can't take everything." Burton grabbed a box from the arms of a baby-faced mover. "The bitch gets half. Fifty-fifty, the papers say. Where's my fifty?"

Generous. Considering she'd cheated on him with half of Washington. He should've squeezed her for more, held her up in court, but he couldn't watch another man step inside, smirking because he'd fucked his wife.

Burton had never asked for a prenup because he'd never seen the deceit in her eyes. Stupid. Dumb. An oaf.

He was all they called him.

He'd thought she was trusting like him. Not a liar. Now he knew better.

"Not the bar," Burton called, storming after the hand turned wood legs of his beloved bar cart. "Goddammit. Is she taking the drinks too? The glasses? My fucking cock?"

"I'd recommend a built-in for your next place," a soft, wholly feminine voice cut in.

Burton spun, teeth bared, ready to destroy whoever dared tell him what to do in his own hell, in his own home. "Who the hell are you?"

Though he glared and snarled, she smiled. Her hair was cut blunt, harsh and dark, thin bangs crowded blue eyes. She wore an oversized T-shirt and shorts like she'd woken a man and transformed into this. A petite woman. A child, dressing up in her brother's clothes.

His eyes stuck to the yellow heels on her feet. Such a sharp contrast to the athletic shorts bunched around her waist.

"What the fresh fuck is this?" He scrubbed a hand down his face. He'd gone mad. He was seeing sirens, visions, hallucinating.

The girl, the woman, he realized as she turned, revealing curves under the billowy shirt, closed the front door behind the movers and flipped the lock. "We won't need them anymore," she said, dusting her hands together. "I think they're putting you in a bad mood."

He snorted. Fucking hell. Another woman to tell him what he needed. To dictate his life. "Get the hell out. Yer trespassing and I'll shoot you."

She made a face. "You lost the guns in the divorce, I'm afraid. The safe's packed behind the entertainment center in the truck outside. Quite a dig. Are your lawyers cheap or dumb? Usually it's both."

Burton didn't have time for chats and tea. He let the Gaelic roughness in his voice, turning him from man to half-grizzly. "What are ye? A witch come to suck me dry? Can ye not see that I've already lost everything?"

"I'm really more of a blower than a sucker," she said dryly, sticking out a hand in offering. "Victoria Steer, I've come to make all of this disappear."

"You'll not be taking my house," Burton insisted, hand fisting at his side. He didn't dare touch a woman. Not now. Not when he was in a fury. "I'll sooner burn it."

Dropping her hand to point at his chest, she said, "You misunderstand. I'm taking *you*."

His fury became ice, a hollow hateful writhing. Another manipulator come to slay him. "Is that how quick ye women work? Inks still wet on the divorce papers, and ye've come to seduce me? I think not."

Victoria Steer offered him a light, breezy laugh that told Burton, plain and easy, she wasn't from close by. Washington women had a particular heft to their laugh, and they dare not be insulted.

"I'm flattered that you think this"—she gestured at her clothes—"is seductive, but I'm here on business. Should we talk in here, or is there an office still waiting to be dismantled?"

He gritted his teeth. "Ye can tell my wife—" Ex-wife. He had to say ex-wife now. His thumb rubbed his marked finger. "Ye tell my ex-wife that—"

"I don't know your wife," Victoria interrupted, no longer sweet and playful, a bite echoed off the freshly stripped walls. "And honestly, she seems like a bit of a B if she's taking all this from you." She raised a hand when she caught his snarl, slim shoulders shrugging. "But it's not my place. I only know what I've read."

The room was empty, but she dedicated herself to absorbing the details, gaze touching the walls, lingering on the dark, sunless spots where frames used to lie as if she could see him grinning in his wedding tux, Bridgit cradled in his arms.

"I'm sorry about your marriage, I thought you divorced a year ago, I didn't expect to meet you on such a busy day but I'm afraid that what I have to say can't wait." She glanced around him, assessing the long arched hallway, the sealed doors. "Are there any chairs left? I think we should sit."

"I'm in no mood for business or otherwise," Burton replied curtly. "Get out."

"I've about had it with impetuous men today. We've come quite far to talk to you, so I suggest you get in the mood. I'm not leaving."

The way she spread her skinny legs, crossed her arms, and lifted her chin had Burton laughing. "We?" He wiped at stinging eyes. "There's another one of ye? Is the whole girls' youth basketball team outside selling cookies?"

They stared, Burton panting from his fit.

Then Victoria grinned, all of her teeth on display, her head barely shaking. "That's a good one," she said, half begrudging, chewing at her lip. "No. No cookies. I brought you a friend."

"I don't have friends." He'd married his best one, and she'd slowly seen to removing the excess fat. He was alone in his cavernous home.

"I don't really have the time for this." Heels clicking against the tile, she unlocked the door and called, "Warren."

Burton's hands fell open at his sides. "That fucking bastard."

***

VICTORIA COULDN'T BELIEVE it. Burton, the man who'd cussed, thrown a vase, who'd threatened to shoot her, and spoken like a damn wildling, had transformed.

One hand-slapping man hug with Warren and Burton was tamed, controlled. The massive Irish tight end had looked at her with soft eyes, offered a nod of apology, and presented a hand for a gentle shake.

"Victoria," he'd said, accent thinning. "I'm happy to meet you."

It was as if she'd said the magic word, pressed the secret button, tapped her feet together at the right frequency when Warren grinned, and Burton's kill-switch reset. Brutal assassin, heartless monster be gone.

If Warren realized his effect on Kilbride, he could overthrow a small country. Better not to point it out until Warren was her puppet. Then she'd unleash the war dog and never want for anything.

They'd trailed up the grand, sweeping staircase to a massive back patio. The craftsman house was dug into the earth, the second floor a walk out overlooking a squat mowed lawn ringed with enough evergreen trees to be a national forest.

She was glad to be in the north again. To smell the needles piled on the ground, feel a cool breeze, and watch as gangs of fat squirrels held turf wars over pine cones.

No more endless prairies. No more stifling heat and relentless sun.

The dense gray sky made it difficult to determine how low the sun sat, a haze of smothered light leached green from the woods. Amorphous clouds threatened to swap the thick humidity for rain, and Victoria wasn't sure which she'd prefer. Rain would send them inside, distract Burton with his dwindling estate, but the humidity, even in the mild heat, made her clothes stick, her hair frizz.

Her cobalt dress would've been perfect. Lightweight, breathable. Warren's shirt was a thick, densely knit cotton, his shorts were so long a nun would call them modest. As she fanned herself, she sent a nasty glare at Warren's back, lauding the mosquito sinking into his carotid.

Burton's swearing had tapered, and the accent thinned. But neither had quite disappeared when Victoria returned from the car with bags of food.

"Steaks seem standard," she said, unpacking the groceries. Warren had added rolls and beer to the menu, despite Victoria insisting Burton probably ate his meat raw with a side of uncooked eggs.

If he chose the civilized route.

Victoria felt like a mother monitoring a play date as she dispersed the beers.

Men did not catch up like women. Women asked how you were doing. If you liked your job. *Are you still seeing that guy with the soul patch?* Burying the lead, desperate for the juicy gossip. For men to be best friends, they didn't have to know a damn thing about each other.

"Saw you eat turf against the Broncos," Burton said.

"Fuck you," Warren returned. "Two knee surgeries. Couldn't even get them at the same time, could you? You had to draw them out, get as much pity as possible."

Burton grinned. "After the first, the second was free."

"You made Mosh's top ten. That's something for an old man."

"I should've been one, but they put me at five because that golden goose you follow threw an interception."

"I would've put you at six, behind the grandma catching the bouquet."

The tone, the lightness, the smiles tugging at their lips was the only indication the two didn't resolutely despise each other.

It didn't matter if they knew the intricacies of each other's lives. They knew they got along and happily lived between the lines.

"Why don't you two go play catch or tag while I cook up dinner?" Victoria nodded at Burton's metal basket of footballs beside the door and reached for the grill lighter.

Warren intercepted her hand. "Absolutely not." With a nudge of his hip against hers, he passed her his beer, and grabbed the parchment wrapped steaks. "I'll cook. You sit down and don't touch anything."

"And ruin this love fest? I wouldn't dream of busting up your reunion. Go on, I'll take care of it."

Warren didn't budge, his grip like steel on the food.

"Don't you trust me?" she asked curtly.

Warren's gaze found Burton's over the top of her head. "Unless you want to eat a thick black disc for dinner, you'll prefer me on the steaks."

Burton waved dismissively, palming a football. "I'm done fighting today. You sort it out. In twenty seconds, I'm launching a ball, and someone better snag it before it shatters my window."

Annoyed, Victoria waved a hand through the air over her head. "No more tall conversations or I'll make you walk around on your knees until camp." She tried to rush the grill, but Warren blocked her path.

Burton rolled his eyes, mouthing *play catch?* as he walked backward into the yard, ball spinning in his large hands.

Warren dropped his chin to Victoria. "Just how badly do you want me on my knees?"

She shot him a sharp glance. "Quit it." Pulling at Warren's ridiculous enormous shirt, she tucked it into the waistband of his shorts. Today alone, they'd crossed more lines than she'd ever had to draw. If they kept at this pace, they'd run out of ink. And Victoria refused to request another pen.

She was too close, spending too much time with him. Her focus was splintering, and it was unacceptable. To finish this job, she needed complete dedication, she couldn't slow in the home stretch, she had to sprint even harder the closer training camp got.

Not to mention, there was a chance she'd have to cut him, trade him off to another team or end his contract dead to rights, leave him teamless. A proverbial death sentence. It wouldn't be her choice necessarily. She had bosses to appease. Bosses that weren't yet sold on a Rose offense.

Flirting with him could only end badly.

A simple wooden picnic table perched on the lawn, the grass below it brown and disparate. Lugging herself onto the bench, she admired the wood, swollen from a Pacific Northwest summer, knots and curves damp to the touch.

Warren divided his focus between the grill and the ball, throwing between seasoning, adjusting the heat before he caught.

Lazing, sipping cold beer and wearing Warren's soapy clean scent, Victoria admired the arc in Warren's whizzing spiral. He didn't throw hard and direct like younger quarterbacks. His throws were easier to catch, gentler on the hands. He covered twenty yards effortlessly, finding Burton's outstretched hands every time.

"Could you hit a target?" she asked him, chin resting in her palm.

"Name one." Cocky.

"How big does it have to be?"

"If I can see it, I can hit it." He turned the steaks.

Over her shoulder, Victoria called, "Burton, toss your bottle."

Three seconds bled into four. And Warren's spiral shattered the glass.

Nerves she hadn't wanted to acknowledge quelled. Warren was an incredible player, but he needed an opportunity to show it.

Time for Foss and Toby and even Gomez to realize Midas was unnecessary for Mountaineer success.

Bringing back Burton would buy time and leverage. She'd be surrounding Warren with all stars. No one could object... right? She swallowed past the lump in her throat.

Warren's voice cut through the slam of her heart. "Impressed?"

"Needy?"

A husky laugh stroked down her back. "I've made my needs abundantly clear, Victoria. What else can I do?" Shutting off the grill, he slid a plate of perfectly browned steaks in front of her.

Leading him away from potential line crossing, she said, "I'd have clapped if you split the bottle clean in half. Anything else is a disappointment."

"High standards," Burton noted, his rough voice right behind her. "I could do it if I was sober." He sat with a grunt, plating himself.

"You've had one beer," Warren accused.

"Did you notice the house? I've been rinsing my toothpaste with whiskey to make it through the days."

Victoria shuddered, stabbing a fork into the biggest slab of meat. "I didn't hear that." She added a roll. "How did you two meet?" Her knife sliced into the steak like butter, revealing a perfect medium rare. She frowned.

"Why don't you tell me why you're here first? What are the Mountaineers offering?" Burton eyed her suspiciously over his plate, fork in one hand, knife in the other, elbows heavy on the table.

Victoria feigned innocence. "No, I insist. I want to hear about you."

Warren grinned, taking a pull of his beer, leaning back as Red and the Boar locked horns.

Burton stared, one, two, three breaths. His eyes narrowed.

Victoria smirked.

"*Christ*," Warren cut in. "Eat. I'll tell the story."

"He loses," Burton and Victoria said simultaneously.

Ignoring them, Warren said, "Burton was a senior when I first started at USC. He was just as mean and big as he is now. Maybe bigger. Maybe not as ugly. He saw me tossing the ball one day with a couple of friends. I had played in high school, but we were bad, never made it to regionals or conference. Never had a winning season. Then Burton storms out, grisly, hungover. He grabs me by my backpack straps and in that fucking accent demands I try out for the season."

"You looked too dumb to take a suggestion."

Victoria smiled. "The boy needs a heavy hand."

"He never told me why," Warren continued. "I thought he was going to use me for hazing. Loser frosh sacrifice. But what choice did I have? He was the biggest motherfucker I'd ever seen."

"So you went?" Victoria asked. "Thinking it was a prank?"

"Worse than a prank. I went thinking I might die."

Burton was grinning. "I didn't even remember inviting him. I'd been plastered the night before. Threw up in my closet."

Laughing, Victoria pointed her knife at Burton. "Why the hell did they make you captain?"

Burton blinked at her, surprise staining his features. "You did your research."

"I don't blindly walk into things."

He gave her an innocent glance. "The C stood for captivating."

"She'll believe that." Warren smiled sardonically.

In return, Burton showed his teeth. "I took it from the previous captain."

"You took it?" Victoria didn't believe him.

"I ripped the damn patch clear off his chest. He didn't stop me. Therefore, he didn't deserve to wear it."

"You take what you want. I respect that."

Warren's dark brows shot up. "When it suits, you do."

Victoria shoved bread in her mouth.

"Anyway," Warren continued. "I got red-shirted. The coaches liked me."

"I'd never seen someone with so much wasted raw talent," Burton told her.

Gaze on his plate, Warren shrugged. "We only ever played two games together, against bad teams, but it's easy to throw to a giant bastard who sticks out."

Burton grinned again, straight, white teeth flashing from his beard as he chewed. "You're catching up on me. If you're lucky, by the time you're forty, we'll see eye to eye."

"Fuck off," Warren shot back, smiling.

Victoria leaned back in her seat, pleased with herself. "How'd you two like to play together again?"

Burton frowned. "Warren warned me."

"We want you." She sat forward. "*I* want you. I want to have Burton and Rose back together."

She could feel it, the whipping wind of the mountaintop as she crested, all of her plans folding in perfectly to make a beautiful origami Pegasus.

"No." Burton went back to his steak.

Victoria fell off the edge of a cliff.

"No?" Her cheeks burned, her shoulders dropped back. "I'm willing to beat your current contract and I can assure you a starting position if—"

"No," he said. "I start here. I've got a life here. I made this home myself. I got a team who knows me. What do I have in Vermont?"

This was supposed to be shooting fish in a tiny, shallow barrel. She should've worn her dress, goddammit. The dress would make him look at her.

"Did Warren tell you that I don't take no for an answer? It's my thing. I get the job done, and the job is you. Tell me what you want, and I'll make it happen. No questions asked."

"You hearing this?" Burton asked Warren.

Victoria stomped her foot, debating ripping her shirt off so someone would look at her. "You're going to be a clincher for this team, so tell me what you need."

"I'll be buried in this yard."

Warren flinched at Burton's brutal tone. "Think—"

Abruptly, a door slammed, shaking the entry's chandelier, sending the chime of clinking glass up the stairs.

"Burton!" screeched a woman's voice. "You motherfucker!"

***

ONE MORE HATE-FILLED, ear-stabbing scream and Warren was leaving.

Or at least threatening to. He'd pick Victoria up and walk out of here. Depending on if he could move with his current hard on.

They'd shuffled inside, Burton directing them to hide behind French doors as the shouts became screams. Night had fallen quickly, cooling the air and starting a drizzle. The room, at one time an office or a dining room, was now a shell. Empty save for three wide based lamps resting on the gray barnwood floors. Rain slicked the windows to the yard, but it was Burton's ex-wife's scream that caused the glass to rattle.

Rubbing his temples, Warren leaned against the wall, one foot raised as Victoria paced in front of him, her mind working overtime.

"I didn't get to finish my steak," he said, trying to drown out the shouts of *whore* and *fuckwit*.

"I've got bigger problems than your diva diet right now. Why doesn't he want to come with us?" Blue eyes snapped to him. "What did you tell him?" She jabbed an accusatory finger in his direction.

"If you'd like, I can show you how good of an eater I am."

Victoria folded her arms.

"He asked if we were dating. I told him you work as a recruiter." He'd also told Burton to fucking back off, stop looking at her, stop thinking of her, and if he knew what was good for his metal knees, to never touch her.

Unnecessary, as it turned out. Burton had assured Warren that he'd sworn off women for good. When most men made the proclamation, Warren dismissed it for a dry spell. Burton, he believed. Half because of the lethal tint in his eyes, half because he hadn't said women, but succubae.

"A party? Are you kidding me right now, Bert? On my last day to say goodbye, you throw a party?"

"I'm throwing a goddamned parade. Finally, after two long years, I have something to celebrate!" Burton's shout rattled the diamond of the entry chandelier again, crystal clattering like an in studio audience.

"Terry said you refused to give him my armoire. That is my favorite piece, Bert. It's mine."

"I bought it."

"For me!" Bridget screamed. "What are you going to do with an armoire? Your thumbs are like sausages. You won't be able to open it. You'll fumble around like you always do."

"I'll find a new woman to use it."

"You're horrible."

"And yer a monster!"

Warren's shoulders tensed at every insult thrown. What was it like to hate somebody you once loved? He'd been invited to their wedding, but he'd been at the top of his career and hadn't been able to make it. If he'd gone, would he have seen the truth? Known Bridgit was insidious?

Probably not. Not then. That was before he'd been trampled, used, before everyone lined up to slot knives into his back. Such is life. You get older, and the world loses its shine, gets harder, you have fewer friends.

Was he becoming a match to Burton? Bitter, holding on to the past? A fucking disgrace of a host.

Victoria didn't remind Warren of Bridgit.

He'd never heard Victoria spew hate, be petty. In truth, she'd been too honest about what she wanted, how she'd do anything to get it.

He wished it didn't hurt so much when she reminded him that he was merely a tool for her to use and discard as she saw fit.

"I need him," Victoria said, sliding off her heels and tiptoeing across the room to press her ear between the doors.

Warren rolled his eyes, following until they were side by side. Chests pressed against the panels, hands raised.

Her pinky brushed his. She smelled like oranges and sunscreen and a swig of beer. "Don't eavesdrop," he whispered.

"They're yelling. They want us to hear."

"Then why do you need to stand at the door?"

She tensed her lips. "I need more information." She closed one eye as the shouting subsided to growls and grunts. A long whine sounded like furniture scraping across the tile. A door slammed.

Another.

Victoria turned to face Warren. "What happened?"

"They left. I think. Fuck, did he forget we were here?" Warren mimicked her, turning, pressing tighter, straining to listen. He'd kill Burton for locking them in here, for telling them five minutes and disappearing for an hour.

"No," Victoria's cheek settled on the wood. "Why did you get moved to second-string?" Her brows pinched. "I can't figure it out. I've seen the game tape. And you were throwing aces at dinner. Loose, happy."

"That was a test?" Warren wished he was more surprised.

"It's too late to get mad, Flowers. You already passed. Did you and the coach fight?"

"It was Randall," he admitted.

Victoria upper lip curled. "The charmer."

"He destroyed me."

"He's a cesspit of a human, but he's not the commissioner. I had him handled in one afternoon. Besides, he wanted you to start."

"Well, I never thought he'd need handling." Warren's voice was low and surly. "I assumed he was doing what he promised, protecting me, looking out for my best interests, communicating with the coach, the GM, progress updates, everything. Then the Texan's drafted a first round quarterback."

"That's not completely uncommon," Victoria reasoned, black brows pinching. "It takes a while to train the college football out of a player."

"I know." Warren all but growled the words, embarrassment forcing him to look away. "Coach Nale assured me I was their top spot. Doyle was being added to the depth chart. He asked me to take him under my wing."

"Like Burton helped you."

"No, Burton was smarter. He didn't train someone to replace him. I taught Doyle everything. I calmed him down, I gave him advice, I helped him—" He cleared his throat. "They blindsided me. Together, Doyle and Nale. The first game of the season. No more starting. Not the game. Not the season. Never again. Midas was QB one."

Anger tightened his throat. "Randell told me weeks, months later, he'd seen it coming. Said Doyle's agent had been hounding the staff, pulling for a spot, calling me complacent, used, old. I was fucking twenty six." He swallowed to even his voice, over-correcting into a rushed whisper. "I thought someone was talking for me. I was overconfident, naïve, trusting. I believed it when Doyle told me he'd need years to learn the ropes, I believed it when Nale said don't worry. I believed Randell had my back."

Victoria matched his whisper. "But that doesn't make any sense. Why would they lie?" She slid closer, her hand closing over his, thumb stroking. "How could Midas convince an entire coaching staff he was better without any proof or argument?" Her voice had taken a defensive edge.

For him.

Warren's helpless gaze followed the elegant bridge of her nose to the bow of her lips. They were close. His forehead hovering above hers, chests rising and falling. He could lean down and kiss her, grab her hand and hoist her into him, taste her, burn his bruised past away with salt and sun.

He didn't. "Come on, Red. You know why. Everyone's only looking out for themselves."

"Exactly," she rushed out, fingers biting his skin. "What—"

The doors swung open. Warren reacted, jumping back, adrenaline rushing.

Victoria didn't possess the speed of an athlete. The hard edge of the door struck her cheek, and she went down in a crash.

Chapter Nine

As Warren carried Victoria into her hotel room, a crash of pained moans rose from the back of her throat. Gently, hands near shaking, he laid her across the bed.

A fighter. More stubborn than a mule. Infuriating, determined. A woman who took what she wanted without embarrassment. Leveled by a door.

The wood had caught her in the cheek, a nasty black bruise already blooming over her pale skin. It should've been hard to look at the mottled patch on her delicate heart shaped face, a horrid contrast to her fair complexion.

It wasn't.

It reminded Warren of a thorn on a rose.

It made her beauty dangerous, deadly.

Utterly helpless. She'd laid sprawled on Burton's hardwood until Warren had carefully turned her over, brushing the hair from her face.

It was lemon juice on a fresh cut, a splinter under his fingernail.

He'd seen her scared, yes. But even with fear in her eyes, she'd risen to fight, at the bar, she'd use her wit to unarm a man twice her size, in her room, she'd armed herself, wielding nail clippers like a poison tipped spear.

Spread prone on Burton's floor, she'd been truly helpless. It had sent an oily roiling disgust over Warren. That he let it happen to her, that Burton hurt her. That he snuffed her fire.

The two had argued, fought. It was when Warren attempted to come to blows, Victoria blinked those exquisite eyes up at him, softly dilated, slightly dazed. As quick as she'd fallen, lost herself, her spark reignited. On his knees beside her, Warren helped her to sit, and she pushed past to stand, leveling those sleepy eyes at Burton.

"Your ex-wife doesn't live in Vermont," she'd said through a rasp.

The bastard found a bag of ice for her and signed the papers in less than ten minutes.

Warren wondered as he adjusted the pillow under her head, smiling at the way her body lay cushioned in the blankets, how much of that weakness had been real, how much of their fight she'd heard, if she'd truly been incapacitated all that time.

Was she the best actress he'd ever known? She'd been hit, yes, but even that could have been planned. Was that why she'd been eavesdropping in the first place? To purposely put herself in a compromising situation.

Brilliant. Devious.

"How's your head feeling?" he asked. "Headache?"

"No, it's burning." Victoria pushed to her side, slipping an arm under the covers. She moaned when she saw the square of chocolate waiting on the turned down sheets. "Hail Gomez and his overpriced hotel." She unwrapped the candy, bit a chip off the corner, and glanced up at Warren, a sweet smile spreading her bruise. "I'm better now," she promised.

He stroked her hair back, thumb gently grazing her ear. "That's it? The chocolate healed you?"

A sly smile fell across her face as she sat, adjusting the pillows to nest around her. "Chocolate is magic. Caffeine, sugar." Her head dropped back as if she were basking in the glow of the heavens. "The nostalgia alone." Her voice was a purr of decadence. "If football doesn't work out, I'll be campaigning for Hershey's to replace the Mayo Clinic."

"I'd say you're improved." Swallowing back unfamiliar emotion, Warren pushed back from the bed. "I'll get some more ice for your cheek."

"Thanks, Flowers, but I'm fine."

"You might have a concussion."

"I don't," she insisted. "I took a little spill, that's it."

"Victoria," he said brusquely. "I've seen linemen walk off the field from lighter hits. You took a door to the face."

She laughed, a dry, bubbling laugh that made her flinch and touch her eye. "I wish that was the worst I would do to take on a client."

Warren didn't want to consider what else she'd endure. With who. His voice went hard. "I'm getting ice."

"Flowers—"

"Dammit, Victoria, I'm taking care of you. The more you fight, the more overbearing I'll become."

She wore a foul face as he scooped ice into a hand towel, tying it off before pressing it along her face.

"I don't need this."

"You do."

Perking up on the pillows, Victoria laid siege the best way she could, with her wit. "So if you got hit, not tackled, not sacked, if an inanimate object lightly brushed your face, you'd let me fawn over you, carry you off the field, inform you that you're hurt, demand you take a nap, and treat you like a big baby?"

"It's not the same," he said in a suffocated voice, fighting the need to look under the ice and check on the tender skin.

"Of course," she droned sarcastically. "Because you're a man and I'm a feeble woman who is destroyed each time the wind changes. Your sexism is showing, Flowers." She pushed him away.

Warren caught her nape, holding her hostage between him and the ice. "It's not the same because I like you, Victoria. I like your fire and spark and it fucking scared me when it faded." With a growl, he replaced his hand with hers and stood back, fingers numb from the cold. "You wouldn't care if I got hit."

"I... would."

He shook his head, slinging drops of water from his fingers with a flick of his wrist. "You care about your bottom line. That's it. If I get hurt, you can't pitch me to the team."

The following silence told Warren enough. He was right. She'd care. Might even offer him a hand if he collapsed with a torn ligament, but not from personal concern, not because of anything they'd shared. Because his injury would affect her contracts, her job.

He was merely a line number on her life plan. Warren clenched his teeth, watching her fingers cradle the ice, nails scraping into the towel.

A sharp ring cut through the room.

Dropping the ice, Victoria shot up from her pillows, adjusting her baggy shirt as she read her phone. "*Shit*, it's Gomez."

"Gomez, as in Fulgencio Gomez?" As in Mountaineers owner, as in the owner of this hotel, the decider of Warren's future.

"Who the fuck else?" she hissed, waving a hand for him to go as she clicked answer.

"Burton Kilbride is in," she answered, voice absent of its usual confidence. As she spoke, she shoved the sheets back and stood. Swayed.

Warren was on her instantly, plucking the phone from her, putting it on speaker and lifting her in his arms.

Delayed movements, lightheadedness, the swirling pupils. Definitely a concussion.

Should've been obvious when she'd nibbled on her chocolate instead of devouring it.

Slapping his hands, Victoria struggled, stretching for her phone, mouthing a sludge of silent profanities.

"Good," Gomez's voice boomed. "Burton will be a valuable asset. How's your progress with Midas?"

She went stiff in Warren's arms. "I have a plan."

"I'll not settle for less than gold, my dear." Gomez didn't threaten, he demanded. "Make it happen. Soon. When do you fly in?"

"I'll be in Vegas tomorrow. When I'm done there, it's straight to camp, with a special surprise in tow. Did you see how dashing Cole Seeder looks in Mountaineer green?"

"And finch gold," Gomez agreed. "He's a fair steal. Foss seems pleased, but time is nigh running out, as is our money. I want Midas."

***

VICTORIA WAS UTTERLY transfixed by the seething man in front of her. The dark slash of his eyebrows, forearms corded with muscle.

His umber eyes flecked with unfamiliar black. A darkness had fallen over him.

How quickly had her soft-hearted savior left?

She mourned his departure. The tender touches she shouldn't have allowed but made an exception for. The way he spoiled her. How he carried her through the lobby like a damned hero. She wanted to strip down and thank him on her knees.

She'd never expected him.

She hadn't had time to brace, to bolster, to prepare before she was dragged under, riptides tearing her asunder.

He wasn't her type. But when he pressed his firm palm against her chest to study her heartbeat, read her eyes... Had a man ever looked so intensely hot? And he wasn't even touching her. Not really. The thick, soft cotton of his shirt lay between them, an annoying, necessary evil.

If he hadn't heard Gomez's unquenched thirst for Midas, she might not have realized how violently she'd been pulled down.

Warren settled her on her feet, stepping back, arms shaking out at his sides. A tick under his eye. The side with his dimple. "We're going to Vegas now?"

Suddenly, Victoria felt weak. "No," she said, settling onto the bed, brushing away the chocolate. She couldn't enjoy it when he was mad. When her head was spinning, and her hands were as dexterous as rubber mallets. Chocolate was good and innocent. She wouldn't tarnish it. "I'm going to Vegas. You're off to Burlington."

"Splitting up?" Warren's eyes darkened to a brassy shade. "I thought we were doing this together. I thought you *owned* me."

"I do, Flowers." A brush off. To keep him at bay, to keep herself from reaching out and demanding a dose of relief from his searing gaze. "I'm the queen, king, and regent. Do what I say. Go to Burlington and stay low. No media, no announcements, no bars." She cut herself off, unsure if Victoria the Businesswoman was in charge, or if Victoria the Jealous had risen.

"The Burton situation took longer than I estimated. I wanted to fly out tonight. Plans change." She cringed, pressing fingertips to her cheek. Nausea began to rise and sweat coated her skin. Locking her jaw, she shut her eyes, refusing to throw up steak and chocolate. Damned blasphemy.

"And how often do your plans change?" Warren's words clawed at her sanity, a bull kicking back sand and dirt before the charge.

There was a sixty percent chance she'd throw up in response.

Laying back, smoothing knuckles over her forehead, she worked to defuse the bomb. "What you heard from Gomez"—she rolled until Warren was in her crosshairs—"he's being stubborn, but I can assure you I'm no longer gunning for Midas. I have you. You're the plan."

"No. Instead of Doyle, you're delivering me, the guy who lost to him. How long do you think it'll be before I'm physically removed from Mountaineer soil?"

"Once you show him what you can do, he'll forget all about Midas."

"And if he doesn't, Red? Where am I left if he doesn't? Back-up quarterback for the fucking golden lion? I already fucking did that."

Victoria held a calm poker face. Best-case scenario, he'd become a backup. Worst, she and Warren would take the same bus out of town to unemployment.

It wasn't the time for daunting truths. Not when she was bedridden, and Warren looked ready to put her out of her misery.

"At least you'll be making more money." She raised a hand to stop his next thought. "It doesn't matter. I know Midas won't come."

Warren snorted. "That's what you're counting on? Not my skill, but Doyle's attachment to Texas?"

"What do you want me to say?" She pushed to her elbows, panting, sweat beading down the slope of her neck. "There's one name on Gomez's list of quarterbacks and it's not yours. We have to wait until camp starts to spring you on him. Once he understands what you're capable of, he'll change his mind."

"*Christ*, Red" —he pulled on his hair—"I'm not a pinata."

"Men like Gomez do not listen to advice. They think they shit rainbows and piss skittles. His idea is the best, so we can't tell him different. We'll never change his mind. He has to do that himself. We'll back him into a corner until he's forced to see how good you are. And by extension, how talented I am."

She pushed to her hands, lugging her legs to the floor. Using the wall as a makeshift handrail, Victoria staggered to the ice bucket, grabbing a handful and dragging it along her throat, around her neck.

The biting cold offered little relief against her hot skin, but it shocked her enough to stay upright. To find the mirror and examine the swollen cheek overtaking her eye, the gnarled purple and black.

Warren's anger faded in the reflection behind her. "You shouldn't be traveling like that. You look awful."

"People can avert their eyes then. Not my problem."

"You have a concussion. You should go see a doctor, at the very least, rest."

"I'm fine, Flowers." She turned, letting the ice melt away on her skin. Two days until training camp started, and she hadn't finished her job yet. Not even close. "It's a black eye. Not a gunshot. With the magic of makeup, no one will notice."

He brushed her hair behind her ear, and blew softly on the wet skin, helping to cool her. As quick as a bullet, her skin tightened, heat overtook her.

"I don't like this, Victoria. I don't want to sit around again while other people make decisions for me. Not again."

She took his wrist to steady herself. This day was endless and nasty. Morgan, Burton's refusal, the screaming, this headache. Warren's lips, his hands, his possession. "Then leave."

"Leave?"

"If you don't want other people to make decisions for you, you're not in the wrong sport." She twisted to face him. "Football players do not have the power. You can play your best, give everything you have every minute, and you still might get traded. That's why I'm here. To balance the politics for you. You have to let me do it. That's why managers exist."

"You're not my manager."

Thank fuck for that.

"You're right, I'm not," she said. "I'm not tied down to anybody. I can do what I want for exactly who I want when I want, and right now, I want you." She closed her eyes, head swimming. "Get some sleep, workout if you need to. Order food, put it on my tab. My flight leaves early." She ordered herself to the desk, to drag the chair to the door, and notch it under the handle.

"What about Doyle? Is he in Vegas?"

"I'd tell you if I wanted Doyle, I promise."

Warren nodded at the door. "Do the chain, too. I'll lock this one."

"Thank you." She paused at her bed, sitting on the corner. "Trust me, Warren. We're on the same team right now."

"Right now." He sounded bitter.

"I *do* care," she said quietly, unsure why she had to admit it. Maybe because he'd held her, carried her, treated her like a friend when she'd been anything but. "If you think I'm immune to the…" She paused. "To this thing between us. I'm not. At all. You…" God she wasn't good at emotions, at this. "You make me feel like I can't breathe, and I know—" She swallowed. "I know all I have to do to catch my breath is walk away and I stay suffocating."

"That's exactly—"

"It's exactly why nothing will happen. This job requires me to be ruthless. If it comes down to the wire and it's me or you, Warren." She made sure he was looking at her, hearing this. "It'll be me I protect."

Walking through the door, Warren said, "That's called heartless, not ruthless."

Chapter Ten

"I KNOW IT'S CUSTOM for women to be late, but there's a certain fucking time constraint in the NFL."

Victoria barely had the strength left to not bite the most sarcastic 'really oh-em-gee, but my nails are still drying' rant to Foss. In truth, he was one of the better coaches she'd worked with. Not that she had a ton in her pocket to pick through. The industry was entrenched in oppressive patriarchy, steeped in misogyny bullshit. Unfortunately, leaning in and being a sarcastic thorn in his side wouldn't fix any of it for her.

Biting her lip, Victoria sat on the blazing hot concrete curb outside The Box. "I'm well aware of our timeline. Why do you think I keep booking trips? There are new players walking through your door every day, courtesy of me. Tell me you didn't embarrass yourself in front of Cole and Burton?"

"All I see is one massive gap in our offense. Once training camp starts, we are fucked. Completely stalled. We'll have to wait weeks until we can try to steal or bribe someone off of waivers, someone's scraps. I'd rather have a team now. A team to build and grow, train before we hit the season."

"I understand that."

"Then stop procrastinating," Foss snapped. "Fill out the roster and get here."

Victoria slammed her phone against her thigh. Foss, the insidious beast. He wanted her there just to point out every person she'd screwed up. The offensive lineman that wasn't wide enough, a weak spined kicker, the tailback with no neck. Never mind she was the one managing the budgets, slinging the deals, throwing up on planes.

She was building a new picture out of twenty different puzzles.

Toby was the only one who really understood, and he'd been letting Foss and Gomez duke it out.

Taking a single moment to breathe, Victoria put her head between her legs. She'd flown out early, before the sun had risen, before she heard a peep from Warren's room.

Hundreds of miles later, it was still early, but her skin baked, heat hitting her from every direction.

Vegas.

She'd love to be anywhere else.

Except Texas. There it was hot and even more misogynistic than Foss. He'd yet to call her a pretty little thing. For that, she wanted to give him a medal.

Victoria had vomited somewhere over Lake Tahoe. That's when she'd admitted to her bleary-eyed reflection that Warren might've been right. Maybe she did need more than concealer and chocolate. Alone, in first class, an assortment of reality television at her disposal and she hadn't enjoyed a second of it.

Instead, she'd tracked Warren's flight to Burlington, sent him his hotel information and the moment she'd landed, she'd stripped off Warren's shirt and shorts, sprayed in regurgitated breakfast burrito, and tossed them.

Now her ass said *Las Vegas* and her tits read *Sin City*.

It could be worse.

Forcing herself to stand, she checked the time. What strip club was even open at ten in the morning? Sure Vegas never slept, but surely, they fucking took a siesta, slowed down for brunch.

Victoria cracked her neck and lifted her chin. With a final, fortifying breath, she pushed through the doors of The Box, swallowing back a wave of fresh nausea as she was thrown into chaos.

A silver tray hit the wall beside her head.

Glass shattered.

Nothing was easy these days, she decided in that moment, nose stinging as vodka and whiskey slid down the black wall.

Flood lights slammed on. A jarring blue-white that revealed cracks on the raised stage floor and made the errant body glitter look like a thick carpet of pink tinsel. The heavy rap music came to a crashing halt. In the mess of it, weaving between glowing metal poles, two men fought, rolling, hitting, groaning.

Half-naked women screamed in horror, in surprise, in excitement, shoving money into their bras, dodging the battle with excited, scared leaps.

Naturally, in the nettle of swinging fists and blood splatter, was Victoria's target: Miles Santos. A running back, a damn good one, save for his reputation. She'd been after another one, a safer bet all summer, but the kid had used her offer as leverage for a bigger, longer contract with his own team.

Which meant she'd had to come here. To steal Santos from the Raiders. Something she couldn't do if he got arrested.

She watched as he swung, arm covered in tattoos, fist pummeling a man twice his size.

A frosted blonde stripper shrieked bloody murder as they toppled, breaking the legs off a plastic chair. Miles' back hit the stage wall with a thud. Grunting, he lifted his arms just in time to protect his face from a right hook.

Victoria puffed air out her nose and shouted, "Stop!"

A bouncer with three gold chains lining his neck, wide as he was tall, snarled at her. "Keep out of it, Mama. I'm taking care of it." He flashed the brass knuckles spread along his fist.

Panic split through Victoria's headache.

No. Miles Santos needed to stay healthy. Unhurt. He needed to stay out of prison. "Wait!" Victoria called before Chains could punch.

Miles laughed through a bloody nose, front teeth pink. "Why prolong it?" he goaded from his spot on the ground. "Hit me, you limp dick."

The running back was enjoying this. The beating.

"Do *not* hit him," Victoria growled, stepping deeper inside The Box.

"Stay out of our business," said the big guy choking Miles.

Victoria had enough of this shit today. A ruined flight, a forbidden dream, the damned heat. "That's my husband. This is my business!"

Miles' smile disappeared.

Spry, as if he'd been faking injuries, he jumped to his feet.

The big guy turned. "Your husband? You sure you want him? He's been coming in here every day, hounding my girl. I'll take care of him for you. You'll never have to see him again."

"I'd agree." Victoria managed another step forward, ignoring the rising smell of sweat and layered perfumes. "If it weren't for the baby." She clutched at her stomach, blinking wide eyes.

Would she go to hell?

Definitely.

But she'd go there as the best sports recruiter in the history of the NFL. And likely be surrounded by friends.

After a moment's deliberation, the big guy shoved Miles to the door. The running back looked grave as he stumbled forward, playing the act of a caught spouse, feigning humiliation and shame, eyes averted, chin lowered.

Victoria caught his arm and pushed him through the doors to face the blistering dry heat.

"Fuck!" Miles shouted to the pale blue sky, throwing his hands down. Unsteady, shaking violently, he bumbled around the building. "Fuck, fuck, *fuck*." He pounded his feet, ripped at his hair.

Victoria folded her arms, frowning, following three paces back as she waited. Scrape off the tattoos covering his arms, his chest, curling up his neck, and down his hands and Miles Santos was precisely Victoria's type. Standing at a solid six feet, he was built wide and powerful, bunched muscle and packed tendons. He had the look of someone who'd endured at a young age, forced to mature before anyone should. Deep, luxurious green eyes could pass for brown in anything but direct sun. His rich chestnut hair curled gently at the ends, soft and inviting, three shades darker than his skin. He was handsome, dangerously so.

And Victoria felt nothing.

No simmering interest, not a flicker of lust.

Slowly, Miles turned, opening his palms to her. "I'm sorry," he said, voice breaking. "I'm *so fucking* sorry. I don't even remember you." He looked like he might cry.

The man laughed at a fist fight and cried at her.

Victoria hurried to his side, clutching his hands. "We're not married," she said quickly. "We've never met. There's no baby. No history."

The running back collapsed against the rough stone wall, sliding into a crouch, rubbing a hand down his face. "Are you insane?"

"I'm industrious," Victoria defended. "Don't look so pissed. I saved you from getting killed in there."

"I had it handled."

She didn't swallow her laugh.

"I did," he insisted.

"At least my way didn't involve the police."

He glanced up at her from between his fingers. "*Fuck.* Thanks, I guess." When he straightened, Victoria realized he wasn't boasting. He was just as much an actor as she was. Those men didn't stand a chance. Miles Santos was all muscle.

Not like Warren. Warren was lean, sinew and bone, a kind of easy athleticism that might've been natural had it been a level less honed.

But Miles, she thought he might live in a gym. Where he lifted nothing under three hundred pounds.

"What can I do to thank you?" Velvet eyes flew to her tits, reading *Sin* over and over.

"I'm Victoria Steer."

"Is that your real name?"

"Real name, real tits." His gaze shot to hers, a self-deprecating smile appearing. "How about we get breakfast?"

Three blocks later, they each had a stack of pancakes and rapidly cooling coffee. Denny's wasn't Victoria's idea of a closing climate, but it had AC, and the hostess didn't scream when she saw Miles' bloody face. Bonus, their waitress Deedee brought extra napkins without asking.

Made Victoria wonder how often Miles got a craving for blueberry syrup.

The running back pointed at Victoria with his fork, syrup dripping onto his plate. "Steer," he said. "I know that name. Where do I know that name?"

"It's pretty common. Why are you hanging out in a strip club?"

Instead of answering, Miles reached across the square laminate table to palm her breast.

Victoria froze, appalled, surprised, ready to smack and maim when he peeled a sticker off, pressing the circled pink *M* to the tabletop. "Why do you still have tags on your clothes? Why am I buying you breakfast? Are you down on your luck? It's not something to be embarrassed about." He sounded oddly sincere.

"I'm not embarrassed. I threw up on my clothes. I have a concussion. Burton Kilbride hit me with a door. Accident. So he says." She gestured to her poorly concealed black eye. "Turns out a concussion doesn't mix with flying."

They locked eyes, understanding moving between them. She'd been honest. Now it was his turn.

He set down his fork, curling long brown fingers over his mug, making it look like a teacup. "I like gorgeous, unavailable women. I make more money than I need, and their breakfast buffet isn't terrible."

"Not terrible?"

"You tryin' to judge me, Vomitron?"

She smiled despite herself. She liked the bleeding, strip club frequenting, fighter splitting diner food with her. "No. I'm considering hiring you and I need to know you're not bothering those women, that you're not a serial fighter and the miscreant people say you are, because it'll affect my offer."

"Have I convinced you of otherwise?" His smile was devious and proud.

Victoria rolled her eyes. "Your nose is bleeding again."

"*Shit*." Miles grabbed a stack of napkins, wiping at himself while shoveling pancake into his mouth. "You're the recruiter," he guessed. "Steer. You hired Laughlin, the lucky prick. We used to play together."

"Correct." Laughlin was a wide receiver she'd stolen from Tampa.

Miles leaned back in the flimsy chair, licking syrup off of a split lip, planting broad hands over his dark jeans, finger slipping into the tear on his left thigh. "Alright, give it to me." He was grinning. "Your offer. Make it sweet."

She pushed her pancake through a river of blueberry sauce. "Why do men always want to skip foreplay?"

"Fine." He set his elbows on the table. "Who have you hired? Who's the coach?"

"Rodney Foss."

A nod. "Foss likes me."

"Toby Zither doesn't," she countered. "We can be honest, yeah? Tell me you're low risk. You're not going to be stirring up trouble in sleepy Vermont before I come up with any kind of offer."

Miles didn't seem a bit flustered as he took a sip from his coffee. "You're quite demanding."

Victoria looked at the swinging kitchen door, waved to their server for the check. "If I were a man, you'd call me smart. We're done here."

Miles switched his empty plate for hers, stabbing a blueberry pancake with his fork. "Please. We both know you're too smart to be working this hard. Even suffering a concussion. Give me the number."

She didn't. With a polite smile, she accepted their receipt and slid it, unpaid, across the table to him. "Can you shape up?"

He raised a brow at her but pulled out his wallet. Two crappy coffees and matching pancake stacks. Ten bucks in Newport, but in Vegas, three times that. "Who else have you got?"

"Just this week I signed Kilbride, Seeder, and Rose."

"Rose." Miles glanced up from counting out a stack of loose, crinkled cash. "Interesting choice. I thought everyone was sucking the golden king's dick."

"He's on a shortlist."

Miles passed the bill to Deedee with a wink and a "Change is yours, beautiful."

In her most annoyed tone, Victoria asked, "Do you have an off switch, or do you flirt with everyone?"

"I don't want Midas."

She smiled, her hunch correct. "Because you're worried he'll throw more than run."

"Because I don't like him. He doesn't care about the team, only himself. Have you watched any of his games?" Miles continued before she could answer. "Of course you have. Wait until they're over. The guys are shaking hands and where is he? Doing interviews, cheesing for the camera. No 'good game' from him." He slid the last puff of pancake between his lips.

Victoria understood Miles' appeal then.

The confident, playful, hometown kid with tattoos to show he didn't have sex, he fucked.

He wet his lips. "Come on. Tell me it."

She did, and the two marinated in the silence after. Miles waiting for her to retract it, Victoria waiting for him to ask for double.

Finally, his smile tipped up. He ran a hand through his curls, leaving them to gently spring back. "I'll warn you now. I look good in green."

"How fast can you pack?"

His grin matched hers. "Let's go right now."

***

WARREN SLASHED ASIDE the reed thin shower curtain and jolted for his phone.

"Tell me everything you know about Miles Santos."

No 'hello'. No 'how was your flight?' No 'Warren, I missed you'.

He'd been in Burlington for an entire day and had yet to leave the hotel. Hadn't heard from Victoria once. Alone, secluded, he broke up the time staring past the crowded parking lot to marvel at the Green Mountains, sweating his ass off in the ten by ten gym, and memorizing the Mountaineers' playbook. He could draw it from memory while listing mountain peaks and squatting twice his weight.

And yet this, *this*, was what he got for playing good boy while Victoria jetted off.

A sharp tone void of patience and familiarity.

At least she was done shunning him.

Fuck, he was soft.

Part of him, the big part, the part that grew rougher, grittier scales each year was convinced she'd tucked him here to find a better quarterback. He'd checked every major news outlet to make sure there were no whisperings of Doyle Heark abandoning the Texans and found nothing.

He wanted to kiss her feet in thanks.

He wanted to spank her for ignoring him.

Her words echoed in his ears, haunted him with every step. *We're on the same team. Right now.*

I'm suffocating.

I'll choose me.

Honest, excruciatingly honest. It took substantial effort for Warren to focus on the *right now* and not the *suffocation*.

Would she warn him when their goals misaligned? Before she buried him to make her own mountain taller? Or would her knife slip into his back as seamlessly as the others, leaving her with clean hands and him bleeding out on the pavement?

Wiping water from his eyes, Warren cleared his throat. "I don't know much. I played Miles a couple of times. Fast hands, knows how to hide a ball."

"I've seen him play," Victoria chided. "I'm asking about *him*."

"Why?"

"Because he's showering off blood in my hotel room, and I'd like to know if that's an everyday occurrence."

Warren's stomach clenched. "You invited him into your room?" He didn't need to tell her what he thought of it. His scathing tone sufficed.

"Did you want me to drop the walking crime scene off at the YMCA?" Her voice remained cool as ice, causing him to wonder if she'd been part of the crime herself. "I don't need all of Las Vegas to know I'm hiring a Neanderthal."

Shoulder resting against the cool, slippery subway tile wall, Warren adjusted the faucet, turning the shower to blazing hot. "You're hiring him? Santos? The running back? That's why you're in Vegas?" Seducing another player.

"Why can't you keep up?" she clipped. "What's that sound?" There was a pause.

Warren let the water beat on his skin, let it sear and sting. She'd do *anything* to get a client. Hadn't she said that? Now she was sharing a shower with one, blood running down the drain.

"What is that sound, Warren? Are you in the shower?"

"One day, and I'm Warren? What happened to Flowers?" Regret filled his stomach. He sounded forlorn, like a scorned lover. He and Victoria were far from that. Gritting his teeth, he aimed for dry as he told her, "You said to answer under any circumstances. I aim to please, Red."

"Get out of the shower," she demanded. "People don't talk on the phone in the shower."

"Are you picturing me naked, Red?" He took her silence as a yes and smiled without shame or remorse. She could chase after others, she could ignore him, she could leave him, but she couldn't make herself not want him.

"You're hiring Santos?" he asked again, swiping a thin rectangle of soap down his chest. Suddenly, he found he enjoyed speaking to Victoria while naked. Hoped to make a habit of it.

She sighed softly and it went straight to his dick. "The contract's signed. I'm having buyer's remorse, but I didn't have time to do any more research. Gomez wants me in Burlington tomorrow."

"You're done then? You're leaving Vegas, coming to Vermont. Not making ten stops in Hong Kong and Argentina first?"

"If you know of a less nosey quarterback in Hong Kong, I'll take the first flight." She sighed again, exhaustion and worry weighing her down. "I hate Vegas. It's—"

"The worst city in America," Warren finished.

"Finally, someone agrees with me. It's over a hundred and ten degrees here. I watched a lizard break a sweat."

Warren chuckled. "I don't agree with you. You said the same thing about Houston and Seattle."

"They're all equally the worst." Warren heard a crash, a shout. Then Victoria called, "Towels are behind the door!"

"Switch to Facetime," Warren ordered.

"Absolutely not."

Her refusal made his heart pound even faster. He switched the phone to his other ear. "What are you wearing?"

"What kind of question is that? We work together, Flowers."

Flowers.

Why did he fucking like it when she called him that?

"Are you wearing a dress? Which one?" He closed his eyes, and his hand sank down his stomach. Lower. "The red one with the miniskirt or the blue with the miniskirt?" His head tipped back as he took the base of his cock in his hand, his tone dropping to a rasp. "I need to see that you're not wearing it, Victoria. That there's not a man showering in your room while you wear napkins for clothes."

A final sigh. "Fine."

He hung up, fumbling with wet fingers on his screen, desperate to see her.

Regret swelled when he saw her face. She wasn't in a dress but cuddled under a thick knit blanket. Black hair pulled back from her face, eyes half lidded, the blue missing its usual vibrancy had become somber, and a deep, mournful bruise covered half her face.

Warren went rigid with anguish at the sight. "Baby—"

"Don't," she began, flicking her eyes away. "I see it right in your face. It's not that bad."

It was grotesque, it was horrible, unacceptable. Warren swallowed his opinion. "How's it feeling?"

Her brows came together, delicate fingers stroking the marred skin. "You mean Melinda? This little minx? Hardly notice her anymore. "

Anger, arousal, frustration, and longing battled for dominance in Warren's chest. "I should've caught you," he admitted quietly, slicking back his hair. "I should've never let you fall."

"You're not a receiver."

"I should've never even let you against that door." No. He should've fucked her behind that door when he had the chance, when they were alone, and she was swimming in his t-shirt. Now, he didn't think he'd ever have another chance. "Did you sleep at all last night?"

"Yes."

He didn't believe her. He trusted the bags under her eyes. She was exhausted and strung out. Something about the lie, white and pointless, given in her soft tone forced him to smile when he really wanted to rage at her, fly across the country and force her to rest, to ice, to relax and recover.

That he could do none of it tore into his chest. Across the country, him in the shower, Victoria in bed, all Warren could do was distract her. "Pan down. Show me your shirt."

With a brief huff of annoyance, she obliged, pushing the blanket aside to let the camera rove across a tight black belly shirt and spandex shorts that better served as underwear.

Delectable. His distraction became too effective as lurid images swept his thoughts. Him throwing back the covers and laying his wet, hot skin over her, watching steaming drops splatter on the swells of her breasts and curve down her cleavage, her stomach.

"You're killing me," he admitted gruffly. "Want to see what I've got on?"

Smiling in spite of her pain, Victoria said dryly, "Seen it. *Sports Illustrated*. Not interested in a repeat right now. Just wanted to check in, not perform a physical."

Warren found himself staring into teasing, blue-gray eyes. "You googled me?"

"*Rose* plus *quarterback* plus *naked* plus *winky face*."

He tried not to let his male pride rise at the news that she'd searched his name. Or the fact that her eyes were glued to her screen, watching his bare chest. "You should get back to it. I know how important research is to you." He nodded once. "Give the phone to Miles."

Her eyes narrowed. "You just want to shower together or what?"

Warren turned off the shower and threw back the curtain, making a show of donning a towel in front of the screen. "I want to talk to him. Come on, Red. Let me handle him so you can take care of yourself."

Looking highly speculative, Victoria slid from bed and knocked on the bathroom door with one last glance at the screen. "Miles, there's a *Sports Illustrated* model on the phone for you."

"You're mean," Warren accused gently. He cleared his throat before he added, "Borrow one of his shirts."

Chapter Eleven

Warren's attention followed Victoria like a heat-seeking missile into a volcano.

She became lightning as soon as she stepped into his room. Crackling with energy and fire. Thrice now, she'd stalked the length of his suite, examined the couch, the table, the television, taking mental notes, methodically adjusting her route around each obstacle.

He wondered if she retained any of it.

Her skin was flushed, her eyes hazy. In less than a day, the bruise on her cheek had faded to an angry purple.

Any chance of conversation was drowned by her restlessness, the smack of her feet, the tapping of her hands on her thighs. Though she'd arranged for him to have a suite, there wasn't enough space to contain a happy Victoria.

The hotel was dated and small, smells of dust and cleaner commingling. The scant furniture seemed to be arranged in a way that hid bald patches on the brown carpet, creating an odd back-to-back chair layout. Stale air conditioning from a high vent showered the room in cold waves of air. Thick curtains were drawn to preserve energy, blocking Vermont's surprisingly formidable afternoon sun.

It lacked the detail of a Gomez suite, but the bed fit if he slept at a diagonal, and the shower ran hot and cold. Both of which he'd put to use after their call yesterday.

Sitting in a three-wheeled desk chair, black fake leather smooth along his back, ankle over his knee, Warren watched Victoria, enjoyed her.

She'd come back.

More than that, she'd come *here*, suitcase rattling behind her, smelling of sunscreen and chocolate.

"I'm done," she said again. Each time seemed to lift more weight off her shoulders. She turned, feet planting, the tips of her heels stabbing the area rug. "I did it."

She bounced on her toes. Lightning, endless energy. It was a wonder sparks weren't flying off her skin. Gone was her Las Vegas paraphernalia. She wore a tight leather skirt and a fitted button down, only half done up. Both were a denim blue that paled in comparison to her eyes.

She was a siren with a nine to five. A business nymph. He tried to picture her in a suit or jeans and failed on both accounts. Victoria Steer didn't do boardroom, and she didn't do casual. She was a machine, a storm that never broke.

Perhaps that's why she'd finally been reduced to monosyllabic words.

A bitter, vicious voice rose up in Warren's head, pricking at his happiness. Why hadn't she worn one of her rippable, indecent dresses for him? Before he could contemplate, she spun again, walking, hips swaying, and he found he didn't care. He watched the toned lines of her calves, the flex of her ankles balancing on glittery black heels.

"I did it," she murmured, grinning, floating.

Warren's low voice undercut the whine of the air conditioning. "If you think you found clothes I can't tear through, you're wrong."

A spiked heel hit him in the chest.

Then the other. The shoes puddled on the floor. Victoria was three inches shorter.

"Training camp starts tomorrow, and I made a fucking team." She brought her hands together, eyes glistening. "I feel like fucking Poseidon shaping the clay of the Greeks, the first people made from the shores of whatever fucking river is in Greece."

"Quite the history buff."

"You can't bring me down, Flowers." A spin and she was winding between the desk and the minibar, prowling straight to him with a grin. "Nothing can bring me down today. I am the winner. After this, everyone will know my name. Everyone will want to work with me. You can suck it."

"Congratulations, I'm proud of you." There wasn't a false note in his tone.

Victoria bent over him, her hands warming his knees, face level with his. Slices of her black hair tickled his cheeks. "Do you know what I've done here? Can you conceive what I've accomplished? What no other recruiter dared to try?" Her eyes shone. Her hands trembled over his knee. "I whetted the appetite of three opposing men and made a goddamn masterpiece."

Heartbeat slamming, lungs empty, Warren asked, "And what am I in your masterpiece?"

"The North Star." Her smile was contagious. Her hands went to his cheeks, thumbs stroking the hard slashes of his cheekbones. "The Mountains. You're everything."

She pulled back before he could kiss her, spinning again, hands finding her hips. "What did you say to Santos?"

"Told him I was excited to see him. He's a good player."

She made a low, disbelieving noise in her throat. "Whatever it was, I appreciate it. He became much less of a handful after." She wove around the couch, her hand grazing the arm. "Aren't you excited?" she asked, stopping to trail her fingers down the starchy beige curtains, watching him from over her shoulder.

Warren tugged his leg higher to conceal the hardness growing in his lap. "Ecstatic." He sounded pained. "I feel lucky to be a single drop on your masterpiece."

Victoria threw back the curtains and froze, arms spread. "Oh... I thought you'd have a lake view." Her shoulders slumped.

His room overlooked the lush Green Mountains, miles of peaks that had thrilled Warren after life on the plains.

Might as well be a brick wall to a girl born on the water.

"I like the mountains," Warren defended, moving to stand behind her.

Ignoring her flinch, he pulled her against his body and fit his hands over the smooth material of her skirt.

Head resting back on his chest, her voice lowered. The adrenaline of victory faded, the slow tug of exhaustion mounting. "I grew up with the ocean as a constant. I couldn't read a map but if you told me to find the coast, I could have my toes in the sand within the hour."

"What will you do now that you're done? Go back to Newport?" His voice was soft against her ear.

"I'll be around for training camp to make sure the roster works, and replace players as needed. Then I'll join the hunt during waivers to finalize the fifty-three." She twisted, leaving his hold to press her back against the windowpane. "The minute the season starts, I'm gone. I don't know where yet. Not Texas. Or Vegas."

"Or Seattle," he offered, trying to keep his tone cheerful.

"Or Detroit."

Warren managed a weak smile as he scrounged two glasses from the minibar, flicking through the bottles. Tequila would sting the most. "You'd let your picks get ousted?" he asked as he poured, ignoring the tightness in his ribs making it hard to breathe.

"Not every player is mine," she told him. "I'm not abandoning anyone. I'll push for my own recruits during camp, if only to ensure none of you make me look bad."

He passed her a glass with two knuckles of gold poison. "I'd hate to be the man who disappointed you."

Instead of replying, Victoria's gaze drifted over the mountains, lingered on the fog shrouding the highest peaks.

A burning ember embedded in his chest. He knocked his glass against hers. "Cheers."

They shot back their glasses.

"It's been a pleasure working with you." Her eyes were glassy, her mouth spread, happy.

Warren brushed his hand over her cheek, caressing the discolored skin before sifting his hand into her hair. Since the day he'd seen Victoria beaming like a devilish seductress in the stifling dank bar in America's worst city, he'd wanted her.

His body came alive for her with only one flash of those blue eyes, one curl of her quick mouth, and he was desperate.

Gently, Warren cupped her neck. "I'm going to kiss you now."

***

NORMALLY, VICTORIA'S MIND was a whirl of activity. Planning, strategizing, a little fantasizing. Now, her head was empty. Every brilliant idea, twenty part scheme, what she'd eaten for lunch had abandoned her. Trickled out like a yolk slipping through the cracks of a shell.

She couldn't bring herself back together, the pieces of logic and reality crumbling to dust at the feel of Warren Rose's strong hand gripping her neck. The way his tongue came out to flick over his full bottom lip as he looked down at her with eyes that made her feel as brilliant as the sun.

"You can't—we can't," she stuttered. An objection, but she couldn't pull out of his embrace. Might've slipped further into him.

In the past, Victoria's celebrations had required strangers and champagne, music to gyrate to, and a hunk of extra thick salted chocolate.

On the plane, her only thought of celebration had involved Warren. Seeing the slow curl of his crooked smile, watching the gold in his amber eyes streak and brighten.

She soaked it up like a lone daisy in the desert, desperate for his praise.

Why? Why did it have to be him? The one person she held most precariously.

Victoria swallowed, tipped her head.

Warren's dark gaze was primal, predatory as his fingers compressed over the delicate skin of her neck.

"You smell like the hotel soap," she whispered, eyes slipping shut. Reaching up his chest, she tugged him down and kissed him until their tongues slid together.

One taste. A reward. She'd earned it.

But his kiss didn't feel like a prize. It felt like a shorn ribbon on a big fat present. A fracture of a whole thing, a scrap, a miserable tease.

Warren slowed her mouth, calmed the kiss until his crooked lips were light and sweet over hers. Not a kiss, a caress.

Pulling her into him, against her lips, he asked, "Why can't we?" He lifted his head. "We no longer work together. Why can't we indulge in this?"

His teeth scored the curve of her jaw. His hot breath hit her neck, and she arched into him, admiring the raw strength of his chest. She wanted to drag her fingers over the grooves of muscle, lick the tan off his skin.

He could throw her around as he pleased. Control her, contort her. Never had she been with someone so tall, so strong. A waste, she'd thought. Awkward, uncomfortable. She was short, a tall man could only give her back problems.

A fucking fool.

Victoria couldn't believe what she was feeling. The tingles of sensation, the sudden flush of warmth. In Warren's arms, she felt as small as a single drop in the ocean. And yet, she had the strength to stain the Atlantic blaze red if she wanted. Delicate and potent and powerful. Things that didn't coalesce, that shouldn't mix.

Warren's words caressed her cheek, his nose drawing up hers. "Celebrate with me."

Her hands anchored to his belt, fingers slipping behind it. "Warren. It's—"

His lungs were working hard, his hand shaking at her neck. "You know how badly I want you and I know, at least when we met, that you wanted me. Has that changed? Has knowing who I am destroyed that?"

Her lungs squeezed. "We work—"

"We *don't*," Warren insisted, thumb stroking down the column of her throat. "We're back at square one, Red. Back in the bar. I'm staring at you, wondering what a girl like is doing in this fucking place. How an angel can stalk the halls of hell."

Victoria let the hotel room fade to darkness, to shadows and shapes. To Warren pushing through a crowd, exuding vitality. Her valiant and brave hero. His soft eyes had been like brass bullets and Victoria had wanted a pretty, pretty scar.

"I'm no angel," she warned. "Especially not for you."

"Thank *fuck* you're not," Warren said wryly. "What do you say to me, in your red dress, last call nearing?"

She folded her hands over his belt, stuck out her chin. "You know what I'd say." Her breath thinned. Her lungs burned. "It's always been what you've said in return. You didn't want me. You said no."

"I was your scraps." His voice thickened with dark emotion. "Unworthy. A passing amusement for you. You wanted Midas and settled for me." His features were more uncomfortable than angry.

Is that what he thought?

"You're the only player I've ever wanted like this, and I hate it," she admitted. "I *hate* it." She fell back into the window, hands sliding from him as the weight of her confession landed. "I *hate* that the minute you say yes, you're going to ruin all other men for me." She pressed her burning cheek to the windowpane. "You did me a favor by saying no."

Warren lifted her chin, his finger stroking the edge of her jaw as he aligned their bodies, a hard heavy length burning her stomach. "I regret it," he said honestly. "I regretted it seconds after I said it." His throat bobbed. "Kiss me, Victoria."

She shook her head, heart beat crashing, lungs empty, sweat building in the dip of her elbows, between her fingers. "I won't be able to stop."

Warren smiled, bending to catch her earlobe between his teeth. Sparks broke across her skin, a shudder ripped up her spine. "I'll make sure of that," he said huskily. "Make sure you can't."

She lurched up then, crashing into him, pushing his lips apart with hers. Her drop of water magnified, multiplied until her entire body was tainted by Warren, drowning, disappearing in every part of his taste—tequila and mint—the scent of soap and sweat.

Rough hands slid under her shirt as he lifted her, caressing the dip of her spine.

Strong.

He was incredibly strong.

The way he held her, she didn't loop her legs around him, clutch at his shoulders to cling, fear for her balance. She sat, full weight in his powerful arms, lavishing in the caress of his tongue, the wicked licks. He took parts of her soul with every breath, inflamed and desperate. As if she was the last piece of his puzzle.

She'd been running for so long. In Warren's embrace, she stopped.

She slaked her tongue against his, trembling as he groaned into her mouth. The hardness she felt along her stomach spurred her on, made her stomach clench and her skin tighten.

Inevitable. She'd known this would happen. That it did today was kismet. The best day of her life, the pinnacle of her career blessed by a man to which she'd compare all the rest.

Lost in a heady daze, Victoria let her hands round over the intense lines of his shoulders, biceps, worshiping the heat and sinew.

"You're like a statue sprung to life," she whispered as she arched against him, swiveling her hips.

Then they were spinning, and she was being carried across the room, past the couch, and tossed onto a massive white bed.

It became a battle for who could undress faster. She unbuttoned her skirt. He ripped it off. She tugged at his shirt. He stepped out of his pants. Her shirt was gone. Her underwear. His. In only her violet lace bra, Victoria sank back against the comforter, breaths rushing in and out.

Standing proudly naked, Warren caught her ankles, wrapping his hands around them like twin shackles. His simple touch went everywhere, throwing thrills of pleasure into her nervous, hyper-sensitive system.

"Beautiful," Warren murmured, gazing down at her. Crooked smile showed his hot, wet tongue licking at his canine, as if he wanted to eat her.

He was glorious. Towering over her, tanned skin pulled taut over flexing muscle. How stupid she'd been to think he was naturally toned. He was nothing but swollen muscles and hard lines. All straining as he watched her. Not bulky, but lean, svelte.

She kicked his hands off and rose to her knees, crawling to meet him at the edge of the bed. A rush of feminine pride urged her forward as Warren's eyes snagged on the lace of her bra. Slowly, she wrapped her arms around him, hands exploring the warmed skin of his back as she took his lips with hers. Slow. Deep.

Her fingers savored every sharp line, every dip and divot and scar on his body.

Work-roughened hands scraped at her skin in return, caressing her curves, teasing the hollow between her breasts. Her nipples pebbled against lace as a flush of wetness wove between her legs.

He was memorizing her, following the smooth skin of her forearm, the contour of her knee. Memorizing the grace in her limbs, like he planned to traverse her in the dark. His fingers counted the chords of her spine. Up, up, up.

The buckle of her bra snapped open.

"Don't," Victoria gasped, pulling back, reaching for the clasp. "I like to keep it on."

Warren's brows came together to sit low over dilated dark eyes. His erection was burning against her stomach, solid and insistent as he reset the strap of her bra. He followed the lace cups with his thumb. "I want your nipple in my mouth. Not your bra."

A bolt of hot, aching desire stuck. Breathless, she caught his cheeks. "Lace is practically porous," she whispered, sucking on his lower lip, hand dragging down his body.

Warren withdrew from her and gripped her chin gently, studying her. "Why don't you want me to see?" His frown worsened as her cheeks flushed with red. "I don't care if they're fake."

"They're *not* fake," she informed indignantly. She'd never pay for them to be this big, this obnoxiously heavy on her chest.

It was exactly the assumption that made her not want to bare herself. She'd gone through puberty, not in spurts, not in a gentle curve, but in one explosive moment. Her body had not been prepared. The stretch marks wrapped around her hips she'd learned to ignore. No one stared at hips, fantasized about them.

But the puckered dark lines on her breasts. The ripples of darkened skin—she hated those. Delicate skin, sensitive skin that never lightened, never healed. He might not stare at the side of her thighs, but men loved breasts. She didn't want his hands pausing on the scars, hovering, couldn't stomach the way his face would twist. Fantasy dispelled.

"They look better like this," she assured. They did, covered up with lace and bows, they were nearly magazine worthy. No need for Photoshop.

"They'll taste better bare," Warren said seriously, hands no longer charting her body, but stroking a line down her forearm. "Tell me why you don't want to take your bra off."

"I—" she stopped. "Warren it's not... I—"

"It's Dimples," he said softly, lungs working hard. "We're strangers in a bar and I'm trying to say the alphabet backward not to come just from looking at you." He chuckled, a dark, self-deprecating rasp. "Take it off, Red and let me embarrass myself."

With a frustratingly hesitant pointer finger, she prodded his dimple, her throat thick.

"Please, Red. For me."

Hardening her jaw, Victoria reached back and undid the clasp. She shouldn't be doing this in the light of day, she should've waited for night, maybe then she could've hidden them. Maybe he could've ignored the feel of the ruined skin.

Carefully, almost reverently, Warren drew the bra straps down her arms, nostrils flaring, eyes sharpening.

Surprise?

Disgust?

He shook his head, a quiet curse parting his lips. "Beautiful," he muttered. "*Fucking beautiful*, just as I imagined."

Then Victoria was moving backward, hair brushing her cheeks as she fell, as Warren caught her and spun, pulled her up his lengthy body and folded her over him.

With her straddling his waist, another brutal curse rippled up Warren's throat. Hands cupping her ass, he blew hot, moist air over her nipples and wet his lips.

Victoria puffed out a half breath at the sensation, squirming. "Did you—" She gasped at the scrape of his teeth. "Did you see it?"

Warren's eyes flicked to her, confusion evident. He flipped them again. The world had no axis. There was no gravity. There was just the way Warren wanted her. Back against the comforter he loomed above her, he flicked his tongue across her nipple, sucked on the skin, traced the stripes of her scars with his fingers.

"Why do you think I'm so fucking distracted?" he asked, blowing air on her breast, watching her nipple tighten, and quickly soothing the cold with his tongue.

"But my stretch marks..." Victoria frowned. Was he blind? Blocking the light?

"What about them?" he growled, sucking hard, hands light, almost restrained, at the curve of her waist.

Her hands came up to cover his. "They're everywhere," she said dumbly, as if it wasn't obvious.

"They're beautiful. They remind me of the way the ocean ripples under the sun." Gently, he pinched her nipple, and licked over the sting. "I can practically taste the salt."

His tongue followed a particularly long line of purple.

"You love salt," he murmured, eyes consuming, words like smoke. "Every time I kiss your lips, it's like drinking ocean water. I know it'll kill me, and I *can't fucking stop.*"

Wearing that crooked smile, dimple a hard divot in his otherwise flat, sharp cheek, Warren dragged his hand down and down. He parted her thighs and stroked once along her core.

"You're wet like it too." His smile twisted to cocky as her hips jerked, desperate for more of him. "I thought you said this state was landlocked." His soaked finger curled against her clit, teasing.

Victoria forgot all about her insecurities in that moment. She *was* the ocean. Ferocious, boundless, graceful, and dominant. She was the roar of waves, the power of swells. She could both erode stone and be a haven for quiet reflection.

Slowly Warren's fingers stroked and circled, his thumb parting her folds as his tongue paid tribute to every ripple on her chest.

The feeling coursed through every part of her, making her clutch at his back, lift her hips. Her stomach twisted as he teased her, pleasure making her pant, making her shiver.

He played her with the same controlled confidence he commanded the field, all of him honed entirely on her reactions, the pulse in her throat, reading each quiver, reacting, pressing tighter when she moaned.

"Say yes again," he growled, flicking his gaze to hers. Amber met blue. The clash like a freshly forged golden ring being plunged in freezing cold water.

Choking out a laugh, she curled her hands into the ridges of his shoulders. "And answer my own question?"

"I sure as fuck know I want you," he told her, half tormented as he teased the first segment of his middle finger into her wet, aching core.

She gasped, stretching, arching. "Yes. Yes. Yes. Yes. *Yes.*" A word so common and yet it stained her. Stuck to her lips, clung there. The way Warren stared... she wasn't sure if she said it right. If she unlocked a new language.

His chest lowered and rose as he looked at her. Ensnared by her, utterly possessed.

This man wanted her with all of his brilliant intensity.

She lunged up to kiss him as his finger entered her, as his thumb hit that tingling spot on her body.

Victoria crashed.

Crashed like waves devouring the shore. Relentless. White tipped waves rushing in rapid succession, punishing and endless. She cried out against Warren's lips, clutching at him, fighting to stay close, hips rocking as another dash of urgency spread through them.

If Victoria was the sea, Warren was a storm breaking along the coast, stirring higher, more vicious waves, begging them to crash, strike, and tear.

Slowly, it stopped. The ocean calmed, receded.

A bolt of feral lightning struck as he kissed her hard, sliding his hips between her thighs. Victoria panted against the skin of his neck, her lips tingling, her body numb and sensitive.

"You want more?" he asked, gently kissing the bruised skin of her cheek.

More. Another new word. She swiped her tongue over his shoulder. "If you don't fuck me, Warren—"

He stole her threat with a kiss, reaching for the nightstand drawer. "Not Flowers?"

"Bad nickname," she groaned, moving to catch his hand. A packet of green foil shined under the slanted afternoon sun. Flowers were lovely and useless, sensitive. Warren was nothing short of a warship demanding she board or drown.

Her thumb flicked the condom. "I'm on the pill." Their eyes locked, his void of the usual umber layer. "I don't mean…" She wet her lips. "Unless you want to—"

"If you allowed me to, I'd never let anything between us. Space, clothes, condoms." He kissed her cheek, her chin, her neck, hand finding its home between her legs, groaning at the wetness waiting. Then he was inside of her.

No.

Pushing. But not quite seated.

He was big. The biggest man she'd ever been with. Rigid length twitching inside her.

Warren swore under his breath, his arms shook. Maybe this was why she avoided men like him. A biological rejection. Her hips rocked forward, almost on reflex, refusing to quit.

Too big, too hard, too much. The storm churning in her stomach stuttered, grasping thin air. Thunder rolled. Tension built deep inside her. She dug her fingernails into the bed.

Warren brushed the bangs from her face. "Relax," he told her, voice like gravel. "Relax."

Sweat beaded her forehead. "If I get any more relaxed, I'll be dead."

"You're not." He clenched his jaw, dark lashes fluttering. "You're thinking." Again, his hand fit between them, strumming the sensitive spot. Victoria moaned, and he rose to his knees, pulling her hips up, forcing her knees wide to hang off his powerful thighs.

Sweat, the lightest sheen, made his tan glow.

Victoria swallowed as the brutal lines of his abs flexed, spasmed, as the vee of muscle that led to their joining tensed. Slowly, he pushed in.

"Oh *fuck*." She panted, gripping his arms as he inched forward.

"No better sight," he grinned, palming her knees, spreading her wide to watch as he entered her. His face twisted in pride and dominance and hunger. He licked his thumb and began stroking, rolling ministrations over her bundle of nerves.

Back bowed over the bed, Victoria gasped his name.

The water had left the beach to build into a massive wave, stacking and folding, waiting, building pressure.

One side of Warren's mouth curled as he tormented her with the tip of his hard length and his thumb. She clenched and pulsed around him, grabbed his knee, dug her nails in. "*More.*"

Too late. It was too late. Not draped over Warren's body. Not yet.

She couldn't do it again, not again, not so soon.

"Warren," she said, desperately. "Stop, *wait*. I want to come with you."

"You will," he promised, letting the wave grow wider and taller, a sheet of rippling energy as he sunk deeper into her. The pressure, the squeeze, the push of him into her—

She couldn't take it—

"I want deeper," she heard herself say, demand, her forehead buried into the mattress, back in a breaking arch, she wiggled her hips. "Deeper, *fuck*."

She came only when he was pressed tight against her, their hips fitting perfectly. He touched a part of her that had never before been touched. A wave with the power to sweep sand off the ocean floor, to disrupt millennia of tranquility, broke.

Crying out, Victoria pulled Warren, pushed. Torn. She wanted his weight, his control painted on her. She wanted to see him, wanted him to see her unwind, crash, and lose control.

Warren grabbed a fistful of hair, dragging his mouth to hers. A mixture of sweat and salt matched the gritty brine scorching her veins.

The air disappeared as he thrust into her again, letting go of his control. His mouth left hers to kiss and nip at her skin, down her throat. "*Fuck*, Red."

With a desperate plea, a growl of command, of begging, Warren withdrew and thrust into her, licking up the arch of her neck.

She said, "Warren" and "yes" and a list of commands left unheeded as she exploded into steam. Warren slammed into her, pounding, unrelenting, fucking. His hand cradled her cheek, kept her bangs off her forehead, holding her there, eyes glued to him, watching the muscles work over his body.

He shook his head in disbelief, dropping his gaze to her tits. "Christ, you are so fucking beautiful," he said it the way she cursed at him, casting blame, demanding retribution. "More beautiful than I ever imagined. And I have imagined it."

Victoria's nails drove into her shoulders.

"I wanted to fuck you against that wall," he breathed, thrusting harder, knocking her up higher on the bed. Callused hands skid over her skin, rough and gentle.

He grit his teeth, holding on, struggling. "I didn't even know your name." He pushed out a short, brittle breath. "I wanted to fuck you at Kilbride's, on the plane. Take you until you were mine." His head went to her ear, lips brushing the sensitive skin as he shifted, hips grinding against her clit. "Beautiful."

She arched, unsure if she was coming again or this was still from before as she throbbed. *Shut up*, she wanted to yell. *Stop talking, stop wrecking me.*

He squeezed her nipple and her lips parted in a scream.

"I never knew I could be furious and possessive and enthralled at the same fucking time. I didn't know it was possible to feel all three at once for a stranger, a vixen." He slammed into her, harder, rougher, unhinged. Waves rippled around them, drowning out sound, life.

This time it wasn't a crash.

It wasn't an explosion.

It was a sequence of meticulously pleasurable events.

It was the way water moved and fit, pooling around rocks and sand to reach the shore. Lazy, indolent, tedious. It swallowed her cries, her moans, the energy in her legs with cool, comforting swells.

Her release was Warren's undoing. Three hard, fast thrusts into her before he shuddered, gripped her, held her together as he fell apart.

Lazily, her mind wandered back to her.

She laid on the bed as Warren cleaned in between her legs and shut the air conditioning off to soothe the bumps rising on her skin. Naked, spent, too handsome, he returned to bed, fitting his body against hers.

It was the middle of the day. Sunlight streaked inside. The news played quietly in the other room. The rooms on either side of Warren's were quiet, empty. Their occupants at work, busy.

Busy, a familiar word Victoria didn't understand as she lay in the cocoon of Warren.

She liked busy but, in that moment, couldn't fathom why. Why anyone would want to be bothered, to get pulled away, to schedules and meetings.

They laid there, quiet, folded together, bare above the blankets, letting the feeling creep back into their toes and fingers. Her hand curled over his bicep, his thigh snug between her legs, just high enough to distract her, to make her skin tighten.

"You..." her voice broke, scratched. A blush heated her cheeks. "You are a deviously good kisser." She twisted her face to his, neck craning. "I knew it from the moment I spotted you. Your smile gave you away."

"Yeah?" Warren drew her closer. "What does my smile have to do with it?"

"It's bold, confident, edging on cocky but not daring to cross the line. It's a cockiness that's earned."

He touched his nose to hers. "Say cock again."

She smiled, reaching around to tease his hip. "Is this what we're doing for the rest of the day?"

"You'll undoubtedly need chocolate soon, but I don't see anything else interrupting my plans."

"Now you have plans?"

"Plans," he insisted. "To show you how I've earned this smile, that my mouth is good anywhere on your body." His hand came to caress her breast. "I got so distracted by these, I didn't get to taste everywhere I wanted to."

Had any man ever been so blatantly, effortlessly sexual?

"You wouldn't," she threatened. "Not after putting that snake between my legs. Not until I devour at least a pound of Hershey's finest, and a bowl or two of pasta." She pushed to her elbow. "It's been awhile since I worked out so vigorously."

Warren caressed her cheek, smile soft. "I don't know which I like more: snake or cock."

"Cobra Commander," she purred, coaxing a wild laugh from him.

"How long has it been for you?"

The question hung in the air.

"Victoria? How long has it been?" He regarded her with worry. Maybe pity.

She squared her shoulders, gathering a pillow to lean on. "Six months." She avoided his gaze. "A dry spell."

His expression was an intense compilation of surprise and disappointment, with a barely leashed edge of hunger. "That's over," he promised, warned. "And I didn't say anything about fucking you again, just tasting you. Satisfying my craving."

Her heart slammed against her ribs. Her thighs squeezed over his. "Maybe I want to taste you."

"You'd keep a dying man from his last meal? I need my mouth on you, on the prettiest pussy I've ever seen. All I want to do is taste it and try not to come while I do."

Victoria's scraped her nails across his pec as her stomach clenched.

His hand rested on her ass, palm hot, territorial. "Don't say cock while I'm down there or I'll finish too quickly."

Then he was sliding down her body, pushing apart her knees. One hand finding her nipple as he scorched a path of wet laving kissed down her ribs, her stomach.

She took a handful of his thick luxurious hair and pulled him up to look at her. "What should I say for you?" she asked, breathless, rising to her elbows to watch him.

There were benefits to him being tall. Like how he could squeeze her tit as he hunkered down between her thighs, propping them over his biceps so he could eat.

"Say 'more'."

Victoria gasped the minute his tongue hit her, and because she wanted to tease and taunt with the same skill he did, she didn't say more. She said his name, over and over. *Flowers.*

Chapter Twelve

WARREN ROAMED THE FRESHLY placed turf of the Mountaineers' practice field. High above, birds pecked and nested on the domed glass roof. The air was warm, sunlight ricocheting across lines and field goals like strobes scattering off a disco ball. Massive whipping fans attempted to suppress the swelling temperatures, but stirred the heat rather than cooled, creating alternating waves of warm and hot air.

The expansive Mountaineers' campus consisted of a massive office building cradling the indoor-outdoor practice field and a gloriously brutal open-air stadium next door.

They called it The Peak

Warren should be stretching, warming up, getting loose.

He wasn't.

He was thinking of Victoria.

Even as he did everything to not think of her, he thought of her. He let his hands fall to his sides, tighten, knuckles throbbing, joints stiff and brittle. Pain pinched at the lack of blood, hands shading yellow. Soreness coated him, sweat lathering overworked skin. He shook his head when offered a water bottle.

He had to hide it, shield the lethargy lacerating his bones, the pants waiting in his chest. If Victoria saw…

It was normal during training camp to suffer. High stakes and endless practices during the hottest time of the year were a fucking awful combination. And he was getting older. The drills wore him down, made his joints stiff and his back burn.

He blew air from his nose, trying to calm, trying to bury the fact that he wasn't as young, as limber, as desirable as Doyle Heark.

Warren wondered how Victoria would look with the glazed sun dancing on her skin, if she'd wish to go outside, open the dome. Let the fresh mountain air fill her lungs.

He missed her.

Missed her like a phantom limb as he crossed the thirty yard line. Training camp was a blur around him. Linebackers rushed in twos, receivers sprinted new routes downfield, a trio of punters compared drop holds in front of a narrow net. Focus and dedication and a thick layer of desperation made the air brittle with nervous energy. All wearing Mountaineer green, they wanted to keep wearing it. To join the team, to stand out and stay.

To hide flaws.

A dozen notes should dominate his thoughts. Reminders to stay loose, play call names, the tick of a countdown clock. He should watch the running backs practice handoffs, talk to the snapper about speed and height. Find the O-line and discuss pocket protection, covering his blind side.

Instead, Warren felt the ghost of Victoria's hand in his hair, the clench of her pussy around his fingers. He planned and re-planned what he'd do to her next, how he'd take her mouth, her body.

Spread across the kitchen counter, crowded in the shower stall, from behind, gentle under fresh sheets and the white summer moon.

Six months, she'd waited.

He'd waited *three years*. Nothing felt right without her wry smile, the dry comments she managed with charm, his damn derogatory nickname.

Even the magnificent Mountaineers facilities—brand new, sparkling with innovation—seemed bland and lackluster.

She'd left late last night, skirt half-zipped, buttons barely together, backing out his door, rushing out excuses. Check into her room, wash her hair, call Foss, make sure Santos didn't need stiches, break it to Gomez that Midas wasn't coming. The last one barely hit the air before the door closed between them.

Sleep hadn't met him. Worry overtook the bliss.

Would he be fired the moment he stepped on the grass?

How would Victoria do it? A plain smile. A brusque explanation, her hand stroking his back.

No. Ruthlessly, just as she promised.

Warren's nails dug into his palms, and he stopped short of drawing blood when he caught Cole striding from the sidelines, mouth tight, dark eyes drifting. The behemoth tackle looked less enormous in the dome. The first week of camp was no contact. No pads required. It was hard to tell if Cole got the memo. He filled his green shirt to the point of gapping stitches.

Stopping at Warren's side, Cole nodded, tugging at a Mountaineer green ball cap, thick swaths of dark hair covering his shoulders.

With one glance, he spoke volumes. *I'm happy to be here. The pressure is nice. I like the green.*

Cole didn't need words to speak, but Warren needed noise to cow his thoughts. More than he missed Victoria, he was ravenous for her. Every slamming heartbeat was for her, every blink and breath.

He was going to get his ass kicked on the field. Unacceptable. He had to perform today, prove his worth, show that he was the right fit for this team. In short, he had to be better than he was.

A gash tore through his stomach at the idea of failing.

If he stumbled, if he dropped a ball, took a hit, Victoria would send him back to the *Circe*. Back to saving pennies while gold streaked down the field, his best friend thousands of miles away. He'd be a miserable bastard—again—lying awake in his dank cabin, breathing in her salt sweet scent day after day

And... he was full circle. Thinking of her again.

Stroking her hair, watching her face contort with pleasure as he coaxed another hard climax from her, thrusting until she gasped, told him she didn't think she could do it again. Until her hands left marks on his forearms, her heels digging into his ass.

Warren forced a smile at his friend. "You're happy."

Cole lifted and dropped his shoulder. "There's a lot to like here."

"The mountains are nice."

They stood together, arms folded, watching as the offensive coordinator scribbled notes onto an iPad. "Is that why you're smiling?" Cole asked. "The mountains?"

"Barely left the hotel room." But Cole knew that. His dry tone pointed and omniscient. "I'm excited to play."

The tackle nodded as up-downs commenced for the defense. Soon they'd break off into skills. The red pinny on Warren's back meant nobody would touch him, but it also meant he wouldn't be left to his own devices. He'd be monitored, watched, and studied by trainers and coaches, by people hiding behind the one way glass office windows looking down at him.

No more shadows, no more second best.

"How *is* Victoria?" Cole asked.

"She's a damn sight, that one. A real firecracker." Burton's voice came seconds before a wide hand slapped Cole's back.

"Well matched last year. We'll be a force together."

Cole nodded his agreement as Burton pulled at the Mountaineers logo on his shirt. "The little devil offered to sell my house just to move me out here faster. As insistent as a fire sprite."

Warren asked, "Victoria's selling your house?"

Burton snorted, scratching at his ruddy, ugly beard. "Fuck no. I'll never sell it. I'd have to split the profit with the sea witch. I'd rather burn it down."

Cole jerked his gaze away, muscles locking. With all the demons that haunted Warren's best friend, Cole never had time for more. For darkness to steal what little light he held. Pettiness, bitterness, anger, it abraded the tackle's calm.

Warren glared at Burton. "Oh," the tight end guffawed. "I've offended the lady." His smile was bitter. "You'll know when you marry a gal how you can hate and love the same person. Switch it back and forth."

"I'll never know that," Cole said sharply, yanking down his hat and stalking off.

Warren level Burton an unimpressed look. "It's day two. Let's keep it light. Try not to talk about torching any houses or the complexities of failed marriage."

"Nothing complex about it. Bitch fucked a bunch of other guys."

"There's a bright attitude."

Burton's laugh was bold and rough. "I don't get paid for my demeanor, I get paid to fill in the gaps, I get paid to catch the ball, so you're going to throw it to me, Rose, because I like getting paid."

Warren shook his head, finally taking in his oldest friend. The jeans, the sneakers, a thick silver watch. "Why aren't you dressed for practice?"

Burton shrugged, feigning casual, but his jaw tensed. "PT said they need to check my knees before I hit the grass." He pulled a face. "I'm surprised you got out of it, considering."

Warren tensed.

Burton clapped his shoulder. "Don't worry, I'll be around later to show the kids how to play. Save all the bullseyes for me."

***

VICTORIA STARED AT the symmetrical white lines of Gomez's office door. Once, not that long ago, she'd considered herself to be bold, rash. A girl who took precisely what she wanted without considering the consequences. It had served her well to be daring, to fuck civility and act like a new breed, a whole new species. A mama bear that would eat her own cubs to survive.

Now... she hesitated.

Had she taken the easy way out by signing Warren? Had her plans crumbled so wholly, she'd forgotten them? Somehow convinced herself she had a grander scheme when waterlogged dirt slipped through her palms? Could she sell mud? Could she mold it and form it into gold?

If anyone could, it was Victoria. Feeling apprehensive and slightly under-prepared, she stretched out her neck and tapped her heel on the glossy stone floor. Show weakness and Gomez would sink into her like a new chew toy.

Warren Rose distracted her, stole her time, her sanity. Had her infatuation blinded her, forced her to make the wrong choice? This, this right here, this swirling in her gut, the shaking hands, *this* was why she'd said no to him.

Now, it was too late for no. For considering consequences.

Victoria crossed and uncrossed her legs, still sore from her thirsty, soul wracking yeses.

Never had she blurred the line between business and pleasure. Never had it been an obstacle. In her head, players were numbers, boxes to check, Pokémon to catch and release at her leisure. Warren had somehow slipped off her spreadsheet and become impossible to ignore.

Her last-ditch idea had exploded into the foundation of her rise.

Victoria shifted in the high wingback chair, back collapsing into the mahogany frame, rigid arms too low to use, deep burgundy cushion sucking her down.

It had to be a negotiation tactic, she mused, torturing his guests with uncomfortable luxurious chairs, raising the question, *are* you *the problem*?

The entire waiting room questioned her sanity. Intricate wainscoting and a frosted crystal chandelier made the large room uncomfortably small, smothering. Sand colored walls invoked the feeling of grit biting her skin, cramming between her toes. Twin grandfather clocks in cream white flanked Gomez's door, ticking out of time. Each swing of their arms raising the hair on the back of Victoria's neck

The only saving grace lounged in front of the glazed windows, a knee folded between her arms, deep teal hair knotted in lopsided buns.

"I'd wait," Zara said, glancing up from her laptop, fingers looping around the screen to pick at the frayed edge of an *Iron Man* sticker. "He's in a bad mood."

"And when, exactly, has your father ever been in a good mood?" The two shared a knowing smile. Two streaks of color in a stylish, lifeless room.

"The day I turned eighteen and he no longer had to pay my mom child support."

Victoria dipped her head, lips quirking. "Please, we all celebrated that. Fireworks, flaming shots, a parade of Go-go dancers. It was a lot to undertake only days after the blowout that was you losing your virginity to Matthew Danson of all people."

Zara faked a gag. "He had the hairiest chest I've ever seen."

"Bigfoot kink?"

"Gross." Her foot dropped to the floor to lean across the desk, soft voice lowering. "I made him wear his shirt the whole time. I have PTSD every time I see the word Yale."

Victoria laughed, a tingle of pleasure weaving along her skin.

The two had worked, in the loosest terms, together the summer before college. Camp counselors for New England's richest. Victoria needed cash for out-of-state tuition, and Zara needed to be anywhere other than her father's empty house in the Hamptons. Two eighteen-year-olds on the coast of Maine, sharing a room with three other girls and shucking oysters by the bucket.

It should've been a nightmare.

Zara made it fun. A lot of fun.

In the last six years, Zara had shed her rounded cheeks, the doe eyes. Striking best described her. Elegantly tall. Dark eyebrows that were sisters, not twins. Rich blue-green glossy hair that had been orange, green, and crayon yellow curled around smooth brown skin. The knockout folded her slim arms. "Did you come here to talk to me about my bad choices? Because I'd love to bring up some of yours."

"If you go after my bangs—"

"You look like a fairy."

Victoria's eyes narrowed. "A sexy fairy."

"No," Zara said. "The kind that promotes changelings and breathes murky lake water."

"I wasn't picking on you. At least Matthew Danson married the real estate agent with the giant mole. My mistakes follow me around." She leaned forward in her chair. "The green-eyed asshole swooped in to mouth kiss me the last time I saw him."

No hesitation. "I hope you punched him."

"It was in the middle of an airport."

"Double gross. If I ever meet him, I'm swinging straight for his balls." Zara stroked awake her laptop. "How hard is it to get someone on the no-fly list?" She squinted at her screen, presumably googling something that would put *her* on a watchlist, when her phone buzzed.

Dark eyes found Victoria's. "Dad's last meeting must have canceled. No one's come out." A light shrug. "Says he's ready for you."

"Right." Victoria stayed seated, frozen. Eyes fastened to the door, trying to see the dangers ahead. Gomez had waited an entire day to call her to his office. There was a chance he'd calmed since the reveal, since seeing a lack of twinkling gold on the lineup.

There was a greater chance he'd been too outraged to manage his schedule, too furious to demand she come in.

Victoria felt Zara's gaze drift over her.

Carefully, her friend said, "I can tell him you have severe period pain. Blood gushing everywhere. It makes him gag. Got me out his second wedding."

No. Victoria wasn't a coward. She took a deep breath and stood, smoothing out her dress. "How do I look?"

"Like a high end hooker who likes the dirty jobs."

Victoria grinned, precisely what she'd requested of the dressing room attendant. Bright, make you squint, lollipop red latex clung to her. Long sleeved, ankle length, and yet decidedly showy.

"Perfect."

One rap of her knuckles against the door and it opened.

Victoria lost her breath.

"Morgan?"

"Miss Steer." Gomez's tone was civil but uncompromising, hitting her like a runaway train. She blinked as the team owner door the shut behind her, silencing the echo of Zara's violent curse.

Morgan flashed white, straight teeth at her, posture deceptively relaxed in the decadent wood paneled office. A spicy, fruity scent encased the room, orange peel and clove. Bright and fresh in the dim space.

"To what do I owe the pleasure?" Victoria clipped through tight teeth. "Did you find my list and swipe the lot from me?" She kept a smile on her face to match Morgan's as her heart thundered and her ears roared.

A trap.

She'd walked into a trap. Gomez had bested her in the most vicious manner. Usurping her with Morgan, handing credit and power and status over to a man who deserved none of it.

"As if I'd stoop down to represent Rose," Morgan said, plucking dust off his lapel. "The man's a dinosaur. Not even a cool one, with an X in the name."

Gomez, in a relaxed, navy suit, gave Victoria a wide berth to stand ground at Morgan's side. The Mountaineers' owner turned to her, the particulars of his face lost behind wire-rimmed glasses and his white, bushy mustache. "Mr. Turaco represents Midas."

Victoria muffled the gasp in her throat as Gomez continued to launch arrows at her.

"He talked the boy out of a very lucrative contract with his previous agent. Of course, Mr. Turaco came to me first to propose a negotiation."

Victoria glared at Morgan, wanting to put her stiletto through his foot. "That's why you were in Houston? You sneaky fuck. I thought you were done stealing from me."

"Language, Vic." Morgan leaned over her, voice condescending. "I'd quit preaching. You leveraged personal relationships to get this job. Why can't I? Great to see Zara again." He winked.

Victoria fought not to flash her teeth, to bite and claw. Suddenly, she regretted the dress, the color, the cut. Too loud, too brash, a blinking neon sign in a church.

Frustration building, she beseeched Gomez, "I brought you an excellent quarterback."

"Morgan represents the only quarterback I will entertain."

Her ex smiled, helping himself to a wide chair in the corner of the room, brown leather compressing under his packed frame. At ease, he crossed his legs, the dark pant leg of his suit riding up to reveal crisp green socks. Mountaineer green. The schmoozer.

"Midas is the best in the league, and now that he and I are working together, I can divulge that he is not happy in Texas." Morgan informed the room. "Did you know he's from Wisconsin? He misses the snow. Now I haven't been around long, but I'm pretty sure Vermont's known for such a thing."

Victoria heard her knuckles crack. Morgan was tossing out delicious breadcrumbs to Gomez like he was a street corner pigeon, and the magnate was greedily pecking at the ground, pleasure tightening his eyes.

Victoria dove into fix-it mode. She needed yellow tape and a bulldozer.

Planting a hand on Morgan's shoulder, she told Gomez, "Midas can say he doesn't like Texas, but I bet he's at their training camp right now, learning their plays, bonding with their team. Why would he want to start over? It would only be more work for him."

"Rose hasn't played in years," Morgan returned. "And what about his surgery? Has he even started since then?"

Gomez looked to Victoria, waiting.

"His surgery..." she began and petered off. She felt ice crack beneath her feet, stretching in every direction, faster than she could follow.

"His shoulder surgery." Morgan explained, smile bending his lips as he caught her. "The reason he lost his spot. Midas said Rose went under weeks before the season. Never recovered. Unless you're referring to a different surgery?" Morgan nodded the possibility to Gomez. "He's old enough to have a few under his belt."

"He's thirty-one," she said sharply.

"He told you, didn't he? Rose?" Morgan pushed, outright grinning. "That he was untested, untrained, recovering."

She lied. "Of course, he told me. But it was so minor, and he recovered so well, it doesn't matter."

"Regardless of recovery, it will always be a weak spot for him." Morgan shrugged as if he hadn't sliced Victoria's future to ribbons. "But what do I know? I'm not a recruiter. Just an agent. Your old friend. To me, shoulders seem important to quarterbacks."

Curling her nails into his suit jacket, Victoria ripped her gaze from Morgan's vile smile to Gomez.

A vein pulsed in his wrinkled forehead, thick black caterpillar eyebrows hung low over his eyes. "Miss Steer will broker the deal for Midas."

Victoria shook her head. "Sir, I spent eighty thousand on Rose already. We need to give him a chance."

"There is one person I want. I have made this abundantly clear." Gomez buttoned his jacket, gold rings gleaming. "Be glad you're not fired for throwing money into the garbage. By my clock, you have five weeks to get Midas here." He held out a hand to Morgan. "Tell your man to dust off his snow boots."

***

VICTORIA FUMED ON and off for several hours. A blinking, rotating ball of hatred spit red across her thoughts, even as she watched the team bond, work together.

A Frankenstein's monster, Foss liked to call the Mountaineers. Not one original part. They made a mockery of the beast.

Messy, destructive, it'd take time to become graceful.

More time than she'd assumed.

Tapping her fingers on the edge of her phone, Victoria nodded to the row of players filing into the parking lot. It was a hot summer day with full, whistling gusts of wind dragging across the asphalt. Stray papers, loose gravel, and puffs of dust skittered along the smooth, freshly poured blacktop to fill cracks in the road beyond.

Latex and sun were a horrible combination. Sweat slicked her body, pooling between her breasts, low on her back. When she moved, it slid down her legs.

She kept still.

From her spot on the sidewalk, the Mountaineers' headquarters was too tall and wide to see in its entirety. A facade of gray and brown stone, it was built to look like a mountain, wider at the base, rising to a narrowed roof. The entrance was an imposing twenty feet high, supported by gold trusses.

Wheels spun behind her, littering the fresh air with the acrid scent of exhaust and burned rubber. The day was over. The players were off to their hotels, where they'd study playbooks and consume their weight in takeout.

She caught a streak of tan skin and dark hair, the flash of sharp canines in a smile. Shorts and a white t-shirt, Adidas slides.

Target locked.

Fury whipped her into action. She balled up Morgan's card in her hand and threw it at Warren, watching it bounce off his chest, catch in the wind, and slip under the footboards of a tesla.

Based on the limited information at her disposal, Victoria assumed Warren wasn't off to study or eat, but rushing to ice his shoulder.

"What the hell?" he asked, gaze darting up and down her body. Back over again.

A lover's caress.

Her body betrayed her, remembered how well he'd played it, how his hands cupped and caressed. If she wasn't already burning, he'd have lit her up with that alone.

Tough shit. She had no room for lust. Humiliation and anger, betrayal covered her like thick, toxic paint.

He'd lied to her, destroyed her future, all while pretending he was the victim.

She stormed toward him. "You took the words right out of my mouth. What the hell *me*? What the hell *you*?"

Freshly showered, he smelled like pine trees and soap. His lashes were extra dark, drooping with water. He raised his hands, all innocence. "I don't—"

"How bad is it?" she asked, her purse smacking the ground as she groped his shoulder, pushing and prodding. "How many pins are in there? How many months of therapy did you have to do?" A pinch made his jaw tense. "How'd you keep it covered up, huh? Is that the real reason you live on a fucking tugboat? You made a big pay off?"

Warren's jaw popped. "Stop." He grabbed her hand and pulled her to the side of the building.

Sharp wind crashed into them, tossing her hair, throwing his shirt.

"You lied to me," Victoria said without hesitation. "I put my job on the line for you. I asked if there was anything I needed to know, and you said no. How could you?" She shoved him, hard, cursing when he failed to move.

Warren kept his chin low to face her, speaking barely above a whisper as he corralled Victoria into the building exterior. "I got hurt," he said. "It's not a big deal. This is a tough sport. Everyone gets hurt."

She shoved again but was too slow. He caught her hands. His touch the antithesis of hers, gentle and aware, mindful of the way his strength could crush her.

He planted a hand on the wall beside her head and with a nudge of his feet brought them chest to chest, stone cool against Victoria's back. The wind lashing at his cotton t-shirt was the only sign it still blew as Warren became a solid wall of muscle and bone.

"I'm fine," he told her. "Better than ever."

"Bullshit, Flowers." She wiggled her hand for him to let go, thrashing, knuckles biting the brick.

He let go but stepped closer, forced her neck to crane upward. "Don't call me Flowers."

"Oh *fuck off*. As if I care about your feelings. You screwed me, Warren. After whining about how you can't trust anyone. Gomez almost fired me today because I didn't know about your shoulder. He wants my neck."

"Almost means he didn't."

"You're right." She jutted her chin out. "Because *Morgan* talked him out of it. Because Morgan said he wanted to collaborate with me. Because Morgan now represents Midas."

"*Fuck*." Warren shoved off the wall, walking a tight circle, shaking his head, hands knotted in fists.

"My sentiment exactly."

"Then it's over." He let out a dark, humorless laugh. "Lead with that next time, Red. I could already be packing."

"You have four weeks and two days to defend your spot," she told him, bangs whipping at her forehead. He'd made her look like a fool. She'd let him. And now, deep in her spiral of hate and anger, she only wanted to talk him out of his own darkness.

Ridiculous.

She pushed off the wall to leave.

Warren grabbed her, spun her around. "Stop walking away. Ask me about it."

"I did."

"No." He clutched her arm, pressed them together until the ends of her hair splashed over his chest. "No, ask me right now. Ask me what happened."

"Why should I?" she bit. "There's no retroactive points here. You lied to me. My entire plan is at risk."

"Ask, Victoria."

She felt like she was chewing glass. "What happened to your shoulder?"

His amber eyes slipped shut, his minty breath fanning her cheeks as he calmed. "I was fishing, reeling in a long cast, and I felt a pinch."

"A tear? *Fuck*." Those were career ending.

"My left arm," he told her, patting it. "My weak side. They barely put me under. Surgery was to twist the ligament around. No pins, no metal, no reconstruction. There wasn't news about it because it wasn't football related, because it didn't have any bearing on my game."

"Then why not tell me?"

"Because of the way Doyle twisted it. He used my recovery days to tell the coaching staff what happened to me after I confided in him over beers and fresh fish. We'd been bonding. I taught him how to properly bait a hook while he was collecting fucking dirt on me."

Warren's jaw clenched. "Conveniently, Doyle didn't mention that it wasn't my throwing arm or easily fixed. He stole the starting spot with a cheap lie. By the time I figured out why they'd benched me, his position was permanent. And the whole team, the entire city, forgot about me."

Every word sounded like a labor, like a pain. A whip against still healing skin. His and hers both.

Her lips parted in dismay. "I should've known that too, Warren. Morgan played the surgery just like Doyle did."

"It's not relevant."

"You're a professional athlete. Everything that happens to your body is fucking relevant." She heaved through breaths, struggling to calm, massaging the skin between her brows. She threw out a hand. "None of this matters right now."

"Because you're getting Midas and sending me home."

"If you hadn't been so damn proud, I could've prevented it," she replied a bit too harshly. "I looked like a novice in front of Gomez, like it was my first day on the job."

Warren curled his arms above his head, neck tight, cords visible. In a rush, he said, "Red, you have to do something. Stop them."

Holding her whipping hair captive in one hand, she burst, "This is why I didn't want to sleep with you!"

Because she cared now, because his plea struck her heart, because she couldn't form a coherent thought other than sheer fucking panic.

Because if Miles, or Cole, or Burton had lied to her, she'd read them their rights and move on, get over it. Numbers. Emotionless, squared black lines. Seven, fifty-four, thirteen.

She glared up at twenty-three. Watched with searing anger as his eyes froze, hardened, until she was staring at her reflection.

If he were a number, she wouldn't be here.

She'd be off working, salvaging her plan, saving her job, not shouting in a wind tunnel.

"You're telling me you didn't want to?" Warren finally said, his voice not entirely his own.

Victoria refused to look at him. "Obviously wanting you wasn't the problem."

She'd begged him, hadn't she? There was no changing that, not enough tequila in the universe to forget it.

Summoning strength, she lifted her chin again, finding it harder to summon the strength as the day wore on. She ignored the heat spreading up her neck and the tightening in her chest. "It was a mistake only because feelings were involved."

"Don't." Two tips of white sank into Warren's bottom lip. His head was shaking. "*Don't*," he repeated. "Be mad at me for lying, fine. Let me suffer for it. Give me hell. But do *not* tell me you regret what happened between us. Please, if—"

Victoria knocked his reaching hands aside. "Warren—"

"If I had another secret to give you, I'd tell it. But I don't, Victoria. You know everything now."

A tight, sad smile fit Victoria's mouth. Cruelty and sorrow winding around her. She believed him. She believed *in* him. As mad as she was, as unsure as she'd been stepping into Gomez's office, she had no other choice but to push all her chips into the Rose pot and bet big.

"I need my computer," she muttered, rubbing her forehead.

Gomez could be swayed, otherwise he would've kicked Rose out of camp immediately. He would've fired Victoria.

She skirted back around the building, collected her purse and clutched the chain.

One day.

She'd taken *one* measly day to celebrate, indulge, forget her purpose and she'd stumbled so far, she could no longer see the light at the end of the tunnel.

"Wait," Warren called.

Victoria turned, wind sending her bangs back.

Warren was on her in six steps. "When I was seventeen, I got caught in the movie theater with Jayme Merman's hand on my dick." He cleared his throat. "It was Twilight, Eclipse. Her hand was clammy, and I held her boob, under the shirt, over the bra. I came when they were sharing the tent on that mountain, and I still get hard anytime someone mentions camping."

A flutter spread up Victoria's spine as she became acutely aware of how crowded the lot remained, how curious eyes watched them, hands paused on keys, eyes peering out rolled down windows.

With both eyebrows raised, she exhaled a long held breath. "All men like threesomes."

A smile kicked at Warren's mouth, that half crooked smile that made her toes curl. He stepped closer, drawl deepening. "I can show you how well my shoulder works." He tucked dark hair behind her ear. "We'll throw your knees over it while I eat you out."

Just as the image flitted across her mind, she tensed.

Warren pulled back, his chest rising and falling, eyes wary. "Red."

"I can't," she admitted. No matter how badly she wanted to. An old, familiar loneliness twisted through her, drawing blood as she retreated from Warren.

She wet her lips, clenched her teeth. Strong. Strong and stubborn, a victor. "I want to," she told him. "I want to so badly, but I have to fix this. I have to find another running back for Foss, because Gomez got to him and now he thinks your arm's going to fall off. They're strengthening the run game."

Warren's eye twitched. "When are you going to be back?"

"When I'm not empty handed." Throwing her shoulders back, she snared Warren's eyes, blue pouring strength and resilience into amber. "Show them they're wrong. Make Gomez question himself. Doyle won't leave the Texans before pre-season ends, which gives us four solid weeks."

Before she could walk away, Warren had her in his arms, sharing his strength, one so different from hers, visible, tangible, hard muscle and vitality warming her as he covered her mouth with his. Not slow or deep, not toe curling. And yet, not a peck, not a press of lips, nothing fast.

He gave her a kiss to remember, to miss.

Victoria hated that it worked.

Chapter Thirteen

H AD HE EVER FELT this irrevocably destroyed? Carefully, Warren lowered himself into the faded, dark leather chair overlooking the pine and birch tree filled atrium. It was, by all accounts, a pleasant summer evening. The sun metered by passing clouds, the humidity stripped after a midnight rain. Because of the mildness of the day, the hotel lounge was empty, guests seeking hikes in the mountains, eating alfresco at one of Church Street's bustling restaurants, or strolling to the lakeside to lose time in the lush, dewy grass.

Warren thought it all sounded terrible.

Two weeks. Seventeen days since the no contact rules ended. Six days since training camp finished and pre-season began.

Since Coach Foss broke out the pads and helmets, Warren had been in a constant state of misery.

Every day aching, pushing himself to each extreme, dry heaving in the last bathroom stall, dumping extra salt in his Gatorade and choking it down. The other quarterbacks, Grant and Ravel, merely watched the drills.

Warren blasted through them, demolished them, red pinny flapping, sweat dripping.

Show them, Victoria had said.

His arm shook from driving spiral after spiral, voice croaked from play calling, even his damn fingers cramped from taking notes during meetings. He evaded every sack. He smashed through every collapsed play. If there was no one to throw to, he took it himself, shoulders hunched, no slide.

After twelve days scouring the country, Victoria had returned to become a fixture on the sidelines, doling stern nods of approval.

Late at night, a soft click of his room key and the turn of his doorknob would wake him.

Under streaming moonlight, Victoria would kick off her heels, peel out of her dress, and cover Warren's skin with hers until neither could move from the pleasure.

Skin sticky with sweat, limbs intertwined. Warren would tell Victoria other embarrassing secrets from his past, waiting for her to giggle and berate him.

He'd become a masochist just to hear her laugh, to feel her body quake with amusement, fingers brushing though his hair, teasing him as she trailed kisses up his neck.

Three days ago, she'd disappeared again.

Vaguely, he knew she was on the West Coast, stalking a rookie. But the more time they spent together, the less she spoke of her job. The less she told him about her days.

Compartmentalizing, he'd realized last night, alone in his bed, hand spread across her pillow.

Warren scrubbed a hand down his face. How he had the energy to think of her was a mystery. He should be consumed by football, but each time his breath slowed, and his pulse steadied, he thought of her. When was she coming back? Was she safe? Was she still shoving a chair under her door?

A month ago, he'd been grateful to be alone, free of shackles, of mind games and manipulations.

He'd play anything with Victoria. Anything to keep her sneaking into his room.

Tonight's loneliness felt acute, slicing him with a scalpel precisely where he ached. Sore from weeks of overkill, the pain had him burn with excess energy.

Today, under the picturesque sky, they'd returned to no contact practice, a flag scrimmage.

The first pre-season game was tomorrow.

Burton, Cole, and Miles would sit. No question. They wouldn't even bother suiting up with helmets or cleats. Power players, top dogs. They had guaranteed roster spots.

Warren's knee jumped. Tomorrow, he'd know if he'd done enough, worked hard enough, shed enough sweat and blood to warrant the respect to sit. If not, Coach would parade him across the fifty yard line on the first down of the game, demand excellence and crow at anything less than complete supremacy.

It felt as if the finish line kept getting farther from him, the bar raised higher.

Warren's worries immolated at the squeak of leather. Shiny, square pointed black shoes, draped in pleated gray, soiled his view.

The entire team was staying at the Green Mountain Hotel, but Warren knew no one, not even Burton the animal, would wear plain, freshly shined brogues.

"When's she coming back?" Morgan dug a hand into a split bag of Cheetos, smirk etched on his mouth. "You know, right? Where she is? She told you?"

Warren gripped at the arms of his chair to stop from mauling the agent.

"I mean, she's been gone all of training camp. Is she going to skip out on pre-season too?" Morgan spread orange dust on the chair back. "Typical Vic would avoid this place until cuts and handshakes, declaring herself the mastermind regardless of the outcome."

Warren's objections crowded in his throat, preventing their escape as he pinched the leather.

Don't make a scene.

Morgan continued without prompting. "But what do I know? She changed after we broke up. Became so focused and bitchy, forgot how to take a joke. It almost makes me miss her."

"Why"—Warren fought to keep his voice level—"are you here?"

"You don't have an agent." Morgan replied coolly, picking through his bag for the tightest orange ringlet. As he chewed, he withdrew a card from his jacket pocket. A twin to the one Warren had thrown out. "I'd love to represent you."

"I'm not in the market."

Morgan tossed his head, flippant, dismissive. More orange streaked on the tanned leather. "Wrong. You need an agent. Everyone needs an agent and I'm the best there is."

"Victoria said—"

"Vic told you not to trust me because she wants to control you." Morgan ditched the bag at his hip, weaving his hands together to face Warren. Light green eyes, boxy jaw, a privileged smugness in the arch of his blonde eyebrows.

"Here's the quick and dirty," he said. "Right now, Vic loves you. You're special to her. You're important. If she gets you the starting spot, well hell, even I'd go to her for help. Because if you start, the jumbled up nonsense plan she's cooked up succeeds. Fuckin' A. Great. Girl power."

Morgan sat back, drumming his fingers together. A smirk, knowing, predatory, made Warren sit up straighter, body alert. Adrenaline seeped into his veins. His pulse kicked into a thunderous beat.

"Really. Great for her," Morgan went on. "Vic wins like she wanted, and she gets the hell out. Forgets your name, your position, your number, forgets the fact that she's ever spoken to you. That's what she wants. No strings, no baggage. I get it, I do." He shrugged as if sympathetic. "On the other end of the spectrum, if I was your agent, I'd care about *you*. Fuck the team. We'd talk, I'd snag you a sweetheart contract, more than four years, massive playoff bonuses, big injury amendments. I'll look after you after she leaves."

Warren shook his head. "I have a contract."

Morgan puffed out a disapproving sigh and shifted to lean forward, pale eyes turning keen. "Until the season starts, that's Vic's roadmap. Let's consider an alternative. Vic changes her mind when she sees that you're not going to make the team. Sad. She cuts ties, abandons you, brings in a hotshot and suddenly you're toxic. A quarterback no one wants. A back-up when the league's flooded with talent. I hope you paid off your house."

Warren felt his jaw grind.

Oblivious or ignorant, Morgan shrugged. He stuffed another Cheeto into his mouth, talking as he chewed. "She's out scoping talent right now, doesn't even know you exist."

"That's not true." He wished he didn't sound defensive. It *was* true. She'd called him last night. Her first question had been 'what are you wearing?' and after that it'd been demands. *Take it off. Touch yourself. Think of me.*

"She's enticing, I'll give her that. I fell for it." As if sharing a secret, Morgan leaned over the gap between their chairs. "You feel like maybe you're the one who can contain all that fire, but nobody can. Try and you'll get burned. Trust me. You're nothing but a number to her."

Warren's mouth went dry, a lump clogging his throat. The combination of overpowering cologne and fake cheese made his eyes water.

Beside him, Morgan was calm as the summer evening, at ease, picking through his bag of synthetic salt and carbs. How much more crunching could Warren endure before he snapped?

Morgan wiped his hands together. "Look, man. I like you. I think you're a rare find. Vic did a good job sniffing you out. I'll help you gouge this team for a fat, juicy contract. I'll guarantee you stay. I'll make it impossible for them to fire you."

"Victoria's doing that right now."

"Yeah, *now*," Morgan taunted. "That's her favorite word. Now. Wildfires don't worry about the future, Rose. She's gone once the roster is set. Then what happens? I'm trying to help you. We men have to stick together."

Releasing the arms of the chair, leaving behind deep divots, Warren stood, hardened his spine, spread his feet, and let himself loom over the square faced agent as he let out a cold, hard laugh. "God, you're fucking bitter. She told me she dated you. I didn't realize she broke your heart." His inflection rivaled ice, hard, uncaring, but Morgan laughed as though Warren delivered a long awaited punchline.

"I see." The agent wiped a finger under his eye as he shook his head. "You fucked her. Hats off to her, that's one thing I won't do. But she's been willing to play that card since I met her. Whatever it takes. I get it now. I've been outplayed."

He stood, digging into his bag for another curly Cheeto, paying half attention to Warren as he added, "Does she still do that thing when she comes? That little bite of her nails on your—"

Warren was charging, hands on Morgan before he could blink, foot crushing the Cheeto bag. "You don't fucking talk about her like that."

Hands grabbing at Warren's wrists, Morgan smiled. "That's the kind of intensity I like to represent." He jerked his shirt out of Warren's hold. "Once she leaves and you're icing your balls, call me."

Warren gave him a rough shove, anger spooling. "The next time you want to drag her through the mud, remember that while you're eating your fucking chips, while you're putting on your generic ass suits, I'm in the gym, lifting double what you weigh, and I have an excuse for bloody knuckles."

"Do you think she's with Midas right now?" Morgan taunted, backpedaling across the empty lobby, lifting his phone. "I can call him and ask, but I'd hate to interrupt whatever they're doing."

Warren's temper snapped. "Get the *fuck* out of here!"

***

THE NEXT MORNING, Warren showed Victoria where they kept the good vending machines. The ones with chocolate.

He'd logged the information away without realizing it. Each time he walked by and thought of her, of her mouth and the way she tasted.

When she'd appeared on the edge of the team conference room, smiling, pointing two watchful fingers at him, wearing a blood red dress, he'd needed any excuse to get her alone. The word *chocolate* tore her away from Miles in a flash.

Where? Now? Milk or dark? The questions tumbled from her full Dragon Red lips as she trailed after him. A sexy Gretel, about to be eaten.

Now that they were alone, together again, Warren turned over Morgan's words. His anger had simmered all night, roiling and waiting, threatening to spill over. The prick deserved a beating, but...

Was Victoria using him? Would she betray him? Leave him?

As of now, she'd been honest, more so than him.

As of now. *Right now.*

Morgan had used the same word. Like it was familiar, an old wound long healed.

Victoria hit D7.

They watched the cookies n' cream Hershey bar fall. When the foil smacked metal, Victoria twisted to loop her arms around Warren's neck, tugging him against the glass as the machine pinged. Chocolate served. "They're playing you today," she confided. "Are you ready?"

His stomach dropped. Coach didn't trust him, didn't think he was a starter. He'd play, they'd risk him. Warren wanted to push back from her, wanted to press closer. Why did she wait to deliver the bad news until she was in his arms?

No. He couldn't let Morgan and his orange fingers get under his skin, break what he and Victoria had.

Warren swallowed, bolstered himself. "I'm ready. Are you?"

"I couldn't be more ready," she said sweetly, pushing closer. "And not just for the game, but for the post game." Her smile was full of dark promise. She rotated, keeping him flush against her as she shimmied down to collect her chocolate. Sunscreen, even in the basement of a football stadium at ten in the morning, she smelled of sunscreen.

Warren clung to her hips. Let go. Clenched his jaw. Before he could ask if anything Morgan said was true, Victoria flipped back around.

"You're going to do incredible out there," she said. "It's going to be dropped jaws, and 'you were rights' up and down the sidelines. Foss will bow and submit everlasting loyalty to me. And Gomez will see that your shoulder is at the top of its game. That Texas made a huge mistake pushing you off the field. That Midas—"

Warren looked away at his name on our lips.

Her fingers caught his jaw, forcing him back, holding him in her clear blue stare. "Doyle's an imposter." Her confidence caught Warren off guard. "Do you know why I brought you here?" she asked, fingers biting his skin. "Do you know why I jumped onto your boat? Why I walked a mile in the Texas heat to get you out of bed?"

He pressed his lips to her hair, breathing her in, feeling heat radiate from her skin. His hands enclosed her waist. "I can think of a long list of reasons. All of which start with the way you kissed me."

Victoria grinned. "Please, football is business. I brought you here because people like you, your team's going to follow you, the crowd's going to love you. It's the same reason I brought you to see Kilbride." She stroked her hand down his neck, lifted to her toes until their foreheads met. "You're good, Flowers." She sucked in a breath. "Better than me, better than most."

"I'm not."

"You *are*." She gripped his arms, the chocolate bar in her palm molding to his form. "You calmed Burton the Boar down. You told Miles-beat-a-guy-bloody-Santos that if he looks at me wrong, you'll never pass him a hand-off."

Warren pulled her closer. "He wasn't supposed to tell you." Pressing his mouth to her ear, he added, "Congrats on the baby."

Victoria smacked him. "Santos has got a big mouth. Now, you're going to go out there and everyone's going to forget that you weren't the first choice. You're going to be the *only* choice. Do you understand?"

"Say you're mine." The command spilled out. He'd meant to thank her, kiss her, question her. Dive into her mind and see how long *now* would last. He meant to make her promise not to destroy him. To spare him.

Surprise widened Victoria's angel blue eyes, her bangs tangling with dark lashes.

Suddenly, nothing else mattered except her response. His hands shook. His eyes closed. He didn't care if he got burned, he'd let skin melt away from the bone, the muscle slide off his body. He wanted to step into the flames with her. "Say you're mine. Say you're only mine. Tell me you're not fucking anyone else."

"Of course I'm not."

He pulled back, relief clearing his mind. "Then you're mine,"

"Warren." Her fingers bit into his torso, knotted his shirt. "Say you're only fucking me." She almost sounded hesitant.

"Yes."

Then he was grabbing her, tasting her. *His.* He wanted her to be his desperately. The idea of her with anyone else repulsed him. A primal need to wash away all the other hands that had dared to touch her rose. An urge to be the only man who knew her, understand her intimately, turned his blood hot.

Their tongues tangled as he lifted her into his arms, fit himself against her.

She took everything and raised the stakes. Poured all of her desire into him, matching his possessiveness with merciless hunger, with bone deep want.

His attention swung to the pulsing vein in her neck, the heave of her chest. Biting, sucking, licking.

Salt, she tasted of salt.

Soon even pepper would make him hard, any reminder of her skin in his mouth. He wanted to swim in her.

Her hand pulled at his hair as her hips ground against his stomach. She whispered against his ear something indistinguishable, something frantic, short, maybe long, gasping. It might've been *yours*. Might've been *mine*.

Might've been *now*.

Might've been all three.

Unable to stop it, Warren thrust against her. The vending machine swayed on unsteady legs, hit cement. Scraped.

An alarm sounded. An obnoxious wail.

Warren hauled her away from the noise, set her on her feet, and glanced up and down the hall to ensure they were alone.

Victoria didn't step back from him, hands still tightly clenched in his shirt, eyes half hooded, lips swollen.

"Four quarters," she murmured through the grating noise, twisting her hands deeper, crushing the soft fabric. "Four quarters," she repeated. "If you let this go into overtime, I'm not going to make it. I'll finish this myself."

Warren smiled. "Four quarters and then you and me." He pressed his mouth to her ear. "Four quarters and then I'm fucking every other word out of your mind."

The alarm stuttered to a stop as they untangled from each other. With a smirk, Warren rescued Victoria's contorted chocolate bar from the floor and tucked it between her breasts. The images it called. Chocolate and her bare skin. Licking it off her.

"Fuck," he groaned, forehead dropping back to hers. "How am I supposed to run with a hard on?"

Victoria's smile was pure pride. "Throw instead," she patted his chest. "I brought you a new receiver."

***

VICTORIA HAD BEEN shocked when Toby sat beside her. No preamble or posturing. He undid his jacket, threw the tie over his shoulder, and bit into a miniature cheesecake, dusted in a green powdered sugar Mountaineers' logo.

She'd been shocked further when Gomez took the seat on her other side.

They were nestled in an executive box overlooking the fifty yard line. A row of high definition screens showed the action on the field in real time, yet the game felt a hundred miles away.

There was no life in the room, no passion, no fans screaming, no clapping. Guests mingled and coughed into napkins and excused themselves profusely. She wasn't stepping in spilled beer and left-over rain. She couldn't smell the baking concrete or over-buttered popcorn.

In three hours, she'd leave as she came, no jersey tan, no blistered feet, no sore throat.

True fans, real fans, Victoria knew, didn't relax once the clock began its thrilling countdown, didn't dine on a spread repast, weren't carting around highball glasses, concerned about overindulging midday.

Football fans were messy and loud. They screamed until their throats sealed, withstood blistering winds and the scorching sun after spending hundreds on nosebleed seats all for the hope of seeing their team devastate another.

Knitting her fingers together to limit fidgeting, Victoria glared at her ceramic plate of samosas, Swiss chocolate, and melon balls, elegantly arranged and refilled each time she stuffed her mouth to stop screaming at the refs or Foss.

She wanted to feel what Warren felt.

Fresh mountain air spiked with the growing sourness of spilled beer and sweat. The heat of a wicked sun slipping in and out of clouds, the tremble of the ground between downs.

It was far less crowded than anyone had hoped. The end zones lightly scattered with clashing light and dark green.

"Expected for pre-season," an unruffled Gomez had explained to the press before the game. The empty seats were not indicative of the season to come. When he'd turned, yanking on his Armani lapel, Victoria saw the ripples of annoyance.

The slash of his eyes across her had stung. He'd wanted to tell the press Midas was coming, that Gomez had snatched the golden god, that the gates of Mountaineer Stadium would soon be flooded.

Through pure force of will, Victoria kept her head straight, rapidly blurring vision pinned on number twenty-three.

The numbers, at least today, were on her side.

Midway through the second quarter, the score was lacking at zero-zero, but there were no interceptions, no fumbles, no sacks.

The colossal disaster Gomez predicted hadn't happened.

Still, her victory was tenuous. A mismanaged third down in the red zone led Warren to hand the ball to the punter. She needed a touchdown, a field goal. Points. Points delivered via Rose's capable—so damned capable—hands.

Out of the corner of her eye, Victoria watched Toby smooth out the corners of a thick notebook and drape it across the lap of his suit. The strokes of his pen were sloppy and looping, a few notes eating up the entire sheet.

"Rose will work," the GM said, flipping his page. "Especially with what you've set up. It was risky to build a team around him. But Moore seems to fit."

Riley Moore, a wide receiver, a rookie, and a voracious flirt, had been a last-minute grab. A necessary addition to supplement Rose's ability.

"Rose built himself around the team," she replied coolly.

Later, she'd admit to her genius. Pretend she'd never wanted Midas.

Now, sandwiched between the men who hired her, those with the power to end her career as they watched the first game wasn't the time to start preemptive bragging.

Toby's dappled gray brows lifted as he smiled, hand soaring across the page, fingers staining black. The man was old school. He didn't like flash, loathed drama. He believed the turtle would beat the hare in every race. That steady and smooth were the quickest path to happiness. That meant more than a star player, he wanted a sound, well-built team.

The mere fact that Gomez—whose license plate was black on black and read *owner*—had hired Toby, spoke of his reputation.

Hope glided over Victoria's skin. Perhaps she'd misjudged the flamboyant owner. If he had enough business acumen to hire Toby Zither, it was feasible he could be convinced of other, formerly contradictory, ideas.

"You've done well here. Managing expectations." Toby's thumb trailed over his tarnished gold wedding band.

Biting her cheek, Victoria nodded, internally curtsying for a crowd of thousands, outwardly following a snap on third and nine.

"There are open positions on the staff. We maintain a few recruiters year round." His pen hovered while he watched Warren's throw connect with Moore. "The pace would slow. You could plant roots. Dare I suggest time off to have a family?"

He could see it on her, the exhaustion, the sleepless nights, the constant state of panic that kept her moving forward. Her stress levels were that of an addict. Self-aware and self-medicating.

Toby blamed stress, but it was worry gnawing at Victoria's nerve endings. Worry over months of work fragmenting. The devastated look on Warren's face when she had to cut apart his contract.

Worry over the fact that she'd do it. Hate it and be unable to stop.

It'd be easier to be an alcoholic. To only destroy herself.

Two small white dots clouded her vision, blurred the field. Warren would never speak to her again when it happened. It would be their last touch, their last kiss.

She'd only just had her first.

None of it mattered. In three weeks, she'd be watching *Love Island* in first class, a pile of rumpled wrappers in her lap.

"No," she told Toby. "Thank you for the offer, but I like the travel and the stress."

Her dad had gotten complacent. He'd wanted to put roots down, promising he'd continue sailing even after he left the sea. It didn't take ten months for him to sell the *Victoria*, his prize winning sailboat. Why? To pay for braces?

She'd been so angry, sitting in the orthodontist's office, declaring she wanted crooked beaver teeth. To pacify her, he'd promised to rent boats, to hit the ocean every weekend. After that, excuses became his main form of speech. *Next week*, his most common promise.

Victoria lived in the now. If she wanted, she did.

Stop moving, stop living.

"I don't want to be tied down," she explained, reaching for an artisanal cantaloupe sphere. "I like the idea of working for the league, rather than a team."

Toby didn't dither, focus glued to his notes. "A smart girl like you will certainly have success. Not many can do what you've done."

"Her work is not yet finished," Gomez cut in, openly glaring at the televisions. The Jets had the ball back. "It won't be until we have Midas."

"Rose—"

"Has not crossed the end zone. Four first downs, and not a throw worthy of highlights. If we had Midas, we'd be winning."

Victoria's heart began to hammer. "This is the first game."

"You'll bring me Midas. I've waited long enough."

Toby nodded. Agreeing or placating, she couldn't tell.

Didn't want to know.

Chapter Fourteen

W ARREN CAUGHT VICTORIA'S ARM before she pulled the stainless steel pin from his weight stack.

"Don't do that. It'll go straight through the floor and crush the PR team."

Together, they looked at the padded black floor as if they could see through it to the offices below, filled with suits and business types marking papers, giving speeches, singing *Happy Birthday* three days late to the creepy nepo intern.

Victoria surfaced first, her eyes vivid in the recess lightning, bouncing off the mirrored walls. Warren had become so used to the blue at night, subdued, pupils dilated.

She pressed a mocking hand to her chest. "Bless their hearts. Who'd be left to spin the tragedy?" She had a southern drawl slow and smooth like refined honey.

"Watch the language, or I'll wash your mouth out with soap."

There was a pause.

Victoria burst out laughing. And didn't stop. She laughed, bright and free, loud, faces turning to stare at the commotion.

Warren paused mid-rep. Terror bubbled up his stomach as she wiped tears from her face, ran out of breath.

Why was she laughing at his bad joke? He wasn't funny.

Why was she here?

No. No—no. Dread sunk over him, yanking down, thickening and burning like tar slicking over his bones. "Here?" He sounded dejected, broken already, as if—

"I—" She covered her mouth to hide a face splitting grin. "It's—" She stopped again. She chewed on her lip, looked at the ceiling.

With visible force, she dropped her chin to whisper, "I just thought, is that why you always smell like soap? You want to wash my mouth out with your big—"

"Red," he interrupted loudly. "Please spare me." Warren shut his eyes as his heart relapsed. Not right now. Not yet. He wasn't cut yet.

"Sorry," she said, not at all sincere. Unaware of where his mind had gone. Maybe she didn't worry over it. Obliterating his life.

She was in another dress today. Thick, with short sleeves and a skirt that'd show her panties if she spun. Sweet, if it wasn't dyed an electric purple rich enough to fade stop signs and streetlights.

She ran a finger over the metal bar laid across his shoulders. "I suppose this means you're lifting a lot of weight."

"Twice what you weigh," he said. "Easily."

A throaty chuckle loosed her lips. Even there on padded floors, a background of linebackers tossing ropes, she looked sexy, a bit mischievous, on the hunt for trouble in the worst place for it. The fine locks of her bangs were parted, curtaining around dark lashes, her skin gleaming in every mirror.

"I doubt it."

When he raised his eyebrows, she raised hers in return.

Honesty, not mocking.

"Baby, I could lift three of you without breaking a sweat."

A sardonic smile cut her lips. "You always seem to sweat when you lift me, Flowers."

They were picturing the same thing. Him standing, hands splayed across her ass, her mouth on his neck as he fucked her, as she cried out, thrashing and begging.

A blink blew away their fantasy. Her voice raised to ask, "How's the shoulder?" Her fingernails tested the tension strings of the lat pull-down machine, strumming them like a concert violin.

Around them, dumbbells hit the floor, people called out reps. Riley Moore's conversation with his mom as he busted out curls could be heard in every corner. It was part of Warren's routine, familiar. He liked familiar, liked a regimented schedule, knowing exactly what was coming.

Instead of a hindrance, a bother, Victoria's surprise drop in had stoked Warren's lust—for her obviously—but also to keep this routine, to stay in the mountains, to be part of a team, to sit down with Victoria and pick sides of the bed. No more splitting the middle.

"Is the demonstration not having its desired effect?" he asked. "Move that pin to the bottom." He nodded at the stack of rectangular black weights.

"Watch it, Flowers. Overconfidence breeds stupidity." The reprimand didn't last. The ferocious light in her eyes faded as Warren stood. He felt her gaze sear his skin, the open slats in his shirt, his arms, down his sore hands.

With flourish, he moved the pin himself and returned to his seat.

"Finally," Burton boomed, whipping a frayed towel across Warren's thigh. The skin smarted. "A real quarterback."

A massive shadow followed the tight end. Dark hair knotted at his neck, Cole's lips pressed in a line. "Too much weight."

Victoria asked, "Is that so?"

Both Warren and Burton barked, "No."

Dragging the bar down, biceps flaring, Warren added dryly, "Cole's mad I'm catching up to him."

Staring at him like a prize sailfish, Victoria said, "I'd love to see your latest achievements."

Warren kept the bar down, muscles straining. "I'm happy to share."

The air bristled with electricity. Noise faded until it was him and her and useless chatter. He'd share his mouth with her pussy, his hands with those breasts. He'd bend her over—

Victoria's mouth parted on an exhale, eyes flaring until the pupils blew. The pleasure of it knocked the sense from him. His hand slipped off the bar.

Weights slammed the floor.

Someone shouted.

Ignoring them, Warren stretched to his feet and stepped over his water bottle, following the scent of sunscreen, the pull of the ocean. Circe called, and he was enchanted.

Smiling, Victoria tipped back her head. Voice laced with sex, she asked, "Can I talk to you outside?"

Burton's coarse laugh made her eye twitch.

Her tone changed, became iron and steel. "I have a list of agents you might be interested in."

Warren might have nodded. He definitely agreed. Whether through a yes or a simple flare of his nostrils as he chased her from the gym.

"Trouble," Burton called to his back.

Victoria gave him the finger, twisting, using her back to push open the door. "What's it like to be a fourteen-year-old stuck in an old man's body?"

The tight end grinned. "Virile."

Warren pushed her through the door before she could grin too.

***

INTERESTING, VICTORIA THOUGHT, snagging Warren's hand and hurrying him down the hall.

She was beginning to like these men.

No one could be more surprised than her.

Friends with numbers.

Warren had been her exception. Football players weren't people, they were numbers and salaries, names to be traded and bargained.

Despite this, she found herself gravitating to Cole on the sidelines, laughing at Burton's absurdity. Hell, even flying back with Riley Moore had been entertaining. And informative. He knew more about *The Bachelor* than the contestants.

It was odd, talking with them. Like naming your chicken before you ground it into nuggets.

Vegetarianism suddenly made sense.

Though problems remained. Namely, Victoria was a carnivore, a predator. She stalked, hunted, charmed into submission, and was gone before her prey realized she'd seasoned their bath with teriyaki.

This position, this undertaking, the career maker, it was unique. She couldn't avoid the Mountaineers. Not that any part of her desired to. She'd sunk into a rhythm, engrossed herself in it, like raindrops hitting a stream and joining the current.

Grinning, she veered left around the saunas, yanked the front of Warren's damp shirt, and hauled him through the first unlocked door.

An office. The only light a blank projector shining on the far wall.

"Perfect."

Turning the lock, she pressed Warren into the door, plastering herself against him, taking his mouth like she owned it.

Who could miss the hunt when she had her very own buffet every night?

Heart racing, she was shoving at his shorts before Warren could kiss her back. It didn't matter. His body was ten steps ahead, hard in her favorite places.

Dropping to her knees, her hands trembled with lust. "I want you so badly," she complained. "All the time." The tips of her nails scored his strong, hairy thighs as her tongue teased the crown of his hard cock.

Salt and musk.

Void of his usual control, lost in shock or sensation, Victoria pressed her luck, gazing up at him as she slowly slid his length into her mouth. Sweat stuck folds and spots of his shirt to his chest, taunting her with its touch. Wet, his hair was darker, longer, messy, sticking haphazardly to his forehead, his temple.

Gorgeous.

A hero of Olympus, fresh from a completed godly task, missing only a gleaming sword.

His chest heaved for air, his hand white knuckling the door-knob. As she licked him, stroked in time with her hand, the stirring between her legs blossomed and bloomed. Her stomach tightened, her body pulsed.

Arching up, she stuffed him in her mouth. Big, even like this, with her stretched and wet and him frozen. She became a medley of motion, hands stroking with her mouth as she watched amber eyes shutter shut and rip open.

Lost in the pleasure and refusing to miss it.

"I woke," he moaned when she squeezed, licking a pulsing vein, savoring. He slid his eyes shut. Through gritted teeth, he tried again, "I woke you up with my cock and now"—his hips jerked, but he caught himself—"this?"

Yes, this. *Only* this.

His taste, his strength and power were useless under her touch. On her next stroke, Warren lost his composure, his body lurched from the door, hands sinking into her hair, pulling it back, away.

He held her steady, at a distance, tender, almost afraid he'd sink too deep, over aware of their size difference.

Digging her nails into his stomach, she pushed down on him, pressing close, taking him deeply into her throat, sucking harder, getting wetter.

She'd thought of this since her eyes cracked open to see Warren's head between her thighs. Since... she'd been trapped in a dream, desire burning steady along her skin, a delicious torture.

She'd wanted him since he pulled out of her, since he threw the sheets over her and demanded she go back to sleep.

Wetness pooled between her thighs as she tasted him, enjoyed him, marveling at the way her body warmed around him, as if his presence scared away her worries.

"*Fuck*, Victoria." He jolted back from her with an audible *pop* and crashed into the door, shorts caught around his meaty thighs. He grabbed the tip of his cock and squeezed, eyes hungry, features tight.

His hands trembled, sliding slowly down his rigid length. He growled. "You're going to make me come."

Sitting back on her heels, Victoria licked her lips. "I assumed you knew that was the point."

"Is it?" The way he said it, she felt much less like the predator she claimed to be.

Under Warren's towering, panting form, she felt like a spider caught in her own web.

Two rough hands pulled her to stand. "Then allow me to oblige."

Warren's lips scored her cheek, neck, her jaw as he walked her back, lifting her, spreading her knees, pushing her dress to her hips as he laid her trembling, willing body across a square desk.

"I have so much energy," she said, head tipped back for his mouth to suck and nip up her throat. Sweat and soap, she breathed him in, her favorite scent. A hard working man.

"All day, I watch you out there, watch you run and throw, and I sit there and want. How badly I want." She gasped as his mouth found her breast through the ribbed fabric of her dress. "I sit there and fantasize about your hot fucking body curled around me. Your mouth burning my skin, the way you taste, what you'll say as you fuck me, that moment you lose control."

She grabbed his hair, thrills crackling through her, desire leaking around the curve of her ass. "Will you call me Red or Victoria? Will you whisper I'm beautiful or tell me I'm a siren? I think about it, and I squirm."

A pastime of hers. Mentally fitting her body under his during the snap, draped over him as he dropped back into the pocket, jumping into his arms every first down.

"*Fuck*, Red." His teeth roved down her neck as he snapped her underwear to the side, fingers sweeping over her core. "I love when you're this wet. I love how you're always this wet." He groaned as he stroked over her clit.

Victoria felt her insides ignite, burn.

Erupt when she dropped her chin to see his hand fisting his cock, still pinching. Stuck on the edge, determined to last for her.

Her legs fell apart, spread wide for him, displaying the token of his pleasure and pain. In the back of her mind, she'd blamed boredom for her up-ticked libido.

Completely wrong.

It was Warren Rose. A flower so sweet, it stirred a deviant, mounting frenzy through her. She reached up to cup her breasts, his hands busy as she stroked the stiff peaks, molten lust clambering up her spine.

"Warren," she gasped, collapsing on the plastic desk, bending up to the ceiling. "I want to finish around you."

A brief laugh escaped him. "You and me both, Red."

"Then fuck me already."

His mouth curved against her ear, his body fitting easily over hers, hand unceasing in its ministrations. "No."

"Warren."

Another laugh, deeper. She moaned. "You're going to come first. Have to." Two thick fingers slipped inside her. "I won't last." His low, dark voice curled in her ear as he murmured, "That fucking mouth. Do you have any idea how sweet it is?"

He kissed her, devoured her, tasting his favorite candy, confirming the appeal with long, searching licks. His fingers began a deliberate, wicked pace, fucking her just as she'd sucked him.

He was shameless in his hunger, calling life to even the most unassuming parts of her body, the bend of her elbow, the hollow under her ear, the bone in her wrist.

Her cry was broken, gasping as she came, a rush of intensity slamming gravity along her bones, holding her down.

Warren thrust inside her, wild, brutal. His eyes half closed. The desk rattled, metal legs screeching across the tile floor. It didn't stop him. The noise, the movement, the way Victoria's cry became a scream of his name. His hands gripped her thighs as he bucked.

Fighting the drug-like pleasure swamping her, Victoria frantically tried to meet him, lift her hips, deepen the angle.

"Every time"—his breath was hot on her neck—"is so. Fucking. Good."

His hand caught her hair, pulled slightly, until her eyes opened, until she was watching him enter her. "Is this why you came to the gym, Red?" The desk hit the wall with a bang. "Is this why you found me? You needed more? *Fuck*."

Their mouths met in a thrash of tongues and promises. "I'll fuck you all day long," Warren promised, arm stretching to brace a hand on the wall as he tilted her hips. "Exactly how you like it, baby."

Good god, Victoria barely finished coming when she felt the euphoria build again, faster, harder.

There was a hurried, desperate edge as they both sprinted to the end.

His gaze locked on hers. "Say you're going to keep coming back to me. For this, forever. You're mine. Say you won't leave."

Warren's hand covered her mouth before her next scream, pressing her down, molding her to the table as she broke into a million pieces. One, two more thrusts and Warren held fast, buried to the hilt, chest shaking over hers.

Victoria bit his palm, and he whipped it away, sheepish, as he let out a long sigh.

"Sorry," he murmured, brushing damp hair off her neck and setting his head there, feeling the erratic pulse of her heartbeat.

With great effort, Victoria's hand found the nape of Warren's neck, caressing the skin with slow, boneless movements.

"I can feel you watching me," he told her skin, arms pulling tight around her. "When I'm on the field, I know where you are." He kissed her clavicle. "I have to wear a cup now."

Almost reluctantly, he rose, pulled out of her, used her underwear to clean between her legs before tucking the silk into his pocket. With gentle hands, he lifted her from the desk, righted her dress, and kissed her. Deeply, indulgently. Fingers gently tangling in her hair.

A stone dropped into Victoria's chest.

A small, smooth stone that had no business cracking a heart like hers.

She hadn't talked her way into the gym for this, for a quickie, for an orgasm. How easy that would have been. She'd come because they had two weeks left before cuts, before rosters were finalized.

Before Victoria zipped up her rollaboard and left.

Warren paused in the doorway, turning to her to say softly, "Victoria, you are—"

"Drink lots of water," she cut him off, patting his chest, lingering, finding she liked how fast it beat still. "I'll be waiting for you in my room after practice. Naked."

New plan.

She'd drown herself in Warren.

Before she starved.

***

WARREN FOUGHT THE smile with all the strength inside him.

Ultimately, he found himself to be a weak man, dipping his chin and scratching at his mouth to hide the grin splitting his face.

Besides, it wasn't as if he could hide the scratch marks on his back, along his arms. He couldn't remember if she'd been wearing lip gloss. His dick might be bright pink, and he suddenly loved the color.

She'd been ravenous.

Drenched and desperate. For *him*. Had sought him out, screamed his name, whispered it.

Victoria, a woman who could silence Burton, coax a smile from Cole, and temper Miles' fucking crazy, wanted *him*. A ridiculous inkling to enter the lottery stroked him. He had luck in spades.

Her undiluted desire was the best pep talk ever given. The near frantic edge to her touch, as if she were on the precipice of careening out of control, of begging for him. Terrified of separation.

As viciously joyful as it made him, as euphorically male, he intended to temper it. Not her, but that feeling, the rush she lived in. It was too fleeting, too transient. Heat of the moment be damned. He'd meant what he said.

Victoria was his.

To make her acknowledge it would take time, care. He'd have to banish her fear of the future.

He didn't miss the irony as he pulled on a pinny he might never see again in two weeks.

One thing was certain about Warren's future: it involved Victoria.

"Holy fuck," Burton said, slamming his weights down and sitting up from the bench press.

Realizing he was standing in the middle of the gym, Warren hastened back to his abandoned water bottle and towel.

Cole found words extraneous, rolling his eyes instead, dropping his hands from spotting Burton.

"You're sleeping with her," Burton gleaned, pounding a fist into his knee, barking a laugh.

"Keep it down," Warren said sharply. Burton's big mouth needed to be contained. There could be no reason for Victoria to run. No rumors, no gossip. "Shut up about it."

"Or what?"

"Or I'll tell Victoria you called her a sprite and she'll bash a steel bat into your knees."

"Fucking tattle," the Irishmen grunted.

Cole nodded once, agreement, understanding, a flash of surprise, and a hint of approval. Warren never felt closer to his friend.

Grinning, Miles snuck a round twenty kilo weight onto one end of Burton's press bar. It was hard, especially when he handled weights, to ignore how stacked the running back was, clad in a skintight black tech shirt, tattoos swirling up and down swollen arms.

"How'd you get her?" Miles asked, leaning an elbow on the bar, genuinely curious. Pretending he didn't just fuck up Burton's next set.

Warren chewed on his cheek. "Shouldn't we be lifting?"

The three men stared at him, expectant.

Apparently, he'd joined a knitting circle.

"She shot me down hard," Miles told Burton, a self-satisfied grin showing a flash of silver on his tongue. "Why settle for you? I was the sexiest footballer alive last year."

"It's a onetime thing," Burton answered for Warren. "He's scratching an inch. You've seen her tits—"

"Enough." Cole's tone brooded no room for argument. His stare didn't leave Warren.

"If any of you say something," Warren warned, finishing his friend's thought with a nod of thanks. "You'll never see the ball again. She's *mine*. Stop hitting on her. Better yet. Don't even look at her."

"When's the last time you had a girlfriend?"

Since it came from Cole, Warren considered answering. Years? It'd been years since he stumbled into a woman who wanted him at face value. He'd been a pariah, a nightmare in football circles.

Wrenching it from a sour, bitter gut, he told the truth, "She's not my girlfriend."

His seething forced the knitting club to react similarly: raised brows, grimaces. Miles hid his face in his hand. It would have been less embarrassing for Warren to admit he'd come in his pants.

In the silence that followed, each man found the floor, his nail beds, the whizz of the ceiling fans to be wildly fascinating. His own fault. Warren was obvious in his feelings for her, his hunger and Victoria was leagues above him.

He was better off catching a sailfish with half of a Nightcrawler.

Wasn't it typical?

Another rising pedestal he'd never reach.

Riley Moore, young, new blood, the object of Victoria's most recent pursuits, sauntered into the middle of their circle. The kid was lanky, extraordinarily tall, and had three lines shaved into the side of his black hair. With meticulous care, the rookie helped himself to Warren's machine. "Sounds like you want a girlfriend."

"Christ, can everybody hear everything?"

Moore shrugged. "Burton's voice is essentially a megaphone. Don't worry"—he waved a hand—"half of its gibberish with the accent." He dragged dark eyes around him, smiling, preening under the attention. He nodded at Cole.

The two men couldn't be more different. Cole wide and brutal, pale as the moon and littered with freckles. Equally tall, Moore was built to run, muscles lean, toned, dark skin use to being a blur on the field.

"There's only one way to get a woman like Victoria Steer." Moore swung his gaze to Warren. "Excellent taste, by the way."

Exasperated, Warren asked, "What are you, twenty-two?"

"Watch it. Youth is preferred in this game." Flashing a wide smile, Moore stood, hands raised. "If you don't want my advice, I understand, what with the endless pool of knowledge already at your disposal." His gaze flit down the line, lethal in accuracy. "Bitter divorce. Perpetually alone. Incorrigible womanizer."

Fuck.

Shifting between his feet, Warren cleared his throat. "What should I do?"

Burton snorted. "Yer asking mama's boy?"

Moore blinked at the tight end. "Honestly, it's like he's speaking another language."

Warren ignored them both. "How do I get her to commit?"

"She's scared," Moore told him. "Which makes it very simple." Pausing, Moore squeezed water from a green bottle into his mouth, lavishing in his time as the center of attention. Someday soon, he'd be a star. He possessed all the charms of a Midas, assuredly cocky, disarmingly handsome. Charismatic.

Warren wanted to dislike him, but he couldn't.

"Do it without her knowing." Moore's tone made it seem obvious.

"What?"

Calmy, Moore said, "She doesn't want to go on a date? Take her out without telling her. Say it's just dinner, pull out her chair, split dessert, buy her tableside carnations and tuck the prettiest one in her hair. If she doesn't ask you to move in, forget your stuff there and keep forgetting. You understand?"

Warren frowned.

"Don't *ask* to be her boyfriend," Moore said curtly. "*Become* her boyfriend and you will."

Anguished, Burton blew hot air through his nose.

Miles made a sound in the back of his throat. "Boyfriend sounds so demeaning. There should be a better word at our age."

"*Your* age," Moore corrected.

Cole remained silent, absorbing, assessing. When their eyes met, they both had the same shocked gleam.

Kid was a fucking genius.

Moore slapped Warren's shoulder. "My jersey's forty-four for reference."

Chapter Fifteen

I f ever Victoria regretted her lust for Warren Rose, it was now.

He'd teased her outside with promises of darkened corners and private rooms, time for them. Intimacy had been implied. Heavily. With that in mind, Victoria had donned her favorite stringy, suffocating, complicated lace underwear and a new bra that unhooked in three places. She'd covered up with a loose white top and black and white buffalo check skirt thick enough to hide the tangle of silk and lace lacerating her skin.

She'd been giddy in the car, teasing the muscles of Warren's thigh, promising all the things she'd do to him, how she wanted to taste him, take him. Slip her hand down his shorts, bite his nipple through his shirt—

There wasn't a shadow in sight.

If she made good on her promises here, she'd be cuffed.

The sun cast a sardonically holy glow over the wide wood planks of the lakefront boardwalk. On their right, the Adirondacks rose above a long, winding lake. On their left, between the boardwalk and the road was an expansive field of trimmed brilliant green grass where innocent children flew kites and played tag. Their high pitched laughter bounced off the water to become a chamber of carefree happiness.

Fresh lake air and the wafting sugary scent of Creemees clashed, natural and artificial, and so ingrained in her body, so familiar, she could almost feel the slide of the soft serve curling around her wrist, sticky and cold.

Victoria wiggled her palm and Warren tightened his grip on her.

Holding hands. It had a lovely ring to it. Until you knew how much more you liked that hand between your legs, fucking you senseless.

As she told Warren this sentiment, he blew out a frustrated breath.

With her.

When she was one dark thought from turning her thong into a sexy garrote.

Staring at the roiling slate blue water of Lake Champlain, Warren ignored her fidgeting, shuffling her past an elderly couple swinging on a slatted bench.

"Behave," he told her gently, nodding to a group of wannabe artists nestled in the jagged rocks abutting the shore, faces wistful, hands still.

Rising to her toes, Victoria dug a hand into Warren's side to whisper, "Do these people even have jobs?"

"I'm sure they do." His thumb stroked over her knuckles. They'd been holding hands since he'd helped her out of the car. Not in an I'm-going-to-steal-you-away-and-fuck-you-against-a-tree hold, tight and sure, on the edge of painful. No. Warren held her carefully as they strolled along the waterfront, as if they were an old married couple. Soon to die, hovering on the verge of a dreadfully meek existence.

Victoria did not like it.

She could barely stomach it.

She wanted Warren. Wanted to fill her days with the smell of his sweat and soap perfection, to suffer the abrasion of his calloused hands and carve her name in the hot hard muscle of his shoulders as he made her come. Under him, over him, between him and the slick tile of the shower wall.

Holding hands while they watched a chocolate Labrador drag his ass over the grass didn't cut it.

"What are we doing here?" Victoria stopped and planted her feet, nearly taking out a knee padded roller blader. "We should be boning," she told him, censoring the filthy images in her mind. "I waxed this morning. For you."

"I'm flattered." His voice held a gently mocking tone.

"I don't think you understand," she said, wiggling her hand, fighting to get free and giving up with a frustrated huff. Changing tactics, she sank her fingers into his shirt, feeling the raw muscle tightening, pushing. She wanted to tear the cotton off, to watch his skin bleach white under her hold.

"I watch you. All. Day. Long. I watch you in those tight shorts, in your red flimsy jersey that rides up on your abs in that sexy impossible way that perfectly displays your god tier body."

Warren's jaw clenched and Victoria couldn't repress a self-satisfied smile.

Balancing on the toes of her boots, she added, "It makes my mouth water."

"Good." He barely looked at her.

"Good?" She shook her head. "I'm obsessed with you. I'm taking a hard stance on pro-stalking. At the very least, decriminalization, so I don't get jail time."

Somewhere, in the chaos of her mind, Victoria was glad they were outside, glad there were witnesses to the complete and utter breakdown of her sanity. Maybe one of the rock hipsters would paint it.

Self-anointed stalker tries to eat quarterback.

"The minute you leave me, I crave your touch. I want you more than my next breath."

"Good." This time, he smiled. "Should we keep walking?"

"Are you on opioids? *Good*?" She'd kill him. Right here, kick his lifeless body into the water to clear her prints from his throat.

Warren tugged her down the path as if she'd said nothing. Her outburst sank into the sludge bottom of the lake, dying in the icy blackness.

"Let's go back to the car," she said. A last effort for a good day. She wound her body around his arm, heart thumping against his elbow as she trotted to keep up with him. "We can test the shocks."

"Come on Victoria, no one actually enjoys fucking in a car."

Her eye twitched. Twitched as failure and indignation coiled around her. Through clenched teeth, she asked, "Why don't we find out?"

"I already know." His arm wove around her shoulders. "I'm too big for it."

"Yes," she purred, gripping his arms. "You are. Let's find out what else you're too big for."

Stopping, taking her cheeks in his hands, Warren stared down at her, eyes hooded. "You're bored," he said softly. "You're not a stalker, you're bottled lightning. You need new. That's all. Hell, I'm bored."

Victoria stilled, willing herself not to shove him away as her ears roared. "No one's ever accused me of being boring." Overbearing? Yes. Vindictive? Yes. Abrasive? Her mom gave her that label.

But boring?

"You wouldn't call me boring if you saw my underwear."

Warren's head fell back as he breathed a low *"Fuck"* that skittered against her skin.

Eyes shut, he muttered, "This is harder than I guessed."

Separating them, Warren sent an odious glare across the water. It was a wonder the mountains didn't quake.

Seeming to collect himself, he returned to Victoria, voice low, calm, a gentle reprimand. "Each time something dirty comes out of that mouth, it's one less night I'm going to fill it for the next week, understand?"

Victoria's jaw dropped.

She blinked. "Am I in an alternate universe?"

Warren's expression showed no hint of disagreement. Even as he decimated all the carefully cultivated knowledge Victoria held near and dear. A man who didn't want sex. She supposed, theoretically, one existed. *Somewhere.* Perhaps sharpening spears in a snow buried cave in the Tyrol peak. Not the guy who—*literally*—fucked her across a room yesterday.

With a tap of his finger, Warren closed her mouth. "I never thought I'd have to threaten anyone into *not* having sex with me, but you've been an exception to all my fucking sense."

His hand covered hers, and when he pulled, Victoria followed, confusion rendering her mute.

"I haven't seen anything other than the practice field," Warren explained, tucking her hand in the curve of his elbow, watching a seagull hang on a phantom wind. "If I'm going to live here, I want to know what it's like, see the sights."

Her skirt floated as a gust of cool air skid off the water. "You're taking me on the great Vermont tour? Are we making our own syrup?"

Her mouth snapped shut before she detailed her enthusiasm for a sticky sweet Warren. She took his threat seriously, biting her tongue. Rather than risk it, she implied it, molding herself against him, fitting his bicep between her breasts.

All he said was, "Better."

"Better than you naked, dripping in organic liquid sugar?"

Warren squeezed her hand.

"It slipped out," she huffed.

"Give me two hours. Please. And then..." A muscle in his cheek jumped.

"Human popsicle?"

His voice was low and surly. "Then I'm finding out exactly what's under that skirt. Christ knows I can hardly stay soft for that long these days."

"One of your many admirable traits."

"Go easy on me, baby."

Fine.

If he wanted two hours of frolicking, hand holding bullshit, she'd glue her hand to his. Talk about climate change, what age kids sucked the least, favorite dog breeds. Whatever boring pointless conversations park goers had. If they ran out of topics, they could watch the grass grow.

While she committed to his grim afternoon, Warren guided her from the boardwalk to a path along the shore.

The air cooled as they neared the water. Goosebumps rose to run the length of Victoria's legs as they passed a narrow bay protected by a stone breakwater. The sand beach was speckled with teetering rock towers and bare-footed kids sorting through worn, knobby driftwood and clumps of duckweed.

In her soul, she longed to shed her clothes and relax in the hot sand, listen to the waves, feel the cold water tickle the arches of her feet, remind her of summers on Narragansett Beach.

Rather than soak under the New England sun, Warren led her down to the marina docks. Sail boats, yachts, and jet boats bobbed against their tie downs, like stallions bucking at reins.

"Are we house shopping?" Victoria teased. "Might be hard to manage. The lake freezes and it'd be a real bummer if you lived on a land boat."

"I lived on the *Circe* because it was cheap."

"Please, I read your contract. It wasn't fuck-you cash, but you made more than enough for a nice home. Especially in Texas. Let me guess, you have a dangerous gambling addiction?"

"When I first signed with the team, I sent my parents a large chunk of my paycheck. Most of it." Warren cleared his throat. "I lived off the money from bonuses and sponsorships."

"Promoting silicon sex dolls?"

"State Farm."

Victoria shrugged. "Still hot."

"Short lived," Warren told her. "They fell over themselves to get Midas when he started. My cash flow stopped, my salary dropped."

Victoria saw where this led. She swallowed. "Oh, Flowers."

Water splashed the hull of a white charter fishing boat, spraying over the bleached dock planks. "I wasn't going to disappoint more people. I still send checks to my parents. I bought the *Circe* at a police auction. Apparently, the old gal was a drug runner."

"So you really have nothing?"

He let out a scraping laugh. "Less. I'm dead broke."

Victoria's stomach knotted with pained sweetness. Admiration and anger. The urge to shake him for being so stupid. And undeniably thoughtful.

His life hinged on the Mountaineers keeping him.

As the realization dawned, Victoria painted a peppy smile over her mouth. "What's the first thing you're going to buy with your new money?" Sheer optimism. She could fake it for him, for his two hours of escapism.

The smooth gray stone in her heart rattled around. How badly did he need today? The distraction?

Warren joined her fake cheer, saying brightly, "A house with a foundation by the water."

A gentleness wove through Victoria's voice when she replied, "I love the water."

Lifting his head to scour the lower, narrow docks splitting off theirs, Warren said softly, "I know. I see it in the way you look out at it, entranced. I love it too."

"It connects everything." She chuckled to cover her excitement for her longest, deepest love. "Not this lake, maybe. But dip a toe in a Newport beach and you're sharing water with a Greenlander. With a boat, the possibilities become endless. You can go any-where."

Small talk wasn't so bad, she thought abruptly. Jolting as the next revelation struck her square in the chest, made her lose her breath. Warren made the most mundane, dreadful tasks—wind-ing coffee lines, stop and start traffic, holding the door open for one person and a thousand rushing in after—bearable. Maybe even fun.

"This is a lake, though."

She surprised herself by saying, "It's so much bigger than I thought. It reminds me of the coast. I promised to hate it on principle. States without coasts? Kick them out of the union."

With a sigh, she closed her eyes, listening to the gentle lap of water hitting the pilings, the squeak of rubber-soled boat shoes, and the distant bellow of boat horns. She inhaled the smell of fish and motor oil, memorized the spray of water offering bursts of cool on her bare arms.

Her voice thickened. "It feels very much like home to me."

Folding his arms around her shoulders, Warren rested his chin on her head. He stayed quiet, letting Victoria relax, remember, miss.

"Did you know my dad was a sailor?" Her eyes stung.

"You mentioned it." His lips brushed her temple. "You are too."

Her hands drifted to the hot metal ladder hanging off the dock. "Not compared to him," she said wistfully. "It'd be like calling myself a football player in front of you. He was incredible. He competed for national teams sailing around the world in these enormous regattas. It was awe-inspiring."

She pictured the once-gleaming trophies collecting dust on the top of their kitchen cabinets, two rows deep. Her stomach twisted, the metal burned her hand. The boats mirrored on the water blurred.

Victoria turned her head to watch the shore. "He quit when I was ten because he wanted to stay home more. Because he missed me and my mom. He promised he would keep sailing, but he sold the boat, the *Victoria*, stopped walking to the docks, stopped turning his face to the water. He became someone else."

He'd stopped being a hero, stopped being the thing she said after she introduced herself. *I'm Victoria. My dad has sailed under the Sydney Harbour Bridge.* Instead, he was her dad, sitting three rows back, two seats in at her clarinet recital.

An engine sputtered twice before it growled, low and thrumming.

"Is he happy?" Warren asked.

"In his way, I guess." She shrugged. "He had the world at his fingertips. Living exactly how he wanted to, and he gave it up to sit behind a desk. He told me it was temporary. But his pause became a stop, which became an end to his favorite thing."

"For some people, once we stop moving, we freeze. It takes something big for us to see it, to pull us out of it. If you're stubborn like me, it takes someone to drag you out." His arms knitted in front of her waist. "When you found me, I was stuck. You got me moving again."

Until the end of pre-season, she wouldn't know if she'd helped him or cursed him.

There was safety in the status quo. Victoria had promised to change Warren's life. What if she'd torn him from his boat only to drown him in a lake? She hadn't known he had no money to fall back on. He'd have nothing.

"You should take your dad sailing," Warren said, not instructing, but supporting.

More guilt piled on Victoria. She couldn't show her dad what he missed, see the regret on his face—

She was strong, fierce, and capable until she stood next to her dad. Then Victoria was ten again, braces rubbing her lips raw, clutching onto his sleeve asking how seagulls floated.

She could only wrench people from safety if she didn't care about them. She could only handle the risk of failure when it was with numbers.

Dread pooled in her stomach.

"Red?"

She never should have brought Warren here.

Warren voice went low and soft, concerned. "Victoria?"

"I haven't sailed in over a year. I haven't been home in over a year."

"Let's fix that."

***

OFF. HE NEEDED to get off. Ice cold water washed over the hull and the boat tipped. Teeth clenched, Warren's yank on the guide ropes made the bolts squeal.

He fucking refused to go down with this ship.

Wind whipped against his skin, vortexed at the back of his neck, and snuck into every fold of loosened fabric, turning him into a flapping, unsteady mess. His stomach dropped to his feet, his pulse throbbed with the flap of the sail, his jaw ached.

Behind him, Victoria beamed.

Beautiful. Unreal. She was blue lightning shattering across an obsidian night sky.

And if Warren wasn't so busy trying to hold on to his breakfast, avoiding the nauseating sway of the boat, the wagging sail, dodging the mast, and choking on wave spray, he'd tell her.

Later, he promised, biceps grinding.

In her fluttering checkered skirt, bare feet, and white silk top, Victoria embodied Circe. A woman with the power to level gods, to cull legions of men. Cotton slapped at her thighs as she bent, heaving the center beam to her chest, angling her cheek to break the wind, her shoulders rigid, strong.

In the depths of his mind, he'd known she was more strong than delicate. It was hard to remember when his hand was able to span her waist, and she hung off him like a koala.

In the light of day, her power couldn't be more evident.

Enraptured, Warren held on and watched. Lean, honed muscles flexed, confidence wafting off her as she guided their skiff along the water, finding a delightful peace in the chaos.

Geoffrey the rental attendant had assured Warren that the boat was the ideal size for two people.

Geoffrey was first on the list of people Warren would haunt after he drowned.

Tiny.

The boat was shorter than he was tall. It rocked under the gentlest breeze. Doubtless, it was the smallest boat on the lake, getting tossed like a feather in rapids.

Undeterred, unnoticing, Victoria weaved them between diesel huffing fishing boats, cruisers, and freights under the power of only her and the wind. Nimble on the water, she approached sailing as she did life.

All or nothing.

Diving headfirst into trouble, but never oblivious of the potential pitfalls.

Bracing a leg on the bulkhead, she laughed as a square white ferry overtook them, bouncing them across its wake.

"I don't think he saw us!" she shouted over to Warren, grinning at the prospect.

Geoffrey would never have a moment of peace.

Warren wasn't a stranger to rough waters. He'd taken sturdy fishing boats far off the Texas coast trolling for tuna and grouper. They'd traversed waves that took minutes to cross. Yet it was sitting in a caution tape yellow sailboat on a lake in Vermont that had Warren checking the weight limits on the orange life vests.

It occurred to him, as sweat slicked his body, as Victoria switched directions, and Warren's hand submerged in the freezing water of Lake Champlain, that he would do this for the rest of his life.

Join her.

Watch.

He'd take her sailing every day. Year round.

In the winter, he'd melt the ice for her, heat the whole damn lake, buy an ice breaker, a pick axe, a flame thrower to see her shine this bright.

In the summer, he'd bring his fishing rod and a tackle box.

If he stayed.

If she stayed.

Both of which had decreasing odds.

A month ago, he'd cast Victoria off, tried to escape her.

Insane.

"Hold on!" she called.

Did she think he hadn't been? Warren's nails stung, the skin along his palms broke and tore under the ferocity with which he gripped. The sail swung, ropes went taut and loose as Victoria expertly reeled in slack, dexterous hands moving too quick to follow.

She was a flurry of action, dropping the cream sail, tying it, leaping from side to side as the boat leveled, yanked, and steadied.

Blinking aware the terror, Warren found the skiff nestled in a protected bay near the Hero islands.

Wiping water off her cheeks, combing her bangs back, Victoria said, "Little boats are so much more fun." Ducking around the folded sail with practiced grace, she added, "They're so easy to move and they fit anywhere."

With an arched brow, she sat opposite him, leaning forward to peel his fingers off the rope one by one. "You're traumatized."

"I'm hard," Warren admitted.

Finding the sun, she smiled. Her hair was like fresh onyx paint, sticking along her neck, eyes twice as blue as the lake behind her.

She glanced back at him, tongue flicking over her bottom lip. Her chin lowered, fingers drawing lines on her thigh. "I believe your two hours are up. If you're up for it, we can do my thing now."

For several seconds, he couldn't manage a response. Yes, he'd fuck her on a boat. He'd fuck her wherever she liked, wherever she let him. But today wasn't about carnal pleasure.

They were good at that. Great. *Fucking excellent.*

But he wanted more. And boyfriends, at least in the early stages, from what he'd gathered from Moore, didn't strip their girlfriends under the raw afternoon sun, and make them beg to come on their hands, their face, and their dick, in that order.

Boyfriends, allegedly, rented deadly boats and suffered turgid erections.

Eventually, Warren would buy her a boat. A big boat with minimal capsize risk. And in that boat, he'd pack a pillow for under her hips and SPF fifty for his white ass. Eventually. When she was his.

For now, he said, "You are so fucking good at this."

Victoria, who danced like sex, spoke the words straight from her mind, who propositioned him every third sentence, blushed.

A faint rosy shade spread from her cheeks all the way down to her cleavage.

"You should see my dad. He actually knows what he's doing. I'm an imposter."

Warren shifted to look over his shoulder. "Where is Victoria?" he mocked. "And who is this humble woman about to win the wet t-shirt contest? Next, you'll say you're not much of a flier or negotiator."

"You forgot to mention fucker. I'm great at fucking." Her smile could clear storm clouds and her mouth could wreck modern civilization.

"There she is."

"How much longer do we have the boat?"

"Less than an hour." He simultaneously thanked his shallow wallet and cursed it. To take Victoria away from the water was like prying stars from the night sky. Knowing how bright the sheet of darkness could get and having to settle for depthless black.

"We'll come back," he promised her sinking face.

Cerulean eyes slid to his, a curve fit her mouth.

Hauling his miniature gas station styrofoam cooler from under his legs, he said, "In the meantime, do you want a soggy ham and cheddar sandwich? Or a soggy turkey and provolone?"

A laugh burst from her, echoing off the shore to caress his back. "Either. They both have my favorite ingredient: sog."

He tossed her the ham, the once stiff sourdough flopping over her fingers.

"Sexy."

"I didn't know the whole boat was going to submerge, or I'd have packed better."

Folding over the plastic, she didn't hide a flash of surprise. "You made this?" She took a bite, impressed. "I won't tell the other women. Don't worry."

Together, they determined the only way to eat without gagging was to chew quickly, before the bread dissolved and plastered to their teeth. He wished he could do better, afford better. The per diem during training camp was thin.

"If I didn't know better," she finally said, rinsing the last of the bread-glue off her hands. "I'd call it romantic. The stroll, the boat, homemade lunch."

Warren braced his forearms on his knees and cocked his head. "But you know better," came his brusque reply. "How?"

She looked up from water logged lashes. "You don't kiss like a romantic." She raised her fingertips to her lips, touching them carefully. "You kiss like there's no oxygen left in the room and your only goal is for me to live."

He went motionless, spending immense concentration not to lunge forward and kiss her. *You'd hit the water*, he reminded himself, *the boat would flip*.

Did he fucking care?

"You kiss like a wife." There was a slight rasp to his voice.

"I've heard people sail on the Great Lakes," she responded, voice stilted, topic averted.

Warren chomped at his sandwich, heart stammering as she went on. "It sounded lame, but it's wonderful. No salt clinging to your skin, no sharks circling, and we're never out of land's sight."

She leaned back, eyes closing. "It's warmer too." She sighed, body relaxed, spent, dried scraps of her hair leaped with the wind to tickle her nose, her lips.

His voice was still low, still wrought with gravel when he spoke. "You have to teach me the names. Jib, mast, helm."

One eye poked open. "You're going to be a sailor?"

"Fuck no." Leaning forward, Warren caught one dark strand off her forehead and smoothed it back. "But I want to be able to tell you to bend over the mast without looking like an idiot."

"Finally," she caught his wrist, pulling him close. "You're on my page."

Her lips covered his, and the feeling of her smile poured liquid ecstasy into his veins. A low ragged groan crawled up Warren's throat. Victoria responded eagerly, balancing them and the boat as she stood, her tongue stroking against his. Her legs slid over his lap.

Warren meant to tell her he liked her, ask her if she'd sail with him again, do more with him. A lot more.

Stay with him.

When she pulled back, lips plump from his, pulse jumping, the golden sun streaking over her jet black hair, she looked carefree. Unrestrained. He forgot the plan.

Forgot his goals.

"I love you, Red."

***

VICTORIA'S HAND TREMBLED, turning a simple twist of the doorknob into rattling metal as she opened the bathroom door. Her throat felt thick, her movements stiff, awkward, steps echoing off the marble and tapping over Warren's bed.

Loud enough for Warren to turn, sheets gliding over his legs. Without a word, he drew back the blankets, circling the open space with his palm to welcome her.

Victoria bypassed the offer to sleep on his other side, checking to make sure both doors were visible before she eased under the covers.

Warren rolled, reeling her into his bare chest, bare everything, her hands lazing over the hard terrain.

Something happened.

Today.

This morning.

On the boat.

Maybe when they returned, sunburned and exhausted.

Victoria turned, prying her hands free, curling them around her stomach as Warren pressed to her back, sheltering her.

If she didn't acknowledge it, it didn't happen.

Warren had said it. The L word. And then asked what the main lines were called, how to hold the rudder and manage the sail at the same time.

The questions had cleared her mind. Heart on lockdown, she'd assumed the role of teacher as they sailed back to the marina, as she buckled into his car, picked up burgers from Al's on the way to the hotel.

Bad.

It was bad, whatever had happened.

Or good. There was a chance it was good.

The way he'd grasped at her with shaking hands when they got to his room, how he pinned her wrists over her head and lavished her with intense, bruising kisses. The curtains stayed open as he stripped her, arms raised, back bowed, on her toes while he licked every stretch mark hidden behind her bra.

His treatment had teetered on holy. A man before his cherished altar, promising blood and eternity.

A reformed sinner discovering the serenity of peace.

He'd gathered her in his arms, gently draped her across the pillows and demanded she stay still as he murmured all his lascivious desires over her skin, as he performed them, eyes ravenous and dark. Gold simmering.

Whatever had changed—good or bad—it made Victoria want to run.

Simply because it made her want to stay. Made her snuggle against him after, bodies bare, wondering what they'd have for breakfast, if he had an early practice, in which case she'd wake with him. For the ten extra minutes over cheap hotel waffles and fake orange juice.

Lips brushed the top of her spine. "What scares you about doors?"

"I am a single woman, alone, very sexually attractive." She wiggled her butt into him, teasing, playful.

Warren yanked back and pushed to his palms to loom over her. The soft glow of the moon cascaded in through the windows, giving him a stark silhouette, a monster in the night. Gently, he ran his nose over her shoulder.

"Wrong," he said. "If that scared you, you wouldn't walk into bars alone or kiss strange men." He dropped a kiss on her jaw. "You wouldn't call rodeo clowns apes."

Victoria twisted to her back to stare up at her gentle warrior. "I call it like I see it."

"What happened?" he persisted. "Did someone—" he stopped, as if unable to form the words, to finish the idea.

"Yes."

She heard Warren's teeth snap together. He reared back from her, hands becoming leaden fists. She watched him under the blue white beam. Saw anger steeped in poison, hatred.

She came up on her elbows. "Not like that," she clarified, fascinated to watch the relief course through his features. "No one's ever taken advantage of me, not like that."

"How?" He gritted his teeth, chest rising and falling.

Her warm hands found the sides of his cold cheeks. "There was a break-in at my room, a year ago, when I first became a recruiter. I had an interview with the head coach of the Ravens. He needed a defensive tackle. I researched the right player for weeks, compiled my results, and ranked them. I was so ready to nail the interview, I went out for a drink and…" She trailed off.

"And a fuck."

She lifted her chin. "Yes." Confused why she hadn't outright admitted it, she paused to sit up fully. Victoria liked sex, she never shied around it. Why had she spared the detail?

"Red, you're stringing me along. Tell me what happened before I tear the room apart."

"I don't know who he had to bribe or threaten, but Morgan got a copy of my room key, broke in and stole all my notes, my research, everything and deleted what was left. He represented a graduating tackle, wanted the Ravens to take him, and I'd refused when he asked to pitch him because he wasn't the right fit. I lost the interview."

"Morgan robbed you?" Warren's voice was dark and shadowed.

"The worst part is, as soon as I noticed the file was missing, I went to the hotel manager and told them. The manager took one look at me, at my clothes, my body, and said I shouldn't give my keycard out so freely. It wasn't the hotel's responsibility to keep track of my guests."

She rolled her eyes, trying to shake it off, but her voice thinned. "He made it seem like I had a rotating door of men that night. Because of how I looked, because I was young, and a woman, and I had big boobs. I was wearing fucking jeans, not that it should matter."

The sheets drew taut under Victoria, Warren's fingers bunching and pulling, bearing down. He seemed to consider his words carefully before saying, "I've never seen you in jeans."

"You won't. If I'm going to be judged for the way I dress, then I'm going to dress exactly how I want to."

"Damn right." Came his growl.

A pause.

"How'd you know it was Morgan?" He sounded distant as if he'd crossed the room, but he hadn't moved. Not a single rise or fall in his chest.

Swallowing past ire, Victoria summoned levity. "He told me, the arrogant asshole. He told me exactly what he did and that no one would believe me, a girl. He said if I tried telling someone, I'd never work again. We'd dated for seven months."

Warren's reply was emphatic. "I'll kill him."

She dipped her chin, one brow arched, chiding, "Flowers."

"He's crossed too many lines already. He deserves it. How does he even have a job? Why haven't you destroyed him?"

Suddenly Victoria felt frozen. Laid bare in the snow and left, all of her secrets hanging out. She pressed a hand to her stomach to staunch a false injury.

Why haven't you destroyed him?

That was what he expected of her, to ruin others for her own gain.

"You think it's cutthroat on the field?" she said sharply. "It's ten times as bad off it. We're a devious, cunning, backstabbing bunch. It's the only way to survive. Morgan taught me early. Only look out for number one. He made it impossible to forget. Win by any means."

A credo for miscreants and she'd happily procured it.

They thought to keep her down because she was a woman, an outsider, and it was for exactly that reason she vowed to rise above them. She let her hand fall to the side, lifted her chin. "I haven't lost since."

"So the chair—"

"A precaution, nothing more."

"It's a reminder," Warren accused, voice thrumming with anger. "Morgan scared you and you won't let yourself forget. He stole your safety, corrupted your mind."

Victoria snapped, "My mind's not corrupted, Warren."

"By any means. He convinced you burglary was expected."

She absorbed his words, the firmness of his tone, the sanctimonious air that rankled deeply, tore on frayed feelings. "There's nothing wrong with going after what you want."

He responded in a low, shaking voice. "By scaring you? Betraying your trust? He's signed his will."

The moonlight drifted up and down, caught and directed by shaking tree branches. The air conditioning turned on, hissed, and shut off. Gradually, the sheets loosened, the soreness in Victoria's throat gave. Their stares became gazes. Time had passed or stopped. Victoria's skin had gone cold. She was tired, her mind, her heart.

Sleep sounded wonderful. Sleep nestled across Warren's sturdy, warm body, wrapped in his arms.

Victoria touched his jaw, stroked to his cheek, thumb tracing his lips. "Flowers the Executioner."

Time snapped back. He slotted a leg between hers and bent forward until his hot breath tickled her ear. "So long as you're not the mourner."

A shiver made her stomach pulse. "Leave Morgan alone. He's annoying, but he's on the mundane side of the scale." She tightened her thighs around his, slowly dragging her core over the muscle. "Imagine his dumb face when I beat him. He'll know I did it with a hand tied behind my back and it didn't matter at all. He's a rock, but I'm a bullet."

Warren let his hands coast down her arms and slowed the pace of her undulating hips with a smirk. "If you were a hundred pounds heavier and a foot taller, you'd make a formidable quarterback."

A husky chuckle escaped her, glad the feelings hour was over, glad Warren and her were living in the present and nowhere else. "God no. Not a quarterback. I'd be a kicker. Low injury risk, high notoriety, long career."

"Wrong," he shot back. "You'd be a punt returner. Running alone against an entire team."

A warmth smoothed over her skin, adding to the heat of their building friction. Warren thought she could face down an entire team. Her chest squeezed.

"Come with me to New York."

"For the game?" she asked, as if she didn't know. As if the Bills hadn't been preparing to host the Mountaineers for six long days. The second pre-season game.

"Yes," he said softly, tipping her chin up to spread light, feathery kisses down her jaw.

The *something* returned.

The good, the bad, all of it spilled between her ribs and found a home in Victoria's soul.

"Say yes. I know you miss flying." Ruthless, he raised his knee higher and ground against her, rough, determined.

She moaned, gasping. "On one condition."

"You could ask me to extinguish the sun and I'd find a way."

Victoria sank her fingers into his hair, molded them to his scalp. Against his lips, she demanded, "Win."

Chapter Sixteen

WARREN'S THREE WORDS PROVED haunting, Victoria realized, as their plane touched down in New York and Gomez called. She didn't need a pocket full of sage and a psychic grandmother to know his summons was an omen. Cold as a brittle, northern winter.

Odd that it offered relief, knowing she was walking into destruction. The rest of her life had become a murky gray, thick fog slipping over the water, daring her to enter.

Warren loved her, promised to protect her, cherished her. He gave himself to her in fist sized chunks hand over hand.

To her. A woman of shreds and dust. She wasn't sure she could return it. Any of it.

Only one thought permeated her mind as she stalked into the Gomez's private jet.

Eat the rich.

A neat, burlywood path led past three rows of cream suede seats. Watercolor orchids wandered over the ceiling, weaving together into a field of pale, delicate petals. The real opulence, though, began in the back of the plane, where a full bar sat. Complete with hand carved cherub corbels, three tiers of crystal decanters, and a wine rack of webbed silver cradling label-less bottles.

Ten to one, Gomez owned a winery.

A draft scented of fresh linen and patchouli, of unabridged decadence, reminded her of the boutique shops by the wharf she frequented before her dad quit sailing. She'd sniff the freshly carved soaps and stand in front of the split units until the salt flaked off her skin.

It was the particular smell of places she never felt comfortable visiting.

Purposefully, Gomez didn't bother to look up at her arrival. The shoulders of his navy suit, complete with deep lush forest green pinstripes, were hunched as he sliced through a yolk-free omelet.

With a sniff, he jabbed his knife at the seat across from him. Victoria sank into the conditioned leather, let it mold to the bare skin of her thighs, her back. With reluctant approval, she knew she wouldn't stick to it, not in the temperature regulated fuselage.

With its custom wide rows and lay flat seats, the Mountaineers' jet didn't manage to scratch the luxury of the Gomez jet. No wonder he traveled separately. Traipsing up the ramp in her new snakeskin (fake) green (moss) dress, she went from New York It Girl to local whore at a lodge in the Swiss Alps.

Silence cloaked them. The click of metal on porcelain as loud as a gun against her ear.

Never speak first.

Sealing her lips, Victoria parted the flutes of untouched champagne and grapefruit juice to smile tartly at her boss. She waited, hands folded, eyes twinkling.

Sweeping a Mountbatten cloth napkin across his mouth, doubling back to clear his mustache, Gomez asked, "Is it typical for a freelance recruiter to travel with a team?"

Letting a shoulder lift and drop, Victoria helped herself to the champagne. "There's nothing typical about our arrangement. When was the last time the NFL expanded? The Jaguars?" She sipped from the wafer thin glass and made her disdain for the cloying sweetness obvious. "That was before I was born."

Gomez's dark eyes could be called plain from a distance. Up close, the narrow black ring around the iris thickened and thinned with his patience. "It's fitting my team should be atypical, as I am not a typical man. I come from an impoverished background, where we had no time for leisure activities. The concept of spending our money on tickets for a game was ludicrous, if not abhorrent. A frivolity we never entertained. To buy a team demonstrates the extent of my rise."

A napkin crumpled over his breakfast as he leaned back in his seat. "Now, I find my time occupied by frivolity."

Victoria's skin tightened. "I'm glad you're enjoying yourself."

"That's the problem, isn't it? I'm not. Do you know why my hotels are so successful?"

"Location?"

"Say 'no' if you don't," he snapped.

Victoria took another sip of champagne, remaining silent.

"I hire only the best," he told her. "I'm not unlike you. I search and study when selecting my employees."

With the tip of his finger, he pushed his plate forward.

Immediately, a server materialized, sweeping the plate, his silverware, the brimming glass away.

Gomez's dipped chin said, *see?*

"I want Midas. I want the team you sold me when I hired you."

A sickening stomach dropping feeling spread as she downed the rest of the bubbly. Her lips pursed. "I—"

"Give me a status update."

Bolstering, Victoria raised her chin. "Foss has requested a new punter. I've found three that will gel well with our special teams."

"Kickers? You misunderstand me. Where is Midas?"

Victoria bit her tongue to keep from matching his seething tone.

Panicked thoughts crowded her mind. Misery tangled up her limbs, stole the iron from her spine, the ice in her veins. She'd danced around it for months, evaded Gomez with the swiftness of an expert sailor on high tide and now—

There was no more wind.

"My hands are tied with regard to any and all players until pre-season ends."

"I'm aware of the logistics. After pre-season, we'll have three days to persuade Midas to join us." A chilling pause. "Procrastination is a synonym for laziness."

She felt herself turning red with violence. Tipping forward, Victoria used all her energy to keep a level tone. "It's very uncommon for a player to leave during pre-season."

"We've just established that my team is atypical, dear."

Victoria looked away from him, nails carving deep crescents into her palm as she searched for something to kick or throw that wasn't the man in charge of her life.

The magnate stood, and waited, his expression bland, until Victoria joined him. The heels of her boots sank into the plush carpet, putting her eyes level with his flattened mouth. No smile lines marred the thick brown skin, no give.

A dark succession of emotions flooded her—anger, frustration, defeat. Hopelessness.

She followed him, using the chair backs as guide rails. Stopping when he retrieved a leather bag from an overhead compartment. His initials were burned into the clasp.

"Midas is the best. To achieve success, I need him."

"We have—"

"We?"

Her fingers dug into the suede. "You have a strong team. Warren Rose is more than capable."

"I have to wonder if my mistake wasn't losing Midas, but in hiring you, Miss Steer."

She closed her eyes, battling down a riot of defenses. "Rose will perform."

"Rose is a nobody. Nothing more than a placeholder until better comes along."

Victoria didn't reply. Hearing Warren's name on his lips drew her to the edge of her fears. The urge to shout, to scream, to rip the handkerchief from Gomez's suit coat and spit on it surged.

"What will you do?"

"The cost alone to retain Midas would decimate half the team. War—" she stopped. "Rose is affordable. He allows a wider spread of talent."

"He's old, riddled with injuries."

"One," she corrected. "That he's overcome."

Gomez waved her off. "Talent will come with time." Shuffling through his bag, he withdrew square framed sunglasses. "If he plays well today, Miss Steer, and is as cheap as you claim, we can discuss his retention. Perhaps on the practice squad. In the meantime, prepare contracts for his dismissal and contact Midas. I'm not waiting any longer. We'll move now."

Grimly, she said, "Yes, sir."

***

WARREN STOOD IN the shadow of his linemen, surrounded in the huddle as the play clock struck down.

A new determination fueled him as he sorted through the plays on his arm sleeve, searching for exactly the right one.

It was the second half. They were up by seven and Warren wanted to bury them.

Victoria had shown him how invigorating it could be to reach.

To push, to leave the known and explode.

His attention slid to the stands, scouring through the lines of blue. Victoria, in green, was hidden within, her gaze devouring, sensuous plans forming. The adrenaline should have kept his focus to the field until all of it—the flashing lights, the pounding music, the screams—disappeared. Until it became him and ten of his team versus eleven of theirs.

But he wanted to see her.

He tore his gaze from the stands, shaking out his hands in the brisk wind. Calm, he felt calm. His breaths were even, light, the edge of his lips tipped. Happy.

"What's the move?" Sixty-seven asked through a white mouth guard.

"Reverse Gambit. Green eighteen," Warren told the circle of men, voice rough to cut through the crowd. He clapped his hands to split them along the line.

Complacency, as Victoria called it, would never fit into his life again. He refuted the concept. With football, his life, the team, her. Especially her.

He'd reach for better, force it with unfettered ambition, find it through blood, sweat, and tears.

Unlike Victoria, he wouldn't live in the now. He'd live for the future. For their future, setting plans to turn fantasies into reality.

Starting now. Buffalo sat on its heels, off-kilter. Few starters remained on the Mountaineers line. Only those who had begged Coach for extra field time.

The rest of the line was pulled from deep off the charts, faces that had never truly witnessed the speed of an NFL game. Seldom would see it again, reduced to the practice team or cut entirely.

Coach didn't consider benching Warren. Not when his position remained so tremulous.

It didn't matter.

Bending his knees, digging his feet into the turf, Warren lifted his arms. He'd show Coach what he could do, why he'd pushed so damn hard in camp.

Third and six, on the edge of field goal range. If they didn't convert here, he'd be pulled, forced to watch special teams score three when he craved seven.

Forward. More. A win wasn't enough.

He'd destroy the Bills, knock them to their asses, pelt them with throw completions until Coach glued Warren's ass to the bench.

Only then would his future be within reach.

Warming his palms, readying for the ball, he checked the line once, ensuring everyone was ready. In the right spot.

This was a scoring run, he felt it.

The clock dwindled down to ten. Nine... Warren shouted out four plays, throat scratching. "Green fifty-six, blue forty-two, blue forty-two, green eighteen. Hut. Hike."

The pitch came fast and high. Were Warren any shorter, it would've soared over his fingers. His fingers missed the laces as he scrambled backward. He reset, adjusted his hold on the ball and scanned for Moore. Couldn't find him.

Buying time, Warren dropped back deeper into the pocket, orienting, searching. He caught forty-four sprinting downfield, cutting a hard route. A defender hung close.

Four seconds, five seconds. He had to get rid of it.

He sidestepped, searching for other options. *Get rid of it.*

Moore was covered, the other receiver tangled up, blue stuck to green.

No other option.

Run. Take it himself. Run it in. Thirty yards.

No. *There.* An opening. He threw, spiral arching with practiced precision it dove for twenty-eight, piercing the air.

The receiver didn't turn, didn't cut his route.

A body struck Warren, threw him sideways into the hard ground.

Warren's shoulder hit first, cracking under the weight of him and a bulky defender. The pain tearing down his arm was secondary to Warren's focus. Struggling to focus, he looked downfield, searching desperately. *Turn. Cut your route.*

The Bills' defense snatched his ball from the air. Warren jolted, tried to move, to get up and get it fucking back, but his arm was trapped under him, the weight of a body dug into his back as the Bills sprinted the ball back for a pick six.

The home crowd roared.

Cheers for his mistake.

The most he'd gotten to date.

Warren buried his face in the turf, black hot anger stabbed his gut. He couldn't block it out. The noise of the stadium was deafening, the smell of defeat putrid.

Slowly, the defender got off of Warren, laughing, calling out congratulations.

More noise barraged him, hollers and screams. Warren stayed down. Hurting, panting, no air in his lungs.

He should've settled.

***

VICTORIA STARED MUTELY at the man laying on the field with horror as her pyramid, her tightly packed scheme disintegrated, broke across her shoulders in waves of ruin, of anguish. Crushed her until her bones wept.

The only sign that she was moving, that she'd gotten to her feet, jerked out of the plastic folding chair, was the flash of faces as she raced through the suite.

This morning, she would've said she could run a marathon in her chunky ankle boots, black leather, a half size too small and surprisingly supportive.

After a single play, her steps were uneven, long and short, stuttering, matching her panic as she rushed to the hall.

He was *down*—*he* was down—*he was down.*

She kept stopping. Kept seeing it, in her mind, on the screens. Flattened by an enormous defender. Two men had to peel him off.

A late hit. Unacceptable.

Punish, Victoria vowed.

She'd ruin that asshole's career with her own, call him toxic, untenable, whisper horrid things in crowded rooms. Loose cannon, sketchy past, violent, subject to outbursts. Rule breaker. He'd bend under her will until he broke.

Still down. Still down.

Adrenaline made her hot as she ran, spots blocking her vision.

Hurt. Of course. Flattened by football's notorious bastard. But how badly?

Medical tent? Ambulance? Airlift?

She wasn't family, she couldn't go with. Heart walloping in her chest, Victoria froze at the door to the stairwell. Elevator or stairs? What floor was she on? What floor was the field?

Points! She had airline points and miles and cash if the rest failed. She'd get on the first flight to Boston. That's where they'd take him. The best hospitals were in Boston.

Weight hit her shoulder. A hand spun her. As quick as he grabbed her, Gomez stepped back, disdain bleaching his eyes of color. "I knew this would happen," he said. "Fix it, immediately."

Remaining still, Victoria's muscles strained, veins constricting. "Not now." She headed for the stairs.

"He's out!" Gomez's raised voice hit her back.

She shouted *fine* or *sure* or *yes* as her heel skidded from under her, her hand crushing the metal stairwell rail. No time to recover, just like there was no time to argue. She kept going.

Why were box seats coveted? She'd never return. The concrete steps stung her feet, sent jolts up her calves. One flight down.

Panting, her fingers trailed over the emergency exit map. Two more flights.

Too slow.

She threw off her heels and became a blur.

Steps melded together until they ended. Then her badge was scanned, once, twice. She repeated her name, her credentials. Whatever they wanted, she regurgitated on command.

"Hurry up," she growled, ducking around security, panic shortening her breath.

Then her bare toes kissed turf.

The game had resumed. Buried in throngs of windbreaker wearing coaches, Foss caught her attention and pointed to the medical tent.

She broke through the tent's curtains as the buzzer sounded. Game over. A tight applause followed. A win? A loss? Tie?

Irrelevant.

Arms shaking, breaths coming out as broken pants, Victoria's hand curved over the limp cleat hanging off the raised examination table.

Breathtaking amber eyes found her, and her heart suspended its beating.

A flashlight jutted between them, shining a white beam into Warren's pupils.

"Enough," Warren groused. "I'm fine." He waved off the medic.

Another hand fell on Victoria's shoulder, and her body sprung back to life. She spun, eyes narrowed, ready to quit, ready to scream.

Foss was faster, howling her out of the tent, spitting his gum in a silver wrapper, eyes darting. "A tie I can stomach." He ran a hand down his lean face, tugged on his short hair. "A loss. By one fucking point?" His fingers showed how close they'd gotten. A vein in his forehead popped.

Victoria didn't look at the scoreboard.

"Grant's playing next week," he said, blowing out an agitated breath.

She recognized the name of their back-up quarterback, a kid from Louisiana. Hers. No spark of joy could fracture through her misery, the churning of ichor in her stomach. "Is it a concussion? How long will Warren be out?"

Foss rubbed the back of his neck, his voice dropping until it was nearly silent. "Permanently."

Victoria fell back, feet staggering, heart wrenching, soul blackening. Her eyes filled with tears, dizziness clawed at her. She looked at the field, the lines, the pylons, passing faces.

Words escaped her.

Warren would never play football again.

A strangled sob escaped her, she grabbed something to keep from falling, Foss's arm.

"He's benched, Steer. I'll have to cut him soon." He tugged his ear. "I'm sorry. You have to let him go. They're not all winners."

"Cut?" Her voice was weak. "*Cut*? You can't fucking cut him because he got hurt."

"He's not hurt. Nothing more than bruises, a possible sprain."

She went still, thoughts jumbling, mouth dry. "What?"

"Rose is out."

Iced venom killed the relief in her veins. She released Foss, stumbling back a step, dragging together flying thoughts, yanking them into ideas, sentences. Arguments. "You're cutting him? For an illegal hit?"

"You told me Rose was stable, steady. He just threw a Hail Mary when we were up by seven with five minutes left in the game. If I have to deal with a flashy, attention grabbing QB, then I'd rather it be Midas." A grimace fit his lips as he shook his head. "At least I'll know how to manage him."

"Are you fucking kidding me, Rodney? *Midas*?" Fake grass tickled the soles of her feet as she stepped into him, finger raised. "You agree with Gomez? What'd he promise you? A bonus? Free rooms for life? A bronze statue of you choking on his tiny dick?"

Foss came swinging back with matching white faced rage. "Watch it, Steer. It's not personal. It's about winning."

"Fuck off, Rodney." She pushed past him.

"I'll have your badge revoked!" he called as she strode inside the medical tent.

Plain blue canvas walls, a line of white folding tables. Victoria scanned the contents: gauze, boxes of disposable gloves, a folded hospital robe, long strings tied in neat bows.

She nodded to the two medics at Warren's side. "I need a moment with my client. Please."

Resting against a black foam square, Warren pulled his jersey back over his shoulder pad. "Red."

She held up a numb hand, waiting until the staff exited. It took years of training to keep her face neutral while Warren sat prone. Sweat-soaked hair stuck to his forehead, his cheeks were bright red, his lips cracked dry. Thick black tape traversed his arm, overlapping and winding around the tan muscle.

When they were alone, Warren tilted his head to the side. "There's no such thing as a tent lock, so if you think I'm going to fuck you right now, you're—"

She ignored him, knocking aside a metal stand holding saline bags. Quick steps brought her to his side, hands featherlight on his wrist. "Is it your arm? How bad is it?" She was whispering, fingers hovering over the sinew. "It looked awful." She didn't meet his eyes. "I could hear the impact from upstairs."

"Not bad at all," he said. To prove his point, he stretched his taped arm in front of him and rotated it. "I overextended my elbow a little. Ice will have it better by tomorrow."

Tell him, her conscience screamed. *Tell him it's over, to go home. He's out.*

Instead, she said softly, "You're benched."

"No."

"Yes."

"*Fuck*," Warren snapped, jerking up, shoving his legs off the table to sit upright, hands making brutal, pulsing fists.

Victoria was at his side before her next inhale, searching for bruises, cuts, readying to catch him at the faintest sway. Other than the ice pack taped to his elbow, she couldn't find a scratch.

He caught her hands in his, shifted to face her, fingers tight over her skin. "It was a hard hit." His voice broke. "It knocked the air out of me. I shouldn't have stayed down. I was pissed off about the interception."

The interception.

Victoria had almost forgot.

She pressed her forehead to his, breathing in soap and sweat and the sting of hand sanitizer. Warren held her as guilt and fear raged in her chest, thrust two electric prods into her heart.

An injury she could talk away, but an interception, the throw.

She couldn't fight *both* Foss and Gomez.

Would Toby be on her side? Or recognize the majority and split? Warren had shown weakness. A stadium had witnessed it.

"You're the face of the team," she spoke so quietly, Warren didn't hear.

"Second game in three years. My first sack and I'm benched." His jaw clenched, forehead pressing into hers. "Isn't that what the pre-season is for?"

"They want you out." She was still whispering, sorting through piles of thoughts, of potential outcomes. A way the both of them could survive.

Foss was serious. Gomez past breaking. Toby. Maybe Toby wouldn't make her fire him. Maybe he'd cleave the axe on Warren's career for her. No. She'd have to tell him. Owed it to him.

Midas was coming.

Others would suffer, her numbers would be snipped away. Her precious, carefully mined numbers.

They'd taken on faces, gotten names.

Feeling hollow, she stared at the curtain walls, folds of light and dark blue undulating. She'd call them to the business center in fifteen minute slots, shake their hands, end their partnerships, draw a permanent, black line through their number.

By the time she got to Warren, he'd know. Burton would warn him. He'd know she was ending it. Two minutes. That's all the time he would need to hate her, to storm out.

She firmed her chin to stave off tears.

It was time. She'd been cornered. No more running, no more pivoting.

Warren wiped under her eyes. She hadn't realized they were watering.

"Everything's going to be fine," he promised, kissing her temple, her cheek, swiping again at her face, thumbs coming away wet. "Don't cry, baby. It'll be fine. I promise."

She took a shaking breath. "Warren—"

"Where are your shoes?"

Slowly, she followed Warren's gaze to her feet. "Uh... the stairwell. I think."

"Were you mugged?" His tone edged on teasing.

"I saw you go down, and I ran. I'm faster without them." Now it seemed idiotic. She blinked. It *was* idiotic. "I'm barefoot."

The Mountaineers had lost, Warren was hurt, his future in shambles. He should be shredding the tent, screaming at her, scrambling for an agent. Instead, he ran his hands up and down her arms, soothing, smiling gently, eyes a simmering sweet caress. "I'll fix it, Red."

Chapter Seventeen

WARREN COULDN'T REMEMBER THE last time Victoria had looked at him. Not a length of time easily measured in minutes. Hours maybe. When she'd hovered over him in the medical tent, eyes glassy, hand cold in his. Worried.

Or so he thought.

His original assessment seemed further and further from accurate as the time stretched.

"You can reach the remote," she said, folding the comforter over his lap. "There's water." A point of her index finger. She chewed the clock. "Tylenol." Her eyes glued to the back of the narrow white bottle. "Don't take any more until six. And you're only allowed three more doses today."

She tilted back to stare at the ceiling. "If it stops being effective, I can get something else." She checked her watch. "When does the pharmacy close?"

"I'm not hurt," Warren repeated, only half believing himself. Victoria Steer was a terrible nurse. From the moment they landed, she'd lost his suitcase, cracked his phone screen, squirted hot sauce in his eye, and flooded the bathroom sink.

It wasn't anything like the tiny nursemaid outfit he'd pictured, the sexy stethoscope.

His sanctioned bedrest involved actual rest, sweating under a mountain of blankets while Victoria scurried around, excusing herself every ten minutes to take a call on the balcony.

"You're in bed. Of course you're hurt." This logic made perfect sense to her as she nodded, self-approving. Her snakeskin dress creaking as she commandeered his remote and changed the station from news to black scrolling movie credits.

"I'm in bed because you told me to strip and lie down." Warren canted forward, blankets sliding down his bare chest. "I thought you would follow."

"When you're hurt?" She shook her head at the TV, adjusting the brightness. "No."

"That's it. I'm getting up."

"Don't." She sounded thoroughly offended as she pushed him flat, forced the covers back up, and re-tucked the corners with tight jabs.

If he were hurt, he'd want her and her flying fists miles away.

"Who have you been calling?" he asked impulsively. "I know it's not a doctor." A doctor would never recommend he use a catheter for a scraped elbow, as Victoria had suggested.

And been flatly denied.

A buzz came from her pocket. Before the ringtone began, she had it muted. "The front desk." She read the screen and frowned. "We need more blankets."

They needed more blankets like he needed more holes in the head. She wasn't worried. She was lying. She was distracted, her mind elsewhere, stealing her grace, her awareness.

His gaze flitted around the hotel room, finding her nightstand empty, the stack of bright clothes cleared from the striped armchair, her shoes waiting impatiently by the door.

Warren felt his throat constrict, his mouth dry, the tightness in his jaw and face began to ache from overuse.

Victoria didn't want to be here.

But she was.

Because she pitied him.

"Come into bed." His tone wasn't inviting but challenging, suspicious. "Let's watch a movie. I have tomorrow off." They always got the day after a game off, time to recuperate. If the weather was affable, he'd take her sailing again, see that sunny smile.

Her fingers twined with his, but her blue eyes remained down, distant. "I ordered soup. I know chicken noodle is the go-to, but sweet and sour was the only option. The concierge will deliver it straight to you, so you don't have to get up. Do you have a spoon? Nevermind. It'll come with the order."

"Red." Warren caught her chin, moving to sit on the edge of the bed until his legs cradled hers. With a tug, her hand flew to this chest, blue eyes sank to his.

"Come to bed," he said softly, absorbing the crystal color in her eyes, hating the puffiness leftover from tears. "Tomorrow, I'll have physical therapy and it'll be clear that I'm in perfect shape. In better shape than I've been in years. Nothing's wrong with me."

"Do you know what can happen between now and your appointment? In sixteen hours?"

"The earth spins two-thirds its normal rotation?"

She gave an unsteady laugh. "You can fly from Seattle to Newport, buy a lobster, and fly back again for your morning coffee."

He pressed a kiss to her cheek, the one long healed from its bruise, absorbing her breathing. Preferring to ease her mind than deal with his, he wound his hands around her waist and pulled her close. Kissed her again. Softly. Murmured endearments between caresses.

His mistakes shouldn't cost her. It was his interception, his fault.

"I can't," she gasped, pushing away, twirling out of his reach.

He all but shouted, "I'm not hurt!"

Victoria didn't flinch at his tone. It invigorated her, armored her. In methodical steps, her spine hardened, her chin raised, a smooth, collected mask took hold of her features. "I can't compromise myself by becoming involved with you." The phone rang and she let it. Bold, stubborn, detached. "Eat dinner, sleep well. I'll be back Tuesday."

Acid pooled in Warren's gut. *Compromised? Involved?* His fingers coiled in the sheets. "Not tomorrow?"

"No. Gomez is lending me his jet to take care of some... restructuring."

Dread lanced through a stomach, vicious and haunting. Despair slackened his arms, needled his temple into a throbbing headache.

"Exactly what kind of restructuring?" The venom in his voice was unfamiliar, bitter and cruel. He wanted to stop it, suck it back, prevent it from reaching Victoria's ears.

"It's not for you to worry about you." No emotion, no lilt or snap. Her eyes were cool, calm water, her face indifferent.

A bolt of rage made him snap, "You're going to Texas."

Victoria flinched. Barely. A flicker in her eyes. A slight retreat. An angle of her face.

"*Fuck.*" Violent, convulsing heat scoured his spine, kindling a need to smash, to wreck. His fist connected with the nightstand, water and pills poured over the floor.

One mistake. And Victoria was gone, done.

"I'm not going to Texas."

His laugh crept through the room like a savage smoke, choking him.

In a soothing, unfamiliar voice, Victoria said, "I need to know you're not going to do anything while I'm gone. Head down. Stay consistent. Regroup and brush this off."

Brush it off. Was that what she was doing? Severing contact, bushing him off before she collected Midas.

If he could see her eyes, if she could tell him what worried her, what she really had to do. "Tell me the truth."

"I've never lied to you!" she burst. Her phone went off again, grinding Warren's eardrums. "I have to answer this."

Warren nodded, staring at the floor, jaw tight. On the carpet, white pills were dissolved into puffs of windblown dandelions. Once sturdy and strong, resistant to the toughest of fertilizers, dismembered by a light breeze.

"Soups coming," Victoria mouthed as she zipped on her boots, read her phone.

The minute she answered, he'd lose her. He knew it. Was too pissed off to stop it. He sat, staring as the water turned milky.

The door slammed, and her voice, clear, firm, missing any softness, slunk through the jamb. "This is Victoria."

Warren jolted. Sprinting, throwing open the door, half aware he was naked. The elevator doors sealed.

Too late.

***

WARREN'S HEAD SPUN from nodding. He'd given a hundred assurances, answered dozens of questions.

He felt nothing amiss. He could play. Wanted to. Needed to.

The world wanted him to be injured. Perhaps it'd be easier if he was. He pinched his shirt and rolled it over his bicep. Nothing but trained muscle. It wasn't in his head. There was no bruise, no scratch.

There was also no announcement of his status. Cursing under his breath, he flicked two fingers at the ball boy and sent the pigskin through a net no bigger than his hand was wide. It didn't so much as ripple. Rain broke in sheets across the glass ceiling of the practice field. Wind rattled imperfect panes.

Cold white lights flooded the field, casting everything in a flat, cryptic light. Shadows chased his arms as he threw.

"Put any more on it and you're going to break it," Burton said, adjusting the strap of his pads over his chest. "Trust me, the worst way to pretend you're not injured is by overcompensating. Hurts like hell, too."

"I'm not injured." Warren raised his hands over his head, blew out a breath. Sleep hadn't come the last two nights. He'd been restless, anxious, paranoid. "The trainer says nothing's wrong."

"Gabby?" With a rap sheet of torn ligaments, fractures and snapped collarbones, Burton considered the PT staff his personal employees. He spent equal time on the field and in their offices. According to Cole's intel, Burton's parting gift to the Seahawks therapist had been a custom pink Rolls Royce.

"She said her name was Gabriella."

The Irishmen smirked. "Gabby to me."

"Hypocrite," Warren muttered. The man ripped apart women as a sex but befriended any who prolonged his career.

"What's with the fireballs?"

Warren signaled for another and launched it. Tuesday and Victoria hadn't called, texted, she hadn't even read his texts. *Call me when you land. Text me when you check in. Let me know you get home safe.*

Each time he sent one, he felt more like an ass. Clearly, she was done with him. Another flick of his fingers, another whistle through the net.

He sent her updates like a personal diary. *Shoulders great. Full elbow motion. No swelling. Good practice.*

The last sent less than fifteen minutes ago.

Three practices left in the pre-season. The final game on Sunday.

Then, the GM, Coach, and Victoria—lead recruiter—Steer, would seal themselves behind closed doors until they had fifty-three names. They'd balance salaries, skills, playability, attitude, trade to supplement open positions, pad the practice squad, and cut loose the rest.

Players lingered longer each day, staying late, doing extra, distinguishing themselves. Anything to get a Mountaineers jersey on their back.

Heaving an annoyed grunt, Burton quit fussing with his straps.

"Why are you still here?" Warren asked, throwing another. Burton wouldn't be cut. He was too good. Probably slept like a baby after getting home early.

Even Cole ditched before cool downs. No one questioned their ability, their worth.

"Don't worry about me." Burton scoffed, nodding behind Warren.

Warren turned, surprise lifting his brows. Across the field, Cole's feet were spread, his chin low, thick arms crossed as he dissected tackles meeting head to head.

From the vacant eyes, the bracket around his mouth, Warren understood why Cole hadn't answered his call yesterday.

Right on schedule. Three weeks. Cole had held it off for as long as he could before his resistance splintered. Another woman had been invited into the tackle's bed.

They were a fine pair, he and Cole, bags under their eyes, jaws sore from clenching, haunted by their own fears.

For the first time, Warren wondered if Cole actually lived for the intimacy, fed off the connection, enjoyed it, and it was the goodbyes in the light of day that coated his heart in tar, drained the spirit from his eyes.

Perhaps, like Warren, Cole was happiest in the arms of a lover. When goodbye came, so did the starkness. Warren was an idiot not to realize it sooner. His friend was kinder, smarter, more sophisticated than him in every way, of course he felt more intensely. The women he selected for his rendezvous were indicative of his true nature. Cole evaded the sparkly gazed young beauties, those boasting tight dresses and flirtatious grins, opting instead for the curvy mature types in jeans and hard eyes.

Burton threw off his pads and shirt in a huff and planted a wide foot on the gear like a king claiming freshly conquered land. "Fuck it. I'm shit at subtlety. What have you heard?"

Burton wasn't asking for his own peace of mind. Only a blind man would release him from the team.

"Is Heark coming?"

A punch to the gut would have hurt less. Burton didn't care about Warren. He wanted to know who QB1 would be. Worried the golden king might bond with a different receiver. Head buried in the game, Burton only cared about his yards, his stats.

Warren threw.

"Are ye deaf?"

Ignoring Burton, Warren strode along the twenty yard line, stepping around the dueling linemen to find Cole's side. The two of them foul-faced and stoic.

"You look like someone ran over your cat," Warren told him, watching Burton flash them his middle finger.

"You look like you ate that cat."

They shared a brief look. Yes, they were both crumbling. No, nothing short of a miracle would fix it.

"Hey man," Ninety-eight, Michael Juárez—a solid guard—lifted from his squat. "My bad about Sunday. I'm damned relieved you're not hurt. Would've been my fault. I missed the call."

"Nah," another burly lineman stood. "It was 'cause of me. I was watching the safety. It's hard, bro. There's a lot going on."

"Shit yeah, it's crazy," Juárez replied enthusiastically. "Feels like I need eyes going every direction. We won't let 'em get you again."

A born mentor, Cole said, "It was a dirty hit. Not your responsibility."

"He's right," Warren agreed with a forced smile. "It's not your job to protect me when I don't have the ball. And you'll get better at reading queues. Save the apologies for when you really force me on my ass."

The linemen exchanged a disbelieving side eye. Juárez rubbed his nose on his sleeve, sweat dripped down his face. "Probably won't have a chance."

To everyone's surprise, it was Cole who blurted, "What? You're not getting cut."

Warren stayed silent, glaring at his cleats as fear crept up his legs, finding holds with thick taloned claws. There was one reason a spry, talented, driven guard would think he was leaving.

A current of nerves slithered through the group, faces straining, hands fidgeting. Juárez thought the stitching on his gloves was fascinating.

Warren's hands went limp.

The swing of the fans threatened to knock him over. He wished lightning would strike and shatter the ceiling, let glass and rain stop the inevitable.

Cole set his jaw. "Michael?"

"Midas checked in at the Burlington airport this morning."

Outrage pinched Warren's cheeks, a lump clogged his throat. His greatest fear come to pass.

And he'd gotten it wrong. It wasn't Doyle's arrival that gutted Warren.

Victoria had lied. Little Red had befriended the big bad wolf.

"That doesn't mean anything." Cole's terse response didn't warm any hearts, didn't assuage fears. His tone was missing its usual confidence.

"He ended his contract," Juárez added. "He walked."

Ripples of disbelief rose. Fingers numb, Warren swallowed hard. Black emotion kept him from moving. Kept him from joining the worried mutters. Kept his burning eyes from shutting. A putrid mix of disbelief, betrayal, longing, and hurt.

Then it stopped.

An icy jolt stole over him, locked the feelings away one by one behind foot thick ice dams. Slowed his heart, froze his blood. He took a deep, stuttering breath.

Cole thrust him backward, hauling him by his pads, shoving, growling under his breath, cursing.

When Warren hit the wall, when Cole snarled low, ominous words, warnings, Warren saw it.

The flash of gold leaving the dome.

***

VICTORIA PONDERED THE wineglass in her hand, wondering how it'd shatter, the stem thin and delicate breaking in two, the clear bowl exploding into a thousand tiny shards of glass. Didn't matter if she had the strength to snap it. She could tap the rim just so on the edge of the table and watch red slip over the polished walnut.

A well-placed nick and everyone's dinner would be ruined.

A late tackle and her future had overturned.

Been decided without her consent. Without warning. If Toby hadn't bothered with his *get here now* text, she'd still be in Baltimore, preparing for war.

Weaponless, a captive, Victoria let the waiter clear her untouched bisque and requested another glass of the cabernet. Dark and bitter, each sip stung her lips.

The mention of Gomez's name had cleared them a table at Green Veins, a Michelin contender serving only locally sourced foods. Rustic at its core, the dining room walls displayed detailed maps of the Vermont countryside, the glasses were hand blown on Pine Street, and not a single chair matched. Hers was low-backed and short. The table felt like a chin rest.

In yesterday's velvet wrap dress, a burst of indulgent indigo, she felt like a child on a timeout. Laughs rang across the table. Deep, rough. Victoria added a commiserating smile, watching texts pour into the phone nestled in her lap.

She felt like a coach on draft day, experiencing the longest ten minutes of her life as she called in favors, brokered deals, offered things she didn't yet have.

Toby nudged her elbow, and Victoria jerked up to rejoin the conversation. She'd pleaded with him as she hustled through TSA lines, begged not to have her entire future blown apart because of one bad play.

Cards close to his chest, Toby had listened until she was barefoot, wallet-less, watching her suitcase drift away on the conveyor belt before he told her the name of the restaurant and the time they were meeting.

On her left, Doyle Heark frowned into his drink. He'd wanted Mountain Dew, but settled, fitfully, for a house made lime and butterfly pea seltzer. Flashing a fake sorry-you-didn't-get-your-drink look to him, she tipped her glass back. There wasn't a worse place to sit.

A lighter, she determined idly. After she spilled the wine, she'd send the table up in flames.

Ta—fucking—da.

Gomez, Foss, and Morgan wore matching smug half-smiles, patting their own backs. The kings of meddling, each thirsty for fame.

Oblivious to the happenings around him, Doyle spun his glass, clearing the condensation to gape at his reflection. Displaying obvious ignorance to the happenings around him. A pretty face with a quirky name. If he could sing, Morgan would cast him as Disney's next princess.

Today, he was the bachelorette, and the world competed for his affection. A darling waiting to be wooed.

Victoria smiled again, wider, laughing at the end of one of Morgan's pointless stories.

Despicable. They were competing for Doyle's hand when they were already fucking married to Warren. Reaching around Doyle, Morgan stole the bread from Victoria's salad plate, plucking it apart and throwing it between shining white teeth, reminiscent of a great white devouring prey.

He leaned back in his chair of welded metal and cream upholstery, indolent confidence oozing. Proud that he'd swindled his own player, tore Doyle from a solid contract. A wasted opportunity.

If Morgan had answered her calls, this could've been avoided. She could've told Doyle that leaving the Texan's camp made him radioactive.

Morgan didn't care. He'd gone over her head, spoke around her.

Fuck that. Victoria winked at her ex, hatred bubbling in her stomach, fueled by bitter wine and a detrimental lack of sleep. She would be unyielding, obstinate.

No more playing chess without the queen.

Toby checked his watch, body angled to avoid Foss's swinging hand gestures.

The only guest who seemed to be enjoying themself was Gomez. "I had a jersey specially made for you," he told Doyle's forehead. "Midas across the back. It will go right next to number forty-seven in the front of the Mountain Shop. Which, do you think, will sell faster?"

Doyle shrugged, slicing his chicken into razor thin strips and dispersing them across his plate. A child pretending to eat. "I thought maybe, I don't know, I could change numbers. I only took forty-seven because it was free."

Based on Gomez's tight expression, he'd already had the jerseys printed.

Victoria swung her attention to Doyle, expression patient and encouraging. "Of course. What number do you want?"

Thinking for a moment, Doyle told her, "Double zero would be cool or maybe seven."

"Seven is cliché," Morgan informed dryly. "So is thirteen."

"Jordan wore twenty-three."

Feeling her hands ball into fists, she snuck them under the table. "Twenty-three is Rose's number."

"Then it's open," Morgan said, either missing Victoria's tone or ignoring it.

"It'll be weird without him," Doyle said slowly. "He's always been my back-up. I kind of liked knowing he was watching me."

In one sentence, one slip, Victoria stopped seeing Doyle as ignorant and naïve, he was as devious as Warren claimed, as cruel.

"The tallest blade of grass gets cut first." Victoria held her smile, cheeks stinging.

"Is that a song?" Doyle asked.

"Don't mind her." Morgan tossed her a murderous glare. "She's angry because she tried recruiting you and failed."

Caught off guard, Doyle's fork dropped. "I'd know if we spoke." He shifted in his chair, arm falling over the back of hers to look at her, *really* look at her for the first time, as if she were suddenly worthy of his appraisal.

Just to piss him off, Victoria wrinkled her nose, faked a half gag, and pretended to cover it with a gulp of wine.

Luckily, a shout from the restaurant's front doors, rattling the hundred year windows, stole Doyle's ire.

Borderline hostile, Gomez stood.

"Isn't. This. Cozy?"

Victoria cringed at his voice, eyes shutting, wishing she were drunk, hammered.

Wishing she imagined it.

Not out of the realm of possibilities. His voice had been in her head for days.

I'll protect you.

I love you.

Foss uttered a filthy curse, throwing his napkin on the table.

"How was Texas, Vic? Fucking productive?"

There was no ignoring the seething tone. Victoria rushed to look over her shoulder, wine splattering from her glass, pouring burgundy into Doyle's lap.

Doyle leaped from his chair, jeans a bloody show, cursing about backordered Levi's.

Victoria met Warren's gaze without blinking. Her heart began to thud as she learned that he'd never been angry with her before now. Not truly. He looked at her in a way he never had before, his mouth twisted down at the corner, amber eyes ringed in tragic black.

"Flowers," she said softly, the way a lion tamer spoke to her charge. "Don't make a scene."

Behind her, Gomez calmed the stirring patrons. "It seems there's a misunderstanding. Go about your business."

"I didn't go to Texas." Victoria held her hands up in a calming motion, pushing Doyle's thigh aside to face Warren fully.

She forced herself to hold his gaze.

He looked feral, stripped of his humanity, chin low, chest heaving, jaw tense. Had he run here?

She reached for his looming form. "Let's talk about this."

Abruptly, Warren's lips ticked up in a hateful smirk. "Are you fucking him too?"

She jerked back as if she'd been slapped. "*Warren.*"

Running a hand over his face, he spat a humorless laugh, raw and vile. "Don't answer. I know you won't tell the truth."

"*Warren.*"

"You," Warren said, shoving Doyle's shoulder. "You'll tell me. Did she fuck you?"

Toby stood. The elderly man's concern shredded Victoria's initial shock, cut through the hole in her chest, freed room for logic.

She stood and became a bulwark between the quarterbacks, back to Doyle, chin raised at Warren. "This is my job, Warren. Stop talking."

"Is. She. Fucking. You?" Warren sent a dark look to Gomez, the table. "That's how she got me to stay." With a wicked curve on his mouth, he shook his head at Doyle. "She probably didn't have to. We both know how much you love taking my job."

Warren's gaze sliced back to Victoria, blowing up her life in metered movements, waves pulling a body to sea. "Sorry, baby. You spread your legs for nothing."

"What the fuck, Warren." She lunged, but Doyle was faster, driving Warren back, knocking him into the arms of a waiter.

Quick as a flash, Warren was steady, pulling out of his reach. "Get your hands off me," he snarled, storming back the way he came without a single glance back.

Leaving Victoria in a mess ten times bigger than the one she'd been drowning in.

She wanted to close her eyes, click her heels together. Landing in fucking Kansas would be better than this. But that was impossible, and Victoria never turned from a fight, didn't quit until she had her man. *You're a hunter*, she reminded herself, *a ruthless predator*.

By any means.

Slowly, she swiveled on her heels and smiled at the five men staring down at her.

Chapter Eighteen

OF ALL THE SCENARIOS in which she expected to address the status of her relationship, Victoria least expected this one.

If it wasn't the overwhelming number of people who had joined this discussion, it was the lack of Warren that surprised her most.

No, she corrected, it was the marked intrigue layered in Gomez's stare.

Holding her spine rigid, Victoria waved a hand. "Should we sit?"

Morgan's smirk shone in her periphery. "You're stalling."

Slashing him a hateful look, Victoria schooled her features. "What Warren said... that's not at all what happened."

It sawed at her to repeat the same things she'd told the sexist hotel manager when he'd suggested her liaisons were frequent and her own fault.

Toby wore sympathy on his wrinkled face, melancholy and grief, as if she was a raccoon on the side of the road, legs catty-wampus.

Her small, scrap of hope went up in flames. Her last ally gone. There'd be no recovering, not if she crawled over broken glass naked, not if she traded her soul.

The stone, once smooth and unassuming nestled in her heart, entered a free fall, grew jagged and heavy as it plunged through her stomach. The fight was over. She'd never be one of them. Never be anything other than the lone woman butting in at the table, included solely because of the kindness of a gentle old man.

Warren had assured her demise, her image set in stone. She'd breathe better if he'd locked her into a coffin and thrown her to sea.

Handing Doyle her napkin for the stain, she began damage mitigation. "War—" She jerked her chin down, sucked her teeth, started again. "Rose and I are in a committed relationship. It began shortly after he signed with the Mountaineers."

"It's fine," Morgan told a blithering Doyle. "They're jeans." He forced the quarterback into his chair and snatched his beer before blowing out a deep, frustrated breath. "You were in a committed relationship?" He sounded... sincere, interested.

She lifted her eyes, wary. "Yes."

Squirming in wet jeans, Doyle frowned. "Girls confuse relationships and fucking a lot."

Gomez balked at the language.

Naturally, he accused her of being doe-eyed and in love, while Warren was the playboy. "There's no confusion here. We were dating and exclusive." They were, in reflection, doing just that, sharing meals, carpooling, strolling in the park, sending *good morning* texts.

"Like how we used to fuck?" Morgan asked.

She was going to kill him. Not right away. With no career, no job, no hope for her future, she would have plenty of time to annihilate Morgan Turaco. Luring him into her clutches, shattering his nose with her knuckles, planting a stiletto in his urethra.

"No," she shot back. "Warren actually made me come."

Doyle bit his knuckles to smother a laugh.

"None of this matters," Foss said from behind his phone. "Did you do anything illegal?"

Illegal? Her thoughts froze. She frowned. "What do you mean, illegal? I..." she drifted off, turned her head away, confusion spinning.

"Did you coerce Rose? Did you bribe him to come with your body?"

Not career ending questions. Life ending questions.

Offended on her behalf, Toby cursed.

"This is important," Foss insisted. "Answer."

"No," she said softly.

"Then it's settled," Foss decided, and she felt like she might get on her knees to thank him when the rest of the table nodded. The matter settled.

Gomez, still standing, face inscrutable, summoned Victoria with two fingers. "Miss Steer, join me."

On quivering legs, she reached his side, lightheaded, stomach wrenching. A dutiful servant ready for punishment, for termination.

Gomez smiled at her, eyes dancing in the low lights. He... loved this. The drama.

At once, Victoria understood why Zara had three stepmothers, why they were all invited to the family Christmas. Gomez loved a show. Any show.

"You will finish this," he told her, retrieving sunglasses from his suit coat. "I will forget this meal when I have Midas." He led her to the doors, pushing one open. "Good day, dear, and good luck." A wave of outside heat followed his departure.

Baffled, Victoria turned, nearly crashing into Toby's chest. He held her purse up. "Unless you want to stay for dessert."

She snatched it. Already her phone was ringing. The screen said Cincinnati.

"I don't like my players making scenes," Toby said, opening the door for her. "It detracts from the game."

"I know." She stepped onto the cobblestone, the evening sun dusting her ankles. "I'll fix it."

"Fix it," Toby nodded, attention veering to a splash pad brimming with kids, pounding feet and laughing, wishing the day would never end. "I'm not sure this mess can be fixed." His thumbs slotted into the belt loops of his dad jeans. "Gomez thinks he has Midas. Midas left his contract. It's a match."

"It's not," Victoria argued. "Morgan was stupid. Now that Doyle's unsigned, he'll be desperate. Money's no longer important. We don't need to outbid anyone."

"There's nothing to do then. Our hands are tied in gold knots." He sounded as defeated as she felt.

"If I don't get Midas, Gomez will fire me."

"No. You already failed to deliver Midas, and you didn't lose your job."

"Because Midas was still signed. There was nothing I could do. Now he's a free agent. Any chance your offer is still good?" Had she sunken so low that she'd sit in the same chair for the next forty years, cowing to Gomez. "Don't answer."

"If Gomez fires you, I can't negate it." Stretching a hand over his eyes, the GM squinted in the direction of the lake. "Know this, if Midas dons the green, *I'll* be the one to fire you."

***

IF HE HAD to identify the most crushing moments of his life, Warren was confident Victoria dining with Doyle belonged in the top three, and would remain there, for...

Ever.

A nasty, crooked hate splintered through him as he bound down the narrow halls of his hotel. Behind each door was a player battling their own problems, worrying over cuts, over moving—again—letting their families down, recovering from injury. The pre-season left no one untouched.

When did football stop being fun?

When did he stop looking forward to hitting the field, to beating a team?

Years ago?

No. He'd had fun tossing the ball with Burton.

With the side of his fist, Warren knocked on the door of 208.

Cole answered without hesitation, asking, "Where did you get that shirt?"

"This?" Warren pulled at the standard Mountaineers shirt, green with the white emblem, soft cotton. "The team sent it. I don't know from where." Moving around Cole's wide stance, Warren paused.

Full house. Moore's feet dangling off the kitchenette counter, Burton's spread legs smothered the couch, and Miles stayed pinned to the wall, fingers splitting the cheap white blinds to peer at the parking lot.

"I didn't get a shirt," Cole said from behind him. Not informing Warren, but the room.

"I'll give you mine if you want it that bad."

Burton let out a raucous laugh, severing the stifling tension. "Do it. It'll be like stuffing a ham in a sausage casing."

"Bad image," Miles grunted, keeping his focus out the window.

"Who else got one?" Cole asked, heading for the mini-fridge.

"They gave me one," Burton announced proudly. There was a pause, and he shifted, sat forward. "Maybe I should leave."

Warren took stock of the room. The sullen mood. The most important players on the team. What were they worried about? "What's going on here? What are you—"

It hit him.

Each one had big, fat salaries. Each one was brought in by Victoria. The door shook under a firm knock. Warren opened it as Cole uncapped a dark beer.

"Asher," Warren greeted the brown-eyed wide receiver. Another whale, another one of Victoria's.

She'd stacked the team with talent, as was evident in this room. At a known cost, a gamble, no money for an all-star quarterback.

Sweeping dark hair off his forehead, Asher asked, "Any news?"

Warren's problems magnified. It wasn't only him at risk if Doyle came. The men in this room, their salaries would be slashed with Doyle's arrival. Their agents wouldn't accept the terms even if they wanted to stay. Another team would make an offer and they'd be scattered across the country while Doyle picked out his visor color.

Packed bags waiting against the wall next to Cole's bed. *Packed.* Decision made.

For several seconds, Warren couldn't think.

Then Burton grunted. "Your girlfriend screwed us."

Moore leaned back, dropping his head against the wall, body slack. Usually chipper, annoyingly upbeat, his brows were pinched together, his lips compressed. He was young. He hadn't been through this yet, this disappointment, the fear of an unknown tomorrow.

Victoria *had* screwed them. She'd taken a risk, a hard, merciless risk with all of their lives to make a name for herself. Having failed that, she pivoted, retreated, recalculated.

She'd looked out for number one.

And yet, Warren couldn't stop the slight growl coming up his throat. "She hasn't done anything to you." So many emotions were running through him he couldn't pin one—defensiveness, contempt, envy, grief. Fury.

He saw Victoria's hand on Doyle, them sitting together, Morgan smiling.

"She brought Midas here," Miles told the window.

Warren fumed. "Fuck off, Miles. Your contract will be bought while you're sleeping. People want you. All of you. I'm the only one losing his spot."

Moore's snort drew attention. No longer was he caught in despair. He perched forward, hands curled over the yellow linoleum counter, lips ticked in a slight curve.

"Got something to say, rookie?" Warren asked.

"Yeah," Moore replied. "This is a sport. You don't get a free pass. Do you know many people would kill for even the opportunity to play pro-ball?"

"She promised Warren he'd start," Burton fired back, anger swelling.

"So start," Cole murmured to the neck of his Guinness. His eyes were hard, unbending as he took a swig. "Midas isn't any better than you, but he battled for it. He begged to play. He fought."

Warren's chest tightened. "By throwing me under the bus. I taught him everything."

"That's the game!" Moore blurted, hopping off the counter, crossing the room. "You have to look out for number one."

"He's right," Asher butt in. "No one will fight for you but you."

Warren looked to Cole for his advice and the tackle shrugged. "They're not wrong," he said. "But if you decide you don't want to fight, it's no trouble for me. I'll go back to Texas. I haven't sold the house yet."

Moore gaped. "That's the most I've ever heard him say."

"You don't like Texas. You're not going back," Warren said gruffly.

Cole wasn't sad or angry, but certain. "I am if Midas comes."

Asher scratched the back of his neck. "Me too. I looked at the caps. I don't know about how Toby Zither will balance the rest of you, but I'm gone."

"I'm staying," Moore said. "They got me on a steal. I'm not worried about a trade. I don't want to play with Doyle Heark. We overlapped in college. He throws low. I'll be the first receiver to have neck problems from scooping so much."

"It doesn't matter. There's only one game left and Foss won't let me play. How am I supposed to fight if I'm benched?"

Burton's head dropped back with a laugh. "I remember the first time a coach told me I couldn't play. Right after I blew out the left." He pounded a fist against his knee. "He said two months and in the second week, I was on the field. The fight for your spot doesn't end when you step off the grass."

Slowly, in the way giants moved, one lumbering limb at a time, Burton rose. "You're a quarterback. Find an option and throw. Block the rest out."

***

FUMBLING FOR HER phone, Victoria refused the call, and cornered Morgan in front of the waffle maker.

"Fuck, Vic. It's a little early to be breathing the same air, don't you think?"

"Cry me a river, Morgan. You think I want to share air with you at any time of day? Your waffle's burning." She reached around him to squeeze the waffle maker clamp tight.

Insurance.

No one dismissed a crazy person when they had hostages.

Having been awake since dinner last night, Victoria felt arson level crazy. "First you steal from me." A strange, maniacal laugh bubbled out of her. "Then you steal from me again, and now you're scrapping my team?"

"C'mon, Vic. I'm hungry."

"I'm mad."

Morgan pulled at his unkempt hair. "I don't care about the team, okay? *Your* boss Gomez called Doyle directly. Without consulting me. After I reprimanded the petulant shit, he told me about the offer. As an agent, I could not in good conscience pass on it."

"How did Gomez even get his phone number?"

"My waffle," Morgan croaked.

Victoria clasped tighter.

Scowling, Morgan said quickly, "Because he's a moron. Some girl he slept with put it on Reddit and it exploded to Facebook and Twitter. I had to change his number."

"His manager didn't?" she asked, hardening her grip on the stainless steel handle. The smell of burned batter permeated the air.

The hotel breakfast was a la carte. Free range on bread butts, unflavored yogurt cups, raspberry jelly, and a single, coveted waffle maker, all artfully arranged on the concierge desk. Diners were provided a selection of fine seating options, including the stone hearth of the drafty twenty foot fireplace, a metal table in the parking lot—no canopy—and the bar. Enjoy your raspberry butt toast with the stench of gin and stale vomit.

In short, it was not a Gomez hotel.

Victoria never wanted to leave.

"He doesn't have a manager." Morgan knees buckled in anguish. "Come on. I'm starving."

"What's it going to take for Doyle to disappear?"

Recoiling, Morgan grimaced. "Is that what you're doing? Is my waffle Doyle? Are you going to soak the golden locks in turpentine and play throw the lit cigarette?"

"Jesus, Morgan. There are kids here." She smiled around his shoulder at the building line of hotel guests. Everyone wanted waffles. "I don't care where he goes. I only want him gone. Away."

He stared at her as if he didn't recognize her, mouth parted, light brows drawn. "You really aren't just fucking Rose."

She flashed him a sardonic glare. "No fucking shit. I'm not a dirty little liar like you."

"Wrong, we're all liars Vic."

"I'm—"

"Ma'am," a squeaky voice interrupted. A woman in pinstripe black stepped away from her spot at the front desk to address the rising black smoke. "Could you please release the waffle maker?"

"Oops!" Victoria gasped, whipping her hand back. "I didn't realize the light went off."

"It's why we broke up," Morgan informed the woman's back. "She doesn't know when to stop."

Hastily, Morgan freed his waffle, groaning at the ribbed circle of black. Taking a plate, Victoria flipped it out for him, and snatched his elbow before he could run. "Let's eat in your room," she crooned.

Devoid of his usual suit, it was harder to hate Morgan. Sleepy green eyes and a sad puppy pout, as if she'd burned his house, not a quarter cup of pancake batter.

Tapping his finger on the waffle, he let Victoria lead him to the second floor, feet stomping. "It's my cheat day," he complained. "I needed this."

It was late in the morning, checkout fifteen, twenty minutes ago. So Victoria guessed. She had yet to spend a single night in her bed. It'd become a walk-in closet, a replica of her abandoned apartment in Newport. Empty fridge, trash can full of clothes tags, perfectly made bed.

The second floor hallway was empty save for a cleaning cart reeking of bleach, and a couple uncollected newspapers resting against doors with *do not disturb* signs dangling from the handles. As they strode down the abstract muddled brown carpet, Victoria wondered how long it'd be before a Gomez Burlington shut the doors on this place. How quickly people would run, sprint, fall over themselves for a taste of luxury.

She'd come to love the brick simple alarm clocks on the night-stands, the hair dryer mounted next to the landline, the scratchy drapes, and the impossible to interpret cartoonish exit plans painted on the back of every door.

Each scratch, stain, and burning clean smell reminded her of what Gomez wanted. A gilded world. He didn't care if Doyle was an idiot who pouted over Mountain Dew and ate chicken tenders. Doyle fit Gomez's aesthetic, like the lilies in the Gomez Houston, beautiful, breathtaking, a sight one had to visit, behold.

Morgan stopped to withdraw his plastic room key, still complaining, "It's my cheat day. Not for the week. The month, Vic. Understand? Imagine getting chocolate one day a month."

"I'll buy you an entire strawberry cheesecake if you help me." Victoria propped her shoulder against the wall, crinkling the textured brown wallpaper.

His hand paused short of the door scanner as he regarded her with a sympathetic smile. "I'm surprised you remembered."

There was no time for nostalgia, not with Morgan, not the hotel. Victoria flicked her attention down the hall to watch a maid dump dirty towels into a hamper. She lowered her voice to say, "The GM and Coach prefer Rose, but Gomez is overruling them."

Morgan was nodding before she finished. "And he wants Midas."

"Yes."

"Then sign Midas."

Annoyance rising, Victoria glanced over her shoulder to make certain no one was approaching, and lowered her voice to a hysteric whisper, "Were you not listening? I don't want him. The deal will blow apart the entire team. Doyle won't even win with the scraps and stragglers."

"It doesn't matter, Vic." Morgan's eyes turned round with exasperation. "You work for Gomez. He wants Midas. End of Story. You're not thinking like a recruiter or an agent," he said, still clutching his key and waffle. "You formed a personal attachment, and it's clouding your judgement. You're trying to win checkers without throwing out any of the pieces."

Victoria felt her face contorting, spasming. "I'm shoving Doyle off the board."

"You shouldn't be on the board at all." Morgan had to shift the waffle to his forearm to gesture above their heads. "You're above it. *We're* above it. We're puppet masters, not their friends. I knew you'd do this," he muttered. "This is why I took your notes. You aren't like me."

"You're wrong," Victoria said acidly.

Heaving a sigh, Morgan banged his forehead against the door and groaned. "Here's what's going to happen." He swallowed, straightened his back and bit into his waffle. Black crumbled down his t-shirt. "Midas is going to be a Mountaineer. I'm going to gouge the team for him and see him again in five years for negotiating. Do I think he's going to like the mountains? No. Do I give a shit? When I'm making bank off his misery? No."

A leaded weight of despondency settled over her as Victoria's lungs squeezed. "Those are my options?" The words scraped up her throat, her eyes burned. "Heartless bitch or fired?"

Another bite stained his teeth a dull gray. He spoke quickly, trying to snap her spine back together. "You wanted to work in football. Unless you want to be a manager, those options aren't changing." He rubbed a hand over his mouth, spreading black dust down his chin. "I tried telling you not to do it."

An indignant snort came from her. As if Morgan could tell her to do anything. "I built this team, Morgan." Her voice broke.

She hated pleading, hated the whine in her words, the rising waiver as she spoke, hated bearing her broken soul to Morgan, a man without one. The race of her heart became white noise as her shoulders pulled together. Sharp spikes drove into her chest, sucked her lungs flat.

"I conquered the impossible task. No one else wanted it. I did it." Her eyes stung. A bleak feeling chilled and blistered her skin. "And none of it matters? It's over because I want what's best for the team? How is that the end? How is that fair? I did everything I could."

"I didn't say you couldn't do it. I said you shouldn't. It would ruin you. Turn you into me."

The waffle stopped midair, inches from Morgan's open mouth, as Victoria belted out a sob. She couldn't hold it back any longer, she let it free. Tears and snot, she choked on her own breaths. A headache bloomed in her temples. Her arms shook. Words collapsed in her mouth, cleared it of moisture, left her in stricken silence.

"Stop," Morgan whispered, checking up and down the hall. "Stop, please." His key card patted her shoulder.

Victoria stared, dumbfounded, taking seconds to realize he was comforting her. She blinked against a burning wet blur. Tears skidded past her cheeks and wet her dress. "I don't know what to do."

"Stop crying."

She shut her eyes, closed her lips, back shuddering with sobs. Pressure built in her body and Morgan's voice became muffled as his face blurred in front of her, a twist of grimace and panic.

"Okay, that's better," Morgan floundered. Something hard and black hit Victoria's toes.

She gasped, the whimpers starting anew. Helpless. She'd torch the emotion off her heart if she could, leave it scarred forever to forget the ache that had no end. The end of her legacy, the collapse of her dream. Her brilliant team wouldn't play a single game together.

And Warren—

With clumsy, paw-like hands, Victoria wiped her face, tears blooming afresh.

Morgan's hands stole hers, pulled them from mopping her cheeks. "Stop. I'll help you. You win. I'll work with you."

She cried harder, feeling hollow and numb. "What's even the point?"

"It's like the *Wizard of Oz*, I'm the Tin Man, you're Dorothy, and Midas's got the mane. Let's kill Gomez."

A hiccupped laugh broke through her. "That's not—" Fresh tears streamed, her back shook.

"Please, for the love of god, stop crying. It gives me hives."

Her fingers slipped as she patted her cheeks. Then it was only the sound of her swallowing down big gulps of air while Morgan stared on in terror. She shook her head and cleared her throat. "I can't believe I actually liked you."

His shoulders sunk with relief. "Enough to memorize my favorite food," he noted smartly. "Relax. I liked the thing you did with your tongue. Magnificent."

Though her slitted eyes, a laugh bubbled up her throat, scraping and scratching. Using her knuckles, she finished clearing her face. Morgan being nice was almost as mortifying as crying in front of him. "Every guy likes that."

"Can you teach it to my new girl?" he asked, tucking his empty plate under an arm and showing her his screensaver. "She's got an ass like a pound cake."

They were back, no more crying, no comforting. They were two survivors trying not to push the other one off the boat.

"Lovely." Victoria's sarcasm dripped. "When's the wedding?"

His voice was dry and edged with mocking. "I'm going to be like Leo. I get older, the girls get younger."

"So you'll never have a genuine relationship because all the good ones will want more." Her mind went blank, and a cautious smile lifted her lips. "They'll want to get married, settle down, find an equal they're better paired for." She touched her mouth, thoughts spinning. "They deserve better than Morgan Turaco."

"Yeah, I'm standing right here."

Yanking her chin up, Victoria planted a hand on her hip. "I need to talk to Doyle."

Chapter Nineteen

Victoria's heart stalled and her hand froze halfway to her hair. "It's fake!"

Morgan shoved her inside his door, kicked the waffle after, and yanked it shut behind them.

"Jesus, have a little decorum," he grunted, securing the lock as he glanced through the peephole.

The room was a replica of hers, down to the wet dog lemon smell. Twin bed with middle school boy blue striped sheets, white Ikea desk, four wide shaded lamps instead of an overhead light, their bulbs leaving dark arching stains on the eggshell walls.

Or so Victoria assumed.

She couldn't look away from Doyle, the golden god. A transparent plastic poncho covered his bare chest, white paste—bleach—clung to his hair. A cloying, burning scent smothered the lingering burned waffle stench. Her own scalp tingled as she beheld the biggest fraud in the history of sports.

Fifteen-year-old Victoria threatened death if she didn't get string highlights.

She'd sat in the hair salon chair for two hours while her skull burned and her retinas bled, the smell striking years off her life. For what? To look like a Jessica Simpson wash out for winter formal.

"You're not a blonde." She turned to face Morgan. "He's not a blonde."

Dryly, Morgan said, "I want the crybaby back."

A smile edged her face as she spotted a red box on the bathroom counter. Ultra-light honey blonde. "I knew I recognized that shade," she muttered, holding the Revlon box to her chest. "I knew it was unattainable."

Midas, six feet of football stardom, hesitated, dark eyes darting between his agent and the intruder. "You can't tell anyone." He sounded like a boy begging his teacher not to tattle to his parents.

"She won't," Morgan assured. "Victoria suddenly understands the value of the gold maker brand."

"How does no one know?" she asked, reading the warning label and divesting herself of the box before she developed ten strains of cancer. "Do you bleach downstairs too?"

"He shaves," Morgan answered, earning a surprised look. "What?" He shrugged, not embarrassed in the slightest. "It was my first question, too."

Delighted, Victoria sat on the bed, full on grinning. "You should wax," she told Doyle. "Less upkeep. No in-grown hairs." Cheeks stinging with humor, she crossed her legs, tapped her toes. Doyle Heark the fraud. She couldn't wait to tell Warren—

"Why is she here?" Doyle whined, scowling at her comfortable on his bed.

With nothing to hide, Victoria let him drink in the peep toe Madden wedges, her baby pink slip dress. After months of chasing him, followed by weeks of avoiding him, when they locked eyes, Victoria felt no rush of emotion, no pleased thrill along her skin.

Her appetite had changed, and now the hunt bored her.

"Is Rose right? Are you here to 'convince' me to stay?" He used air quotes for *convince*.

Normally, she'd punch him, but she'd already suffered a windfall of polarizing emotions. Today, she laughed at the absurdity. Doyle midway through a dye job trying to demean her.

Impossible.

Patience not so thick, Morgan sent his client a harsh look. "Watch how you talk to her, or I'll let it slip that the dye boxes are from room 212, not 213."

"Not before I fire you."

"Victoria won't let you," Morgan said, waiting for her to pick up the baton.

"He's jealous he doesn't have a signature look," she crooned, tracing invisible numbers on the bed sheet. "I've got my bangs. You, the color. We're visionaries."

Doyle gave her a skeptical glance. "Why are you here?"

Behind Doyle, Morgan scrounged the mini-fridge, muttering about light headedness.

Victoria's gaze returned to Doyle's face. "I want to talk about Rose."

"Your 'boyfriend'?" Again with the air quotes.

"Yes," she hissed, feeling territorial. "And much more."

Morgan fake vomited into his hands. "I told you, you were soft."

Bestowing her ex with a familiar, offensive finger, Victoria didn't miss a beat. "How long until your scalp starts to burn and your eyes water?"

Playing tough, Doyle shrugged. "Ten minutes until I rinse and deep condition."

Deciding to humor him, she flashed an impressed, you're-so-strong look. "Great. I'll wait and then we're going on a walk." At Doyle's questioning glance to his agent, she added, "Alone. Morgan still needs breakfast."

Always on, always a bastard, Morgan stood. "And cake since you're buying."

It took twenty minutes for the golden-haired lion to shower, blow dry, apply a thickening mousse, tweeze out stray dark strands, and make out with his reflection. With great care, Victoria pampered and preened alongside him, removing the runaway mascara, rolling hotel ice under her eyes, plumping her bangs until they said sexy chic.

Warren didn't preen. He stepped out of the shower looking devilish and handsome, crooked smile, thick hair extra dark, water gliding over sinew and bone. The mere fact he didn't care how he looked made him sexier.

Fresh and clean, black and blonde, Victoria and the southern lion departed.

The morning sunlight fell with bright menace onto the cobblestone sidewalks of downtown Burlington. Church Street, the center of the city, awoke slowly, taking time to warm and welcome.

Arms wrapped around her waist, Victoria pointed out the landmarks listed on google maps: city hall, an oldish church steeple, a big plain rock in the middle of the street.

As she finished her tour, explaining to both herself and him who Ethan Allen was, two University of Vermont students, early for the upcoming semester, stopped Doyle for a photo and a handshake, promising to tag him, to watch him play, welcoming him to Vermont.

"You're going to like it here." Chattering with cold, Victoria stopped in an alcove between buildings, hands sliding up and down her arms. "Did you know this is the biggest town in Vermont?"

Doyle's eyes went wide with surprise. "No shit?"

"Yup. In fact, we're on the busiest street."

"No." More than disbelief colored his rejection.

"Oh yes," Victoria continued as if she hadn't heard the change. "It's smaller than your old college." Barely, she didn't add. "If every single person in this city right now went to a Mountaineer game, only half of the Texans stadium would be filled. How quaint."

Striding forward, ignoring the fall of his features, Victoria led him south, heels clacking against the cement sidewalk. "Isn't it nice to walk without being swarmed with fans? After a big win, you could go to any bar here and have a nice, private drink."

Doyle followed her down College Street, head lowered, hands buried in his jean pockets.

They passed a closed brewery and a closed coffee shop as the terrain tipped downward, Lake Champlain overtaking the horizon.

Before Doyle had time to admire, Victoria prattled on, doubling down. "I assume Morgan explained the benefits of rural living. No press, no jersey chasers, no drama. Who knows if Vermont even wants a football team, the market's untested." A cool breeze coasted up the street, nipping her skin. "Don't worry. An empty stadium doesn't mean you won't get paid."

"I'm not dumb," Doyle said crisply, irritation evident. "Stop trying to make me leave. I can't. I left the Texans. This is the only team with a QB slot."

Victoria swung around, cutting off his next step. He figured her out, *fine*. Time to Ross Geller this shit and *pivot*. "You're the most well-recognized player in the league right now. You could go anywhere. Pick a city and I'll make it happen. Denver? They have a rabid fan base. What about Pittsburg? They sell out their stadium win or loss. They like football more than teenage girls like K-Pop."

"Why should I listen to you?" Doyle asked pragmatically. "Morgan wants the Mountaineers, you want the Steelers, what's the next person going to tell me to do? Dolphins?"

"Morgan is only motivated by money." Later, she'd feel bad about trashing him after he helped her.

"You're not any better," Doyle accused, running a hand through his hair. "You just want Rose."

Victoria considered Doyle for a moment, looking past the rich brown eyes, the perfect unattainable hair, the cheekbones, the movie magic. She peeled it back, laid down the pieces before her and... Doyle Heark wasn't dumb. Quite the opposite. He was damn smart. He'd cultivated a vapid, childish image to further his own agendas, to be forgiven for stupid mistakes, to protect his ass.

"Yes," Victoria said plainly. "I promised Warren a spot, but that doesn't mean that I can't help you too."

He laughed quietly, disbelieving. "How can you do both?"

"Are you hungry? I haven't had breakfast. You eat bagels or just mainline Mountain Dew?"

A spark came to his dark eyes. "I hate Mountain Dew. Signed a three-year sponsorship with them. If a place serves it, I have to order it."

"You keep surprising me."

He sucked his teeth, nodding over her head. "C'mon, let's get you out of the cold."

***

IN BLEAK SILENCE, Warren stood shoulder to shoulder with Cole, watching as Coach strode across the field.

Anger flooded Warren's system, thick bands of spiked rope lashing around his lungs, tightening, pulling, and yanking.

Poison swam in his veins, stark and savage, hateful and terrorizing.

Doyle Heark had pulled his last straw. Warren could stomach the blows to himself, to his life, but he'd build a cage of his own bones before he let Heark rip apart his friends.

"Don't go easy on him," said Cole, voice more monotone than usual. Disgruntled, because he'd discovered the team had, indeed, stopped sending him new gear, new clothes, and playbooks as if he'd already been cut. For Cole, it wasn't the threat of being traded that angered him. It was the underhandedness.

Dismissing him without dismissing him.

The offensive tackle respected honest, straight talkers. For the team to dance around the truth—there wasn't a worse insult.

Across the field in a matter of seconds, Warren felt Cole's stare follow him as he called, "Coach."

Coach didn't slow his pace for Warren, eyes pinned to his clipboard, head shaking. "Don't ask," he began. "I can't say anything about *you know who*."

Warren measured out a carefree smirk. "Doyle Heark is the last person on my mind."

A snort from Coach. Guess Warren wasn't selling casual.

The Mountaineers' head coach stopped, lifted his ball cap and set it down again. "You're worried. I get it." He tucked the clipboard under his arm, fingers wrapping around the corded whistle at his neck. "But I coach whatever team I have. I give opinions and try not to drink when they're ignored. Doesn't matter how loud I yell. Understand?" He took off again, bounding to the goalpost, whistle fit between his teeth.

Warren chased close behind, sending a backward he's-in-a-mood glance to Cole.

"I'm only asking," Warren said, "for you to play the team you have. I'm on your team. I want to play."

"No." The pierce of his whistle set Warren's teeth on edge. Coach thumped the clipboard against his thigh. "Round up!"

A team huddle, the end of the day.

Warren stepped in front of Coach, cutting him off as a human blockade. "I understand more than anyone how frustrating it is to have no say."

"I've seen you play. I don't need to see any more. Out of the way."

Warren didn't move. His nerves writhed with frenzied panic. The instinct to step back, to defer, to quit, surfaced. He strangled it and sucked in a measured breath. "I'm here. I want to play."

"I need to evaluate Grant, determine his range."

"Fuck Grant. I'm ten times the quarterback he is."

A slow, echoing clap silenced the chatter on the field.

"Spoken like a true quarterback." Doyle's lilted voice rolled over Warren like a swell of thick exhaust gas.

Gritting his teeth, Warren turned. The team had gathered in a nebulous blob, mouths shut, eyes peeled as the gold king and his former back-up went toe to toe.

For the first time, Warren found Doyle lacking. Truly lacking. A good three inches shorter than himself, legs thin enough to be scrawny, tight purple bags under his eyes. Even the smell of his aftershave, an acrid bitterness, was offensive.

Knocking his shoulders back, Warren licked at his canines, preparing for the taste of blood. "Doyle," he greeted in a cold tone, taking on the confidence of a king.

The quarterback dipped his head in return, blonde hair sliding in layered waves across high cheekbones. He sidestepped, stretched his arm out.

Victoria trod forward, steady—*beautiful*—indifferent as Doyle claimed her shoulders as a personal perch for his arm.

Pressure built in Warren's chest, absorbing each part of her like flipping through the pages of a book. Her face, clear of makeup, black hair tangled, bangs blown back. Razor thin straps held up a slippery looking dress the same color as her rare and cherished blush.

Without calling the image forward, he saw her in his bed, squinting with one eye as her phone rang, the light of dawn a transcendent glow caressing the skin not covered by his. The tender smile that followed, the press of her lips on his shoulder before she abandoned the sheets, skin breaking out in goosebumps at the chill.

Exactly how it did now.

A corner of Victoria's mouth curled in a reluctant hello. "Flowers."

She looked calculating and utterly self-assured, and Warren understood how, precisely, this woman broke him free of his contract, how she could sit across a table, smile and win. A deck up her sleeve.

Heat flooded him, the kind that scorched rather than simmered, lashed and corroded, heat that consumed and killed.

He was shaking his head, frantic, lungs failing. Worse, seeing it the second time, it was worse, seeing the easy touches between them, Doyle's palm skating up and down Victoria's arm.

Warren wanted to twist away, run, smash a brick wall. Steal a ball and throw straight up to shatter the ceiling.

Because he couldn't, in that moment, as furious as he was, fault her.

For pivoting to keep her job, to protect herself. For overflowing with the very thing he lacked. Action, agency, drive. Spirit and stubbornness. A will to move mountains.

For years, Warren had been pissed at the world for turning on him, and not once did he ask them to turn fucking back. Victoria did.

She'd part the sea if she had to.

Does Cole like Texas?

Her question surfaced from his memories.

It'd seemed conversational but wasn't. She wouldn't have moved Cole to Vermont if he'd liked Texas. Burton had been miserable too. She'd discovered Miles fighting and blood covered. She'd rescued them.

The thought set Warren's every internal rhythm off-kilter, heart and lungs stuttering and shrinking. Expanding.

For a ruthless, manipulative woman, Victoria had betrayed herself.

She hadn't built a team. She'd constructed Utopia.

Plucked players from unhappy existences and corralled them to a new start.

The inanity that he'd fought her abraded his bones, severed ligaments. He'd emerged from his grief and snapped at a visionary, when he'd never, not fucking once, tried to fight for himself.

Desolation and defeat had weighed on his shoulders, those of his friends. With a fire too bright to behold, Red had torched the black emotions. Replaced them with pride and twinkling hope.

"I don't care," Warren mumbled, heart bounding, hurting, barely able to stop from sinking to his knees. He understood now. "I don't care."

And *Christ*, he'd missed her. How he missed her. He'd been miserable without her.

He didn't care if she fucked Doyle.

She could fuck half of teammates. It wouldn't stop him from wanting her.

He would never hate her for fighting, for shredding through problems, refusing to quit. Standing up for herself. Seizing when asking didn't work.

Betrayal stained his past, and he'd let it.

Betrayal fueled Victoria. She'd harnessed the feeling of defeat and suffocated it with power.

"I think we lost him," Doyle joked, waving a hand over Warren's face.

"Stop," Victoria hissed. Her voice, even angry, was like aloe soothing a deep burn.

Doyle's hand continued to stroke up and down Victoria's arm, as if he wanted to hide the goosebumps. "Good to see you, Rose. You look lean."

Playing with the ends of her hair, Victoria gave Warren a side-long glance, a flash of hot, infinite blue melting him.

"Is Grant my number two?" Doyle asked Coach Foss, grin cocky.

Warren bit his tongue as Foss and Doyle interacted. His attention was on Victoria, his body begging him to reach out, to touch, to hold. *I'm sorry*, he tried to say. *I won't interfere anymore. Do what you have to. Keep fighting. You're so close.*

He knew how important this job was to her. She'd told him the day that met, it was all she lived for.

A strangled sigh wrenched from his throat, earning odd glances, a flash of blue.

Victoria needed Doyle.

Warren's knees buckled. He felt his body sway forward. He shook it off, firmed his jaw.

He'd been fighting her. Trying to stay. The harder he pushed, the less chance she had. He had to fight *with* her. First—

"I can teach Grant," Warren blurted at the mention of a green QB two.

Surprise colored Doyle. "You *are* quite the teacher."

Confused, but distracted, Coach rolled his eyes. "Fine. Rose will teach Grant. But Heark, these are closed practices, until you sign—"

"That's why I've brought Victoria, my new manager. She's here to start the process."

Blowing a breath through his nose, Coach rubbed his temples. "Shit, this feels like high school football again. Miss Steer knows where the GM's office is. I'll see you Monday, Heark. Good luck."

The rest of the team followed Coach to the locker rooms, grumbling, casting last, interested peeks over their shoulders.

No one spoke until it was only the three of them. The buzz of the overhead lights, the whirr of the fans.

Disregarding Doyle's existence, Warren faced Victoria, asking softly, "Can we talk?"

Doyle's hand slid off her shoulder as she stepped back, retreated. "I'm late for a flight," she told the ground. "Are you taking care of your shoulder?" She checked her phone, flicking her gaze up at Warren's silence.

Enemies. That's what he'd let them become, because of jealousy, because of pride, ignorance, and selfishness. "Victoria. Will you look at me? For one second?"

Her fingers paused on her phone, but her head stayed down, her body rigid.

"Red?" One last broken plea.

"I don't have the time for this," she said sharply, spinning on her heels, calling back, "Midas."

His name on her tongue. Strength born of a surge of violence sent Warren charging forward.

Doyle filled the space between him and her. "Let's not make another scene."

Chapter Twenty

WARREN FELT LIKE HE'D been thrashing and bucking the frigid grip of the lake's bottom for three damn days, on the cusp of the end.

And in a handful of seconds Doyle Heark drowned him. Defending Victoria he understood, though she'd never admit it, there were times solid brawn won.

But defending her from Warren... knowing he deserved it, he'd hurt her, knowing Doyle had, for once, the high ground.

Black, oily disgust stirred in his body, throwing sparks, blistering. Warren detonated, shoving the golden usurper back, wild rage slipping its leash, slinking to a bloodlust prowling alongside him.

Bind his hands, take his sight, his legs, he bade the Olympians. Otherwise, this fight would not be even. A maelstrom of emotions revived sore muscles, smoothed unfamiliar movements, caressed a lack of self-preservation.

Hand balling into a fist, Warren crowded Doyle, caught the collar of his shirt. Funny how he'd forgot Doyle was smaller.

The reminder brought menace in its wake. Towering over the so-called king, Warren said coldly, "You better believe I'm going to make a fucking scene." Something dark filled his veins, something unyielding and thick. "You're not leaving me," he told Victoria. "You can't push me away."

"She can't, but I can." Doyle threw his back into a push.

"We'll see about that." The thought of despising Victoria for leaving became foreign weeks ago. Half insane, he vowed to follow her. First, she'd been an incessant nuisance, a tease, and then a prude, and finally something else entirely. She'd become the light in his mornings, the peace in his nights, the most important thing in his life.

Being apart hadn't diminished her importance but revealed it. She'd become *more* important.

Not like football.

He'd survive without football.

To live without Victoria's lewd humor, her quick asides, seeing her face break from pleasure, impossible.

She was better than him, baring her truth, not correcting people's assumptions of her, wearing them like a scarlet letter, and refusing to quit.

The vicious recruiter who rescued players from themselves.

Who beamed at the prospect of capsizing. Flew like she'd been born to the skies, and loved like a purveyor of sin and seduction.

"She's had enough of your scenes," Doyle muttered, smoothing his shirt.

When had Doyle ever raced to the defense of another? Doyle, the golden narcissist. He loved her too. Of course. No man could resist Victoria Steer on a mission.

Warren switched tactics. "I get it, okay? I know how intoxicating she can be, but I won't hurt her, I promise you that I just... a little time, we need—"

"No."

"Five minutes. I need to tell her," he stopped. "Fuck this." He jerked to the side, avoiding Doyle's hands. "Victoria. Stop."

Resilient to her core, her steps merely slowed, the hem of her dress fluttering as she glided forward.

"I'm not going to fight you anymore," he told the lovely curves of her shoulders. *Turn around. Look at me.* "Move who you want, take me off the roster. I don't care."

Blue flashed over her shoulder, tens of yards away and it struck him like white, hot lightning.

Pushing the phone back from her mouth, she looked past Warren, "Midas, we're late."

Warren started forward, desperation peaking. "I love you, Red. Please, stop, I love you."

Her lips were red and puffy, as if she'd been biting them, swallowing back arguments. "Do your job," she said, no hint of emotion, no break in her determined expression as she peered up at the executive offices overlooking the field.

"No," came Warren's flippant response. "No. I don't care about it anymore, I—"

"Do. Your Job." This came from behind Warren, in Doyle's low timbre. His elbow clipped Warren's ribs as he passed.

Victoria's phone rang against her ear, jolting her.

Four yards later, Doyle hovered at her side, head bowed in deference. Almost reluctantly, Victoria turned to face the golden haired wonder, lips moving.

How Warren used to hate Doyle. Despise him.

Now, he wanted to be him, befriend him, warm the bench for him.

Victoria offered one final glance to Warren. Eyes piercing him with the intensity of a heat storm, crackling energy, whipping at dry air.

Then she was gone.

***

ACCORDING TO VICTORIA'S calculations—minimal and mood based—she approached the limits of her sanity. Shuffling from building to building, plane to plane, she felt like a trained seal launching itself through flaming hoops. Red nose included.

The clock was getting to her. She heard the swing of its hands when she blinked. The gentle slash struck her like a gong, forcing her to focus.

Saturday night was lost on a red eye. Each bump, hell, every sway of the plane had sparked a tremor. Fear that things she once believed in, trusted—her gut, planes, the whisk of a sturdy wind from the east propelling her home—would crumble, disintegrate.

The engines of the plane would seize.

The wind would die.

Her plan would fail.

Would Warren understand if it did?

I don't care, he'd said on the field. Muttered with loathing stuck to his throat. Exhausted, freezing, the three meaningless words unraveled her, stole her air, her mind. Doyle's warm arm on her shoulders had saved her from collapsing. His composure steeled her to conceal the inner turmoil, the awakening storm.

Then Warren had said three different words.

Which did he mean?

The question packed tightly against her, encasing her in a shroud of worry.

In the darkness of her mind, she thought he could only have a reason for the first. He hated her.

Perhaps that was the reason he'd used love. A brutal weapon. He'd sunk down to her playing field at last. *By any means*, Morgan reminded her on every phone call. Look out for number one, win by any means.

But the risk of explaining, of stopping to tell Warren, the risk of being talked out of her plan kept her backing off, swallowing her questions. She'd stared. The same way Morgan had after robbing her.

Heartless, she'd finally mastered it.

She'd envisioned it differently. Pictured a cold, hollow place in her chest, a calculating, cruel mind operating at maximum efficiency.

What she got was a solid stone scratching at her organs, painfully busting holes into her lungs. She struggled to breathe, to eat, to sleep, for fear that the stone would implode and eviscerate her entirely.

Because under the black abrasive rock, deep in the center, was a raw, ruinous truth. She loved Warren.

His voice, his smile, even the way he smelled like soap and sweat, made her heart stutter.

Could he forgive her for this?

For hurting him in the worst way, for bonding with his greatest rival, his hated enemy?

Sunday morning stirred somberly, umber sky bare, no moon, no stars, a fledgling sun striving upward. Six windows were lit in the building ahead, fourteenth floor, conference room *Onyx*. A mist suffused the air, wetting the pavement under her feet.

An omen, or a blessing. Wearing white after labor day, she'd done it to herself.

Victoria peered up as Doyle, signature golden hair hidden under a black beanie, came through the doorway of Wawas with two tall brown disposable cups.

"Do I smell like grease?" he asked, coming forward to hand her one.

Tamping down the panic, the despair, Victoria took the cup and uncapped it, sniffing cautiously. A surprised smile crossed her lips. "A mocha?"

"You have a sugar addiction," Doyle said flatly, smelling his shirt, frowning and yanking it to her. "Smell."

Rolling her eyes at his neuroticism, she huffed at his cotton pullover. "French fries."

"No." Doyle groaned. "I have to change."

"No time," Victoria said, flapping his shirt in the smoggy, city air. "It smells good. It'll make everyone hungry. The meeting will end faster." He was shaking his head, a tendril of spun gold spilling onto his forehead. "The other option is we switch clothes."

Together, they assessed the feasibility of a swap. If they weren't trying to keep a low profile, Victoria would insist on stuffing Doyle into her dress. Cut in a Grecian style of folds, the white skirt had a slit from ankle to thigh and the bodice was pleated enough to forgo a bra.

He'd look like Hercules.

Her excited gaze met his frown. "You suck," Victoria whined. "I'll slip in that I super-sized my breakfast."

A wry smile edged Doyle's mouth. "You're a good manager." At Victoria's snort, he said, "You *are*. I'm fed, freshly clothed. I know who I'm meeting with, and what to expect."

Victoria shrugged, trying to conceal her pleasure. One was more likely to be screamed at than complimented in recruiting. If she wasn't patting her back, no one was. She squinted down the street. More windows began to glow from within as the city stirred. "I'm not a manager."

"Alright, give me the three percent back."

"No, and three and a half." They hadn't finalized the contract. No time. "I'm a recruiter first. You're an exception."

Sipping his coffee, Doyle watched the streetlights change from red to green, a slog of commuters leaving the peace of the suburbs. "You act like Rose's manager."

She faked a knife to the stomach. "Might as well call me his mother. It'll hurt the same."

"Fine, don't listen to me, nobody does."

She stopped and placed a comforting hand on his arm. In his quest to cultivate the image of the golden boy, Doyle's intelligence was overlooked. Victoria herself had assumed he was an idiot pretty boy, but beneath the shimmering façade, the two of them had a great deal in common. Drive, ambition, awesome fucking hair. "I'm listening. I am. I'm just working through the forty stages of grief."

"Five," he said without thinking.

Victoria smiled into her cup, taking a deep drink, chocolate and coffee and milk foam wrapping her in a warm, delicious hug. "I knew you were a brunette. You're smart."

His head whipped around, as if stray reporters and pop up camera crews ran rampant. "Stop saying that. I'll fire you."

She made a faint scoffing sound. "You won't believe how many times I've been threatened with unemployment. I don't even register it anymore."

Doyle checked his phone. "Should we go? It's almost seven."

"I was going to send you with Morgan so I could get to Indianapolis on time."

"He's perpetually late."

"Because all he cares about is payday. He'll appear from the gates of hell at the first whiff of a check." She threw her skirt to the side, thigh puckering in the cold. "Let's go. I want to make a good impression."

The clock struck zero.

Chapter Twenty-One

Warren was dead. He breathed, his heart beat, blood—presumably—flowed through his veins, collected in his arteries.

The coldness in his chest leached him of anything to live for. He ventured he had hours to live and then he'd continue on as nothing, a lifeless body stumbling through time.

"Holy shit." Miles gasped, flashing his bare ass as he sprinted for his locker.

Someone yelled, "Clothes, man!"

Retinas burning, Warren dropped his face into his hands. Nothing could lift his black mood, melancholy weighed on him like weights chained to a swimmer.

"Holy shit," Miles repeated, foot stomping the locker room carpet. Speed Blue. Trademarked. The same hue as the lockers, the benches, the pad under Warren's ass.

A near match to Victoria's eyes.

Beautiful next to his green pants, like a lush forest hovering over a coast of smooth, deep water. An eighty-foot cliff keeping them apart.

Restlessness made his knee bounce. He was dressed, had been since they landed. Cleats double knotted, jersey loose on his shoulders. His helmet hung off his knee, strips of silver outlining the green mountain emblem, a white mouth guard was clipped to the facemask.

Around him, a cacophony of pre-game rituals weeded out nerves.

Some ate packed lunches, some—Moore—called their mothers, a few stretched, beat their favorite level of candy crush. Miles showered and air dried. A long-standing superstition.

"Clothes!" shouted another voice when Miles spun, phone raised.

Ever confident, Miles ignored it. "Look," he said, shoving the screen into Burton's face.

Strategically placing his gloves, Burton did, in fact, bend his head, reading slowly. "Holy fuck," he croaked, grabbing the phone and squinting.

"He doesn't have glasses," Moore called, spreading black tape up his calf. "You have to read it to him!"

Burton scowled, twisting the phone. "Read this, you shit. Doyle 'Midas' Heark joins the Baltimore Ravens."

At Warren's side, Cole stood. "Bullshit."

"Read it yourself." Burton launched the phone across the room, ignoring Miles' yelp of protest.

On instinct, Warren intercepted it, palm stinging as he swiped at the screen. *Baltimore. Midas.*

Midas had been traded.

Midas was a Raven.

Cole hit Warren's shoulder. "You're the quarterback."

"He's *our* quarterback," Miles amended. "No one's leaving."

An explosion of relief went off like a firework. Helmets dropped, hands slapped, Cole dragged Warren into a bear hug.

Starting quarterback. Warren was staying, everyone was staying. The golden bomb had been defused.

Cole's deep chuckle shook Warren. "Holy shit."

Miles gave hoots of triumph as he jumped into his pants. Moore was on the phone again. Asher smiled into his hand.

Burton, a closer friend with bad news than good, stared at Warren, waiting for him to get there, to find the darkness.

Victoria was fired.

The phone fell from Warren's hands. That's what the headline should say. *Victoria Steer loses everything*. Dreams crushed.

She lost her job because of him, because he couldn't stomach being second place.

Reality hit hard enough to make him stumble back. Breathless, heart pounding, Warren lurched for his jeans, his phone.

Coach entered the room with a piercing whistle. "Who's ready to win?"

***

THEIR STEPS ECHOED off the concrete tunnel walls, made them sound like hundreds marching to war. Legions off to battle for love and country, strong in the face of death.

Deceiving.

Warren struggled to place one foot ahead of the other. Cole's toes bit at his heels. Refusing to let him stop, turn around, run out of the stadium, and find her.

"Congratulations," Coach had told him, shining his whistle, expecting him to be happy.

By all standards, he ought to be.

He'd gotten precisely what he'd wanted, exactly as Victoria promised. Starting position, a spot in the limelight. Money, fame. A head to head with Midas. Prizes, yes, but she hadn't stopped there.

She'd surrounded him with friends, compiled a team of refugees and given them a safe place.

Cole's knuckles dug into Warren's back. *Keep. Going.*

Flashes of white and blue sparked at the end of the tunnel, a mix of hard rap and cheers filtered through the pounding march.

"How dare you show your face here," Fulgencio Gomez's voice snuck between the sounds, a hiss of violence amidst the merry.

"There," Cole whispered, pointing over Warren's shoulder.

In a midnight black suit, Gomez stood over the most beautiful woman in the world, a vision in flowing ivory. The stampede slowed, quieted, interrupted Warren's view.

Immediately, his feet found purpose. He was shoving, excusing his way through the team, to the mirage.

Victoria turned to look at him, eyes sparkling, even in the darkness. After days apart, she was looking at him, a tremulous smile on her Dragon Red lips.

"You have ruined this organization by explicitly acting against my wishes," Gomez's anger was directed at Victoria's shoulder, his face beet red, fury making his r's roll.

She lifted her shoulder, dropped it, head shaking ever so slightly. "I quit," she said without looking away from Warren.

Gomez's neck jerked back. "You—"

"I quit." She turned her chin to Gomez, back ramrod straight, hands loose. "I made you a team, and it's spectacular." A growl crept into her tone, wrapping her in a sheet of ice. "Stop fucking with it."

An incredulous look came over Gomez's face.

Pushing through the stalled team with his clipboard, Foss faced Gomez. "She doesn't quit," he heaved. "She shouldn't have sworn, but she's right. You've got a good team here, Fulgencio."

Warren found his voice. "Victoria," He elbowed past the last of the gawking bodies between them. He knew Cole was filing behind from the way people shifted to make room for the tackle.

"No." Victoria patted Coach's clipboard. "I appreciate it, Rodney, but I do quit."

Coach lowered his voice. "I wouldn't if—"

"Who will work with you now?" Gomez was seething, roaring.

Unaffected, Victoria regarded the billionaire with a perturbed frown. "Midas."

"Victoria." Warren reached for her, but drew back before contact, scared she'd disappear.

"Don't quit," Coach repeated.

"What have you done?" Warren asked her. "What'd you do to Midas? This is your dream."

A vicious and ugly light glowed in Gomez's eyes. "Not anymore. You were never suited for this."

"I know." Victoria was watching Warren again, gaze drifting between the hand that didn't touch her and his face. "I'm not a heartless asshole who plays with people's lives for my own entertainment, as much as I wanted to be."

"Please, stop." Coach was going to tear his hair out.

Her smile was soft, hesitant. "Hey Flowers."

Warren's heart lurched. His life clicked back into place.

Reflexively, he started with Gomez. "Victoria Steer is the best person on this team. She works harder and has better vision and insight than anyone."

Gomez sneered. "Be silent. We know how she got you to play."

Warren didn't back down. "All she had to do was speak. She's fucking smart—"

"I quit," Victoria reminded Warren. "Don't bury yourself for me. I was always going to quit."

"No, you weren't," Warren said sharply. "Steal Midas back."

"I can't." She was still smiling, a few loose strands of dark hair caught on her cheek. "He doesn't like Vermont."

"So this is for him?" Jealousy reared its ugly head at the worst time.

"Yes, I'm his manager."

Gomez went still.

Flicking a smug glance at him, Victoria explained, "Midas will never be a Mountaineer. I've made sure of it."

"You arduous bitch—"

"Finish that sentence," Warren interrupted darkly, "and I'll quit too."

A sea of murmured agreement followed, a team united.

***

VICTORIA HADN'T CROSSED the distance to Warren, had no idea how she could. Suddenly an ocean felt as big as it was, and a voyage across treacherous.

She wanted to shout, to tell him he was the one she cared about, the one she'd defended, the one who made her realize her true purpose.

Not to scheme, but to protect, to covet. Admit that she never would've brought Midas here, never would've spoken with him, dealt with him, signed her life to him if it weren't for Warren, to ensure *his* fate. To fulfill a promise she hadn't yet made.

The crowd beyond the tunnel quieted. The music on the field paused. Confusion rose as thousands of fans wondered if the Mountaineers had vanished, forfeit.

Not her problem.

Victoria watched Warren, feeling her heart in her hand, holding it out to him.

"Will you be my manager?" Cole asked.

The first tear sprung from Victoria's eye and then Warren was in front of her, brushing it away, grasping at her waist, heat scorching through her dress. "I'm—"

She kissed him.

Too long had she gone without. Too many nights she'd stayed up with her thoughts on him, unable to talk. He crushed her to his body, tasting, then pulling back. Victoria gave chase, needing him.

Warren gaze snapped up, scanned the tunnel. "Get on the field." A deadly command.

Victoria lit like gasoline on the water, undulating and ferocious.

As the cavernous tunnel emptied, she pulled at Warren's chest. "I'm so fucking sorry. I didn't mean to ice you. I went into fix it mode. And I— I didn't want to get your hopes up if I failed. I promised you the starting spot."

"I'd trade it for you," Warren said softly. "I'd trade football for you. I still will. Say you want me to. I'll get Midas here myself." He pressed his forehead to hers, bending his body over hers.

"No." She cleared her throat. "No. This is good. I'm a manager. I never liked dealing with these people anyway. Morgan is an ass, but he was right about me."

"Morgan"—Warren growled, his lips scorching her jaw—"doesn't get to express any opinion about you."

"He said I care too much. And I do."

"That's not going to stop me from tearing him apart. No one scares you and gets away with it."

"About that." She clutched at him, stomach fluttering. "I had to make a deal with the devil. Morgan's your new agent."

"Red."

"It was the only way he'd give me Midas and I had to send him away, send him far away or your position would be threatened. Don't be mad."

Warren's fingers twined gently in her hair. She shoved her face into his neck, inhaling the fresh scent of him. "I'm furious. You're making yourself deal with a bastard for what?"

"For you." Her nails scraped his abs. Harder than she'd remembered, perfect. "I love you. I'll invite Morgan to every date if it means we get to be together."

Warren pressed tighter against her, taking her mouth in a wicked tease. "You buried it there." He stepped back to kiss the pulse in her neck. "Go again."

She pinched her lips, breaths hard. "I love you, Warren Frederick Rose."

A faint smile curved Warren's lips as he looked down at her. "I'm not going to correct you."

"Because I'm right?"

"Because if we start arguing," Warren's voice rolled over her like warm rain on the beach. "I'm going to fuck you"—he grabbed a handful of her ass—"even though I know there are cameras in the tunnels. Come on." He kissed her, pulling away too soon. "Let's go watch the game."

"Watch?" Victoria pulled back, noticing for the first time she was touching his real shoulders, pressing against *him*, not pads. "I thought you were better. What happened? Why isn't Foss playing you? I'm going to murder him."

"Down girl," Warren drawled with a wry twist of his mouth. "Coach said he doesn't want to risk the star for a pre-season game. I'm already prepping for next Sunday."

She melted against him, limbs heavy, heart full. "Next Sunday." She pressed her ear against his heart. Her fingers trailed down his stomach. "Should I paint my chest?"

"You want me to play with an erection?"

She laughed, memorizing his heartbeat, memorizing this feeling. "And risk injury to my favorite appendage? I'd never." She nuzzled her cheek against him. "What if we dashed back to the locker room quick? Five minutes, I promise."

He steered her to the field. "I love you, but you're going to kill me."

Chapter Twenty-Two

W ARREN WAITED UNTIL THEY hit a red light before he looked right. "Just tell me."

Cursing loudly in the passenger seat, Victoria twisted, batting at her bangs, which were now, according to the note stuck to his chest this morning, being transitioned out. "I want to. God, do I want to." Soft fingers danced over her lips. "I can't though. I signed a sixty-page contract affirming my silence."

"What's the worst that can happen?" He had to know why she stared off, got that amazed, amused, brilliant smile before chuckling.

"Honestly, nothing short of an apocalypse."

"You're giggling at the nuclear codes?" Warren asked, guiding them down Lily Street. Sun drenched the road in warm yellow, but somehow the dash read sixty.

Eight years in Texas, and sixty warranted a sweatshirt, a sturdy set of jeans.

His northern girl bared more skin than she covered in a matching flowery skirt and shirt, a good four inches of her creamy, soft belly on display. He could even spot the beginnings of her tiger stripes. Made him want to follow the trail.

"I don't giggle," she insisted, tracing a purple flower on her hip. "I'm not six." She stabbed indignantly at its yellow center.

Warren signaled onto Lake Street, effectively stealing Victoria's attention as Lake Champlain filled the windshield. A dog and a bone.

Next week, fall would start. Victoria promised cascading ruby leaves, apple cider doughnuts, and pumpkins as big as Cole. Maybe even Burton.

"Chiefs next week," he reminded her, putting the Rover in park, squeezing Victoria's thigh. The SUV was a new purchase, long overdue.

Warren swung his gaze to her. She was damned beautiful, midnight hair, pulsing blue eyes, an explosion of color. Unintentionally, his thumb snuck under the hem of her skirt. He bet it'd match great with the carpet in the backseat.

"Are you done guessing, just like that? Now we're on to your thing?"

Warren grinned, anchoring his elbow on the console to span a hand around her waist. "Murder hornets."

"No."

"Tupac's Alive."

"Colder."

"Denver."

"It's the *worst!*"

"You had a vision and know the exact score of the Superbowl but you're not sure which year."

She pinched his forearm, unbuckling her seatbelt. "I'll have to meet you in Kansas. I'm meeting Lincoln Wray, that quick pocket quarterback in California first." She slashed him a wicked smile. "Fox Sports called me a quarterback whisperer."

He couldn't help but smile back. "I'm sure they didn't mean it literally."

"Quiet is boring." She lunged out of the car, glancing left, then right, and promptly crossing the street.

Warren should have guessed. Should have known she'd disregard all but the water. She stopped at the dock, read the private property sign and with the daredevil glint in her eyes, stepped over it.

He was going to marry this woman, spend his life chasing her.

Sunday, he'd introduce her to his parents. He'd gotten three seats together. He and Cole had an escalating bet on how long it would take her to realize who they were. If she didn't have them pegged and charmed by the end of the first, Warren was covering steaks for the next year.

With Victoria managing six players, they'd have to wait until the season finished before he'd convince her to take him home. Sail the ocean blue.

He gave her thirty more seconds before he was out of the car. He was going to lose the bet. When Red focused, she hyper-focused.

"Baby ducks," she said when Warren stopped at her side. She kept her voice low as if to not scare them and grabbed for her miniscule purse, pulling out—

"You carry bread with you now?" he asked as she ripped it to pieces and chucked it in the water.

"Don't be ridiculous. I carry stale bread."

Explained the slices she'd left bare on their counter, why she'd threatened life and limb if he touched them. "Why stale bread?"

"Takes longer to sink that way. Is this our date? Ducks and fucks?" She looped her arms around his torso, cheek brushing his chest. "You've outdone yourself."

Fuck, he was raging hard. "Absolutely not. I have much bigger plans." He wrapped an arm over her shoulder, casting his gaze over the water. "Guess."

"It's too cold to swim." She turned, smile curling. "Is a boat coming to pick us up? Can a yacht fit through the breakwater? Does it have jet skis?" She tugged at his shirt, crushing the bread, jumping with excitement.

"I knew the minute I had money, you'd find out."

"Please, I'm way more loaded than you. And I'm the one who processes your paychecks. After taking my incredibly fair eight percent cut."

She'd negotiated him down from fifty.

His hand landed on her ass. "We're not going on the water. Not today." Stroking her hair behind her ear, he turned her to face the cape style home nestled across the road. "This is the view I wanted you to see."

Her head tilted. "The house?"

He held up a key.

Red lips parted. "You bought a house."

Warren kissed her, slipping the key into her palm. "Next date's boat shopping."

"Doyle bleaches his hair."

Thank you for reading.